THE HAREM

NOELLE MACK
EMMA LEIGH
CELIA MAY HART
MELISSA MacNEAL

APHRODISIA
KENSINGTON PUBLISHING CORP.
http://www.kensingtonbooks.com

KENSINGTON BOOKS are published by

Kensington Publishing Corp.
850 Third Avenue
New York, NY 10022

Praise for the authors of THE HAREM

"A truly sensual story that will captivate and titillate readers."
—*Romantic Times* on Noelle Mack's THREE, 4 stars

"Smoldering hot, naughty adventure . . . a deliciously
kinky read."
—*Just Erotic Romance Reviews* on Noelle Mack's THREE

"Loving and sexy . . . a bawdy delight . . . this is must-read
historical erotica."
—*Just Erotic Romance Reviews* on Celia May Hart's
SHOW ME

"Highly erotic . . . captivating characters. Melissa MacNeal
is taking erotica by storm!"
—*Romantic Times* on Melissa MacNeal's EVIL'S NIECE,
4½ stars

CONTENTS

THE SECRET DOOR

NOELLE MACK

For JWR, the magic man

1

The deep blue of twilight suffused the garden where Yasmina walked alone. She stopped at the black-tiled fountain at its center, bubbling with water that rose from an ancient, buried spring. Only she came here—the other odalisques of the Topkapi harem shunned this place, convinced that the strange shadows cast by the garden's old walls had enchanted the water and the flowers that drank from it.

Yasmina had listened to these tales and then, left to her own devices, dipped her fingers in the fountain, not caring if the water was poison, and found it pure in taste. Still, it was whispered that evil spirits, djinns and ifrits, lurked in its dark depths. For that reason the garden had been neglected, and for that reason she preferred it. Here, sweet white roses sent out thorny shoots, climbing up and over the walls with wild abandon, as if they might someday escape the earth in which their roots were buried.

But the roses could not. Nor could she ever leave this place, she thought with bitterness. Though she wanted for nothing in this golden realm, nothing belonged to her—not her beautiful gowns, not her embroidered slippers, not the jewels that hung between her perfect breasts, bared under silken gauze.

Yasmina shivered. A cool breeze wafted through the garden, enlivening the air and clearing her mind. Her nipples stood out against her white skin, white as the roses she walked among. Here in the harem, no one considered such display of female flesh immodest. There were only women to see. Like them all, Yasmina was the property of the sultan, a debauched and repulsive old man whom she glimpsed only rarely from behind a latticed wall of precious marble, under the great dome of the palace, holding court among his viziers and eunuchs.

His chief wife and favorite, the plump and lovely Gulbahar, made a great show of enjoying his company, as did the kadins, his lesser wives. The odalisques did not have to, as a rule. The sultan Suleyman was too old to visit many beds, and weary of the quarrels and vicious rivalry among the women.

Left to themselves, watched over by eunuchs and attendants within the harem walls and armed guards without, the young odalisques entertained themselves with storytelling and poetry, and games of chance and skill, and songs that extolled the prowess of legendary lovers and erotic bliss. When those amusements palled, there was always gossip. And for some, hashish and opium, which allowed their minds to flee the lovely bodies that had brought them to a state of bondage.

Yasmina wanted only to be by herself. As no one spoke her dialect, she was ignored and avoided, and some thought she was deaf and mute. A few seemed to look at her with pity in their beautiful eyes, but she cast her gaze down, not wishing to be entangled by an emotion as useless as pity.

Being alone was her fate. And there were far worse fates, she reflected, sipping from the crystal cup a harem servant had brought her an hour ago, filled with sherbet that had melted by now, made with berries and herbs and fine white sugar.

It had been prepared in the harem kitchen, made from snow that was brought down from Mount Olympus every spring. Before she had been sold into slavery by her avaricious uncle—whose clutches she had been glad to escape, knowing nothing of what awaited her here—she had seen the caravans of the snow men and marveled at the sight. They wore turbans piled with snow, driving teams of fifty and sixty mules, who strained to pull white mountains of the stuff, piled into wagons. Yet even a miserable mule had more freedom than she, though many might envy her fine clothes and jewels.

She set the crystal cup in a niche that had once held a vase and sat down on the edge of the fountain, soothed by the rhythm of the bubbling water. Yasmina stared down, focusing on an elusive blue light in its depths that seemed to come and go. A minnow, she thought. With scales of a hue to match the twilight. The blue light vanished and the water grew calm. She drew in her breath. For two years she had come here and never in all that time had the water been still.

She saw a white rosebud reflected upon its mirrored surface, tiny and tightly furled, and so perfectly like a real one that she touched the water, thinking that it had fallen there. To her surprise, the bud opened, becoming a huge, full-blown rose under her fingertips. Its stem shot above the water, and an unusual fragrance filled the air. Yasmina drew back.

Come to me. The deep voice was male. It came from everywhere—and nowhere. Yasmina looked wildly about the shadowy garden and saw no one. If she were caught with an intruder, she would be killed with him, her throat swiftly cut. Or she would be tied into a sack and drowned in the indifferent sea, depending on the whim of the executioner. She had no friends within the harem, no wise woman to plead her innocence.

The huge rose sank back into the fountain and vanished by a magic beyond her understanding, yet its fragrance lingered.

The air grew still and warm, oppressively sensual. Yasmina put her hand into the fountain, craving a few cool drops upon her forehead and her lips. Her mouth was suddenly parched.

A goblet made of ice rose from the depths of the fountain, brimming over with its water. Her hand clasped it and could not let go.

Drink, Yasmina. On a hot night, cold water is as intoxicating as wine.

Compelled by an unseen presence that seemed as male as the deep voice, she drank it dry. She closed her eyes, letting the enchanted water slide down her throat—and gasped when a man's hand covered her mouth. He was behind her. She could not see him and she dared not scream.

You must be quiet.

He took his hand off her mouth, and she whispered a reply in her own language. "Who are you?"

Shall I reveal myself?

"Yes."

The intruder came around to stand before her. Clad in black rags, his body was outlined by the same bluish light she had glimpsed in the fountain's depths. His eyes, blacker than midnight, held that unearthly light as well.

Yasmina was spellbound. Yet she could still hear the distant chatter of other women within the harem walls and could still see and smell the smoke of the nargileh, the many-armed water pipe they shared to be sociable, drifting out into the air. Silent and lonely though she was, she would be missed. And she would be found with him.

His bold stance and the tight wrappings around his strong legs left her no doubt that he could easily overpower her. He was tall, far taller than any man she had ever seen, with the sensual grace of a panther and an air—a very odd air—of courteous menace.

Come with me.

"I cannot."

No one will see us. There is a door—a secret door. It leads to another garden.

"This garden is my refuge. I have walked here scores of times, in the sun and under the moon. There is no door."

For answer, he reached out his hand to her. Yasmina took it, lifted to her feet with magical lightness.

You need not be afraid. The women inside will not miss you for a while longer. I have seen to that.

She followed him. She had no choice. The ragged man raised a dagger from his girdle of black rags and stabbed it into the stone wall. The stone gushed forth a river of blood that ran down to the roots of the white roses, which bent and sighed, filling with blood until they were crimson. A door appeared behind them, carved in an intricate pattern and inlaid with mosaic.

Now do you believe?

"Yes," she whispered. "But what is your name? What may I call you?"

Rustem. It is not my name but you may call me that. He took her hand and pushed aside the red roses. She glimpsed blood on his skin where he touched them, and she shuddered.

"I did not know roses could bleed."

All living things bleed, Yasmina. But I do not.

He drew the tip of the dagger along his neck. A wound appeared and closed up again, quickly. She gave a little cry.

It is kind of you to feel pain for me. I cannot.

"Is there nothing that you feel?"

He pushed the climbing roses farther away from the door. *Loneliness. And for a little while you and I shall keep that at bay. Enter.*

He drew her through the secret door into a garden she had never seen. It was much like the one in which she walked, though hers lay in shadow, and this one shimmered with light.

It boasted something her garden did not: a small pavilion, strung with pierced lamps, in one corner. On its floor were cushions of silk. A young woman, naked, sat upon them and strummed an oud, singing melodies that hung in the air and repeated themselves. Yasmina came closer. The singer's flesh was transparent, her body as insubstantial as the notes of her song.

A ghost. She cannot see or hear you. But the music is pretty.

The transparent singer rose and floated to a different part of the hidden garden, where birds had begun to echo her melodies. They flew over the wall and she flew away with them, abandoning the two mortals who had dared to intrude upon her music-making.

Yasmina sighed with relief. Her companion motioned her to sit beside him on the cushions, offering her more water in another goblet of ice, and unfamiliar fruit. She refused both.

The black-haired man shrugged and helped himself, eating with evident pleasure. His gaze traveled over her body, resting longest on her face. But the sight of her breasts, concealed not at all by the fine gauze that she wore, seemed to arouse him.

Are you a virgin, Yasmina?

The bold question surprised her. "N-no," she stammered, unable to lie. Like all the other women who entered the sultan's palace, her legs had been spread open and the most intimate parts of her body carefully inspected. She had been sold as a virgin, and, because of her youth, it had been assumed that she was. But she had not passed the shameful test, though her beauty had persuaded the kizlar agasi, the master of the girls, to keep her in the end.

Yasmina had been consigned to the lowest ranks of odalisques, forced to share a room with coarse, strapping young women who tried to rape her with a thick rod of ivory they had stolen from somewhere. They'd bound Yasmina's wrists, clumsily. One had stripped naked and tied the rod to a string around her own waist, letting it dangle in front of her as her companion tightened other strings at its base, running those through her buttocks and knotting it at the small of her back. That one had held Yasmina's legs apart, eager to watch the other violate a new and vulnerable member of the harem.

But Yasmina had bitten through the bonds around her wrist and fought them hard, twisting the heavy ivory rod from the strings that held it around her tormentor's waist and bruising her with no more mercy than she had been shown. In the years since then the two women had left her mostly alone, preferring to play their wicked games with each other, although they invited her to join in when they had drunk too much wine.

So you have known a man.

"A man knew me when I was far too young."

Ah. Then the experience was an exercise in cruelty, not tenderness.

"Yes."

Now I know why you seem afraid of me, although I have little more substance than your own dreams.

"I am not so sure of that," she said, trembling. She felt powerfully drawn to him, all too aware of the disparity between the sensual languor of his pose and the coiled strength that was hidden by his ragged clothes.

I will not hurt you, Yasmina. Undress me. I will let you go as far as you like and touch what you will. Allow yourself to know pleasure.

Unwilling but unable to refuse, she lifted her hand and stroked his face. Rustem closed his eyes, enjoying her tentative caress. Without her being quite aware of it happening, her hand drifted down, and the black rags that bound him flew open to reveal a muscular chest. His skin was bronzed and gleaming, like soft, warm metal to the touch. But he had no heartbeat. She pulled her hand away, as if the increasing heat she sensed in his flesh would scorch her.

"What are you made of?"

I cannot explain it now. But I was once human. He took her hand and rested it between the juncture of his legs. *As you can see. Or should I say feel?* He smiled without showing his teeth, pushing his groin up slightly so that her hand pressed down. So. He was a man like any other. She could feel something she had felt before: a rigid shaft of hot flesh.

The black rags unwound from around his groin and he was fully revealed to her wide eyes. She could not look away any more than she had been able to stop herself from following him to this strange garden, from caressing his face and touching his chest. Under her gaze, his cock grew long and thick, the heavy head resting on the bare skin of his thigh at first and then rising as the shaft rose. The sight was mesmerizing. He was not a man like any other. He was made of pure gold.

Touch me. However you like. Your soft hand is soothing.

Yasmina clasped his cock. He cupped his balls as though he were offering himself to her. The rags that bound his legs stayed in place, but she glimpsed his skin where there were openings. It was as bronzed as his chest. He lay back in the cushions, moving just enough to do so but not so much that she lost her grip on the throbbing golden rod between his legs. The veins that curled around the shaft pulsed with a slow fire. Compelled to caress him again, she lay her white hand over the middle of his chest. Now she could feel, very faintly, the beating of a heart.

The sight of him, whatever he was, man or spirit, aroused her—and Yasmina had never been aroused. Everything that touched her skin excited a potent, animal desire. The delicate friction of the sheer silk over her breasts, bare beneath it, was unbearably stimulating. She let go of his cock with a soft cry and clasped her breasts, then her nipples, pinching them until the silk was torn to shreds. Her nipples were fully revealed by the ruined garment and she rubbed them frantically.

Ahh. Such sensitive breasts and such beautiful nipples.

Startled, Yasmina sat back on her thighs, ashamed that he had seen her fondle her own flesh so wantonly, and she tried to draw the shreds of silk together. It was no use. She could not even cover her breasts with her hands or the sensation of pure sexual excitement would overwhelm her again. No, she must sit before him in rags of her own making and be devoured by his hungry eyes.

Should she return to the harem, she would be publicly punished, perhaps even whipped by order of the kizlar agasi, the master of the girls. The kizlar agasi decided which woman was brought to the sultan's bed at night, and if any were so bold as to forget that her body and the clothes that displayed it were his property, she would be corrected, forcibly if necessary. Though many odalisques indulged in private stimulation, alone or with each other, a woman of low rank could not be so willful as to rip her clothes in the throes of sexual pleasure, private or public.

She blushed furiously. Rustem sat up and caressed her hot cheeks.

Ah, pretty one. I enjoyed seeing you tear your clothes. Your bare flesh is much more beautiful than your finery. And your excitement is building more quickly than I thought. He put his mouth on hers and kissed her long and deep. Yasmina moaned, helpless with lust for this strange man. If he was a man.

He picked her up as if she were a flower petal and placed her on his lap. *Such tender nipples,* he murmured into her ear. *And yet, how hard you pinch them. Sometimes pain is as irresistible as pleasure, and as sweet. Am I not right, Yasmina?* He grasped the sheer material and ripped the last of it away from her. *There. Your breasts are as bare as your soul.*

She cried out, knowing that he was right. He cupped her breasts in his golden hands, and a sensation of warm fire shot through her. Able to curve around her with uncanny ease, he brought his head down to suckle her nipples and nip them until she cried out again.

Yasmina arched her back and her hair flowed loosely over the cushions. Her lover moved his body over hers, separating her legs, clad in billowing pantaloons sewn to a band about her narrow waist. He drew his dagger, holding the point precisely at the wet spot in the soft silk where her cunny had been enfolded by it. Her sexual arousal had been intense and uncontrollable.

She held still. He pressed the point of the dagger into the yielding place between her legs . . . but he cut only the cloth, in a deft slice that bared her from her navel to the soft double moons of her behind. Her cunny tightened when he bisected the silk and tossed the dagger aside. He spread the rich cloth and gazed upon her no longer hidden flesh. Yasmina tried to cover herself with her hands, but he pushed them gently away.

As I thought. Your cunny is beautiful, whether or not you are a virgin. As beautiful as life itself. And sweet and juicy as a plump little peach.

His eyes were burning with supernatural desire. She felt their odd radiance warm her most intimate flesh as he looked his fill, not touching.

You have been nicely shaved. The hamam attendants take good care of the sultan's women.

Yasmina nodded. She had left the ritual bath late that afternoon, ignoring the gossiping women who drifted through the hamam, taking turns being scrubbed to perfect cleanliness, massaged and oiled. A silent slave had shaved and plucked her cunny, deftly removing every single hair as was the custom in the harem.

Was the slave young?

"Yes," she said, startled. Had this golden djinn seen her and the slave in the hamam? It was said that supernatural beings lurked in water, and perhaps he had been there.

She was gentle with your tender skin. Sometimes the older women are not. But perhaps that is because they enjoy punishing the new ones.

"You know much about what goes on in a hamam," she said. "But no men may enter. It is forbidden."

Men have always found a way to watch such sport. The erotic games of frustrated women are highly arousing. Some men have died for risking a look, just one look.

Understanding opened her mind. "Oh," she said. "And were you such a man?"

Rustem sat back on his thighs, his erection subsiding. He rested his hands on her open thighs as if he were her lover, tenderly possessive, separating from her after prolonged and pleasurable intercourse. She was almost as wet as if he had climaxed inside her.

Yasmina wondered dreamily if his semen would be as golden as the rest of him, pouring forth like a hot river from the little hole in the heavy cock head. She had watched the play of illicit lovers in the harem. Once. The culprit had been caught and castrated.

Yes. I looked often and long, and I loved a woman who was a sultan's favorite. I met death soon enough. And now I have met you. And I would taste life. He reached forward with one hand and spread her cunny lips with his finger and thumb. *Allow me to kiss you there, beautiful Yasmina.*

His mouth came down on the shaved, sensitive flesh between her legs and he wasted no time in thrusting in his tongue, tasting her fully. He was gentle but masterful, and his otherworldly skill gave her exquisite pleasure.

He quickly brought her to orgasm. Her first.

Wave after wave of sensation coursed through her shaking

body. Hot tears rolled down her face as he continued his tender lovemaking, putting the tiny bud above her swollen cunny into his mouth and sucking it until she reached orgasm again, writhing, pushing helplessly against his soft lips, begging him for more. He stilled her with a hand upon her belly, stroking her there until the pleasure ebbed into a feeling of utter contentment.

He straightened and kissed away the tears on her face. *There. You remind me of the woman I loved . . . and died for.*

"How did you die?"

You will not like the answer.

"I must know."

The sultan immersed me in a vessel of molten gold. I am of royal blood and he could not kill me by ordinary means, though I had dared to love the most beautiful woman in his court. A jadi, a witch, betrayed us to the sultan and he saw to it that I did not die quickly. My skin burned away and became gold.

"And what happened to the woman you loved?"

He didn't answer for a long time. *You must be careful that you do not meet her fate.*

"Our fate is sealed at the moment of our birth," Yasmina said softly. "It is written on our foreheads."

Rustem nodded. *God can see such writing. And sometimes the dead can too. Which is why I came looking for you. You must be my eyes, Yasmina, and my hands.*

"Why? Oh, Rustem, why? You are crying tears of gold. . . ." She trailed off. The sight of his strong face racked with fear and sorrow was infinitely sad.

My younger brother is a prisoner in the Topkapi Palace. He is alive, but I can see his fate as well. But there is a chance. You alone can free him, Yasmina.

She scarcely wanted to reply, fearing for her own life, for what little it was worth. "And what if I refuse?" she said at last.

He caressed her body with those magical hands, sending

tremors of scorching desire through her. *Though you are not virgin and not entirely willing, I shall make you mine. And you shall do my bidding.*

She stiffened, suddenly wary. "You did not penetrate me. What you have done to me is what women do to each other. I am not yours."

Not yet. But your orgasms nourish me, and I am a little stronger now. You shall have more. My kisses will open your helpless mouth, and my hands will fondle your soft breasts and nipples. My tongue will lick your nether lips and the throbbing bud above them.

You held my long cock in your soft hand and felt it throb. Imagine how it will fill your mouth. My balls will be next. How sweet it will be to feel your obedient tongue upon them. And when I am slick, I will penetrate your swollen, shaved cunny as I please and satisfy your womanly need to be taken with strength, as a stallion tops his mare.

"But—"

But that will not be enough to satisfy me. My hands will spread the round halves of your behind, and you will cry out to have me in that hidden hole as well, and deeply. I will possess your body in every way I can. I will possess you.

"Only by sorcery," she whispered.

Yes. A very loving sorcery. And now you will crave, desperately crave, more of what only I can give you: a sexual pleasure so intense that your fears are burned away and your past is obliterated. You cannot say no, my beautiful Yasmina.

She wriggled backward, away from the golden stranger, who only smiled.

2

His softly spoken words—had they been spoken or had she just thought them through his sorcery?—unnerved her far more than the sensual attention he had lavished upon her. Sold into slavery, she understood its nature too well, and would never become a slave to desire, that most capricious of masters, all the more so because it resided within the mind. Truly, her body was not her own, but she would never be tamed, not even by a djinn. Her loneliness had taught her strength.

Yasmina restored herself to a measure of decency by wrapping her upper body with an embroidered shawl that had covered one of the pillows. The split in her pantaloons, still wet around the edges from her sexual excitement and his hungry mouth, she could hide by pressing her thighs together. But doing so caused the sensations he had awakened to thrill her afresh. She called down a thousand silent curses upon Rustem.

"Tell me, Rustem," she began, searching his face for a sign of the tears he had cried. But gold had melted into gold and left no trace. "Can you not free your brother yourself? You have powers of magic far beyond the tales of wonder that the old women tell."

He reclined upon the pillows of the pavilion, restoring his rags around his magnificent body with a wave of his hand. *Here I do, in the open air. But not inside Topkapi. There is one who lives there whose magic is a match for mine. Like you, she can see me. I am sure you know her.*

"What is her name?"

Leyla.

Yasmina shuddered. Leyla frightened all whose paths she crossed, whether she deigned to look at them or not. Her gaze was hypnotic and her eyes a bright shade of green. Not the fresh green of new leaves or young herbs, but a green that had the distilled purity of venom.

"Yes, I know her. I wish I did not." Leyla had a particular dislike for anyone whose intelligence equaled her own, and Yasmina had soon sensed that the green-eyed woman saw her as an enemy and wished her harm. But from this at least Yasmina had been spared from the day she entered the harem. Brought after some months to the Hunkar Sofasi, the luxurious hall of the sultan, Yasmina had instantly caught the old man's jaded eye, and Leyla had thought it unwise to have her poisoned or drowned.

Leyla had seen to it that the dark-haired new girl received the customary training in deportment and dress, music and dance, and games of chess and backgammon, that Yasmina might someday serve to amuse master and mistress. But Yasmina excelled in all these things, so much so that Leyla became uneasy.

As the years went by, Leyla made trouble for her, falsely accusing Yasmina of minor misdeeds, assigning her to help the herbwoman, Kosem, as punishment. Kosem's chamber was off a gallery that ran under the roof, far from the society of the other odalisques and far from Suleyman. Leyla entertained the hope that the sultan would forget Yasmina in time.

Yasmina had been grateful enough to escape the necessary fawning upon her lord and master and the spoiled Gulbahar as well. Patient and quiet, she learned much by assisting the herb-woman—as always, saying little.

"Who is Leyla to you?" Yasmina could not help but think that this strange man might have shared Leyla's bed.

My cousin. A distant one.

"I see. And is she the one who betrayed you and your lover to the sultan?"

Rustem gave her a long look. *No. But she was sorry she missed the chance to do so. And Leyla was glad to see me die. She laughed when I was lowered into the molten gold, screaming.*

"Why?"

He met Yasmina's horrified eyes. *She is cruel. If you know her, then you know that.*

All she could do was look away. Leyla was the confidante of Gulbahar, the sultan's chief wife and favorite, and held great power in the harem. When resentment festered between two women, Leyla and her eunuchs had the least lovely of the two sewn up in a bag and drowned, on the grounds that it was the swiftest cure for jealousy. When a shy neophyte was discovered penning love poems to an imaginary swain, Leyla made sure that the girl's hands were beaten black and blue. She was feared and hated, and she gloried in it.

"Has she had your brother imprisoned in Topkapi?"

Yes. Mehmed is held somewhere within those walls. The golden man looked at the palace fiercely, as if his gaze could pierce the marble. *Leyla intends him to serve as stud for Gulbahar, who hopes to give the sultan a son.*

"The sultan is old and ill. And he will know that her child does not spring from his seed."

But no one else will because our great ruler, the mighty Suleyman, is too vain to let such a secret escape. But he must and will have a son. It is his dearest wish that his direct line continue. All his relatives are dead, save for his nephew, who has gone quite mad, you know.

Yasmina nodded. The wails of this unfortunate man, caged in a closely guarded tower for twenty years, could sometimes be heard in the night, like a jackal's howl.

"Why did Leyla choose your brother?"

She dallied with me once. I suppose I proved myself worthy in her bed, and now she assumes my brother will be able to do the same with Gulbahar.

Rustem fell silent for a few moments, gazing up at the latticed roof of the pavilion in which they sheltered. The birds had returned and were singing again, a lonely melody the ethereal musician had taught them.

Ah, Yasmina. I did not enter your body and so you did not realize that I am hollow. Give me a breath of a breeze and I can drift about. And I go where I wish, since I also have the power to make myself invisible.

"I can see you."

You are a strange one, Yasmina. From whence do you come?

"Circassia. A remote province." She named it in her own tongue.

He gave her a surprised look. *My father's family came from there. No wonder we can understand each other. And my brother will as well.*

"Could you not foresee that he would be taken, if you can see even a little of the future?"

As I said, Leyla's magic is a match for my own. Her men dragged him from my family's palace in the night. I tried to stop them. It was no use.

She wrapped the shawl more tightly about herself.

But I followed. And I learned Leyla's purpose soon enough.

"When was he taken?"

He sat up and then stood up, towering over her. *Last night. There is no time to waste. Leyla is preparing the sultan's wife for the great moment—decking her out with little bells, as if Gulbahar were a prize cow. And the musicians are tuning up.*

Yasmina could just hear a discordant series of irregular notes begin. The birds ceased their melodious singing and listened too.

They will play incessantly and loudly to cover up the sounds of the secret lovemaking.

"What if Mehmed cannot make love? The penis of a frightened man will shrivel between his legs," Yasmina pointed out.

Leyla can make any man grow hard. There is no pleasure she does not know. And Gulbahar is a beauty who has been trained in the erotic arts. Yet, sultan's favorite or no, she is a slave like all of you. Worth nothing.

Yasmina's eyes grew hard. "Why should I help your brother?"

Because you must. It is kismet. Your fate and his are intertwined.

Rustem reached a hand to her, and Yasmina took it without thinking. He pulled her to her feet and drew the shawl from her shoulders.

Leave this here. He dropped it back among the pillows.

The cool night air stiffened her nipples and Yasmina covered them with her hands. "I cannot go back with ripped clothes."

One brush of his golden hand drew the delicate fibers together. It also caused her sensitive flesh to thrill under his warmth, and Yasmina was assailed by sexual sensations once more. But her sheer silk garment was miraculously new again.

He reached between her legs with breathtaking speed and reopened the split in her pantaloons, putting a finger to her cunny and then licking it as if he tasted heaven. *Sweet as honey. You could not help surrendering to such pleasure, beautiful Yasmina.* He squeezed her there, and the cloth was restored to silken perfection, as if he had not made that bold cut with his dagger and revealed her excited cunny to his searching eyes.

Yasmina shivered without the shawl. Rustem looked down and brushed her nipples, erect once more, with the palms of his hands, a sensation so strong that she arched backward and let her hair flow behind her. With infinite gentleness, as if they were locked in some strange dance, he put his hands about her waist, then lifted her up, kissing her lips as chastely as a boy. She wanted to weep, overwhelmed by his tenderness, and knowing that it was far more dangerous than the animal urges he had described in rough whispers.

"Ah, Rustem. . . ." She could not tell him what was in her heart. Whoever and whatever he was, this golden man was not of her world and might pull her into one of whirling spirits and far fiercer djinns than he, lost forever among the souls not risen.

He said no more but put his arm around her shoulders with a lightness that made her remember what he had said: he was hollow. He brought her back through the garden to the secret door, and they stepped through it.

I will be with you from now on, but you will not see me.

"Yes," she whispered . . . and he vanished.

As the night wore on, Yasmina retreated to a windowed chamber off a high gallery three stories above the main floor of the great palace and its endless warren of rooms. Here, where it was warm and sunny during the day, the herbwoman could dry flowers and plants to make her potions. It was a pleasant enough place.

Yasmina lifted the curtain to enter and let it fall back into shabby folds, looking at the herbwoman. Old Kosem, a venerable crone who had resided in Topkapi since her birth to a kitchen slave, was uncorking a small bottle and sniffing at its contents, wrinkling her nose.

"This will do. He must wake up, and he must be virile."

Kosem spoke freely, assuming as so many did that Yasmina did not understand much. Being hard of hearing, Kosem barely noticed her assistant come into the room, but she did look up when Yasmina stood in front of her to ask, "Who?"

"A guest." The herbwoman dismissed Yasmina with a wave of her crabbed hand and went back to talking mostly to herself. "An unexpected guest, but an honored one. He will spend the night in the sultan's private apartments. The slaves are rushing about, bringing in silken pillows and soft carpets through the doorway to there. Perhaps Suleyman desires to view an orgy."

The old woman's frankness did not shock Yasmina. But the mention of a "guest," who very likely was none other than the kidnapped Mehmed, sent a shiver down her spine.

"No, that cannot be," Kosem muttered. "The sultan would never let an outsider see his odalisques. He reserves that pleasure for himself." She swirled the uncorked bottle in her hand as she mused aloud. "One man might service many women with this. The eunuch said our guest is deep in some strange dream. Whether from wine or opium . . . who knows?"

Yasmina knew he might have been given both against his will.

Kosem tipped the bottle over her grimy fingertips and poured a few drops of a foul-smelling dark liquid upon them, rubbing and sniffing. "Yasmina—come here. Taste this."

She shook her head. The old woman was not strong enough to force her to swallow the stuff, and she would not. Yasmina busied herself with straightening the glass phials and jars that lined the shelves, pausing to put a pestle back into a stone mortar and run a rag over the edge of the shelves, brushing away a few insects that had crawled out of the drying bunches of herbs.

A commotion on the floor far below rose to where they were, and Yasmina went to the curtain and pushed it aside, but only a little. Even from this height the half-dressed, beautiful young man she saw bore a very great resemblance to Rustem.

But his face had a beaten, groggy look, and he was gasping. He looked up wildly and then around, hearing his pursuers gain on him. A slave came into the room through an arched doorway, a massive man with bulging arms and thighs, cutting off the only avenue of escape.

The young man backed off and was captured at once by several more slaves who gagged him and tied his hands behind his back.

Yasmina knew at once that this was Mehmed. Her heart went out to him, as humiliated and ill-used as she once had been. Yet, though Rustem had said it was kismet for her to help him, she could not.

Yes, you can.

She looked around for the golden man with the burning eyes but did not see him . . . and remembered his parting words to her. Rustem was here but invisible.

Yasmina dropped her voice to the merest whisper. "Rustem . . . how came you here?"

Over the roof. This high chamber is far enough away from Leyla. She does not sense me. But I cannot stay long inside the walls of Topkapi.

She clinked the little bottles with a swipe of her dust rag to keep the old woman from hearing her almost inaudible replies. "What must I do?"

Follow old Kosem when she brings the potion to Gulbahar's private room.

"I cannot. She will insist on going alone," she whispered. A glance over her shoulder told her that Kosem was still preoccupied with the potion in the bottle.

I will see to that. She will need you to help when I twist her arm.

Yasmina sensed Rustem moving swiftly away from her. Then the herbwoman cried out, "Ay!" and clutched her arm. Her withered muscles stood out, contorted in a painful spasm, and her knobbed fingers clawed the air, as though an unseen someone had her by the wrist. "Ay! Ay!"

Yasmina rushed to the herbwoman and reached out, but Kosem shrank from her. "Get away from me! Ay, what has happened? Has this strange brew crippled my hand? But I poured out only a drop. . . ." She extended her fingers with excruciating slowness and tested her sore wrist by picking up the bottle.

Wincing, the old woman dropped it but righted it awkwardly with the other hand. Then the invisible Rustem twisted that arm too.

"Ay!" Kosem flailed at the air, then dropped her hands into her lap. Yasmina did not reach out again, knowing that she would be rebuffed as before. As the pain ebbed away, Kosem shook her head and returned her thoughts to her assigned task. She wrapped a cloth around the little bottle to protect her skin from the contents and motioned to Yasmina to stay.

Yasmina only nodded as she watched Kosem lift the curtain. Once the old woman was shuffling along the gallery to the long staircase that led down to the lower floors, Yasmina followed.

I cannot go with you, but I will be able to read your thoughts and guide you.

She nodded to the unseen presence. The old woman scuttled like a spider down the upper stairs, with Yasmina not far behind, making no noise at all in her soft, embroidered leather slippers.

No one was about as they reached the lowest floor, and the corridor to the sultan's private apartment lay unguarded. The portals, however, were flanked by two tall, turbaned black men, garbed in saffron silk robes, each with a pistol thrust into his sash and a curved, double-headed ax as well.

They let Kosem pass and only narrowed their eyes at Yasmina as she quickened her steps and followed close behind.

The sultan's rooms were luxuriously appointed, almost overwhelming to Yasmina's eyes. She had never been called here and had never wanted to be. The great ruler was elsewhere, evidently, and only Gulbahar and Leyla were present. Both were nearly naked.

Gulbahar wore only long earrings and jewelry upon her neck. Her rich, impossibly red hair flowed in waves over her white back, though it was constrained to some degree by a pattern of braids woven into each temple. A cabochon jewel on a delicate cord hung at the widow's peak that defined her heart-shaped face.

Leyla, black-haired, with skin the color of milky coffee, wore only a little more: a wide strap of silk, decorated with a beaded fringe, adorned her waist, and from it, other, narrower straps without beads ran between her buttocks, around the tops of her thighs, and disappeared into her cunny.

Yasmina shrank behind a fringed drape of magnificent brocade before either could see her, peeping through its fringes. Kosem made the customary obeisances and scuttled into a room farther on, averting her eyes from the sexual sport of the chief wife and Leyla.

Rustem spoke silently in Yasmina's mind.

The old woman is tired and in pain. Their play does not interest or excite her, and it will not take long before Mehmed is brought out.

Leyla was caressing Gulbahar's plump behind as the sultan's wife sprawled on a divan, her lips sucking one tube of a nargileh. The pungent smoke of the hashish it held filled the air.

Gulbahar giggled drowsily, raising her rosy-pink rump under the other woman's hands and letting Leyla push her down again and again, in a sensual imitation of intercourse.

Her small feet had been hennaed in elaborate designs, Yasmina noticed, and her hands too—designs that were used to beautify a bride for her groom.

There was no sign of Mehmed. Since erotic pleasure would

increase Gulbahar's chance of conceiving a son for her lord and master, no doubt Leyla was preparing her mistress's body. The terrified Mehmed might be forced to spill his seed, but that would be all he could do.

Lelya left off her stimulating fondling of Gulbahar's bare behind and stroked her legs, capturing her feet and tying her ankles together with a twist of a light silk scarf. Gulbahar only laughed and took another puff from the nargileh.

Leyla began to stroke the bottoms of Gulbahar's feet, not so lightly that it tickled but in an erotic, deeply soothing way that made her spoiled mistress moan softly. Then Leyla began to pinch the pads of her pretty toes, a sensation easily felt by such smooth and pampered feet.

Gulbahar spent most of her time lolling about, Yasmina knew, being waited on by her women and slaves. But Yasmina had not known how much Leyla liked to do so. The glittering look in the woman's green eyes, the flushed cheeks, her evident passion for a beautiful female body—yes, Leyla's sexual arousal was clear.

"Untie me," Gulbahar said lazily.

"But I have only just begun, my lady," Leyla replied in a soft voice. "Do you not wish your beloved Leyla to give you more pleasure?"

"Of course. When I am on my back. Or—I might get up. I like to see you on your knees, Leyla. Humbly asking if you might touch your tongue to my cunny. And being whipped for asking."

Yasmina saw Leyla's eyes widen with excitement. She untwisted the silk scarf from about Gulbahar's ankles and rubbed them tenderly.

"Enough of that. Get my whip. And the other things."

Yasmina heard Rustem's amused voice in her head. *Ah. Gulbahar is more wicked than the bitch who serves her sexually. I should like to see Leyla humiliated.*

As Gulbahar stood and stretched, cupping her full breasts with sensual self-absorption, Leyla got on all fours. She reached under the divan for a long box, carved, Yasmina could see, with a demure scene of lovers in a garden. She drew it forth and lifted the lid, removing things that were anything but demure: a many-tailed whip with a penis-shaped handle. A set of large, smooth beads spaced on a string. And several shafts of ivory and wood, smooth and gleaming.

As if offering tribute to a goddess, Leyla set all these objects at her mistress's bare feet, crouching to press kisses upon Gulbahar's hennaed toes. Yasmina saw that the delicate bands about Leyla's waist and the tops of her thighs held a dildo in her cunny—a dildo that eased out an inch or two in her abject position. Gulbahar bent suddenly and rammed it in all the way, making Leyla cry out with pleasure.

"Yes, my mistress," Leyla murmured. "I desire only to submit to you. If you are not pleased with me, I ask for the whip."

Yasmina drew in her breath. The beautiful bitch would be humiliated indeed. That Leyla wanted to be did surprise her.

Leyla reached up to stroke and caress Gulbahar's flawless thighs, then pressed her face against the favorite's shaved cunny and clasped her buttocks.

Gulbahar stroked her lover's flowing black locks and tightened her fingers in it, using Leyla's hair to pull her away and make her look up. "Not yet," was all she said. She slapped Leyla and none too gently.

Leyla put a hand to her reddened cheek and sat back on her haunches. The glowing look in her eyes, her air of eager submissiveness, puzzled Yasmina but only for a second. Then Rustem spoke, dryly amused as before.

Leyla worships power, my dear Yasmina. Even though his words were silent, Yasmina sensed the contempt in them. *And Gulbahar wields it well as the sultan's wife. I wonder if the vile Suleyman is watching from some hidden place.*

Gulbahar looked over the things at her feet and touched a toe to the whip. Leyla handed it to her, caressing the penis-shaped handle. The sultan's wife ran the strips of leather through her hand, twisting and untwisting them as Layla watched.

Though the strips of leather were numerous, all were light and fine and held no hidden stings at their tips. Yasmina supposed it had been made to provide sexual excitement and not to injure or wound those who felt its lash.

"On all fours, Leyla," the sultana said softly. "And spread your legs very wide."

Leyla opened her mouth in an inaudible moan, anticipating the intense pleasure she craved. She did Gulbahar's bidding, turning her buttocks to her mistress and pulling her hair over her shoulder so her back was bare.

Without waiting, Gulbahar brought the many-tailed whip down upon Leyla's back, again and again, but so lightly that her submissive lover's skin only glowed. Yasmina saw no welts and no blood.

The sultana concentrated next upon Leyla's bare buttocks, whipping her there so sensually that it was all Leyla could do to hold still. She was moaning incoherently, begging for more and begging for it to be done harder.

"No," Gulbahar said imperiously. "You whispered to me last night when we lay in each other's arms that you wanted the beads in your behind."

"Yes," Leyla whispered.

"And that you wanted me to pull them out at the moment of climax." Gulbahar rested her bare foot on one of Leyla's buttocks, brushing her back with the tips of the whip strings. "You are a slut, Leyla. A hungry slut who wants to be used."

"My mistress, to be used by you is all that I want. . . ." Leyla hung her head and said no more.

The sultana took her foot off Leyla's behind and set the

whip aside. She picked up the string of large, smooth beads, oiling them with an unguent from a small jar. She dangled them in front of Leyla's face. "Look at them before I put them into your little hole. I shall push them in slowly, watching the tight ring of flesh open for each until all are inside you."

Leyla gasped, looking up at Gulbahar with frantic desire in her eyes. "I wish it so, if that is your pleasure, mistress."

The sultana nodded and turned to straddle Leyla, bending over and spreading her trembling buttocks with one hand. She carefully inserted the smooth beads into her lover's anus, smiling when Leyla moaned as each sphere slipped inside her. Gulbahar left the last one outside so that the string might be pulled out. Whether by her or by Leyla, Yasmina did not know.

They are unbelievably wanton. Does this arouse you?

Yasmina was glad that she did not have to answer.

"There, Leyla. Now I shall lie back upon the divan and allow you to lick my cunny. You are not permitted to touch yourself until I climax. And I want to see your face when you do. One hand on your cunny and the other pulling the beads out of your tight hole with each pulse. One by one."

Gulbahar returned to the divan, lying across it with her thighs fully spread. She slid a ringed finger between her shaved, slick labia and pleasured herself lazily. Layla stared. The sultan's wife was the picture of erotic elegance, from the jewel upon her forehead to her decorated feet. Her rosy-tipped breasts were high and firm even lying down, and her redhead's skin was pure and white.

The darker woman kneeled between her spread thighs, licking and sucking the tender flesh that Gulbahar was teasing with her finger. Leyla's tongue soon supplanted that finger, and Gulbahar threw her arms back over the rolled side of the divan, pushing up her hips into Leyla's wet face.

Her submissive attendant brought her to a moaning climax within moments, and Gulbahar pressed Leyla's head against her cunny with both hands. Then she lay back, gasping, while Leyla wiped her mouth and awaited the next command.

"Now," Gulbahar murmured. She rolled on her side and motioned for Leyla to begin. Her lover buried a hand in her own cunny, pushing in the strapped dildo and rubbing her pleasure bud with slow strokes and reaching around to hold the last bead that she would use to pull the others out. Leyla's eyes closed, and her mouth opened.

Gulbahar slapped her. "Look at me. Come for me."

The masturbating woman opened her eyes again, very wide, only a second before her climax began. Leyla began to moan softly, rocking on her knees and pulling out the beads from behind, one by one, as she had been commanded. Gulbahar reached between Leyla's legs to keep the dildo in and feel her orgasm and smiled. "Ah. That was good. Very good, Leyla. You have pleased me."

Leyla subsided with one last, low moan, and Gulbahar stretched out again, looking pleased enough and a little bored.

"Now bring Mehmed to me. But get dressed. I would not have him desire you or see these things."

The other woman scrambled to obey and soon stood before Gulbahar, clad in plain, roughly woven shawls and the dress of a peasant, her hair covered.

The sultan's wife laughed. "You are the picture of modesty. Go." She waved her attendant toward the far room into which Kosem had disappeared, and Leyla left.

She soon returned, holding Mehmed by the hand, who was now completely naked. Yasmina felt a flash of inexplicable jealousy. So close, still hidden, she could see that he did indeed resemble Rustem in every particular. He was tall, with the smooth body of a man of twenty, lithe and strong.

His chest was broad, and it tapered down into a flat belly, with a large cock nestled in the dark curls of his taut groin. His thighs were well muscled, and his legs were long—surely he had spent much of his time in the open, hunting and riding and enjoying himself as a young prince should.

He seemed utterly, fully alive. The shadow of blue-black death that Yasmina had seen in his older brother's eyes was absent from his. No, Mehmed's eyes held a warm fire and a mingled look of terror and fury. His hair was also dark, in loose curls that gave him the look of a statue of antiquity, a perfect kouros made for sexual worship.

She noted the wounds on his body with a fury of her own. Leyla brought him to stand before Gulbahar, not explaining who the magnificent woman on the couch was. Mehmed did not look away.

Kosem's drug had stiffened his cock, and Gulbahar reached out to touch and stroke it. She spread her legs and reached up her arms to him. He could not be in his right mind—Yasmina wondered what Kosem had put in her potion. Mehmed leaned down, aided by Leyla, who inserted the tip of his cock into her mistress's cunny. Nature compelled him from then on, and the beautiful young man thrust furiously into her softest flesh, making Gulbahar writhe beneath him, aroused in a very different way than she had been by her servile female lover. Her curving hips and thighs cradled his body, and the sultan's wife clutched his tightening buttocks, pulling him deep inside her.

Leyla stood by to watch, sulking.

Mehmed grabbed Gulbahar's white shoulders and fucked her hard, banging her down against the cushions of the divan until he spent, bucking and moaning, his eyes closed and his dark curls sweating with the intensity of an orgasm that must have seemed half nightmare, half dream of pleasure.

Yasmina bit her lip. She desired him. They might die together this day, but she desired him.

Mehmed lifted himself, the drug in his blood wearing off, and looked down at Gulbahar and then at Leyla. The words he was about to utter died in his throat when Leyla dragged him by one hand to his feet, possessed of a strength made fierce by her own jealousy.

And now . . . darkness comes, Yasmina heard Rustem say. A black fog began to swirl in the corners of the room, unnoticed by all save her. *Go to Mehmed. Lead him away and to Kosem's chamber. You two will not be overcome by the black fog, but the others will be—just long enough for you to escape.*

3

Yasmina was grateful that Mehmed followed her when she took his hand, supposing it the work of Rustem's magic also. Perhaps his brother could hear him too, but there was not time to discuss such things. They had to flee the chamber where the sultan's wife and Leyla had collapsed, not breathing. Rustem's last words had been to tell her that in the room beyond, Kosem had suffocated, along with the guards and nameless servants.

Worst of all, the black fog had brought death to the sultan, who had been watching the debauched play of his wife and Leyla as Rustem thought he might. But the old man's hiding place, outfitted with every comfort and luxury but windows, had filled up first. He had swung open the pierced door too late, and the great ruler of an empire, of Constantinople, the potentate at the center of the glittering palace of Topkapi, had died as miserably as a rat smoked out of a tunnel.

Yasmina guided Mehmed to the stairs, noticing that his wounds were bleeding. What strength he had seemed to have been absorbed by Gulbahar in their intercourse. She put her shoulder under his arms to support him most of the way, praying that no one would see them.

The black fog had swirled into the corridors but not as thickly. Those who breathed it lay prone upon the mosaic floor to the right and the left of them, but were not dead. Not yet.

If she could get him back to the chamber under the roof, where Rustem might yet be, Mehmed would have a chance to escape and to live. Unlike her . . . but when Yasmina stopped to get her breath, she remembered that all who had been present in and about the sultan's private rooms were dead. There would be no one to bear witness against her.

A fleeting thought crossed her mind: might she also escape? She knew of no one who had done so. The women who entered the harem of the sultan through the Gate of Felicity never left it. Except through the Gate of Sighs—and then only if they had been singled out for murder.

Mehmed moaned and sagged against her. Yasmina summoned all her strength to keep him moving, putting an arm about his waist and encouraging him step by step. He scarcely seemed to hear her.

They reached the herbwoman's chamber at last, and she guided him swiftly to Kosem's old bed, finding a pillow for his head and helping him to lie down. She took one last look at his prone body, grateful that his breathing was steady. If only she could make the marks of his torture vanish and restore him to his natural perfection. She was familiar with many of Kosem's medicines and potions; she prayed she knew enough. Yasmina drew a light cover over him and then turned when the air in the room stirred suddenly.

My brave Yasmina. Rustem appeared in all his golden glory, undimmed by black rags, at least above the waist.

"Do not praise me," she said frantically. "Mehmed is grievously wounded. Leyla's men have tortured him and Kosem's potion still runs in his veins."

Rustem lit an oil lamp and brought it to the bed. He kneeled by his unconscious brother and pulled off the cover. He inspected the wounds—dagger slashes and rope burns and a very small puncture that oozed a black liquid. He looked closely at it and shook his head. *This little wound may kill him.*

"But the others look much worse—"

For now we must stanch the bleeding. Show me which to use. Yasmina looked quickly through the phials, selecting one and then the dry herbs. She crushed aromatic leaves in the mortar and pestle and poured the contents of the phial over them, adding sweet oil to bind the mixture.

She crossed the chamber to kneel at Mehmed's side, anointing the bleeding gashes and the rope burns with the salve she had made. He moaned when she touched his injured flesh, and Yasmina wanted to cry. But she would not; her tears would not save this beautiful man.

She sat by Mehmed's side when she was done. Rustem had not said any more about the smallest wound but had gone to the secret garden behind the magic door to seek a remedy. The blackness was no longer oozing from the puncture—it spread, slow but inexorable, an evil stain.

The young man lay uncovered, his skin hot to the touch. Yasmina watched in silence, awed by his beauty. He was young but not so young as the boys the eunuchs sometimes kept. No, there was a shadow of beard along his chiseled jaw and a dusting of dark hair upon his chest. Mehmed was in the early years of manhood, still lean but with the same powerful body and natural virility his brother had once possessed.

His vulnerability touched her heart. Laid low by violence, he was, for a few stolen moments, safe in her keeping. She had cleaned him intimately as best she could, gently washing away all traces of his semen and Gulbahar's juice.

His cock rested over velvety balls she had touched as she cleaned him, making him stir, though he was still in a trance.

Yasmina ached to caress him there. To serve as his nurse was a strange experience: her awakened desire had to be restrained, which only made the yearning stronger. She had done all she could for him by now; watching over him was all that was left. He opened his eyes for only a moment, and the strange glitter in them told her that a fever was rising in his brain.

She lifted the lamp and brought it closer when Mehmed closed his eyes again. There was a high, unhealthy color in his face. Yasmina rose to prepare herb-infused water, placing a cool cloth in it and wringing it out to place upon his brow. She was deeply afraid that he would die.

Mehmed, in his nakedness, was more beautiful than any richly attired prince. Her whole body ached for him and longing pierced her heart. She hoped he would not remember that he had been forced to serve as stud to the wicked Gulbahar.

For a moment Yasmina's jealousy got the better of her, remembering how the sultana had enjoyed the remarkable beauty of Mehmed's strong young body, spreading her flawless thighs and greedily getting all of his cock into her cunny as she undulated beneath him.

He was both the object and the victim of lethal desire. Gulbahar and Leyla had used him as they wished and would have killed him in the end. Still, if the sultan's wife had conceived and Mehmed had met his death—or if he did not live to see this dawn—his seed would have lived on. And Yasmina would have found a way to be close to the little son Gulbahar had hoped to bear. Yasmina, an odalisque of low rank, would never have a child of her own.

Mehmed was young and strong. Made to live . . . and to love. Yasmina pressed her palms to her face to keep all evil away, then pressed them together and prayed to Allah for his recovery. There was not much time. Some of the surviving victims of the dispersing black fog were groaning below, not knowing what manner of calamity had befallen them but not yet able to raise an alarm that would rouse the two thousand and two people who lived in Topkapi: odalisques, servants, guards, courtiers, and all.

She heard Rustem's light footsteps upon the roof above and turned as he came into the chamber moments later. He had in his hand a few sprigs of a plant she had never seen, and again, he knelt by his brother.

"The last wound is worse. He is feverish."

The blackness is spreading. I feared this would happen.

"What causes it?"

Leyla's magic.

"But she is dead," Yasmina said, suddenly afraid that the green-eyed woman who had ruled the seraglio by subterfuge and secret terror had somehow lived. In the guise of a snake, perhaps, or something smaller—a spider that could be hanging nearby on a single thread of silk, watching her and Mehmed and Rustem.

The look on Rustem's face confirmed her fears. *Yes . . . and no.*

"What do you mean?" Yasmina felt the cloth on Mehmed's forehead. It was burning hot. She exchanged it for another that had been sitting in the basin of water.

It may be that this black wound contains a trace of her. I am sure she watched Mehmed being tortured. Leyla enjoys that.

"Giving it and taking it," Yasmina murmured bitterly.

Yes, as you saw. And Mehmed is too like me for her to be able to resist hurting him. Her fingernails are strong and razor sharp. It would be nothing for her to pierce human skin.

Yasmina shuddered. "Is there nothing we can do?"

Rustem did not answer but busied himself making another potion. She looked long at his young brother, willing Mehmed to stay alive, wishing there was some way she could draw the poison from the evil wound Leyla had inflicted upon him.

The golden man knocked over a phial, and she glanced his

way. Rustem was clutching the edge of the table and shaking. His skin began to shimmer like molten metal in a crucible.

Leyla. She is near.

The shimmering stopped and his body ceased its trembling, but Yasmina saw the blue-black light flicker wildly in his eyes. He drew in a long sigh and then relaxed. But he seemed perceptibly weaker.

She has gone on.

"Is she dead?"

I do not know. He came to sit by his brother and dipped a soft cloth in the potion he had made, touching it to the black wound. Mehmed screamed and convulsed, and Rustem pulled the cloth back, cursing.

My strength is ebbing. And this potion is not strong enough to counteract Leyla's magic.

Mehmed's beautiful face grew pale and drawn. Yasmina stroked his cheek and a faint flush of color appeared again.

Your hands, Yasmina . . . you have a healing touch.

"But it is not enough. The blackness still is spreading under his skin. Your medicine does not work and my touch cannot save him. Unless . . ." She hesitated.

What?

"You said that my orgasm gave you strength. Make me have another."

Rustem shook his head. *But you do not want me. You loved Mehmed from the moment you saw him.*

"I did not know that I would, or why I do. But it is true. He must not die."

The golden man was silent for a little while. *I also do not want to die. When I saw you in the garden, I believed that I might live.*

Suddenly she felt him forcibly penetrate her consciousness, and she saw, against her will, through the eyes of Rustem, the moment when he had been lowered into the molten gold. She saw Suleyman looking on impassively, his wrinkled face sweating in the reflected heat next to Gulbahar's, beautiful and indifferent. And Leyla's green eyes, glowing with evil.

Yasmina covered her face and wept for all the wickedness in the world. Was it wicked of her to desire the living brother, when she had sworn never to feel that emotion at all? The question tore at her heart.

Mehmed moaned and she laid a soothing hand upon his brow. The pulse in his temple throbbed under her fingertips. He opened his eyes and looked into hers. Yasmina felt a wave of sudden, passionate love for him that rose from deep within her soul, as the fountain in the garden rose from deep within the earth.

I will do as you wish, Yasmina.

Rustem's memory of his own death dissolved in her mind as he stood up. He took her hand and led her into an alcove outside the circle of light cast by the oil lamp, bidding her to lift her dress and reveal her cunny to him. The first time he had taken her with his mouth, employing a tender skill that had nearly undone her. His rough words afterward, his careless reminder of her enslaved state, had steeled her resolve not to let him penetrate her. She had half believed, in the twilight garden behind the secret door, that Rustem was real. For a little while.

Whatever reality the golden man still possessed was an illusion—a dangerous one. A woman whose body had been entered by a djinn would be owned by him in this world and the next.

To save his brother, she would give herself to Rustem. Despite her unspoken, fleeting hopes, Yasmina knew she had little chance of escaping alive from Topkapi . . . but Mehmed might. Let me do one good thing before they come for me, she thought wildly. Before I die.

She touched Rustem between his legs and felt the black rags fall away and his golden cock spring up. He kissed her roughly this time, not bothering with sweet words or allowing her to caress him.

He held her against the wall and spread her legs, thrusting hard, ramming the huge cock head as far as it would go. The pleasure was intense, and her cunny pulsed around his shaft. He tore at the embroidered bodice of her dress, pulling out her breasts to suckle upon them, bending his head down and writhing around her. Yasmina was seized by a powerful climax, trembling as he ran his hands over her half-clothed body. She moaned faintly and drew back from him.

Rustem looked more alive than before, more golden—and more sad.

Thank you. His tone was unemotional. *Now I—or should I say we?—can minister to Mehmed.*

He left her with her dress still up around her waist and her breasts bare. She leaned her weary head against the cool wall, aware of the hot liquid from his ejaculation trickling from her cunny onto one thigh. Yasmina touched herself there and looked at her finger in the flickering light. Pure gold.

He had set her on fire and then quenched it. Why, if her desire strengthened him, was she so weak? She felt only emptiness. And exhaustion. Then, from the chamber where Mehmed lay, she heard his voice for the first time.

He was talking to Rustem, somewhat incoherently, covering his brother's golden hands with kisses, telling him of his nightmare and the beautiful angel in it who had led him away from two she-devils.

Yasmina arranged her clothes and went into the lamp-lit chamber. Bare-chested, Rustem looked quite real in its glow, golden in the way that anyone would be by the light of a lantern. But surely Mehmed did not believe that his brother had come back from the dead. Perhaps his ordeal and Kosem's potion still fogged his mind.

Or the deathly taint where Leyla had pierced his side was

doing worse. Rustem pulled back the covers and looked at the ever-spreading blackness. He motioned to Yasmina to come to them. *Place your hand upon his side.*

She did, feeling the cold poison under his skin ebb away, drawing it into the warmth of her hand. The younger man looked at Rustem. "I am still in a dream, I fear. I am talking to my dead brother, and here is the angel again." He looked around the herbwoman's chamber. "Heaven is a shabby-looking place."

You are not in heaven.

"Then where am I? Brother, explain."

Rustem tried his best. When he finished, Mehmed only nodded.

The three of them, the living and the dead, sat in silence for several moments. Rustem spoke at last. *Leyla's spirit is riding the clouds above us. We are doomed.*

4

Rustem's golden body shimmered and the light in his eyes dimmed.

She will kill us all. Starting with me. He gasped, unable to draw in air, and Mehmed rose from the bed, restored to vigor, wanting only to help his stricken brother.

Go from this place. Rustem breathed out the words.

"Not without you." Naked, Mehmed lifted his brother. Yasmina gazed at them through a mist of tears.

"Rustem, you could not enter Topkapi in your spirit body," Yasmina said softly. "Then she cannot."

I have tried to explain this. Her evil magic counteracts mine. Your good magic seemed to strengthen me and so I could follow you for a little while. But you are not as strong as Leyla. The oil in the lamp was low, and the light flickered as though a spirit were in the room with them. Rustem's head dropped back and his arms and legs hung limp. Yasmina fought a sickening wave of fear. Was Leyla's vengeful spirit descending from the heavens? She heard a faint howl in the sky above and shook with fear. The sound died away, and she realized she had heard the night wind begin to blow as it always did. If only it would push Leyla far, far away. . . .

Mehmed turned to her, holding his brother with ease, a question in his eyes. "Why is he so light?"

"He is hollow, Mehmed."

The younger man nodded. "Then I can carry him, even over the many roofs of Topkapi. If Leyla's spirit is riding a cloud, the wind may yet push her away. Or drop her screaming into the sea, where ifrits and djinns belong. Yasmina—come with us."

She raised a hand to caress his resolute face. A hero's face— but she could not be a heroine. If she went with Mehmed, it would slow him down, and both of them would be murdered.

Better to stay. She could live out her days in the harem if Leyla's spirit could not enter. "No. But I will clothe you. In Kosem's dirty old dress, with charcoal upon your face, you will not be easy to see."

Listen to her. Rustem's voice was weak. Very weak. *Put me down, Mehmed.*

With reluctance, the younger man did, settling his brother upon the bed where he had nearly breathed his last. Yasmina looked at his body again. The black wound was a faint shadow now, and the skin had closed.

Mehmed's long, muscular legs were made for running, and his strong arms could hold his brother while he ran. There was hope. Rustem rested as she brought out the dress and garbed Mehmed, dusting his handsome face with charcoal and tying a ragged shawl over his head. She heard Rustem's silent, bitter laugh.

You can beg your way back to our family's palace, Mehmed. If by some miracle you escape.

"We shall. You are too weak to fight me off. Yasmina, is there a sack I can put him into?"

No.

"Yes," Mehmed said.

Wordlessly, admiring the younger man's stubborn courage, she found a huge sack. Mehmed slipped it over Rustem's feet and drew it up the length of his body, stopping at his chin. He pulled it up over his brother's glowering face, bunched the top of the sack into folds, and tied a rag tightly around them.

An ignominious way to leave the palace. But I suppose it is better than boiling to death.

Mehmed ignored this complaint as he hoisted the sack over his shoulder. "Which way to the roof, Yasmina?"

"Come with me." She pushed aside the curtain, peering down at the floor far below. The semiconscious guards sprawled on the tiles were still there. No one had come to their aid, though she could hear distant shouts from the far corners of the palace. No doubt everyone was afraid of ifrits—or whatever and whoever they imagined had brought a mysterious pestilence into Topkapi, visiting death upon the sultan and his wife and the loathed Leyla—if anyone had gotten past the guards and seen their corpses. It was possible no one had.

She stole out, leading Mehmed and his brother, who was quiet inside the sack. The opening that led to the roof was unlocked and unguarded. She drew down a narrow ladder and went up first, climbing out after first peering around, not sure what she would do if she saw Leyla. But there were no clouds in the starry sky. And no moon, by Allah's mercy.

Yasmina reached down to assist Mehmed. Despite his awkward burden and Kosem's dress, he moved up and through the opening with ease. Once upon the roof, he closed the door and stood upon it. "You are coming with us. I have decided. Do not argue, Yasmina."

She gaped at Mehmed, half expecting to hear a few words from Rustem on the subject. But the golden man in the sack was silent.

Mehmed reached out his hand and she took it. Warm and

strong, his fingers clasped hers, and Yasmina felt a surge of hope. From where they were standing, the starry sky seemed infinite. The sea glittered darkly in the near distance, its immensity pierced by the slender spinarets that adorned Topkapi's roof. Quietly, slowly, they began to walk over the roof to freedom.

They paused only once, by the tower that had held Suleyman's nephew imprisoned for so long. Impelled by animal instincts that had survived the disintegration of his human soul, the poor madman came to his window when he heard their approach. His toothless mouth opened in an O of shock . . . and he began to scream.

Far below, his guards screamed back, telling him to hold his tongue unless he wanted them to cut it out and stuff it down his throat.

He screamed louder. The trio moved on.

Rustem stirred within the bag and Mehmed set it down.

Go another hundred yards, brother. The old wall there is cracked and there will be footholds for you and Yasmina.

His silent voice seemed . . . almost audible. Yasmina felt an uneasy stirring in the air. But they kept on, not talking, aware that they were in far more danger of discovery at the last moment of their escape than they had been for all this time.

Again Yasmina felt a stirring in the air and whirled around to see . . . nothing.

She is near!

Yasmina saw two green eyes, entirely disembodied, glowing in the air in front of her. She stopped and choked back a shriek of terror. Leyla had found them. Mehmed saw the eyes next, looking his way, glittering with hate. He clung to the neck of the bag as though he might protect his brother from her evil.

But her spirit, far stronger than her earthly body, tossed Mehmed to the ground and took the bag. The bag vaporized at her touch. And there stood Rustem, her golden nemesis. The black silhouette of her naked body appeared in the air, made visible by the absence of stars within it.

The two spirits circled each other, feet not touching the roof of Topkapi. Then Rustem, summoning the last of his strength, grabbed the last of Leyla—and hurled her into the night sky. There was no sound. No star fell to earth.

Go!

Startled into action, Mehmed grabbed Yasmina's hand, and they ran the last hundred yards to the wall that was the last barrier to their freedom. They looked over it. The guards had gone, perhaps to torment Suleyman's mad nephew. But Mehmed and Yasmina looked back before descending.

Leyla had fallen back upon the roof—heaven would not have her. Once more Rustem picked her up, but his strength was fading. They whirled about each other, gold and black, and rose above the roof, locked in a battle that neither could win. The force of their fury spun them into sparks that shot out in all directions, rivaling the stars for brilliance . . . but not for long. In a moment there was nothing there at all.

Mehmed and Yasmina watched in wonder for a moment longer—and then disappeared over the wall.

"It will be a tale to tell our grandchildren," Mehmed said.

"May they never know it." Yasmina brought a rose down to inhale its fragrance, not wanting to cut it. Since their escape nine months ago, the white rose that had risen from the fountain in the Topkapi garden and the red roses that had wept blood by the secret door still bloomed in her dreams. Here in the garden of Mehmed's palace, the walls were made of solid, unchanging stone and the fragrance of the flowers did not unhinge the mind.

"But you are safe with me, love. And there will be only one beauty in my harem. You."

"Ah," she said softly. "So I have escaped one prison to end up in another. A woman has no choice in these matters. It is her duty to please her lord and master." She said no more. A sudden commotion in the street below distracted her and Yasmina surrendered to the irresistible temptation to peep through the filigree inset of the garden wall, knowing she was unseen.

Two foreign women, their faces unveiled but shaded by

enormous hats, walked in the street, followed by a manservant who kept curious men at bay with a thick club, cursing at them in Turkish. "Come and see, Mehmed."

He came to look out with her. "They are English. Perhaps of the ambassador's household."

"Ah." The women's garments, though beautifully made, seemed odd to Yasmina, with great swaths of material caught up to make a sort of artificial rump and close-fitting bodices with high necks and long sleeves. A cur ran up and sniffed at one woman's skirts, lifting a leg to urinate upon them. The woman emitted a nervous little scream and the manservant sprang forward and cuffed the dog before it could sully her dress.

Yasmina giggled. "No doubt the poor beast thought she was a moving house. Her clothes confine her. It seems that all women are imprisoned somehow."

Mehmed laughed. "That is the way of the world. Someday it may change, and women will be as free as men. Would you leave me then?"

She reached up to stroke his glossy hair. "Never, my love."

He kissed her tenderly, then led her to a shady arbor hung with honeysuckle and more roses, and sat with her there upon a wrought iron bench of fanciful design, caressing her body underneath the light, multilayered robes of silk that she wore.

Yasmina sighed with pleasure, letting him fondle her breasts and kiss her neck as much as he liked. The fragrance of the flowers made her drowsy and she barely protested when he pulled her onto his lap without a word of warning. Her pantaloons billowed out and her embroidered slippers flew off. He kissed her with lascivious abandon. Yasmina responded, desiring him more than ever. He broke off the kiss and began to nuzzle her neck.

"And you have taken me to wife," she murmured. "Surely your mother will object when she returns from Alexandria."

"My mother will rejoice. She fled to her family there after my brother's death. She will return to see me married."

"Alas, to a lowly slave woman."

"In our country every sultana is a slave, and our sultans are the sons of slaves. It is a question of degree, Yasmina. You are lovely, accomplished, trained in palace etiquette—ah, I cannot tell her that you were a Topkapi odalisque. Nor that we met there. She will never believe it. We escaped by a miracle."

"By magic."

His face grew somber. "Whatever you wish to call it, I did not meet my brother's dreadful fate. Few men have ever entered the harem and left it alive."

"Entered? You were kidnapped."

"So I was. I remember almost nothing of the inner apartments and what you said happened there."

His body bore no signs of his wounds. Mehmed was strong and healthy. Yasmina had seen to that.

"Topkapi is a terrible place. A beautiful and deadly prison." That she had left it alive was beyond a miracle. She said a silent prayer of thanks for the madman who had distracted the guards. "And what news is there of the new sultan?"

Mehmed grew more serious. "They dragged Suleyman's lunatic nephew from his tower and declared him ruler. Poor mad puppet. The viziers and the chief eunuchs will pull his strings. And loot the treasury. Imprison and murder whomever they please."

Yasmina sighed, swinging her feet as she sat on his lap. Her newfound freedom was bound by the walls of his palace, but that was a woman's lot in life. Mehmed too was a prisoner in a way. There might be a guard or a servant left who remembered his clandestine arrival at Topkapi. He could not go out without concealing his face. Rumors would swirl for years about the mysterious events of that strange night, and the sudden death of the sultan and his sultana.

"I will have to tell her that I bought you somewhere," Mehmed was saying. Yasmina turned her head to pay attention. "So long as she sees that I am happy, she will be happy."

"Ah, my love." She patted his cheek. "And do I make you happy?"

"If I might have you now—and if you would be so kind as to disrobe completely—and tempt me with your bare breasts and your beautiful buttocks—and open your silky thighs—yes, I would be happy. Yasmina, I desire only you."

"Then let us go in."

To love, to know that she was loved, was Yasmina's first joy. And to give Mehmed the utmost pleasure was the second. She danced for him as he sat upon a divan and smoked, the light tendrils of smoke drifting as sinuously as her body.

One by one, Yasmina shed her artfully arranged veils. She pushed down her belt to just cover her pubes, turning her back to him and making the tiny gold coins upon the belt tremble in sensual rhythm with the song she wailed. Wantonly, she pushed the belt lower still and bared her buttocks, tightening and releasing them with smooth sensuality. Her sheer pantaloons fell into voluptuous drapes over her legs as she stepped her feet apart, then stepped out of them, bending forward from the waist to fully display her succulent cunny to her husband.

Mesmerized, Mehmed cast the tube of the waterpipe aside, and the nargileh ceased to bubble and smoke. He sat forward to kiss and nip her soft, womanly behind and thrust two fingers roughly in between.

She cried out, craving something larger still inside her tender flesh, but he made her stay where she was with one strong hand, parting her love-lips and penetrating her more gently but more deeply with the other, spreading her juice when he pulled his fingers out. He put them in again, all four this time, with infinite slowness and care.

With his fingers completely filling her cunny, Yasmina could not move and did not want to. He teased her arsehole with the fleshy tip of his thumb and slid it in when she begged him to, eager to be doubly penetrated and experience his sensual skill.

"I have you in my hand, sweet Yasmina," he whispered, pressing kiss after kiss upon her trembling buttocks. "But I shall not permit you to reach climax just yet." For minutes more he continued to thrust his fingers and thumb into her pliant body, making her moan and cry out his name, over and over. "Submission is your secret pleasure, my darling. You are mine . . . all mine . . . taking what I choose to give."

Yasmina held back a sob but tears ran down her cheeks when he released her at last—tears of sexual longing for him, a longing so intense her entire body was shaking. The hollow man, his brother, had made her feel only a shadow of the pleasure Mehmed gave her now.

He turned her around to face him, kissing her belly now, and lower, kissing her cunny and her pleasure bud, so stimulated it stood out from her flesh like a tiny penis.

Mehmed put his lips upon it and suckled it tenderly, reaching around to squeeze her bare buttocks. Yasmina gasped. "No more! Not if you wish to have your pleasure first, my love!"

He lifted his head, and pushed her back upon the divan, spreading her legs apart and staring down as he removed his own robes. Mehmed's large cock stood out, pearly drops coming from the hole in the tip. He stood over her and she opened her mouth, tasting his sexual essence, then taking his hard rod between her lips and running her tongue around it.

He cupped his balls until she pushed his hand away, teasing him with fingertip strokes that made his sac tighten. Mehmed made her stop, clasping her wrist and holding it over her head as she lay there. He rubbed her exquisitely sensitive nipples with the palm of his other hand, one by one, then pinched them sensually. "My beautiful naked prisoner. My hands shall be your bonds—and you shall not escape the pleasure I will give you. Raise your legs."

Obedient and willing, she lifted her legs high and he gently clasped her ankles and wrists together with one hand. Supporting himself with easy strength, he placed his cock to her cunny lips and pinned her with one bold thrust. She was nothing more than his plaything now, overmastered by her ardent lover, wishing to have no name, to be only woman incarnate . . .

But Mehmed gasped, shuddering with pleasure, and let go of her, allowing her to move however she would, unable to control himself or her. They writhed together in a sensual heaven beyond imagining, and Yasmina exulted when his hot seed spurted deep inside her at last . . .

Later, much later, her husband, rested, bathed and fed, reclined upon the same divan, naked and waiting for her. Yasmina paused in the doorway of their bedchamber to admire him.

He laughed, covering his cock and balls. "Your immodest gaze arouses me again, Yasmina."

"Then why do you hide yourself? Let me see."

Mehmed lifted his hand. It was as he said. His cock was long and thick, on the verge of standing up from the curls at its base. She came closer and he lay back, cradling his head in the crook of his muscular arm. The fine hair in his armpit matched that on his chest, and Yasmina reached out to stroke him between his dark nipples, which were taut with the excitement of being gazed upon by a woman whom he knew wished to please him.

She ran her hand down his flat belly, following the brush-strokes of body hair to that from which his cock sprang, then took him suddenly in her mouth, sucking strongly and fluttering her tongue against the underside.

Mehmed murmured his appreciation. Yasmina repeated the tonguing, slowly this time, then fast again. She sat back and her soft hand held his balls, loving their wrinkly, velvet feel, and the heat of the seed they held.

She was glad for her thorough tutoring in the erotic arts, begun in the harem. But the intercourse she had witnessed there was rarely loving, however passionate it might be. Every perverse desire of the body might be satisfied, but the soul wanted something more.

In becoming Mehmed's wife she had found that something more: the connection between two hearts that deepened every erotic sensation. His regard for her, his openly expressed love, his compelling sensuality, only made her want him more each day . . . and each night.

Yasmina sighed with pleasure and resumed her worshipful attention to his body. She stroked and massaged him from his shoulders to his thighs.

"Mmm. Ah, Yasmina. Your hands are magical. I would be happy to spend hours being caressed by you."

"Lazy one," she chided him gently. "But we have all the time in the world, so I will. Turn over."

Mehmed looked down between his legs. "You have made me too stiff. I will do myself an injury if I roll over."

She laughed. "The soft cushions of the divan will prevent that. Imagine that you are lying next to another woman . . . while I rub your back and buttocks. She is soft and round, spreading her thighs for you to see her cunny." She thought for a moment. "Which I have licked to perfection."

He looked up before he complied. "Not jealous, dear wife?"

"Of an imaginary female, one of my own invention? No. Not at all."

Mehmed settled himself on his belly, adjusting his stiff cock, and burying his face in his crossed arms. "How delightful."

Yasmina began long, slow strokes over his shoulders and down his spine that ended in her cupping his muscular buttocks, and stroking in an upward direction again. "The woman beside you has no name, but she knows yours and cries it out when you thrust inside her. Her fingernails trace delicate patterns upon the skin of your back, love scratches that arouse a fiercer desire in you. Your cock goes deeper into her. Her hands clutch your buttocks and spread them so that I may see your balls beneath, and your long, thick rod in her cunny, going in and in."

"Mmm."

She reached for a bottle of sweet oil and dripped just enough onto her fingertips to massage his balls. "Open your thighs, my love."

Keeping his face hidden and staying on his belly, he obliged. Yasmina touched her oiled fingertips to his balls and he spread his legs wider. His fine buttocks were muscular and tight, as were his thighs and strong calves. His willingness to spread for her and be vulnerable to her probing touch from behind delighted her.

"Now come up," she said softly.

Mehmed got on all fours, hugely erect. She caressed his balls with one hand and stroked his cock. His thighs trembled and he stiffened them, deepening the hollows at the sides of his buttocks. He kept his head down, his dark curls tumbling over his folded arms.

Yasmina smiled. She dripped a little more oil into her palm and applied it to his cock, clasping him tightly, stroking him up and around with a twist of her wrist, then down. Mehmed began to rock with the rhythm of her stroke, pushing his shaft into her tight, circling fingers.

"Come for me," she whispered. "Show me how you will fill my cunny. Let me see, my love."

He pushed harder and faster, thrilling her. Yasmina touched his balls again, working him both ways, until she felt the heavy sac draw tight against his body, and he shot forth a stream as hot and juicy as life itself. He collapsed and rolled over, spreading his legs apart, a vision of satisfied, virile masculinity. She soothed him, easing the tension in his body with gentle strokes of her hand, thanking the fates that such a man had been set aside for her, and only for her.

Yasmina soaked a soft cloth in a porcelain bowl of water, cleaning him with feminine tenderness while he luxuriated in the attention.

Mehmed rose up on one elbow. "Yasmina! What about you?"

She patted his chest. "Rest. We have all the time in the world."

"And our imaginary houri?"

"It seems we did not need her after all." She climbed on the divan and stretched out next to him. To be fully clothed and held against his warm nakedness was bliss. Soon enough he would disrobe her and worship her as he loved to do.

"Ah, Yasmina. But you are her. You are many women in one. And I want them all. Will you stay with me while I sleep?"

"Yes, my husband."

He bent his head to whisper sensually to her, and reassure her of his love. Yasmina smiled, safe in his arms from all harm and all sorrow. The golden light that streamed in through the latticed windows enfolded them.

THE PLEASURE GARDEN

EMMA LEIGH

1

Peking, China 1859
The Forbidden City

Garrick MacDonald stared at the unconscious young woman who lay naked on the table. There was no denying the fact that he had felt almost immediate lust for her. Her skin was like ivory, and her hair was long and full, a tangle of stunning auburn curls. Her body was sheer perfection; he checked himself—his words, his expression, could betray him. He had to appear totally uninterested. It was vital to his life and hers. In the Forbidden City, intrigue was a way of life, and there was truth in the cliché that "the walls have ears."

She was European, as was he. Until now, he had been the only European behind the walls of the Forbidden City. He shook his head. As tempting as she was, he was far from pleased with her presence. At the very least she would complicate everything.

His thoughts drifted to the carved ivory Chinese ball his mother had owned. How it had fascinated him! Carved from the outside in, it was one ball inside another, the center one being smaller than a marble. It was said that a man could carve only three before going blind. The Forbidden City was like that ball, circles within circles within circles. Each ball was intricate, delicate, and filled with conflicting images—dragons and Buddhas, snakes and flowers, suns and moons. He had penetrated the center of the Forbidden City, and now this! This stunning woman could ruin all his hard work. He was furious at her presence, furious that her arrival might give Wan Shi, his sworn enemy, the opportunity to destroy everything he had worked so hard to achieve. He clenched his fists and turned on his heel and left. He would return when she was awake. For now, he left her surrounded by a bevy of curious young concubines who had never before seen a European woman.

Julia stirred ever so slightly, though her eyelids remained closed. She felt imprisoned in darkness, cognizant of her body but unable to control it. She could hear strange, mysterious sounds. She fought to concentrate on the soft padding noises—they were like footsteps made by small creatures. And there was an odd yet pleasant aroma. It was like nothing she had ever smelled before. It was perfumed yet somehow mouthwatering. Perhaps it was some exotic fruit.

Two things were certain. Wherever she was, wherever she was laid out, she was not dead, and she was not alone. There were others about, and somehow she felt as though they were caring for her. Had she been hurt? She was unaware of pain, even though she felt pleasantly paralyzed, if such were possible. But, no, she was not truly paralyzed. She forced herself to concentrate and succeeded in moving one of her fingers ever so slightly. She felt a smooth, rich material beneath her finger. Was it satin? Was there any place in the world where a sick or injured person might be placed on a material as rich and as expensive as satin?

She tried to lift her arm. Then she felt a series of pricks in her neck. It felt as if a small insect was biting her—more pricks, tiny pricks without pain.

In seconds she felt a greater heaviness flood over her. The fingers she could move before could not now be lifted. The pleasant odor disappeared. All sound, even the mysterious shuffling, evaporated into absolute silence until she was floating in a soft fog through the darkness, a wandering spirit held captive in a still body.

The fog through which she floated suddenly dispersed, and there was water. Great waves swept her across a frothy surface; hard rain pummeled her exposed skin. She was swept away as dark clouds obliterated the moon. Then there was sand. She was dragged across it, the course grains scraping her skin while jagged pebbles tore her clothing. She couldn't breathe; she clutched at the sand, trying to stop herself. It was no use. She was propelled faster and faster and at last deposited in a cloud of darkness, unable to move, unable to speak.

Julia, I'm Julia Martin; I'm from London. A flood of memories filled her dreams. They were unpleasant memories accompanied by fear. Her father was William Martin, a sea captain in the employ of the East India Company. He was an unspeakably cruel man whose violence was responsible for her mother's death. She was his only daughter, and in exchange for his command of a new vessel, he had promised her in marriage to Jason Hamilton, a man three times her age, a cruel man like her father. Her father was to deliver her to Hamilton in Shanghai. Then there had been a storm. She tried to erase her frightening thoughts, but she could not make them go away any more than she could move. Still, the details were gone. She could not remember how she had gotten off the ship, how she had gotten ashore, and she did not know if any of the others had escaped. Again, it all began to fade, and darkness closed in around her as she floated into a deeper sleep.

How long she remained in this deep sleep, she was unable to

calculate. But then she was again aware. The sound of the shuffling not only returned but also became clearer. The tantalizing aroma returned, too. She sensed that someone was leaning over her, and the person's breath was filled with the odd but pleasant perfumed aroma.

She lay still for a few more seconds, and then she tried again to move her fingers. Yes, there could be no doubt, the sheet beneath her was made of satin and so was the one that covered her.

Feeling was gradually returning to her body. She opened her eyes and looked about. What she saw was surely a dream.

She closed her eyes quickly, thinking that the faces would disappear. But when she opened her eyes again, they were all still there. Dark, expressive Asian eyes, intent eyes, all staring at her as if she were a butterfly pinned on a board.

She was lying flat, not on a bed, but on a table of some sort. Young women surrounded the table; their faces were round and their eyes bright and dark like shoe buttons. They had jet-black hair, and each wore a semitransparent, diaphanous gown made of brightly colored orange material trimmed in gold. They were all Chinese, or at least she thought they were Chinese. A sudden horrible panic filled her. Had she been rescued and taken to Shanghai to the home of Jason Hamilton?

"Am I in Shanghai?" she suddenly asked, surprised by the sound of her own voice. A silent prayer filled her; no matter what the danger, she wished to be anywhere but Shanghai.

The women all jumped away as though they were afraid of her. None of them answered her, and she thought it likely none had understood her question.

After a moment the women came back, surrounding her with their curious faces. They moved about her, and she looked at them more closely and saw they wore sandals and shuffled across a stone floor. She had not been wrong. They had been here all the while she was lost in the darkness of unconsciousness.

Then, as if silently commanded, the women all stepped back and parted, making room for a man to pass through their ranks. He was a small Chinese man with a long white goatee. He wore an ornate pink robe embroidered with temples and dragons and trimmed in black. It looked as though it were made of silk.

He ran his fingers up her arm to the side of her neck and deftly removed a series of something that felt like pins from her neck. As he deposited them into a silver bowl, she saw that they were needles—long, slender needles—needles as light as silver feathers.

"What have you done to me?" she asked in a panic.

The old man did not answer. He simply backed away from her with his head down.

She looked back at the women, studying them. They wore nothing beneath their silken gowns, and while one could not actually see their bodies in detail, one could easily make out the shape of their breasts, the shadows of their nipples, their curves, and, indeed, the tufts of dark hair in their most private regions. Yet they had shown neither shyness nor modesty with the man who had just been there.

With a second sudden surge of panic she realized she was naked beneath the satin sheet that covered her! Absolutely naked! The thought caused her skin to flush. In England a woman did not appear naked among others, even among other women. She strained to look beyond the curious women who surrounded her, and it was then that she noticed the men. There were twelve in all. All were dressed in long gray robes and wore stiff three-cornered hats. All had sharp goatees, and each stood, their hands folded in front of them, at perfectly spaced intervals along the far wall of this large room.

As though pushed with considerable strength, great wide

doors on the far side of the room opened, and a man passed through them. He dwarfed the oddly dressed men who stood against the wall and the men who were in his wake; the women scattered like feathers in the wind. They ran in groups and huddled together, covering their faces with gaily decorated fans.

This man was like Gulliver among the Lilliputians. He was tall and muscular with broad shoulders. His eyes were dark and his expression seemingly angry. He was not Chinese nor was he even Asian. He was Caucasian, as was she. The only relief she felt was that he was far too young to be Jason Hamilton, whom she had never actually met but knew only by reputation.

Automatically she drew the satin sheet tight under her chin as the tall man strode to her side.

"Where am I?" she demanded. "Where are my clothes?"

For a long moment he just stared at her. His expression softened slightly, though in some way she still felt he was angry.

When he did speak, his tone confirmed her first impression.

"You are in the Royal Palace within the Forbidden City. You are among the emperor's concubines, and you are fortunate to be alive."

A wave of relief swept over her. Peking was a long way from Shanghai. She cursed the fact that she knew so little about China. Peking was the capital, but what was the Forbidden City?

And why was she among the emperor's concubines? As far as she knew, a concubine was a kind of mistress. Still, she was grateful not to be in Shanghai. "How did I come here?"

"I thought perhaps you could answer that question."

Tears welled in her eyes, and she shook her head helplessly. Why did he sound so angry? What had she done?

He looked away from her face. "Do you remember anything?"

At once she wondered how much she should tell him. It was

her understanding that Jason Hamilton was a powerful man. If this man learned her true identity, he might turn her over to Hamilton. Perhaps if she did not reveal too much, she could escape the fate her father had planned for her. "My name is Julia. I remember no more," she whispered.

His voice softened ever so slightly. "Obviously you're English."

"I suppose I am. But I remember nothing," she reiterated.

"You were not sent by the English?"

"I told you, I don't remember anything." Did this mean the English were his enemy? She was puzzled; he had a strange accent, and she decided he must be American.

"I don't remember anything," she said again. And then, for good measure, added, "But I'm sure no one sent me."

He stared at her as if he were trying to see through her.

"I would like my clothes," she said firmly. "And some privacy to get dressed."

He looked as though he were going to laugh. "My dear young woman, you do not seem to understand. You are in the Forbidden City. Women do not leave the Forbidden City. You belong to the emperor now."

Julia felt a cold chill fill her. What did he mean? Had she gone from bad to worse? No, absolutely nothing could be as bad as Jason Hamilton. "I don't understand," she managed.

He leaned over her very close and whispered in her ear. "I have to say these things. I will try to help you escape; I will see you get back to the English in Shanghai."

"No!" Her objection was loud; it startled the women, who all jumped away, their expressions fearful.

"No?" he repeated.

She could hear the incredulity in his voice.

Seldom in his life had he felt taken aback. But he was taken aback now. Had she not understood him? Again he leaned over her. He whispered urgently, "You will be trained as a concubine and given to the emperor as soon as you learn how to desire. Don't you understand?"

"I understand," she whispered. "I won't go back to the British. I would rather stay here." She did understand, and while she feared the unknown, at this moment she feared what she knew more. Here, she might be able to buy some time.

He shook his head. He had just risked everything to promise to help her, and she had rejected his offer! He could only hope there was no one about who had heard or understood his whispered promise to her. Why was she afraid to be sent to Shanghai? Did she understand what she was getting herself into by not accepting his offer? He could not risk trying to explain the situation to her now. It was simply too dangerous.

"It is your decision," he hissed in her ear. Then he said in a normal voice, "Quite simply, you are in China, in the Forbidden City, in the House of the Concubines. You will be given new clothes, and you will be trained."

"Trained?" She could barely speak. Again she wondered if she had she gone from one terrible fate to another. Was she wrong to insist on staying here? "Trained for what?" she finally managed.

"For the emperor, of course."

"Will I be raped?" Jason Hamilton would rape her. He would beat her, too, just as her father had beaten her mother.

"No, you will not be forced. When you are ready, you will not only desire a liaison, you will cry out and beg to be touched. I can assure you that after a time you will probably not even want to leave."

"I don't want to leave now," she said, fighting back her own uncertainties. After all, she had nowhere to go and no one to go to. But she did not really want to be a concubine to the emperor either. "Isn't a concubine a mistress?"

"Something like a mistress. As I said, you will be trained."
He could say no more. There were too many eunuchs in this
room, and then, too, one could never be one hundred percent
certain of the women either. "The fewer problems you cause,
the easier it will be."

It was a warning, and she recognized it as such.

"I am loyal to the emperor," he said coldly. "You will stay
here, and you will do exactly as you are instructed."

"How long will my training take?" Again she thought of
buying time. *When the time is right, when I know some Chinese,
I can escape on my own. I will not go to Jason Hamilton,* she
silently vowed, *and I will not end up a mistress to the emperor
either.* As for this "desire" he spoke of, she was sure she would
not develop it, regardless of the training. "How can one develop desire by being trained?" she asked, not hiding the defi-
ant tone in her voice.

"Desire must be awakened. It will take longer because you
are a virgin."

She felt her whole body flush. "How do you know I'm a
virgin?"

"You have been examined."

Her hands flew to cover her face as tears once again filled
her eyes. "Who . . . ?" she said softly. "My heaven, I was violated in my sleep."

"You are a typical example of Victorian womanhood!" he
snapped. "You were not violated, you were examined by the
court physician."

He scowled at her. She would represent a challenge, but he felt
certain any woman could be awakened. What mystified him
was her reluctance to accept his whispered offer.

She stared up at him. "There are men here. Were they here
when I was—was examined?" She indicated those who still
stood impassively along the wall.

"Eunuchs. They have no interest in women." He noted her expression and then added, "They've all been castrated. That is why they are allowed among the concubines. Frankly, I don't know if they were here or not when you were examined."

She felt both ashamed and confused. She could not look at him or at the eunuchs. Instead she looked about at her opulent surroundings. This was a strange world where women were obviously kept for sexual pleasure and men were castrated. "And you?" she asked, tilting her head. "Are you castrated, too?"

"No, I am not a eunuch. I am an adviser to the Hsien-Feng emperor. I am only allowed here on special occasions and then only among these women who are secondary concubines. I can assure you that those women who are the emperor's favorites are kept in well-guarded quarters."

She listened but did not respond.

"I have arranged for a woman called Ming Li to come to you. She speaks English and will tutor you."

Julia wondered if she should tell him what she remembered, but he seemed so angry, she decided against it.

He turned abruptly and walked away, followed by the eunuchs who had stood so silently for so long. As soon as he and his entourage of eunuchs had passed through the great doors, the women came to life, crowding about her, touching her hair and running their soft hands across her face. They giggled like small schoolgirls when her hair kept springing back into curls. For a few moments she let them satisfy their curiosity, and then she shooed them away with a wave of her hand and a firm, "Leave me!"

If they did not understand her words, they understood her gesture and quickly scattered.

She sat up and wrapped one of the satin sheets about her. She began to cry, and she wiped the tears from her face with the back of her hand. Then she slipped off the table, standing still for a moment until she regained her sense of balance. What was she to do? Surely there was some way to escape this place without help. She pursed her lips together; she was in a satin-lined prison, a velvet jail filled with people she could not understand and men who frightened her—frightened most of all by the one who was her own kind and who had just left.

2

Garrick MacDonald strode purposefully down the corridor, ducking as he passed through the low portals that were the hallmark of Chinese architecture. "Damn!" he muttered. "Why did this—this Julia have to appear now of all times?" Her presence would have been inconvenient and caused great difficulty at the best of times, and this was hardly the best of times.

It wasn't simply the complications she would cause. There was the matter of controlling his desires. An ordinary woman would have been bad enough, but this one set his imagination afire. From the moment he had seen her naked body he had imagined her pressing against him, touching his organ as he took her essences and fondled her till she cried in his arms. He momentarily forced thoughts of having her from his mind.

From what he had been told, she had apparently survived a shipwreck, and she had been brought here only because of the manner of her survival.

The story, according to the local prefect who had delivered her to the gates of the Forbidden City, was that she had been found on the beach. She was unconscious and tied to the broken mast of a vessel that had obviously been lost in the recent typhoon. The prefect, one Sun Chi Ling, who wished to curry favor with the emperor, was a highly superstitious man. He brought the woman to the emperor as a gift. "Washed up on the beach the very morning of the New Year," he proclaimed. "She is the harbinger of the Year of the Cock. And look at her hair, it is the sacred color. She will help us rid ourselves of the foreigners who plague us, I know it."

She should have been turned over to the British immediately, he thought. Her accent was British; she was no doubt from London or its environs.

Doubtless the prefect realized that by Western standards, she was a beauty and might be worth some ransom. But Garrick knew that on that score the girl was worthless. She was probably only the daughter of some sea captain. It was not uncommon for them to take a family member to sea with them. "The British will not stop their activities simply because of one woman," he cautioned the prefect. Nonetheless, the emperor's other advisers had seen merit in keeping her—whether for the emperor's personal pleasure or for ransom. They, too, felt that the day and time of her arrival was somehow providential. The Turks might have called it fate, while the Buddhists considered it karma. One of the advisers also mentioned her red hair. "The sacred color," he had intoned with awe. "She is sent by the gods."

Not as far as I'm concerned, Garrick concluded. All he knew at this point was that a beautiful young woman had been washed ashore and taken prisoner. And the emperor, who had not even seen her, and indeed had refused to see her until she was properly educated and trained, had ordered her sequestered among the young concubines of the court. Worse yet, he had made it clear that Garrick was to be in charge of her education and training. *I shall have to help her somehow,* he thought angrily. Again he reminded himself that helping her could easily undo all the work he had done. It had taken him years to gain the confidence of the emperor and his inner circle. Foreigners were never allowed in the Forbidden City, and none had ever attained his position. His entire plan was built around the trust the Chinese had in him; now this girl with her red hair, deep green eyes, perfectly shaped body, and porcelain skin threatened everything.

He entered his own quarters and closed the door behind him. He supposed he was wrong to blame the girl, when it was Wan Shi who had suggested he be put in charge of seeing to her training. The emperor had readily agreed, so now he had no recourse. Wan Shi mistrusted and disliked Garrick, and the feeling was entirely mutual, though he kept his feelings to himself. *This is a test,* he decided. If he could train one of his own without having her and turn her over to the emperor, he would pass this final test. If he failed, all would be lost. Perhaps even China would be lost. Unhappily, the Forbidden City was so well insulated from all reality no one here gave that much thought, save Wan Shi, who no doubt dreamed of controlling empires.

Garrick spoke aloud to himself, "And so, Miss Julia whoever-you-are, I will oversee your training to enter the Jade Bedroom. I will do it because I have no choice. If you change your mind, I will help you if I can, but you will not know that."

Julia paced around the ornate room, clutching the satin sheet to cover her body. "Where are my clothes?" she said loudly. But there was no one who understood. The Chinese women huddled together, watching her somewhat fearfully and in utter silence. Then at once they turned. Julia turned, too, and saw an older yet truly lovely Chinese woman enter the room. She wore a red gown but one that was far more beautiful than the robes worn by the women she had thus far seen. Over her gown was a kimono. It was embroidered with Chinese symbols. Her rich, dark hair was piled high and held in place with elaborately carved ivory combs. She wore makeup that was artfully applied, and her movements were incredibly delicate.

She walked directly to Julia. "I am Ming Li," she said softly.

"I want my clothes."

Ming Li smiled and nodded knowingly. She waited a long moment before speaking, and then she reached out and touched Julia's hand. "Think," she said softly. "Your clothes were destroyed during your ordeal."

Julia stared at her and decided that, indeed, it was likely her clothes had been destroyed. Then, just to make sure Garrick had told her the truth, she asked again, "Where am I? Can I leave?"

"You are in the Imperial Palace inside the Forbidden City in the center of Peking, far to the north, away from the sea. There are none of your kind here, save Garrick MacDonald. No one leaves the Forbidden City. If you left the Forbidden City, you would be attacked immediately, and your fate would be far worse than if you remained here. Give yourself to learning, bide your time. What was intended shall be. You cannot control fate."

Julia looked back into Ming Li's soft eyes. She was obviously intelligent, and her words seemed to hold out some hope for the future. Perhaps her words were necessarily veiled; still, the phrase "bide your time," was something to cling to; it was indeed what she had thought herself. Moreover, Ming Li seemed entirely logical. It was true that Julia had no idea what lay beyond this city. She had never been to China, nor had she even read much about it, and certainly did not understand a word of Chinese. If set free, where would she go? The cold truth filled her mind. There was no place to run, and if she left this place, Hamilton might find her. She would have to stay and, as Ming Li suggested, give herself over to learning. Not just learning how to be a concubine, she thought, but learning how to speak the language, how to find a way to escape both this place and Jason Hamilton.

"Will you be teaching me?"

"I shall be helping. It is Garrick, the giant, who will train you."

She frowned. "Is Garrick the man who was here, an American?"

"Yes, we call him a giant because he is the tallest man in the Forbidden City."

She did not really want to know more right now. In fact, she did not want to ask more about this so-called training and what it entailed. Heaven only knew what strange rituals these people took part in or what outrageous things might be demanded of her. For the moment she decided to put it all out of her mind. She would take one step at a time and hope for some escape opportunity to arise. If she worked hard, if she applied herself, perhaps she could acquire the necessary skills to escape when the time was right.

"If I cannot have *my* clothes, may I have *some* clothes?" she finally said.

Ming Li nodded and spoke to the other women in Chinese, and they quickly turned and scurried off. They were nine in all.

In moments they all returned, each one carrying a garment that was folded neatly. Each one bowed in front of her and deposited her offering. There were four semitransparent gowns and two kimonos to cover them. They also brought covers, which she assumed were for her bed. Each of the garments was a different shade of gold or saffron, and the kimonos were red and embroidered with green thread.

"There are no undergarments," Julia protested.

"No, no, of course not. You are always to be naked beneath your gown. It is nature's way. It is Tao."

"Tao?" Julia repeated.

"*Tao* means 'the way.' You will be trained and taught Tao."

"I thought I was to be trained to be a concubine."

"The way of Tao is the way concubines are trained. You must eat properly and do certain exercises. You will learn how to enjoy having your lute played by a master. You will learn 'the way,' and I think you will not be as displeased as you now believe."

"I want to learn Chinese."

Ming Li nodded. "Yes. You will be taught, though foreigners have a difficult time with our language."

Julia did not answer. She reached out for the clothing and picked it up. The gowns were transparent except for the areas where designs had been embroidered with gold thread. Mercifully, the kimonos were not transparent. "Where can I put these on?"

Ming Li laughed lightly, musically. She nodded toward a door. "In there, if you must have privacy. Rest assured you will soon learn the advantages to being naked, of being free of constraints, of being available."

Julia could not even respond. Instead she opened the door and closed it behind her. The room was not a small dressing room but a dormitory of sorts. Along each wall were sleeping mats. At the foot of each mat was a carved trunk. No wonder Ming Li had laughed. It seemed there was no real privacy here. Obviously the women all slept in the same room, dressed in the same room, and probably shared some kind of communal bath. Silently she chastised herself for being so prudish. In spite of her father's cruelty, and indeed even when aboard ship, she had always had a place of her own. She also knew full well that the privacy she had always known was not available or even the custom in most countries. "I will adjust," she said aloud, though she was not sure she would adjust to the eunuchs. Their hostile eyes troubled her.

Quickly she shed her satin sheet and adorned one of the gowns. Then she wrapped the kimono around her. The material felt odd against her skin, or perhaps it was the absence of a corset and endless petticoats and pantaloons that felt odd. Still, being without her restrictive undergarments was not entirely unpleasant. She went back to the larger room with her sheet folded, leaving her other gowns for the time being. *I am a prisoner, but my body feels a new kind of freedom.* Corsets, she silently admitted, were a dreadful fashion.

Ming Li smiled when she emerged. "We shall have to tame your hair," she said, touching it.

Julia said nothing. At present her hair was a tangle of wild curls. "I can do it with a brush. Do you have a brush?"

"Oh, yes. I shall explain everything to you. You are fortunate—your hair is the sacred color. I think it was part of the reason you were brought here."

"What is the other part of the reason?"

"You were washed ashore on the day of our New Year."

"Why did the other women want to touch my hair?"

"We have never seen a woman with hair that color. It is why the others wanted to feel it, to touch it. They have never seen curls either. Still, I have seen men with curly hair, so I am not surprised. You must be patient with the others. They are very young."

Immediately Julia thought of Garrick. His mass of dark hair was curly. Was he involved with this Ming Li? She did not ask the question. It would have been too impolite.

At that moment Garrick returned, striding through the great double doors as he had before, followed by the silent eunuchs.

As before the other women scattered, leaving him alone with her and Ming Li.

"I see you're dressed."

His tone still sounded angry, and she wondered why. Surely it was she who should be angry. Worse yet, his dark eyes examined her in a way she found discomforting. She did not reply, but neither did she turn away from him as the other women did.

"Ming Li will show you where you will sleep and eat; she will remain with you until you learn the rules of the palace and know where, when, and how to perform your toiletry. Then she will come only for your lessons."

He turned then to Ming Li, but he continued to speak in English. "She will be taught the level-one exercises and prepared for the ceremony of the jade egg."

Jade egg? What on earth was he talking about? Ming Li only bowed her head and acknowledged his instructions.

"I thought I was to be taught the lute," Julia said forthrightly.

Garrick actually laughed. His dark eyes danced. "No, you misunderstood. You shall learn to have your lute played."

She stared at him blankly.

"Not *the* lute—*your* lute, the place most intimate in lovemaking, the center of all female pleasure. In other words, your clitoris."

Julia felt her face flush more deeply than ever she could remember in all her life. She turned, aghast, and fled back to the sanctity of the dormitory. Men did not speak to women of these things!

She heard the door behind her and turned, only to see that Garrick had followed her. "Go away, leave me to my shame."

He stared at her trembling hands. He had been too abrupt, too forthright, and had spoken openly too soon of things she was not yet ready to discuss.

"You have nothing of which to be ashamed. I apologize for embarrassing you, though I can assure you that Ming Li will think nothing of my words."

"Is she a concubine? A fallen woman, too?"

He wanted to laugh but restrained himself. This ravishing

beauty was sheltered and had been repressed all her life. This could not be rushed. It was not *the way of Tao* to force women, but rather it was *the way* to make them truly desire.

"Ming Li is a teacher. She has had a husband and lovers, but she is not considered to be 'fallen.' Indeed, Ming Li is held in high regard and respected for her intellect, her charm, and her many talents."

"I don't understand this place. I don't want to be trained to have—to have sexual relations with strangers or with the emperor."

"Training includes sexual knowledge and experience, but this is not all about sex. '*The way*' is total. It is dress and diet; it is exercise, belief, and much more. It is as much about restraint as it is about pleasure. Yet there is much pleasure, and when '*the way*' is followed, there can be unparalleled pleasure, especially for women."

She looked up into Garrick's face. His expression was softer now than it had been before. It crossed her mind that he was, in fact, a handsome man, and the kind of man women often looked to for protection. But he was not protecting her. He was prepared to train her and turn her over to the emperor. Though, she reminded herself, he had offered to help her escape. It was she who had made the decision to remain.

"I will not be a whore," she said with conviction.

Again he forced himself not to smile. Every woman was a whore to some man. His father had taught him that. "One man's virgin is another man's whore." It was his father's favorite expression, and he knew it was true. Vaguely he wondered if he wanted this woman to be a whore with him—that is, to show him unrestrained passion. Was that a partial reason for his anger at her appearance? Once again he vowed to show restraint, not to be tempted by this beauty who had been washed ashore, this lovely woman whose hair was the sacred color of

Tao and whose body was deliciously formed. She presented a distinct temptation. She was indeed a test.

He turned back to her. "Stop thinking in terms of whores and fallen women. You are to be trained in an ancient religious practice. Give yourself over to learning. You will regret nothing and cease to be afraid."

It was what Ming Li had said, too.

"Then I will be forced into a liaison with the emperor."

Garrick inhaled deeply. "You will be forced into nothing."

A look of relief covered her face. "Then I shall try to learn."

He nodded and took one long last look at her. She had wrapped her kimono around her tightly, but he knew that beneath it she was curved and tempting. He had seen her full pink-tipped breasts and her buttocks as round and as succulent as ripe melons. It would indeed take time, but the day would come when she would open her kimono and beg to be touched. When that moment came, she would give of her essences and in return receive sublime pleasures. It was his duty to make that moment come. And if fate ordained that she be returned to her people eventually, well, he knew she would be a happier woman for what she had learned.

3

The hazy winter sun cast a muted light as it fell through the windows of the long, narrow room in which the thirteen women slept. Julia turned restlessly, opened her eyes, and sat up.

Nothing had changed. She had gone to sleep hoping her reality was nothing but a strange, frighteningly real dream. She sighed; it was all as it had been.

The walls of the long room were decorated with paintings that portrayed stylized trees and mountains that seemingly floated through a misty space. There were small tables inlaid with mother-of-pearl, and at the end of each sleeping pallet, there was that handcarved trunk. Hers contained the changes of clothing she had been given as well as sandalwood soap, a sea sponge, a towel, a brush and comb, and three sets of decorative combs made from ivory, mother-of-pearl, and tortoise shell.

She looked about the room and saw that the others were also awakening. They looked at her curiously but quickly looked away if she returned their glances.

"Good morning," Ming Li said from the adjacent bed pallet. "It is a new day, a new beginning."

For a moment Julia hesitated because beneath the covers she was naked. Holding the sheet, she sat up shyly. "Yes, a new day," she replied, glancing at Ming Li. Then, as quickly as possible, she pulled her garment, which lay on the end of the pallet, over her head. As she stood up it fell about her, and she quickly put on her kimono.

The others were not so modest. They emerged from their beds naked, nipples erect in the cold morning air. They had not left their clothes on the end of their beds but rather had put them away. They dressed without urgency while they talked. Next they made their beds and then hurriedly ran to the door and stood in a line.

It was, Julia thought, like a private girls' school or an orphanage. Yes, this place—was it called a harem?—seemed like an institution. She made a mental note to ask what it was called, and then she followed Ming Li and stood in line with her.

"Are the doors locked?" Julia asked Ming Li.

"Yes, every night they are locked by the guard, and each morning they are unlocked by the chief eunuch, Tung Shu."

In a few moments the doors were opened and Julia followed Ming Li and the others through the room in which she had awakened yesterday and then down a long corridor and through double doors into a courtyard.

The girls all assembled on a patio in the center of the courtyard. They stood far apart. "First we perform our morning exercises," Ming Li whispered. "Exercise is one of the pillars of longevity."

"We do not set aside time for exercise in England," Julia said.

"I have heard this," Ming Li answered. "Madame Chin will lead us in our tai chi. Watch the others, and do as instructed."

In a few moments an elderly woman appeared. They all bowed to her, and she in turn bowed back. Without hesitation she began a series of strange and highly complicated movements. More than once she came to Julia's side to help her master a specific movement or to slow her down. The exercises were not arduous, but Julia was aware of stretching in ways she had never stretched before. This tai chi was like a slow dance without music, and it involved every part of the body.

Julia was unsure of how long the exercises took, but she was glad when she was told to sit down. She was instructed to sit cross-legged with her back straight and her hands resting on her knees.

Madame Chin then led them in deep-breathing exercises. At first Julia found these difficult, but as soon as they were finished, she was aware of feeling strangely invigorated.

When the breathing exercises were over, the girls climbed to their feet, talking to one another and laughing. Julia's gaze strayed to a balcony that overhung the courtyard. Garrick MacDonald was there, watching her with his intense dark eyes. Immediately she wondered how long he had been there, and though she had not felt self-conscious before, she felt so now. She had been instructed to take off her kimono for the exercises, and she was well aware of the fact that he could see through her gown.

"Time for our baths," Ming Li whispered.

Julia glanced toward the balcony. "I trust there will be no observers," she replied.

Ming Li did not look up; she simply shrugged.

In moments they were back in the long corridor. They made their way into a tiled room with a great clear pool surrounded by smaller steaming pools.

As quickly as they had adorned their gowns, the women discarded them and slipped into the water of the steaming pools.

"I cannot. I've never bathed with others," Julia objected.

"Come along. You must learn to bathe with others. It is the only way to bathe."

Ming Li prodded her along. Julia drew in her breath. She wanted to submerge herself in the steaming water and wash with the soap that gave off the aroma of a thousand blossoms. She stood motionless and then suddenly whipped off her gown and slid into the water, crouching down so only her head was visible. Her hair grew damp and formed a thousand ringlets.

The water did indeed feel wonderful. The perfumed soap caressed her skin, and in moments she felt silky all over, as though covered with some wonderful oil. It really did not compare to her lukewarm baths at home, where by the time she had filled the great copper tub, the water had cooled down. And she felt freer in this great pool. At home she had to fold herself up; here she could stretch out.

The others washed each other, giggling innocently and relaxing in the warm waters. But there were two who appeared not so innocent. One, a young woman taller than the others, bent and kissed the breasts of another. Almost immediately the one whom she touched slid her hand between the legs of the other. Their faces were flushed as they fondled each other.

"Do not look at those two," Ming Li warned. "They are pleasuring each other, and without specific instruction to do so, it is strictly forbidden. We call it rubbing mirrors."

Julia frowned. "What will happen if they are caught doing this forbidden act?"

"They will be punished by the chief eunuch, Tung Shu."

"But this 'rubbing mirrors' is allowed sometimes?"

"Only when ordered by a trainer or the emperor. The same is true of pleasuring oneself. You will learn when such things are permissible and when they lead to punishment."

Julia said nothing more.

After a time, as if summoned by a silent signal, they all climbed out of the water. Glistening bodies shed great droplets of water. It rolled off their soft flesh as gently as trees shed leaves. The young women ran to the great pool and splashed in, playing in its cool water like children. The two who had been rubbing mirrors continued to hold hands. They seemed to glow with satisfaction.

Julia followed Ming Li, once again submerging herself.

She looked up at the sound of the door opening. Eunuchs! Julia almost screamed as the oddly dressed elderly men paraded into the room.

They would see her naked in the clear water! How could she get out and dress without them staring at her?

"They have come to help dry the others. They will also massage those who are in need of pleasurable stimulation," Ming Li explained.

Ming Li called out in Chinese to the men. As if they were one person, they obediently turned away from the pool to face the wall.

"You may get out now. Wrap yourself in a towel, and put on your kimono. They will not turn about until I tell them."

Julia, her face burning with embarrassment, climbed out of the pool and did as Ming Li told her. She waited as close to the door as possible, wondering if Ming Li would take her away, or if Ming Li would be one of those who were in need of this so-called "pleasurable stimulation." Curiosity welled within her in spite of her embarrassment.

Ming Li again spoke to the eunuchs, who turned about. Julia watched as the other women came out of the water unashamedly and were dried with great towels offered by the eunuchs. She followed them all into an adjacent room. Most of the women climbed onto tables such as the one she had lain on yesterday.

They lay on their stomachs, and the eunuchs deftly applied scented oils to their upper backs and began to massage them. Ming Li did indeed submit to the massage while Julia watched, fascinated and yet horrified at the same time.

The faces of the eunuchs were seemingly impassive. They worked hard, but nothing in their expressions betrayed lust. Julia gasped when some of the women turned over on their backs, exposing their breasts without the slightest concern. The eunuchs rubbed their breasts with the scented oils. It was most certainly an intimacy she could never allow! Never! But she did note that not one of the eunuchs ventured to touch any of the women below the waist, and she decided she would ask Ming Li why this was. After all, there seemed to be no modesty whatsoever among these women. If this was true, were there in fact rules that applied, rules about which she knew nothing?

Julia watched in utter fascination as light switches woven from heavy grass were used to beat the women's nipples. But clearly they did not hurt. No one cried out, nor did any seem in pain. Still, their use clearly had a purpose. The women's nipples seemed to grow even larger and were taut and filled with blood.

"It makes them like tiny, hard rosebuds," Ming Li said as though she sensed the question on Julia's lips. "Repeated use makes the breasts more sensitive than usual."

Julia said nothing. But she was aware of feeling a vague excitement, a strange desire she had never before known.

Gradually the eunuchs finished their work, and the women once again dressed. She could still feel the warmth in her own face, and she knew she had experienced another sensation as well. She had been unable to take her eyes off the women who were having their breasts massaged. She had almost been able to feel someone's hands on her own breasts, and, to her surprise, her nipples had grown hard, and she knew that deep down inside, she, too, had wanted to be touched. She shook her head, trying to dispel these disturbing new thoughts as all her Victorian instincts fought with this new sensation of arousal.

"It is time for the morning meal," Ming Li told her. "After we eat we will do some gardening and then some different kinds of exercises. In the afternoon we rest for a time and then study and read."

"Is that when I will begin my lessons?"

Ming Li laughed lightly. "You have already begun. Each day is a lesson."

"Then I shall ask a question."

"Ask anything you like."

"When the others were being massaged I noticed that the eunuchs never touched them below their waists. Is there a rule about that?"

Ming Li smiled. "How very observant of you! Yes, the area below the waist is reserved for one's lover. Only he may climb the sedge hill, play the lute, and continue to the jade gate. These are acts to be controlled and yield pleasures of great magnitude. Our external pleasures must be regulated in order for us to control our inner passions."

"I'm not sure I understand," Julia confessed.

Ming Li smiled. "Perhaps Garrick MacDonald can explain more clearly than I."

Julia did not say so, but she knew that she could never ask a man the question she had just asked Ming Li. But, then again, she marveled at the change in herself. If she had been told yesterday what she would see and do today, she would not have believed it. It did not seem prudent for her to ever say "never," because everything was changing. She was changing.

Ming Li escorted Julia to a garden. It seemed as though this remarkable palace had gardens everywhere, hidden gardens with surprising rivulets, miniature waterfalls, and flowers the likes of which Julia had never seen. And all in spite of the fact that it was winter! It was amazing that the gardens flourished so, but then, she concluded, they were sheltered, just as were the women of the Forbidden City.

"Garrick will come to you here." Ming Li turned and disappeared through one of the four round portals that led to this secluded and quite lovely garden. Julia sat down on the edge of a pool and stared at the fascinating multicolored tropical fish.

"Do you like flowers?"

Julia stood and turned abruptly, realizing that Garrick had silently joined her—or perhaps he had been there all along, hiding behind one of the gnarled trees or one of the ever-present stone Buddhas.

"You always look like a frightened deer."

"You startled me," she replied.

"I startled you because you are filled with thoughts about yourself. You were not listening, and, if you were, you were listening only with your ears."

"That is the usual way to listen." She could hear the edge in her voice. Doubtless he was trying to impress her with his vast knowledge of the "mysterious East."

"It's the usual way, but not the only way. When you are more sensitized you will be able to feel my presence."

"Only yours," she said with deliberate coolness.

"No, others as well. It is a matter of using all your senses to augment any one sense."

"I thought you were here to instruct me."

"I am instructing you. I am trying to tell you that you know a man not simply by his appearance but also by how he feels to your touch, what aroma his body gives off when he is near you, how his voice sounds."

She said nothing, but when he sat down on the stone bench, she sat down beside him, though not close to him. He still frightened her, even angered her, but she was willing to admit that he had a certain attractiveness, that he was in fact handsome and that his eyes were compelling.

"If you are blindfolded, you should be able to still know your lover."

"I do not have a lover and do not intend to have one. You said I would not be forced."

"You won't be. Think of this as another kind of exercise."

She said nothing as he withdrew a long, slender black cloth. "I'm going to blindfold you."

She did not resist, for her curiosity had overcome her reluctance.

"Stay here," he commanded.

Julia heard him walking across the stones. In a moment she heard him return. She then heard him unwrap something from a crinkled bit of tissue.

She sniffed at the familiar aroma. It was the same smell she had been aware of yesterday, the smell that was like perfume but somehow fruity.

"Open your mouth," he said.

When she did, he placed something on her tongue. She tasted a most unusual taste. It was rather like a large raisin with a stone in its center. And yet it had the aroma of perfume.

"Eat it," he said. "What do you think?"

"It's good," she said, and she meant it. "But it smells like perfume."

"It is a li zhi—'lychee' in English. Its aroma is unusual; some say sensual. It has a reddish outer shell and sweet, edible flesh. Some believe it is sacred because of the color of its outer shell." He smiled. "Like a woman, the deeper you go, the pinker the flesh."

Julia felt her face flush hot. She struggled to regain her composure. "And the point is, I should be able to know you are present even if I cannot see you."

He admired her ability to regain her composure. "Yes, that is precisely the point. And just as this nut has a special aroma, so, too, does each person."

He stood up but did not remove her blindfold. Then she felt

his hands on her shoulders, guiding her to her feet. "Stand still," he said softly. "Do not move, do not step either forward or backward."

He positioned her and stood in front of her. He stood close but not close enough that they were touching. She could feel the heat emitted by his body, hear his breathing, and sense the nearness of him.

"Inhale," he whispered. "Breathe deeply as you have been taught."

In no way did he touch her or move closer. Yet she felt almost as though she were in his embrace. It was a strange, incredible feeling. Perhaps only a piece of paper could be passed between them. It was as if they were apart and yet together at the same time. And he was right; she could smell the saltiness of his body and something else, something she could not describe other than to define it as his maleness. Then she wondered how she knew so much about the scent of men. Perhaps it was because she had lived among so many of them aboard ship with her father. But she said nothing to him and did not comment on his male scent.

As if he read her mind, he whispered, "You smell my essence. You will learn to recognize it when you are blindfolded, even when you are asleep."

It seemed they stood there together for a very long time. Then she felt him leave, and, from a distance he said, "Remove your blindfold."

Julia lifted off the blindfold and looked about. Garrick was gone, and, in his place, Ming Li stood by the far portal.

A great bolt of lightning struck the vessel, and it heaved and was dashed against rocks. The last sound Julia heard was that of splitting wood and her own scream.

Julia sat upright, beads of perspiration on her brow. She

shook violently with the memory of her dream, aware only of the other women in the darkness. She knew they were staring at her.

"You screamed," Ming Li said softly as she put her slender arm around Julia's shoulder.

"I had a dream," Julia whispered.

"Ah, you remember."

Julia knew she was trapped by her own scream. She could no longer lie to Ming Li and Garrick. They would know now that she remembered, that she knew who she was.

Ming Li said something in Chinese to the others, who lay back down immediately. "Wait here," Ming Li advised. She padded away into the darkness.

In a few minutes Ming Li returned with a cool, damp cloth, with which she wiped Julia's brow. "Tomorrow," she whispered, "you must tell Garrick everything you remember. He wants to know all about you."

Julia lay down and drew the sheet about her. She shivered. What if he did send her to Jason Hamilton? It was then, in the darkness of the night, that she knew she had to tell Garrick everything and pray he would not send her to Shanghai. She could not go on being afraid.

Julia sat on the low, curved bench by the lily pond. *Tranquil* was a word both Ming Li and Garrick used often, and she knew that, sitting here, tranquillity could almost be grasped. The pathways, the arrangement of the flowers, the pond itself—all contributed to the extraordinary atmosphere of peace. It was, as Garrick had said, "a whole," a tranquil reality.

This afternoon Garrick did not appear mysteriously when she least expected to see him. He came through the portal she was facing and walked to her side.

"Ming Li says you have remembered."

She stared into the pond, afraid of revealing so much of herself, of her emotions, by looking into his eyes.

"My father was a sea captain. We sailed from Portsmouth more than two years ago. I did not want to accompany him, but I was made to do so. He was to give me in marriage to a man I despise, a man I greatly fear."

Garrick ignored her comments about the man she was to marry. "Surely your marriage was not the main reason for the trip."

"No. My father was a trader. He had cargo to deliver to Shanghai. The man I was to marry was also in Shanghai."

"And your mother?"

"She died. My father was cruel to her; he abused her in every way. I remember."

Her voice had grown small, and it faded away as she spoke about her mother.

"Were you mistreated as well?"

"I was afraid of him. My mother used to hide me when he returned at night, after he had been out drinking."

He watched her carefully and saw that she trembled slightly. "There was a terrible storm, and we were thrown off course. We hit rocks—I tied myself to the mast because I was afraid to go below deck. Oh, please, you must let me stay here. You must not send me to Shanghai or back to the British. He will come to claim me."

Garrick did not speak for a long while; then he turned to her.

"The fisherman who found you was right. It was a miracle you survived tied to the mast. As for going to Shanghai, surely this man cannot be that bad."

"He is old and cruel and drinks like my father." She looked up into his eyes. "So, you see, it doesn't matter if you give me to the emperor or train me to do whatever he wishes. My father was to give me to a horrible man. It seems I'm destined to be given to someone! It doesn't matter!"

Tears had flooded her eyes, and he put his hands firmly on her shoulders. It was the first time he had actually touched her, and he felt his own emotions surge through him as he connected with her even in this slight physical way. "Given? No, you are being educated to know desire. I told you, you will not be forced." And, as he spoke, he acknowledged for the first time how much he hated the idea of preparing her for another. Still, he had no choice. He had pledged himself to help this country, and to do so, he had to remain close to the emperor. If the emperor wanted this woman, he would have her. Once again Garrick reminded himself that her life would not be unpleasant. Indeed, apparently she had been delivered from something worse.

"You won't turn me over to the man in Shanghai, will you?"

Garrick frowned. "Who is this man?"

"Jason Hamilton."

Garrick felt himself go stiff. He clenched his fists at the sound of Hamilton's name. But she need not know that Hamilton was an enemy of China and Garrick's own personal enemy as well. "I assure you, I will not."

He watched with some admiration as she drew on some inner strength and again regained her composure. "Forgive me. I'm feeling sorry for myself."

"It seems you have cause. But now you must close the door on that part of your life and begin anew. When you are in a state of balance and harmony, you will know happiness; and, I assure you, it is not a happiness anyone can take from you."

He let his hands drop from her shoulders, and yet it was as if he still held her. She was filled with a sense of release from fear as well as a feeling she could only describe as longing. It was at that moment that she realized she wanted this strange man to hold her.

"I must go now, but I'll return this afternoon for your lesson."

She drew in her breath. Obviously he was not attracted to her, and she reminded herself that he was preparing her for the emperor. "I want to know about you," she said firmly. "I want to know why you are here among these people and how you came to know so much about them." She did not add that she wanted to know about his relationship with Ming Li.

"Observe," he said, looking into her eyes, "and in time you will not need to ask such questions." It was an evasive answer but a truthful one. There were things he could not tell her, things he might never tell her. Again he wondered if there was any hope that the emperor might not claim her. He forced that thought from his mind. It was a dangerous thought. He had to remain focused. He could not allow this woman to take him off course.

In the afternoon light the garden took on a new beauty, a different tranquillity.

"I'm ready for my lesson," Julia said, looking up into Garrick's face.

"Sometimes lessons must be based on observations. What have you seen here that you want to ask about?"

She thought for a moment and wondered if she could ask such a question of a man. She had asked Ming Li only half the question; could she ask Garrick the rest? But who could better answer her than Garrick, who said he was her teacher? She decided she would simply have to overcome her shyness if she was truly to learn.

"I have watched the other women in the morning, after the bath. They allow the eunuchs to rub scented oil onto their breasts and beat them with woven grass switches. Sometimes they make sounds of great pleasure. I wonder why this is done and how it feels."

"This question would best be answered by trying it."

"I don't think I could."

He half smiled. "I think you could."

She did not argue. "Then at least tell me why it is done?"

"Ah, that question I will answer, though you may not fully understand till you are further along with your lessons. When a man and woman make love, they exchange essences. A woman's breasts give off female essences. There is a great deal to learn about Tao lovemaking, and you are getting a bit ahead of yourself, but, simply, we believe that prolonged sucking of the nipples during intercourse causes increased excitement and thus increases the essences secreted. A woman's breasts can be made more sensitive by frequent massaging and by the use of the grass switches."

Julia felt almost hypnotized as he spoke. Her throat was dry, and she felt strangely weak. Suddenly he laughed.

"Why are you laughing?" she demanded. "I'm only trying to learn."

"As you are naked beneath your gown, I am quite sure you can feel that your own nipples have hardened. How do they feel as the cloth of the gown touches them?"

He was right! Her nipples had hardened, and she felt nothing so much as that strange longing she had felt before. But he was making fun of her, and she turned away, her face hot with embarrassment at this frank conversation. She had managed to steel herself when he spoke in the abstract, but as soon as he had involved her personal reactions, she retreated.

Shock may have filled her eyes, but Garrick could easily see she was aroused. Ah, this little puritan was a woman of fire. He had guessed as much from the beginning, in spite of her protestations.

He touched her arm and leaned close, whispering, "A fire burns far too quickly. You must learn the secrets of smoldering till you are completely overcome. That is how mere physical pleasure becomes ecstasy."

She could not bring herself to look again into his eyes, though he continued speaking.

"Yes, the eunuchs rub the breasts of the women after the bath so that their breasts will become more sensitive, and eventually all the women have their nipples swatted lightly with woven switches. It does not hurt, but it increases blood flow and makes them a darker color. And, yes, the women enjoy this even though the eunuchs cannot satisfy them in any way."

She nodded, even though she stared at the ground. She wondered what else there was to this Tao lovemaking. "Are you going to explain all the lovemaking to me?" she asked.

"As I have told you, there is more than lovemaking. Tao is a whole, it is 'the way.' You cannot separate lovemaking as though it stands alone. Lovemaking is central to Tao thinking, but it does not define Tao any more than the lily pad defines the pond."

"All my life people have taught me that lovemaking was wrong, that it is sinful."

"I know what you have been taught."

"But those who taught me those things forced themselves on women and were cruel. I cannot return to a man like my father. That is why I have agreed to stay here and to try to learn."

He did not say that in truth she had no choice but to learn, just as he had no choice but to teach her. He was grateful for her willingness. It made things easier, though as he thought about the look in her eyes, he knew it would not all be easy.

4

As was the custom in the late afternoon, the women all gathered in a brightly lit room to sew. Most did delicate embroidery, and, as they did so, they chattered among themselves.

"I shall never be able to do such fine work," Julia lamented.

"Do the best you can. As with all things, practice brings proficiency."

Ming Li was always encouraging. "I'm curious about Garrick," Julia confessed. "How did he come to live here in the Forbidden City?"

"It is not my place to tell you Garrick's secrets. You must ask him. But I will tell you that he is a most unusual person and the only foreigner in the Forbidden City, except for you. He is also a kung-fu master who for many years lived in a Taoist monastery in the south of China. He is much respected and also a master of our language." Ming Li paused. "Of course, he is not respected by all. Everyone in the Forbidden City has enemies."

Julia stored away the intriguing comment about enemies. Her curiosity was centered on Garrick as well as on Ming Li's relationship with him. Ming Li did not say that she did not know Garrick's secrets, she said only that it was not her place to reveal them. Julia decided to try to find out a little more. "A monastery? Does that mean he is some kind of monk and cannot take a lover?"

Ming Li laughed lightly. "Oh, no, I am sure Garrick has had many lovers. It means he was taught by monks. Even so, Taoist monks may have women. They are not like the monks found in Catholic monasteries."

Ming Li was truly educated. She knew about Catholicism and seemingly many other aspects of life in the West. Julia knew little of China save the fact that spices and silk came from China, and upper-class English ladies had Chinese dishes. She drew in her breath; there was so much to learn. "What is kung fu?" she asked after a moment.

"It is a skill. I shall try to explain. In our language, *pinyin 'gongfu'* is a skill exercise that involves the spirit. It can be any endeavor undertaken without interference from the intellect or from the emotions. Usually the term is used to describe a form of personal combat that involves no weapons. In involves four stances or fighting positions—the dragon, the frog, horse riding, and the snake. It has been practiced by Taoists for many centuries."

"Do you know how Garrick came to study this skill and to live in a monastery?"

Ming Li lowered her eyes. "You must ask him. I can only say that his mastery of *'the way'* has made him acceptable to the court and to the emperor."

"Is he then a master of Taoist lovemaking?"

Ming Li did not look up. "He is," she replied softly. "One cannot master *'the way'* without also mastering lovemaking, because exchange of essences is central to Tao."

Julia frowned and tilted her head. "I'm still not sure I understand."

"The arts of the bedroom constitute the climax of human emotions. They encompass the totality of Tao. A man regulates his pleasure in order to conserve his strength. A woman must have as many orgasms as possible in order to develop her essences."

For a moment Julia thought of Alice and felt that she, too, had fallen down a rabbit hole and entered a world of opposites. Men in her world, in the world her mother had known, cared only for their own pleasure. A woman's sole purpose was to keep a man happy, to work for him and to have his children. Here, at least among those who called themselves Taoists, it seemed quite the opposite. Women were endlessly pleasured while men learned restraint. In spite of all she had been taught about the evil of sex, she found this new teaching truly intriguing. In her innermost thoughts she had already admitted that she wanted to experience this kind of lovemaking.

Again Julia wondered if Ming Li and Garrick were, or had been, lovers. Garrick was a Westerner with a true grasp of China. Ming Li was Chinese with a grasp of the West. It seemed reasonable that they were lovers or had been. But she did not ask, and she knew it was because she was beginning to care for Garrick and did not really want to know the answer.

On this occasion Julia was not sent to the tranquil garden where Garrick usually met her. Instead she was taken to a private altar located in yet another courtyard.

At first she had not realized it was an altar because it was different from the kind of altars found in Western churches. It was made of stone and blended perfectly with the garden that surrounded it. It was almost as if it had grown like the trees and flowers.

Usually she sat and waited for Garrick to appear, but when she arrived he was already waiting for her.

Garrick watched Julia carefully as she passed through the

portal into the garden. Her hair was tamed and was held tight with tortoiseshell combs. Her silk kimono covered her thin, gauzy gown, and she walked taking small steps, her head down. Each day she seemed to absorb more of her surroundings; each day she behaved less like the reserved English prude she had been and more like a young woman ready and willing to experiment, to learn, and even to practice what was learned.

Curse Wan Shi! Wan Shi had suggested that he train the girl. It was a test; now he knew how serious a test it was. As her tutor in matters sexual, he could, and indeed would have to, demonstrate all manner of intimacies. But he could not have the ultimate joy of intercourse. When she was ready, when her sexual desire was at its peak, after the ceremony of the jade egg, she would be delivered to the emperor. She would be blindfolded and made to lie naked and prostrate on his bed, waiting for his decision. If she pleased the emperor, he would deflower her and keep her sequestered with his favorite concubines. *I will never see her again,* Garrick thought. He knew she would be miserable, for she would not have Ming Li's company or his. *I warned her. I warned her again and again. It was her choice!*

Her choice or not, he still harbored the hope that she would let him help her escape if the opportunity arose. But he could not even discuss it with her. Wan Shi had spies everywhere. Even in this sacred garden someone might be hiding and listening for him to reveal his slightest disloyalty. *And I am disloyal,* he admitted. His own controlled desire for Julia was disloyal because he should have no desire at all. He should have no need to be with this woman of passion, no desire to exercise his Jade Stem, to hold her, to watch her, to feel her tremble and pulsate as she knew the ecstasy he knew he could make her feel. He closed his eyes as she approached and forced his thoughts aside. She had much to learn; she was not ready. When he again opened his eyes, she was standing in front of him.

"Were you praying?"

"No, not in the sense that you know the word *prayer*. But this is a Taoist altar we stand before."

"Am I to kneel?" she asked.

"No, it is not necessary. Simply tell me what you observe about this altar."

"My first thought when I saw it was that it seemed to grow here."

"It is one with the garden, one with nature. That is the very essence of Tao."

"It seems very old."

"It was built by Li Lung-chi, the greatest of all the T'ang emperors. He ruled in the sixth century. One day, while burning incense at this altar, he had a mystical experience and was mentally carried to heaven."

"Do you believe that?"

"I believe the experience changed him forever. He abolished capital punishment and ordained the humane treatment of animals. He became one with nature."

"One with nature," Julia repeated.

"Think on your modesty. Think on what you were taught about lovemaking. In England you were made to feel shame when your body was exposed. Do animals blush at one another's bodies? Sex is both natural and necessary to man's well being. When you feel the fires of desire smoldering inside you, your body secretes hormones that give you health, life, and youth."

He was not looking at her as he talked; rather, his eyes were on the altar and the surrounding garden. She listened, feeling strongly that there was truth in what he said. Although she would not admit it, his very words had excited her yesterday, and for the rest of the day she had felt alert and filled with inexplicable energy. She wondered if he was aware of his effect on her, of how when he discussed lovemaking or even the intimate parts of the body with her she felt both embarrassed and elated.

"A man's sexual secretions come mostly from his penis," he said, turning to look directly into her eyes. "A woman emits her essence from her *three peaks.*"

"Three peaks? What are the three peaks?"

"The tongue, the nipples, and the vagina."

She could not prevent her face from flushing, no matter how hard she tried.

Again he withdrew the blindfold from his pocket. She said nothing as he tied it over her eyes, leaving her only with the aroma of the garden, the sounds of the insects, and her own acute awareness of his closeness. She wondered if he was going to stand close to her again, to make her feel him without touching him.

He did indeed stand close to her; close enough so that even through the heavier material of her kimono she could feel his chest against the tips of her breasts.

They stood in that position for what seemed a very long time. Then he leaned closer, and she felt his mouth on hers. His lips moved against hers until he forced open her mouth. Never had she been kissed before, never had she dreamed a kiss could be like this one. She could not pull away. Could one be violated by a kiss? If so, the probing of his tongue had violated her.

His tongue explored her mouth, darting around even as he sucked on her lips, just as she imagined another part of him might probe her most intimate region. The shock of the image that filled her mind both surprised and flustered her. She had a fleeting sense of guilt, but it did not persist. His tongue was too warm, too soft, too deep inside her. She could not wrench herself free of him. These "lessons" were far more than she had bargained for; they aroused her in ways she had not even thought possible. Did he know the effect of this kiss? Then, with agonizing slowness, he withdrew from her mouth and stepped back and away from her. She shivered ever so slightly, aware of the dampness between her legs, aware of an indescribable feeling of longing, aware of how desperately she wanted him to touch her in that special place. How could she have been afraid of him? She only wanted him to go on, to show her more, to awaken her fully.

He took off her blindfold. Then, refolding it, he handed it to her. "Wear it tomorrow morning when you allow your breasts to be massaged for the first time."

"I cannot allow that!" she objected in the slightest of whispers.

"You are ready. Wear the blindfold, and imagine the hands of whomever you choose."

His words chilled her. When he kissed her as he just had, was he kissing another? Was he perhaps kissing Ming Li? She could not ask, and, regrettably she knew she could not ask, because she wanted him to be kissing only her. Just as regrettably, she knew she would do exactly as he asked. And she would think of him.

Julia was filled with nervous energy. She bathed and swam with the others. But no matter how hard she tried, she could not forget what Garrick had told her. Was she ready? Could she allow one of the eunuchs to touch her bare breasts?

When the time came for them to adjourn to the room beyond the baths, she steeled herself. She then went to one of the tables and noted that, as she did so, Ming Li smiled at her proudly.

As Garrick had suggested, she put on the blindfold, and then she took off her gown, lay facedown, and pulled up the satin sheet to her waist. She waited for one of the Eunuchs to come to her, still unsure if she would be able to turn over when the time came.

She inhaled the scented oil before she felt the eunuch's strong hands on her back. At first his trained fingers danced on her flesh, and then he applied pressure on each side of her spine and on her shoulders. The eunuch's massage was wonderfully relaxing. For a few moments she was lost in the wonderment of it; in fact, it was so relaxing she almost fell asleep. But, after a time, the eunuch poked her, and she knew she had either to get up or turn over. She closed her eyes even beneath her blindfold and turned over slowly. In moments she felt the warm, scented oil applied to her breasts. *"Imagine the hands of whomever you chose."* Garrick had said. *Heaven help me! I can only think of him.*

She was massaged only gently at first. She marveled in the sensations caused by his hands. Then both nipples were taken between thumb and forefinger, and they grew taut. Garrick's face filled her imagination. The fingers of the eunuch, if they were the hands of the eunuch, became Garrick's fingers teasing her pulsating flesh. Her mouth was ever-so-slightly open, and she tried to breathe deeply as she had been taught. Oh, it was an indescribable sensation, this massage. Her nipples were pulled gently and rubbed till she thought she might well scream aloud. She wanted someone to touch her elsewhere—no, not a stranger, not the eunuch! But she did indeed feel desire welling inside her, and as she moved she wondered if this was the slow, smoldering desire of which Garrick had spoken.

Garrick looked on his pupil, aware only of the dryness in his own mouth and of the hardness of his own organ beneath his loose-fitting garment. Her breasts were the color of cream, and her rosy, hard nipples were turning an even a deeper red as they filled with blood. She was excited, and he signaled the eunuch to step aside. He knew as he watched her breathing heavily that she was thinking of him just as he had almost felt her breasts beneath his own fingertips while watching the eunuch work on her. She was a beautiful, sensual woman. She was a brave woman, and he wanted her for himself, even if it was forbidden. But she was not yet ready, not for him nor for the emperor, should he choose her for a night.

The eunuch stepped away from her, bowing, and Garrick stepped to the side of the table himself. With a wave of his hand, the other women, who were finished in any case, hurried away.

He leaned over Julia and applied more oil, and doing exactly what the eunuch had done, he began again to massage her breasts. The flesh beneath his fingers seemed hot to his touch, and watching her writhe beneath the sheet held the sweet promise of things to come. He worked on her for a few more minutes, all too well aware of the beads of perspiration on his own brow and the throbbing of his own organ. Desire—yes, he felt desire for her, but he would not fulfill his desire. "*The way*" was much more fulfilling. He had learned the lessons of patience well. Again he reminded himself of just how dangerous it might be to keep this woman for himself rather than give her over to the emperor. It would jeopardize everything! He lifted his hands from her hot flesh and stepped away from her, fearing she might prematurely come to orgasm from the stimulation and her own obviously fertile imagination.

She did not hear an order given, but she felt her legs spread and her ankles bound to either side of the table.

When the hands stopped massaging her, Julia lay still, trying to regain her composure. Was she going mad? Or had more than one person massaged her? There had been a slight pause, and she felt certain that larger hands had taken over—Garrick's hands? Or was that a dream; was it merely wishful thinking? Her skin was on fire. She had wanted Garrick to feel her breasts; she wanted him to be the one who so aroused her. But she could not be certain that it was he who had given her such pleasure.

She lay still for what seemed a long time and then felt the freezing cold. Ice? Had the eunuch put ice on her nipples? They again hardened, and again she felt the pleasure of touch. Lips fastened on to one and sucked and teethed, drawing and withdrawing. She writhed and felt hands holding her down as ice was applied to her other breast, and again her nipple was drawn into the mouth of the unseen man.

Her breath came in short gasps, and she strained against the bonds that held her legs apart. She moaned, and then the mouth withdrew. She felt exhausted as she lay there, and, slowly, her nipples returned to normal. Her legs were released, and she heard Garrick say, "Tomorrow she must be bound throughout the massage in order to prevent her from coming to high tide on her own."

She said nothing even though she shivered. She was past objection.

As if awakening from a dream, she heard Ming Li's whisper, "It is time to go."

She opened her eyes and sat up. The others were gone, and so were the eunuchs.

"Did you enjoy it?" Ming Li asked. Her bright eyes danced, and she smiled ever so slightly.

"I did," she replied honestly. It was an understatement of vast proportions.

As was their routine, Garrick met her in the garden. He came while she was sitting by the lily pond, her kimono drawn about her.

"It is warmer than usual," she said. Perhaps he would not discuss the massage, about how she had felt. He really did not need to ask; he had been there and seen or even caused her response, which she knew she had not hidden, indeed could not hide because she had had no control over it.

"It is the last gasp of winter. Spring is coming to Peking," he said slowly. "Soon it will be warm in the gardens, and the blossoms will bloom."

"But there are flowers now." Julia felt mystified.

"All grown inside and transplanted outside to create an illusion. You must learn to recognize illusions. In spring there will be fresh flowers, and gardens you have not yet seen will be opened. You will see there is much in the Forbidden City you have not seen. There are surprising places, places where we can be quite alone."

His emphasis was on the word *alone.* A chill ran up her spine with the promise of things to come. Then, as quickly as she had climbed the upward spiral, she spun downward.

"I must leave for a short time. Ming Li will continue your lessons—in Chinese and in culture."

"And my other lessons, the ones you give me?"

"You will need time to absorb what you have already learned. The breast massage will continue."

"Why must I be bound?"

He smiled ever so slightly, "So you will not experience too much too soon. We will continue when I return."

He did not say how long he would be gone, and she did not ask. He drew her to her feet and into his arms. Again he bent over and sought her mouth, quickly forcing it open and inserting his tongue. As before, the motions he made were suggestive, and as he flicked his tongue in and out of her mouth, her imagination conjured up images, images she never dreamed she could or would imagine. She knew what a penis was, but she had never seen one. Yet she imagined it like a tongue, moving in and out of her, in and out until . . . She almost fainted in his arms as he withdrew from her mouth but continued to lick her lips, sucking gently on them, allowing his hot breath to caress her neck.

She shivered as he held her, marvelled at her boldness as she pressed against him. Was that his organ she felt? Another chill passed through her. It could not be! Such a thing as she felt could not possibly fit inside a woman.

But she had no time to ask, no time to savor what she felt. He released her and without another word turned and left.

One did not enter the Forbidden City easily, and leaving was no less difficult. Garrick MacDonald did not choose to pass through the main gates; rather he made his way through the maze of royal buildings and used a little-known underground passage. A passage that might become very important. When he emerged he was on a dark, narrow street, part of the labyrinth of streets that surrounded the Forbidden City.

Garrick dressed in drab clothes, and he walked rapidly. Soon he was on a wider street filled with people. All his senses were assaulted simultaneously.

Street vendors roasted duck and chicken. They poured meats and vegetables and aromatic spices into deep, round pots of sputtering grease, and an aroma-filled vapor of steam filled the air, beckoning the hungry to buy a dish full of their concoctions. Even as the combined smells of food and filth filled his nose, his ears filled with the sounds of the street. The roads were filled with clattering rickshaws. Loaded Peking carts rattled along, pulled by human pack animals, a caravan of camels plodded on, and a hundred thousand feet tramped on the ground. Beneath the constant traffic, the earth had long ago turned into a thick layer of gray, fine, powdered dust.

It was still winter, but when summer came dust storms would blow in off the great Gobi Desert. Then it would seem as if the desert itself hung over the city. The blue sky would turn a sickening yellow like pale urine. If the winds did not carry it away, the desert dust grew thicker by the day until the sun faded and then disappeared altogether. Then even the protected and most secluded gardens of the Forbidden City were covered with dust, their bright blossoms tinted with yellow. The dust was remarkable, an airborne invader that sifted through every crack and crevice, piling up against doors and windows. During such storms, Peking became *the City of the Faceless.* No one ventured forth without scarves and wraps.

Garrick's thoughts returned to China and what was happening. On the one hand the Europeans wanted to carve up China, subjugate the people, control all trade and commerce, and have the right to spread their religion. And the English were the worst. They had deliberately imported opium, thus creating millions of addicts and untold misery. The Chinese, on the other hand, regarded the foreigners as beneath contempt. They saw them as drug-distributing, uncultured barbarians and thought them inferior.

The emperor might have changed the course of history, but he made no attempt to do so. He was a victim of Ching bureaucracy. It was a stifling Confucian-based bureaucracy that had done little but alienate the people. To make matters worse, those who wielded power were divided between the War and Peace parties. Prince Kung, the emperor's younger and far brighter brother, led the Peace Party. Garrick favored the Peace Party. A war would only bring endless bloodshed. He hoped that on this trip out of the Forbidden City, he would make important progress. Prince Kung must take over; it could make all the difference.

The situation had grown far more tense, and it was the growing tension that had sent Garrick on this mission. Inside the Ching bureaucracy even the factions had factions. Danger lurked everywhere, and war was a distinct possibility.

Garrick turned his thoughts to Jason Hamilton and cursed under his breath. Who could have guessed that a woman from half a world away would be living in fear of his sworn enemy? Jason Hamilton wanted war. He wanted no government, not even the British, to regulate his opium trade or to try to close down the houses of prostitution he ran in all of China's port cities. Drugs and slavery . . . small wonder the Chinese were suspicious of foreigners. Hamilton was the worst kind of criminal. Garrick shook his head; it was no wonder Julia had chosen life in the Forbidden City over life with Hamilton. He drew in his breath. Hamilton must not learn of her whereabouts; it could create just the sort of incident that was to be avoided at all costs.

No, he vowed, Julia would never be Hamilton's possession. Sadly she might have to remain in the Forbidden City. He thought about her and felt longing and desire so strong the emotion was almost painful. She was young and needed protection and guidance. She was beautiful—at least to his eyes—and though he might never possess her as he desired, he had to find a way to protect her. Daily he knew she was overcoming her inhibitions. It was a joy to see, but Wan Shi would learn of it; then Julia would be given to the emperor. Unconsciously Garrick gritted his teeth. He wanted her, but he had a duty. He felt desire, but he had to exercise the discipline he had been taught. "Ready her," he commanded himself. It was what he had to do.

Julia, her kimono wrapped around her, stood outside, letting the warm spring breeze caress her. She had never walked this way before and was surprised to emerge from the maze of interconnecting gardens and corridors into a large, open space. Far across this space she stared at the great gates that guarded the main entrance to the Forbidden City. Had Garrick passed through those gates on his mysterious journey? How she missed him! She continued to stare at the gates, wondering first when he would return through them, and then if she would ever pass through them herself.

"You have walked far today," Ming Li said.

Julia whipped around, startled by Ming Li's voice. She had not even heard Ming Li approach, just as she had been unaware that she had been followed.

"I've never walked this way before."

Ming Li bowed her head. "I suspect you are curious about your surroundings. I am surprised you have not explored more."

"I haven't been all over the Forbidden City, and I have no idea what lies beyond it."

"Not beyond it, but all around it. We are totally surrounded by Peking."

"I should so like to see the rest of the city."

"It's very large and very old. There has been a city here for more than forty centuries. Peking was here before Kublai Khan. Once it was called Chi, Yu Chou. Come, follow me! I shall take you to a place where you can see most of Peking."

Ming Li motioned to her, and Julia followed. It seemed as if they walked for miles through the intricate corridors, along garden paths and outdoor passageways. At last they reached the outside of a tall tower. Ming Li motioned her inside, and the two of them climbed ancient, winding stone steps to the top. Once there, they emerged onto the roof and into the sunlight. A low parapet surrounded the circular roof. One could see in all directions, and Julia was taken aback by what she saw. Peking was as large, if not larger, than London!

"To the west and north are the ridges of the Purple Hills. As you can see, there is a city within a city and beside a city. There are two great rectangles."

Ming Li pointed, and Julia saw groups of buildings, each surrounded by tall walls. Behind the walls the rooftops were blue, green, red, yellow, and gray. It was a great canvas, a painting on which the artist had used the full spectrum of colors on his palate.

"Nearest is the Chinese part of the city, and behind that is the old Manchu district."

"What is that round building?"

"Ah, the Temple of Heaven. It is believed that the altar is the center of the universe."

Julia nodded, thinking that considering the size of the domain they ruled, the Chinese were justified to believe the center of the universe might be there. It was a huge city; it frightened her, and she knew now that escape would be far more difficult than she had originally thought. She could not simply go over the wall or under it. She had to know where she was going, and she had to know some Chinese—certainly more than she knew now. Could she even go alone? If only Garrick would take her, if only they could run away together. Run from the emperor, run from Hamilton, go somewhere where they would be safe and could be together forever. But that would never be, and what made her think that Garrick would want such a thing? He had already warned her that he was loyal to the emperor. For all she knew, he had trained many women as he was now training her. No, she was not his lover. She was his pupil, a woman destined for the emperor's bed. Still, she wanted Garrick to return. If nothing else, she longed for another probing kiss—a kiss that set her afire.

5

Julia walked along the bank of the winding, narrow stream. It had a rock bottom and was so clear she could see its population of tiny black fish darting to and fro. It fascinated her that this city within a city had so many secluded gardens and court-yards. This garden was the largest of the three she was allowed to frequent. An oval-shaped wooden bridge crossed the stream. On either side of the bridge, a profusion of multicolored flow-ers filled the air with a heady aroma.

It was warm, and, thinking she was alone, Julia slipped off her kimono and sat down on a wooden bench. Then, to her sur-prise, she looked up and saw Garrick walking toward her. He had been away for more than a week, and though he had told her he was leaving, he had not told her when he would return. Her heart raced as he drew close.

"You are without your kimono," he said when he reached her.

She only looked down. It mattered not. She no longer cared if he could see the shadow of her pubic hair, the erect state of her nipples, or the curve of her buttocks. Since the morning she had submitted to the massage, she knew her body was no secret to him. Indeed, so strong was her desire to be touched by him she would have stood naked before him.

He put his hands on her shoulders and motioned her to stand up. Again he withdrew the blindfold and secured it. It was as if he had not been gone at all. Clearly he intended taking up exactly where they had left off.

"Are you being massaged daily?" he asked.

"Yes, daily."

"And you are bound so you cannot cause yourself the greater pleasure?"

"Yes."

"And now you are more sensitive, are you not? Can you feel the material of your gown against your nipples?"

"Yes." She did not say that virtually as soon as she had seen him they had gotten hard, and that, once again, she had felt the moisture between her legs and that extreme sense of longing— that desire she could not truly define.

"Are you beginning to feel the smoldering of which I spoke?"

"Yes," she said, her voice barely audible.

He reached across the small distance between them and brushed her neck with the back of his hand.

A chill went through her whole body.

He toyed with her ear, circling it slowly with his finger.

He had touched her much more intimately, but this motion sent repeated chills through her. It seemed as if all her blood had rushed to her face. It felt as if her cheeks were on fire.

"You react well," he said before dropping his hand and sitting down.

She wanted to scream, "For you!" But she could not, she could not tell him how she felt. Of course she did react when massaged, but that was because she thought of him.

"Sit down. Take off your blindfold."

He sat still, and as was often the case with him, she could actually feel his mood changing. "I've been to visit your countrymen," he told her.

She frowned. "You mean Englishmen?"

"Yes."

All her warm, delightful emotions fled in the face of fear. Was someone looking for her? Had her father survived, and were he and Jason Hamilton trying to find her?

"Is something wrong?" she ventured.

He turned quickly, almost angrily. "Have you no idea what is going on in this country?"

Her mouth opened slightly in surprise. "No. I know nothing of what is going on."

His expression softened. "I'm sorry. Of course you don't. You've been sheltered in more ways than one."

"Is something bad happening?"

"Something very bad. Do you know of opium?"

"It is a drug. They say it kills slowly."

"Very slowly. It gives sweet dreams to those who live a nightmare. Your countrymen have taken it upon themselves to import opium into China, to enslave a whole population with drunken dreams while making themselves rich all at the same time."

She stared at the ground, unable to think of what to say. "It's terrible," she finally managed.

"You cannot imagine how terrible. And as if that was not bad enough, foreigners have decided to divide the coastal cities into their own little kingdoms. Soon every city in China will have a foreign enclave. Mind you, there is precedent for that in Chinese history, and most of the people would not object. But the British want more; they want to subjugate all of China. They want war. America and Russia do not want war."

He could not tell her everything. He certainly could not tell her that the man she so feared had somehow learned where she was and was attempting to retrieve her. That it was this man who was his sworn enemy and whose personal power was the greatest of all threats.

"It cannot be all the English who do these terrible things?"

"Men like your father and the man he would have married you to are among the worst. These men must be stopped."

She could hear the passion in his tone. "How have you come to know and care so much about China?" It was among the questions she had yearned to ask.

He turned and faced her, and she looked into his eyes. At first she had disliked him; then she had been deeply aroused by him. Now she saw that there was much more to this man than she had imagined. Listening to him, hearing him talk about this country, made him even more attractive to her.

He sat and stared at the ground, his hands together. "My parents came to China many years ago. They were honest traders. We lived in the south of China. My mother died when I was nine, and my father and older brother were killed in a battle with the English. A wealthy Chinese man adopted me and sent me to be educated in a Taoist monastery. I came here to advise the emperor on the way of our people, to try to negotiate a settlement in order to prevent the country from being taken over."

"You are like a prism," she said thoughtfully. "You're many-sided and change in different lights."

He laughed gently and lifted her hand. "That's a very Chinese observation."

"Have I no more lessons today?"

How easily he could lose himself in her, how very much he wanted to give her the ultimate lesson! "Not today, but tonight. Have you any questions?"

"When a man and woman are making love, does he massage her breasts?"

He lifted his hands and touched the sides of her breasts through the thin material of her gown. "The man begins with massage. Then he kisses the entire breast. He suckles on them for many hours. This is how he receives the essence of the second peak."

His very answer made her feel weak. The look in his eyes was a promise. She wanted to touch him, too. She wanted to know all his secrets. Her face was hot, her desire overwhelming. "Touch me," she suddenly said. "Bind me, do all the things you have talked about. Please, let me feel the pleasure." She had surprised even herself with her words, how she wanted him to ravish her, to give her what she so longed to experience.

"Tonight your lesson will take you to a new level."

Garrick's words had become sweet torture. "What will happen tonight?" She could barely speak.

"I have prepared a surprise for you. Your progress is excellent, and it is time for a reward."

He lifted his hand and touched her breasts, brushing across them quickly, furtively.

She drew in her breath and closed her eyes.

"Not now," he whispered. "Later."

A reward! Through the entire day she had been unable to concentrate. Garrick's promise returned to her again and again. Was he going to kiss her breasts? Would he suck on them and take her essence? All day she felt excited, expectant. All day she was moist, and she ached for his lips, not just on her mouth, but on her entire body and in her most intimate area. She yearned for his sensual, experienced touch. It was as though this very sensitive part of her body, this second peak, as he called it, was waiting for him to suckle the essences from her, to pleasure her as he had promised she would be pleasured.

* * *

The moon was full and the night unusually clear. Not that Julia was used to wandering outside at night. Indeed, the women who occupied the house of the concubines were usually sequestered before the sun sank.

But on this night Ming Li escorted her to an inner courtyard to which she had never previously been.

They entered it through a perfectly round portal called the Moon Gate, and she was shown to a low wall. On the ground beside the wall were a series of satin kneeling cushions, and she was told to kneel and to wait.

It seemed a long while that she remained kneeling, and she noted that where she knelt it was pitch black due to the overhang of the building. But below her, on the other side of the low wall, it was quite bright from the moonlight. It was, she imagined, rather like being in a theater, because the lower garden was illuminated just as a stage might be, while she was in darkness, as an audience would be.

In a moment two figures entered the lower garden. They were quite easily seen silhouetted against the bright night sky. One was clearly a woman. Her gown was flowing and her hair piled high on her head. The other was a man, who led her by the hand.

The man stood in front of her, not touching her, just as Garrick so often stood in front of her. She could not tell if the woman was blindfolded or not.

Then the man bent and kissed the woman. It was an exceptional kiss, a kiss of great length. She was sure it was a probing kiss such as the ones Garrick had given her.

Suddenly Julia turned, sensing Garrick even before he knelt beside her. He lightly brushed her hand with the back of his knuckles. It was barely a touch, yet, like a falling domino in a long line, it set her responses in motion. Heat rippled through her body, her nipples stiffened, and the longing in her lower regions, the sensation she could not describe, returned to her. She turned to him.

"You are to watch," he whispered. "Watch and feel."

She looked back into the garden, and, to her surprise, the long kiss had ended, and the man was removing the woman's gown. He did so slowly, revealing a voluptuous silhouette against the purple sky. Light and shadow . . . she could see, but she could not see.

The man held the woman at arm's length and toyed with her breasts. She could not see the detail of the woman's nipples, but she could feel her own. They were hard and tight and rubbed against her gown.

"Watch and feel," Garrick had said only seconds ago. To her surprise she could feel; it was almost as if what was being done to the woman was being done to her.

Next the man shed his own upper garment; then he stood closer to the woman, allowing her breasts to caress his chest. Julia wondered what it would feel like to have her breasts pressing against Garrick's broad chest. Did he have hair? She was certain he did, and it occurred to her that hair would add to the pleasure she would feel when he came into contact with her taut nipples.

Next the man released the woman's hair, taking out her many combs. Her tresses fell down over her bare shoulders. The man had seized the woman's breasts in his hands and now bent to draw first one and then the other into his mouth. As he did so, his hands held her buttocks tightly so that the lower half of her body pressed against his.

Soon the woman's groans of pleasure were competing with the crickets to fill the night air. Watching, listening, Julia was aware of the dryness in her mouth and throat, aware of the dampness, aware of the longing, of the desire even to touch herself.

The man spent a very long time kissing and sucking on the woman's breasts; then he did what she had never thought of before. He dropped to his knees in front of his lover and, still holding her buttocks, buried his face in her pubic hair.

No sound could equal the sound made by the woman. It was a kind of gasping, yet Julia could tell it was an expression of pure pleasure. The sight was extraordinary, but her own ever-building desire was nothing short of painful.

Soon the woman was writhing; then she let out a cry, and her hands gripped the man's shoulders hard.

When at long last the woman seemed to relax, the man swept her into his arms, carrying her through yet another portal and out of the garden, away from view.

Julia closed her eyes as she felt Garrick's hand resting on her shoulder.

"Touch your lute strings," he whispered.

She could not see his face in the darkness, nor could he see hers. She quivered slightly. *How could she?* Yet she wanted to, she wanted to feel something. . . . How stupidly naive she felt; she did not even know what she wanted to feel.

She felt his hands lifting her silk gown. She was kneeling, and in the darkness she was naked to the waist.

"Touch your lute strings," he said again.

Shakily her hand went to that hidden place.

"Close your eyes and remember what you just saw. Replay it in your mind, relive the vision while you touch yourself."

He was there, near her, breathing on her neck, touching her ear, rubbing his knuckles over her neck. What she had seen played before her closed eyes, just as his fingers played on her neck.

She touched herself as he instructed and was both startled and delighted by the sensation.

"Rub it gently, caress it," he whispered. "Your lute strings will play for you. You will like the tune."

She was lost. Her only response was a slight groan.

"A little more pressure," he whispered.

Julia felt the building tension. Then, as she thought of the man nestled against his partner, his hands on her surging buttocks, his mouth sucking on her breast, drawing pleasure from it, from her, from—Julia could not breathe as the throbbing started, and she felt her own release.

She shook with it, and Garrick put his arms around her, letting her lean against him while she pulsated with a pleasure she had never known before.

"You have just experienced the Tide of Lin. As you will learn, the pleasure is not as great as when a man brings you to high tide. But playing your own lute sensitizes you and readies you for the firing of the canon, as the Chinese say."

She nodded, still trying to regain her composure and still breathing in short gasps.

"You are only to play your own lute when you are granted permission. At least not until after you have been deflowered by the emperor."

She was torn between the joy of this experience and his last words. She had the desire to cry out, "Don't you want me for yourself?" How could he give her to another? Did he not realize that the source of her excitement was the thought of having him for her lover?

He touched her hair gently. "Stay here till Ming Li comes. You are almost ready for the ritual of the jade egg."

"What is it?" She felt apprehension creep through her. Did this mean she would soon be given to the emperor? No, she was not ready to run away yet or even to try. She could speak only a very few words of Chinese, and she had no idea how to get out of the Forbidden City or where to go if she did get out.

He touched his finger to her lips. "You will see. Be patient."

He drew her close and again sought her lips, opening her mouth, inserting his tongue. She pressed against him, feeling the strength and size of his penis, which the Chinese called the Jade Stem. She knew with certainty that if he took her, his Jade Stem would rub against her and move inside her. It would pleasure her even as it filled her. She shivered in his arms. What could be left to teach her? Was tonight not the ultimate lesson?

6

Two days had passed since her extraordinary experience in the garden, but not a single moment of it had faded from her memory. It was early evening when Garrick appeared and summoned her to follow him.

He led her down winding corridors, through connecting rooms, and finally into a dimly lit bedchamber. As soon as they passed through the door, he turned the bolt and locked them inside.

The room was richly decorated with gold and red embroidered tapestries. The bed was huge, a heavy mahogany four-poster bed with satin sheets. Garrick moved about, quickly lighting candles and incense. Then he turned to her and smiled ever so slightly. "Take off all your clothes," he said.

She felt as though she were going to faint. She undid her kimono with shaking fingers and let it slip from her shoulders. He had seen her without clothes before, but this seemed different to her. They were alone, absolutely alone. What did this mean? What did he intend?

Then she lifted her thin gown and lifted it over her head. His dark eyes seemed to devour her, and when he reached out and took her nipples between thumb and forefinger, her mouth grew dry, and she felt her lip quiver with anticipation. He toyed with her breasts for some time, and then he led her to the bed and told her to lie down.

"I must bind you," he whispered into her ear.

Quickly he attached her wrists to thin leather straps, which in turn were attached to the two posts on either side of the bed. Her ankles were attached in the same way to the two posts at the foot of the bed.

"You are now completely open," he said, looking down on her.

"Am I not to be blindfolded?"

He smiled. "Not tonight. Tonight is about seeing and feeling."

He turned away from her and poured some of the perfumed oil, with which she had become so familiar, into a small copper container. This he held over the candle flame for a few seconds. Then he poured the warm scented oil onto her, and she groaned slightly, unable to control herself, as he began massaging not just her breasts but here entire body. She moaned many times and shivered as he aroused her, torturing her with brushes of his knuckles over her nipples, her lute strings, and on the inside of her thighs. He massaged her for more than an hour, straying into all her hidden crevices and now and again sucking a nipple into his mouth. She strained against her restraints, wanting to touch herself, wanting to touch him. "Oh, please," she whispered, "play my lute strings, I beg you."

It was then that he withdrew the jade egg from his pocket. It was truly beautiful, a smooth, perfectly formed egg made of dark green jade. He held it to her lips and then covered it with oil. "Soon," he whispered. He then slipped the egg inside her vagina, which he called the Jade Gate. "Feel it fill you," he whispered in her ear as he stretched out beside her on the bed.

She shivered again as his lips fastened on her breast. The combination of his fingers, his mouth, and the feeling of being filled with the jade egg was incredible. Yet he did not touch that place that gave pleasure; instead he taunted her again and again till tears were running down her cheeks and she was unashamedly begging him to satisfy her—to even allow her to satisfy herself.

"Close yourself around the egg," he commanded. "Keep doing it again and again."

She breathed deeply as she felt his body move lower on the bed. His tongue was suddenly on her lute strings, and it moved in such a way that she cried out. He stopped and started, stopped and again started. His fingers pinched her nipples, his tongue moved quickly, and she squeezed the egg again and again.

Again his tongue touched her, and this time he did not stop. She wanted to embrace him, but she was bound and could not. She wanted to wrap her legs around him, but she was restrained and could not. She cried out and then felt the beginning of the release. She cried out with pleasure, and her whole body shook with her orgasm—"High tide" as Ming Li called it.

He wiped her brow with a silk cloth and smiled down at her. "Very good. You have reached the second level. There now remains only the final level."

She felt unable to speak—could there be more? Was there something more pleasurable than that she had just experienced?

"You are still not to play your lute unless given permission. But you are to insert the jade egg daily and practice over and over closing tightly around it. This is an exercise that will make your muscles strong. When the Jade Stem enters you, you will close around it, giving your partner much pleasure. You will want to do this in order to thank him for the pleasure he has given you."

She looked back into his eyes and felt emboldened. "I want

to thank you," she said. "I want you to give me the final lesson."

"If it is me you want, then think of me, and it will be me."

His answer was immediate and firm, but the look on his face spoke of longing. At that moment she knew he wanted her but that he had to restrain himself.

"There are things you do not know. Things I cannot tell you now and perhaps may never be able to tell you."

Then, without further conversation, he unbound her and told her to dress. He silently led her back to the room where she slept and gave her the jade egg. "Use it daily," he said. "It will make you strong so that you can hug the Jade Stem of your lover."

She nodded, her eyes full of tears and her thoughts on all the things she had wanted to tell him.

"A warning," Garrick said slowly. "When you are taken to enjoy the greatest pleasure, speak no man's name. Not mine, not any man you have ever known. Your lover will be the man you want, but the name of the man you want must be kept silent."

She did not ask why because he turned quickly and left.

Days slipped by and, as instructed, Julia used the jade egg daily. Garrick did not return, and Julia began to worry that his role in her instruction had ended. It was on the night of the full moon that she went to search for Ming Li, only to discover that she, too, was nowhere to be found.

Dejectedly she returned to the room where the concubines slept. Hardly had they all begun their nightly ritual when two eunuchs appeared. They came directly to her and motioned her to follow them. Were they taking her to the emperor? Her heart began to pound, and she bit her lower lip. Garrick and Ming Li had been gone for days. Was she now to be alone? Her Chinese was still limited to only a few words and phrases. Without Garrick and Ming Li she had no one with whom to talk.

As they walked down the long corridor, she wanted nothing so much as to run. But run where? The Forbidden City was a maze. It seemed as if they had walked for ages in what might well have been circles, when they stopped in front of huge double doors. One of the eunuchs produced a blindfold—it was exactly the kind Garrick so often had used. He deftly covered her eyes and secured it. Her world became dark as well as silent. Then she heard the doors open, and, with one eunuch on each side, she was escorted into the room. There her kimono was removed and her hands gently tied behind her. They led her to what she assumed was a bed, sat her down, and then left without a word. At least, she thought they left. She heard their steps on the floor, and she heard the doors open and then close.

Another door opened, and Julia knew she was not alone. She wanted to say Garrick's name but feared, if it was not Garrick, she might get him into some terrible trouble. "You will not suffer or be harmed," he had told her many times. "You can imagine whatever you like, whomever you like. You will be ruled only by your sensations."

She felt him close—was it Garrick or was it the emperor? If it was Garrick, why did he not speak? Still, there was a familiarity to the man's touch, the way in which he brushed her neck with his knuckles.

She felt her gown being parted, and she felt the warmth of his body as he pulled her to her feet and held her close to him. He was naked, and it was with surprise that she felt his Jade Stem. It was large and strong. It pressed hard against her thigh. She wanted to embrace him, but she could not because her hands were tied behind her. He held her there against him for a long while, and then he pushed her gently onto the bed.

She smelled the heady aroma of the oil and felt light-headed with the memories the familiar scent brought to mind. He began to apply it to her. He rolled her over and untied her wrists, only to gently roll her over again and tie her wrists and ankles to the four posts of the bed. She was open and vulnerable, yet she was unafraid.

As before, she was now just as she had been when Garrick had given her the jade egg and taught her how to use it. That night he had instructed her that no matter whom she thought of while being pleasured, she must never speak Garrick's name.

Memories and questions disappeared. The sensations she was feeling overcame her, and any hesitation she might have felt earlier on her way to this assignation also vanished.

The warm, scented oil felt wonderful; her skin tingled with the desire it caused, and she groaned ever so slightly as unseen lips fastened on one breast while thumb and forefinger pinched and squeezed the other. She felt herself become moist and knew she was giving off her essences. She jumped when she felt a sudden stinging and realized her partner had struck her with the woven switch she knew so well. Again he snapped it across her taut nipples. Whatever slight sting there was, it was instantly replaced by the tenderness of the warm, caressing tongue of her unknown partner.

All sense of time was lost to her. The stinging of the switch was alternated with warm suckling and tender touches. She felt as if she were drowning in her own essences, so great was her arousal. And she knew now why she was tied. Had she been able to draw her legs together, she would have reached the first level on her own. Clearly, her lover did not want this.

Then there were a thousand kisses and caresses to her ears, to her neck, and finally to her mouth. Deep, long, incredible kisses combined with more caresses to her breasts and quick, furtive movements over her zone of greatest pleasure. She moved beneath him, lifting her hips shamelessly and moaning and begging for more intimate caresses. Surely this was Garrick. The kisses, the movements, the size of the hands—oh, it must be him, and she saw his face in her mind. It did not matter that in reality her world was all darkness.

Fingers still pinched her nipples as he slid down her oiled and perfumed body to that hidden place. Then, to both her shock and surprise, she felt his caressing tongue. She moaned loudly and shivered uncontrollably, and he sucked and flicked his tongue over her lute strings. Then just as she felt she would scream aloud, the release came—a release that seemed to last forever.

She lay panting and was only barely aware when her bonds were undone. He waited till her pleasure entirely subsided, then he rolled her over and lifted her to her knees so that her round *derriere* was up and her head was down.

He grasped her firmly around the waist, and she felt him tease her inner passageway with his Jade Stem. One hand moved to her center of pleasure and held it while he moved within her. She squeezed him as she had squeezed the jade egg. For the first time, she heard him groan. Then he withdrew from her and held her while once again he brought her to climax with dancing fingers and his playful, probing tongue.

How she wanted to speak his name! How she wanted him to know the pleasure she was having! But his warning had been serious, and she took it seriously.

She was still breathing heavily when he turned her and laid her on her back. This time she was not tied but was left free to move. After a few minutes he began again. More scented oil was applied, and again he began the movements that so aroused her. But this time she moved with him, felt his broad back with her hands, touched his Jade Stem with wonder, and returned his kisses with kisses and caresses of her own. This time when he entered her, he loomed over her, lips on her breasts, his Jade Stem moving inside her with agonizing slowness, each movement also caressing her pleasure zone. Every part of her sought him, held him. He breathed heavily as he moved inside her, holding himself for a long time while her own pleasure mounted. Then, as though completely able to read her sensations, he shook into her, filled her in a way she never imagined, just as she began to tumble into her own abyss of pleasure. For a very long time he lay there, deep inside her, his hands caressing her gently now. Then she felt him withdraw and cover her with a soft blanket. Footsteps on the floor, doors opening and closing, he was gone, and she was alone and more satisfied than she had ever dreamed possible.

7

Julia opened her eyes slowly and then, sitting up, looked around the dimly lit room. She shook her head to clear it. In her sleep the blindfold she had worn had come off. It mattered not; she was quite alone. Was she to stay and wait for someone to come? Or was she to try to find her way back to the other concubines on her own? She pulled herself farther up in bed, aware of how deeply she had slept and how wonderfully satisfied she felt.

She wondered who her lover had been. Oh, surely it was Garrick! Surely no other could have inflamed her so and made her feel so wonderfully complete.

At that moment she heard the door being unlocked. It opened, and, in absolute silence, Ming Li slipped into the room, motioning her to be quiet.

"Oh, good, you are awake," she whispered. "Quickly put on your gown and kimono, and come with me."

Julia heard both the urgency and the distress in Ming Li's voice.

"What's wrong?"

For a moment Ming Li looked as if she was considering her explanation. "You must be silent, and we must hurry. It is Wan Shi; he has caused Garrick to be arrested."

"Arrested? I don't understand."

"I shall try to explain, but right now we must hurry. Time is of the essence."

Was Garrick in real danger? She knew she could not ask now; she knew she had to trust Ming Li. Quickly she put on her gown and kimono and followed Ming Li, who cautiously looked both ways down the long corridor before leading her away.

They walked in silence down one hall and then turned into another, working their way through the Imperial Palace and then through other buildings within the Forbidden City.

Ming Li stopped suddenly before a door. She opened it cautiously and then motioned Julia inside. The room was not well lit, and Julia watched as Ming Li moved her hand along the wall and then bent down and seemed to apply pressure to a baseboard.

"Oh," Julia said in surprise as the wall moved, revealing a secret passageway.

From the pocket inside her kimono, Ming Li produced a candle. She lit it and led Julia into the dark interior of the passageway. She handed Julia the candle, bent down, and again pressed on the floorboard. The door swung closed, leaving them in the passageway with only the flickering light of the candle.

Again Julia followed until Ming Li stopped before another door. She opened the door, and they both entered a small room lit by the natural light that came through a narrow slitlike window. The room was furnished with a chair, a bed, and a table piled high with clothing. In the corner there were weapons. In her lessons Julia had learned a little about kung fu, and she recognized the vicious metal weapons as those used in the ancient Chinese art. There were a variety of curved swords, daggers, axes, whips, and darts.

"What is this place?" Julia asked in amazement.

"It is an unwise person who does not plan for the unexpected. Garrick is not unwise."

Ming Li dug in the pile of clothes. "You must dress as a man," she said. "And you must darken your face and hide your hair. I will help you. We must disguise ourselves and rescue Garrick from the prison before Wan Shi returns to the Forbidden City with Jason Hamilton and the English soldiers."

Ming Li's words cut through Julia like a knife. "Jason Hamilton," she repeated. She could hear the fear in her own voice.

"Garrick has told me your story. I know you fear this man. We must free Garrick—he will lead the men loyal to the emperor's brother. The emperor must be deposed, or all China will be subjugated."

"Garrick has spoken to me about these things, but he did not mention Jason Hamilton as being specifically involved." What had he said? He said they were "men like Jason Hamilton."

"He did not wish to frighten you. Hamilton is an opium dealer. He is a man of great power. He heard there was an Englishwoman here. He bribed the prefect and persuaded Wan Shi to tell the emperor that Garrick had taken you for himself—before the emperor even saw you."

Julia's heart leaped. It was Garrick! He had taken her! She felt certain that Garrick wanted her and that they would be together again. But Garrick was in danger, and she had to help him. "Tell me what to do. I will do whatever I can."

"Dress as I told you, and we will go to the cells. I will bring the guards a tea, which I will drug. They will fall into a deep sleep. I will guard them while you set Garrick free. He will know exactly what to do."

Julia nodded and began to dress as Ming Li had instructed.

"Hide this dagger in your clothing, and give it to Garrick. Be silent, and keep to the shadows."

They walked for what seemed like miles through a tangle of dark, dank tunnels beneath the buildings of the Forbidden City. They emerged in a semidark corridor and finally into a large room that was obviously used for food preparation. It was quite deserted, and Julia watched as Ming Li prepared the tea, adding to it the contents of several small packets she withdrew from her pocket. She put the teapot and the tiny cups onto a tray and beckoned Julia to once again follow her.

In a few moments they entered a large room, behind which an armed guard sat.

Julia kept to the shadows as told, her head down.

"I have brought tea," Ming Li said in Chinese as she set down the tray.

The guard did not look at Ming Li but rather concentrated his gaze on Julia.

"My guard," Ming Li said, gesturing toward Julia. "He is mute."

Julia could not understand but surmised that Ming Li was explaining her presence to the guard.

Ming Li poured the tea and served the man behind the desk. "I am sent to reward you for guarding the illustrious prisoner so well."

The guard smiled and nodded.

Julia did not understand the words, but the look in the guard's eyes as he looked at Ming Li was one of undisguised lust. Instinctively she knew that Ming Li was offering herself as the primary distraction or at least until the drug took effect.

The man was gross, and it was the kind of sacrifice a woman would make only for a man she loved. Did Ming Li love Garrick, too? There were so many questions, but this was not the time to ask them. Garrick, no matter which one of them he loved, had to be saved.

Julia watched as the guard drained his teacup and motioned Ming Li to his side. He stood up, pushing his chair across the floor. He pulled Ming Li into his arms roughly, and, looking over his shoulder, he shouted in Chinese for Julia to leave. Julia hesitated for only a moment. Again she had not understood the words, but his meaning was clear, and she slipped back out of the room and toward the cells, hoping for Ming Li's sake that the brutish guard would quickly fall into a drugged sleep.

There were cells on either side of the corridor. She stopped at each one and whispered, as loudly as she dared, "Garrick?"

At the fifth cell she heard a tapping answer. It took all her strength to push the huge bolt that held the door to one side.

He pulled the door open from the inside and stared at her. "Ming Li is with the guard," she whispered urgently. "I am to give you this." She handed him the dagger.

His lips brushed hers, and he whispered, "Soon." He slipped the dagger into his belt, and she followed as they returned to the guard's room.

Inside, Ming Li was pulling her kimono around her. The guard lay still, not in sleep but in death. His head rested in a pool of blood, a dagger protruded from his throat. "He did not fall asleep soon enough," Ming Li whispered.

"You are an accomplished woman," Garrick said. "Take Julia, and meet me in the appointed place."

"We will be there," Ming Li promised.

The night reminded Julia of London. A dense fog had closed in over the city, obscuring the gaily painted lanterns that normally glowed from the windows or danced in the breeze as they hung from tree branches.

Julia had seen those lights from the tower in the Forbidden

City, but tonight there were no lanterns, just a fog that shrouded everything. It was as if they were lost in a cloud.

"We are fortunate," Ming Li said. "The fog is like a cloak. It will help us in our escape. You must say nothing; if we are questioned I will say what I said before, that you are a mute."

"Where are we going?"

"Out of the Forbidden City. We are going to travel far away to the place where Garrick was raised. He will join us when the new emperor is on the throne. But our trip is long and arduous. You must be patient."

Julia nodded and helped Ming Li up onto the cart that waited for them. Clearly this escape had been planned. Just as clearly, Ming Li was a master of disguise. Both were now dressed as men.

"First we will travel by cart and then later by water," Ming Li explained.

So many questions. . . . Julia buried her curiosity for the time being. Ming Li was anxious, as if the monster Jason Hamilton were pursuing her, too.

They traveled many nights by cart, sleeping during the day in the houses of peasants. Ming Li clearly knew just where to go. Julia could only assume this was a prearranged route. After a time, they began traveling on a *sanpan* down a river, through deep gorges and past many villages. Ming Li indicated that it was safe enough to travel by day, so each day Julia could see the scenery changing. It was almost as if they were in a different country.

Ming Li stared into the water. She looked tired but was still, in spite of the hardships of their journey, composed and beautiful.

"How long have you known Garrick?" Julia asked. The question had lingered on her lips almost since they had met.

Ming Li looked up at her. "I fear I have kept much from you. I have known him since we were children. I was his brother's wife. My husband is dead. Garrick has always kept me close to protect me."

At once Julia's hesitation fled. She had imagined many things but not that Ming Li was Garrick's sister-in-law.

"I told Garrick you should know about me, but he wanted to make sure of you. Now we will go to the monastery where he was sent to be educated after his father and older brother were killed. We will wait for him."

"I'm afraid for him," Julia whispered.

"He is strong. He has many allies. He will come."

"I love him and want him," Julia confessed.

Ming Li nodded. "You have exchanged essences. He is made stronger by you, just as you are made stronger by him. Be patient, and have faith. You have excelled at all your lessons."

8

More than a month after leaving the Forbidden City, Ming Li and Julia arrived in Guilin. To Julia's eyes, Guilin was like a village straight out of a fairy tale. The meandering river wound through the countryside, irrigating the fields and periodically enriching the soil when it spilled over its banks. The entire valley in which the city was located was filled with odd rock formations that, in English, she learned, were called karst towers. They were tall and rugged and seemed to guard the valley like giant sentinels.

In the monastery, smiling saffron-cloaked monks silently meditated, studied, or went about their work in the gardens. Julia's days were spent in study, but thoughts of Garrick filled her thoughts, her hopes, and her dreams. Never could she forget the feel of his hands on her moist body, never could she forget him swelling inside her again and again as their essences mixed in the last final swelling that resulted in a wild climax of throbbing delight. Each day after the evening meal she was given a lychee nut. Its aroma, its exotic taste brought a rush of memories—of Garrick placing it on her tongue while he taunted her with slow caresses until there was moisture flooding from her Jade Gate, until tears ran down her cheeks as she begged him to let her know the relief of the Tide of Yin. Would he ever return to her? The thought of not seeing him again, of not having him lie by her side, was almost more than she could bear.

On this night the moon was full. Its light flooded the valley and the terrace outside the house on the hillside in which she and Ming Li stayed. The karst towers looked like giant ghosts in the moonlight, appearing and disappearing as the moon danced now and again behind night clouds.

Julia was staring at the valley when she felt his presence. She did not even have to turn to know that her wishes had been granted and that Garrick had come to her.

"Ah, you remember me."

"I could never forget."

"The emperor has fled, and his brother is now emperor. Jason Hamilton is dead, and, for the time being, China is still free."

"And I am free of fear." She paused. "But not free from undying desire."

His arms encircled her from behind. The warmth of his body filled her, her mouth was suddenly dry, her hidden crevices damp with anticipation.

"I have been trained to withhold my essence many times in order to better pleasure my lover, but on this occasion I have waited a long while, traveled far, and thought too much on the pleasure of losing my essence."

Julia turned and stood close to him so that her already erect nipples pressed against him. "I have continued my studies. I know what must be done."

A smile crossed his lips, and he rested his strong hands on her shoulders, guiding her body downward so that as she dropped slowly to her knees, he felt her against him.

It was she, to his amazement, who lifted his tunic and, with trembling hands, freed his hard, erect Jade Stem. Her lips closed around his organ; her tongue darted here and there as he grew even stronger. He put his hand on the low wall of the garden to brace himself as she performed her magic with tender, moist lips and soft, magical fingers. He burst forth suddenly, not even trying to stop himself. There was much time, and now he could taunt her for hours before again he was filled with the essence that would bring her such pleasure. How stupid Westerners were! Lust was negative in the Western mind, but here it was absolutely positive and meant only that both partners were alive and healthy.

She continued to hold his Jade Stem in her hand, but she looked up and sought his face, her eyes filled with her craving.

"And now we will go to bed, and I shall possess you as never before."

"And shall I be blindfolded and bound?"

"Only if it gives you pleasure."

She smiled, and he felt her skin warm to his touch. "It gives me pleasure."

He carried her to the bed and laid her down. Then, as she requested, he blindfolded her and bound her gently. Caresses, as always, began with her ears, her mouth, and her neck. Now and again, he furtively touched her nipples. They were hard and erect and hot with the fire of absolute passion. Gradually, slowly, he worked downward. He pinched and suckled on her breasts and then slid down the length of her body as he had done before. His lips touched her divine field—her clitoris. "Tonight," he whispered, "I shall play your lute strings till they tingle with unbearable tension."

The sensation was incredible. She moaned with pleasure and squirmed against him, her breathing fast from her own excitement as he mounted that sedge hill, all thought given over to sensation as he stopped and started many times until she let out a scream of pure pleasure. The release could no longer be held, and she panted as the throbbing pleasure overcame her.

He unbound her and turned her over, placing his swollen Jade Stem between the cheeks of her buttocks. There he played for a long time, his Jade Stem touching and rubbing her Red Pearls, known in the West as the labia. The sensation was taunting, and she moved about, feeling him grow larger yet as his own excitement increased.

When he again turned her over on her back, he plunged into her, moving the base of his Jade Stem against her gateway. Again she felt the mounting tension, the desire, the need to tumble once again down the hill—to feel the release. She did so, clinging to him and writhing against him.

He was the absolute master of control. He did not lose his essence inside her. He withdrew and sat up. He opened the aromatic oil that sat on the bedside table and began applying it to her body.

Twice now he had pleasured her, while she had pleasured him once. But she knew this was Tao, "*the way*." They would know pleasure together again this night, but not before he had taken her many times up the mountain and allowed her to plunge down into the valley of wild pleasure.

"Will you always be by my side?" he asked as once again he entered her and began to taunt her.

"Yes. I will always desire you."

He smiled. "Then the master has become the slave."

EAST MEETS WEST

CELIA MAY HART

1

Struggling up the ornate carved walls of the *zenana*, Lieutenant Benedict West muzzily wondered for the umpteenth time why he persisted with this insane course.

The effect of drink still muddled his senses, yet the words of his fellow lieutenant, Gerald Smith, rang in his ears: "The eldest daughter of the old nabob Camberton, a real looker, that one, and a *bibi* ripe for the picking. She's been trained, I heard, in the Indian erotic arts."

The drinking officers oohed in salivating desire for a fresh bird's flesh. Another toasted the girl's beauty. A third toasted the girl's mouth.

Somehow, amid the raucous laughter and endless glasses of arrack, they dared West to sneak into the girl's bedchamber. Somehow, he'd accepted the task.

His fingers scrabbled for a hold in the crumbling stonework, plasterwork falling away. He found the granite underneath and held on. The *zenana*, the women's quarters, stood behind an even taller wall, scraped smooth and whitewashed.

At least with the outer wall his fellow officers had offered to give him a starting hand.

Within the compound, he was on his own, skirting the household guards and now making this crazy ascent. Lieutenant Smith had made a map—how the man knew the layout of an area off-limits to men, West didn't want to ask, but Smith muttered something about a little *bibi* of his own.

Idiot. Fool. West looked down to the black maw of ground twenty feet below him. Of course, this little *bibi* princess had her own tower. The white gravel of pathways far below spun in a dizzy circle.

Grunting, Benedict gazed out at the city. Flat rooftops mingled with minarets, candlelight glinting behind intricate screens. Beyond stood the hulking square houses of the British colony, the lines clean, classical, familiar. He glanced upward, his goal a small balcony jutting out from the wall.

Just a few feet more.

Chandari waited for sleep. A cool breeze wafted in from the balcony, the heavy woolen drapes pulled back to reveal a moon three-quarters full.

Through the gauze draping her bed, Chandari stared at the imperfect silver round. She let breath escape in a long sigh. She wished she might escape to the moon.

She lay on her cushioned sleeping couch and stared up at the netting gathered into a simple point. She had complete training in all the erotic arts, a very model of aptitude. She'd even taken a lover, a half caste like herself, to practice with. It had cost her mother a fortune.

It had been pleasant and even fun, but without the attachment, it seemed to Chandari to violate one of the tenets of the Kama Sutra.

The clear night air carried sound. She heard distant conversations, the rattle of carts on the streets outside the *zenana*, the sound of someone grunting, hard at work. It sounded like it occurred right out her window.

She rolled over, hugging a pillow. She must sleep.

A thud brought her upright. She stared at the balcony, the shadow of a man straightening. He was tall, slender, and most definitely not Indian. He wore the tight trousers and loose white shirt of the East India Company's army, not the flowing traditional Indian robes.

Chandari held her breath. Who dared enter a *zenana* uninvited? He strode toward her bed, which was centered in the octagonal shaped room, with stone stairs twisting down the outer wall behind her.

If she ran, would he catch her? What did he want with her?

He pushed the net curtains aside and sat on her bed. The moonlight lit his face, bringing his contours into sharp focus. No Indian, the moon turned his blond hair into a shock of shining white, rendering his eyebrows almost invisible. His light-colored eyes stared at her.

She turned away, ducking her head. She knew she didn't possess any great beauty, the lightness of her skin being the only benefit of having an English father.

"No, don't. I won't hurt you," the stranger whispered. He neared and his fingertip touched her chin. With that light touch, he drew her out of the shadows.

She stared at him, trembling. Why was he here? Was this some sort of test created by her mother? How else had he managed to escape notice from within the compound?

"Beautiful," he breathed, stinking of the English alcohol. "I had heard . . ."

He kissed her. His cool lips warmed upon contact. He sat back, tucking behind her ear a strand of her long dark hair which had escaped her sleeping braid.

Chandari thought to protest against his description of her, but her training prevented it. If that's what he wanted to see, then let him see it. She knew the truth.

"You are even more than I was promised," the strange Englishman continued, the backs of his fingers smoothing along her cheek.

So her mother had sent him. Was she meant to seduce him or send him away? That he was English suggested the latter, for Mother had little time for the English these days, but—

"Do you not speak English?" The stranger interrupted her thoughts, speaking in stilted Bengali.

"I do," she returned in his native tongue. "Forgive me."

His hand waved in a vague, drunken benediction, and he leaned in to kiss her again.

This time, she opened herself to him. The Englishman expected her acquiescence, to cede to him without any protests. Had her mother sent him as a test to see if she could bury her repulsion of the English?

Truly, even a detailed search found little to repulse her. His fairness disconcerted her, a blond beacon in the dark, but Chandari didn't doubt the handsomeness of her stranger.

She twined her arms behind his head, discovering his linen shirt stuck to his body with sweat. He had climbed her tower? Englishmen *were* mad.

She opened her mouth, teased her tongue along his teeth. He moaned, her mouth filling with alcoholic fumes. Could she get drunk just by kissing him?

He took over, plundering her mouth with no rhyme or reason, ignorant of even the smallest erotic art. Still, his command excited her.

Pushing her down against her cushions, he covered her body with his. He lay on her, all hard muscle, forcing apart her legs.

Swiftly, she hooked them around his waist, her anklets tin-

kling with the sudden movement. Let him untangle the petticoats trapped between them. He showed no inclination to push
aside her clothing, instead humping her groin.

Squirming against him, Chandari wondered at this stranger
plundering her mouth and trapping her against her bed. Was
her mother trying to prove a point that all *firingi* were bad
lovers? Or was this the Englishman's way of delaying consum-
mation?

The stranger cradled her in one arm, his hips still thrusting
against her. He folded back the flat lapels on her simple tunic,
shoving the delicate fabric to one side, revealing a breast.

He broke off the endless kiss, her wistful sigh escaping into
the night. He gazed at her in the moonlight, the areola of her
nipple almost black in the white light. She licked her lips, thick
and swollen with his kisses.

His gaze lifted to her face. "You will not scream?" he whispered, lightly thumbing her bared breast.

What a curious question. Without words, she shook her
head. Why did he worry she might scream? Was his presence
not sanctioned by her mother after all?

She drew in her breath to cry out a warning, but the pressure
of his mouth upon her neck reduced it to a gasp. His kiss made
her forget to scream, his heated desire seeping into her.

He slid his mouth down the slender column of her neck,
pausing to press openmouthed kisses along the way. He nipped
at the base of her throat, just by her pounding heartbeat.

Chandari gasped again, all concern fleeing in the face of his
sensual assault. If her mother wanted her to learn a lesson that
the *firingi* made bad lovers, she'd picked the wrong man for the
job. Oh, heaven! She came alive beneath him, clutching his
head close to her bosom.

He nipped at the sensitive flesh, drawing the hard bud between his teeth and tugging. His breath escaped between his

bared teeth and fell hot upon her skin. His hands traced a line of fire from breast to hip and back again, passing over the bunched linen of her tunic and skirt.

Slowly, ever so slowly, he hitched up her skirt, until the trapped material between them refused to give. Chandari squirmed against him, letting herself fall into the sweet sensations the stranger wrought.

The man might not know the tenets of the Kama Sutra—he had not washed nor shaved before coming to her, nor had he allowed her to prepare herself for him—but his raw enthusiasm made up for it.

He reared, pushing away the wad of skirts between her legs. Through slitted eyes, she watched him unbutton his breeches, fumbling with the metal buttons.

His *lingam*, his cock, sprang forth, shadowed by the night. She expected him to enter her at once, in his eagerness and ignorance of the Kama. She reached for him, wanting to drag him back down upon her, but he eluded her grasp.

He dipped his head lower, his breath hot upon her inner thighs. Falling back against the pillows, Chandari squeezed her eyes shut. She hadn't washed or purified herself!

He swiped at her shaved *yoni* with one lick, sending a jolt through her. His mouth pressed against her *yoni*; he teased her budding clit. A thousand joyous bee stings rocked her, spiraling up from her groin to her belly.

She ached for him, wanted the release that came too fast, too fast. The relentless stranger continued his oral barrage, licking and sucking at her *yoni* until the first shuddering wave of release hit her.

With one last lick, he backed out, sliding his body up against hers. The blunt end of his *lingam*, thick and wet with his arousal, pushed against her *yoni*, sliding into place against her convulsing hole.

He penetrated her easily, her wetness lubricating his way. Chandari cried out, her muscles tight and spasming around his invading cock. He stretched her being larger than her hired lover. She sobbed against his shoulder, lost in the wonder of it.

His thrusts made her come and come and come. She dug her nails into his back, clawing at him through the white linen shirt he still wore.

Capturing her mouth with his own, he thrust his tongue inside in time with his *lingam*. He possessed her, filled her, encompassed her. Nothing else existed except for him, his *lingam*, and her endless orgasm.

He stiffened against her, his *lingam* pistoning in and out of her in staccato bursts. He let loose a low groan into her plundered mouth, his *bija* squirting against her cervix.

Panting, he lay atop her, his *lingam* still twitching inside her throbbing *yoni*. Chandari held him tight, this stranger who had invaded her room and taken her to the heights of sexual desire in a way that made her head spin.

She held on to him, not knowing what else to do, not wanting to do anything else. She knew not his name and would never see him again after this night. She didn't want him to leave.

The stranger stirred at last, sliding his softening *lingam* from her. He kissed her perspiring brow. "My thanks," he murmured, sitting up to fasten his breeches. He rose, looking over his shoulder. "Is there not something of yours I may take to remind me of this night?"

Chandari's mind raced. She reached over to the small table beside her bed and retrieved one of her bangles. She'd made the highly lacquered papier-mâché bracelet herself.

Taking it from her, he tried to put it on, but it wouldn't pass the knuckles of his large hand. With a rueful smile, he tucked it into his breeches.

Smiling, Chandari observed his skintight breeches made it unlikely he'd lose her gift. Indeed, he might bruise himself with it.

He padded barefoot to the balcony. Propping herself on an elbow, she watched his shoulders straighten and then haul himself over the stone railing, grabbing the carved outer wall to help his descent.

In a short time, he had gone.

Chandari slid a hand down her sex-slickened body, still heaving with the tumult of release, and plunged a finger into her soaking *yoni*. His thicker *bija* mingled with her own seed.

She lifted her hand to her nose, inhaling his salty male scent, letting it fill her nostrils, imprinting the memory of it upon her brain.

She'd never see him again, this Englishman, but she would always remember.

She sucked on her fingertips, tasting him and herself, and slid to lie down. Every part of her body still throbbed with the memory of his touch and of her fast-paced release, and yet she had to sleep, for tomorrow, she left her home forever.

Lieutenant Benedict West hauled himself out of bed. It had taken him the better part of an hour to reverse his climb, descending the *zenana* tower wall, finding his boots, and escaping over the outer wall of the compound.

Being so pleasantly exhausted after his interlude with the half-English *bibi* hadn't helped his concentration either and he'd more than his fair share of bruised shins and skinned knuckles.

He'd made it back to his quarters, which he shared with Lieutenant Smith, stinking of sex and exertion. He'd slumped into a camp chair. "Hope you're satisfied," he had said to a snoring Lieutenant Smith.

Gaining no response, Benedict stripped for bed, wearing

nothing but his shirt. The girl's bangle clattered on the wood flooring. He bent and picked it up, marveling at the pretty design of flowers against an azure background.

What had possessed him to ask for a souvenir? Benedict collapsed upon the lumpy feather mattress, supported by ropes across two thick slats of wood. What use did he have for this bracelet? Nevertheless, he tucked it under his pillow.

Within a minute, sleep claimed him, his dreams filled with his dark-eyed *bibi*, whose gaze both remonstrated and pleaded with him to give her powerful releases again and again.

He woke with the dawn, having gained only a few hours' sleep. Dressing, he gave the still sleeping Lieutenant Smith a shove with a booted foot and proceeded to complete his toilet, shaving in the small mirror propped against a chest of drawers.

Lieutenant Smith groaned and then came awake at once. "Did you?" he demanded, bouncing out of bed.

Benedict regarded him out of the corner of his eye, his razor poised to take another swipe at his bristled, scarred cheek. "You saw me go over the wall."

"But—but did you?"

"Look under my pillow." Benedict ignored him, finishing the trickier part of shaving his dimpled chin.

Lieutenant Smith waved the bangle in the air. "This is hers? Really hers? You didn't just hop back over the wall and head for the nearest brothel?"

Rinsing his razor, Benedict turned to face the younger lieutenant, still brandishing his razor. "I completed my dare. You owe me."

His roommate chewed on his lip, reddening. "Next payday?"

Benedict sighed. "Very well." He finished dressing, pulling on white gloves that concealed his battered hands. "You better hurry and dress."

Smith looked out the window at the rising sun and cursed,

tossing the *bibi's* bracelet to Benedict. Benedict caught it one-handed and tucked it into an inner coat pocket.

A rap sounded on the door.

"Enter," called Benedict, amused by Smith's hasty attempt to don his breeches before another entered.

The colonel's ensign entered. "Colonel requests your presence, Lieutenant West, sir."

"I am ready." With a wave, he departed his room, grabbing his pistol belt and buckling it around his waist while he followed the young ensign.

His colonel sat drinking tea at his campaign desk. He looked up at their entrance. "Ah, good. Ensign, thank you. You're dismissed." He waited until the door closed behind the young ensign. "West, you've been a lieutenant longer than anyone else in your age bracket. Most men get promoted after three years. And it's been, what, six or seven years?"

"Six and a half, sir." Benedict kept his tone flat, burying the insubordination that threatened.

"You're a good soldier, West. If you stopped these hare-brained capers of yours—"

Benedict blanched. The colonel had heard about last night already?

"—you might have a chance at promotion and making proper money."

Loot. Divvied according to rank, or sheer luck if you found treasure on the body of the man you just killed. West hadn't seen enough offensive action to benefit from the latter.

"Lieutenant West, I have a commission for you. This is not East India Company business, you understand, but a favor to one of our former members."

Benedict nodded and listened with an attentive expression. If the colonel pitied him, why not just put him in for promotion?

"He has asked for an escort for his daughter to the maharaja of Jenalapur. There will be a reward from both our former member—and the maharaja, if you're fortunate."

"I know the kingdom, sir." Benedict perked with interest. "The way between is rife with bandits."

"Precisely, and that is why Camberton has asked for an escort."

Benedict swallowed. "Camberton, sir?" Dear God, had he already despoiled his charge? "I understood he had returned to England."

"Indeed. His letter arrived some time ago, asking to assist his wife in this. She submitted her request just yesterday, saying her daughter is ready to leave at any time. I see no reason for delay." Colonel Chesterwood noticed Benedict's hesitation. "Things are quiet around here at the moment, so I don't think you will miss any action."

It seemed easier to have the colonel think the thought of missing loot put Benedict off this babysitting errand. "Yes, sir." He grinned. "And who knows what booty those bandits have?"

The colonel shook his head. "Don't be getting any ideas, my boy. It's a simple escort. Take the girl there and come straight back. No heroic nonsense." He paused. "Oh, and keep your hands off her. She's for the maharaja's harem. Heaven knows, I can't condescend to allow such barbaric practices, but she is part Indian and better off with her own kind, what?"

His stomach roiled, the thought of his *bibi* pawed by the far older maharaja. "Yes, sir. Leaving at once, sir?"

"Yes, lad. Go pack and be on your way. If Mrs. Camberton is true to her word, the girl will be waiting for you."

West saluted and bowed his way out of the tent, his footsteps quickening. Good grief, he heard Lieutenant Smith's laughter now. Had the rat known of his assignment and decided to put him in this messy pickle?

What if the girl wanted him to continue bedding her? A smile tweaked at his lips. Well, what the colonel didn't know wouldn't hurt him.

With a cadre of twelve volunteers from the regiment, Lieutenant West stood to attention in the eye-watering heat of the Camberton courtyard. The white walls of the gateway to the women's *zenana* glared in the rising sun until West had to squint in order to spot his charge's arrival.

He glanced at the tower behind the gateway, wondering for the umpteenth time what on earth had made him agree to that ridiculous dare.

Inwardly, he shrugged. He'd find a way out—or play along with the new scenario. Would the girl recognize him?

Forms moved in the shadows of the gateway, and at last a tiny creature stepped out and down the stone stairs, a servant holding a large fuchsia umbrella over her head. She wore a sari of saffron yellow over an emerald-green *choli* and flowing saffron skirts. Her bare feet tinkled with belled anklets.

Benedict's heart flipped. Good God, it *was* her. How absurd to hope, even for a moment, that he escorted some other Camberton daughter. He touched his coat, feeling the circular outline of her bracelet before coming to attention and saluting.

The girl ignored him, turning to exchange tearful good-byes with a plump woman and two much younger girls, the eldest barely a teen.

Wiping her tears with the edge of her sari, the girl stepped into the curtained palanquin waiting for her. A cart pulled by an ox contained her camping gear, her few possessions, and a horse tied to it.

The plump woman advanced toward him, her white sari almost as blinding as the walls behind her. She wagged her finger at him. "Take care of my daughter, sir! She is my precious jewel and our sole hope. I rely on your honor!"

West managed a tight smile and a salute. "Of course, madam," he said in cool, even tones, hiding his laughter. Honor? What was that?

The cavalcade at last took off, a source of much interest in the crowded streets of Calcutta, an overheated version of the somnolent city of Bath back home. Yet Indian architecture had made inroads here—the locals had built their own quarter in their accustomed style.

Four men from his unit marched ahead of the bobbing palanquin. West followed behind on horseback, gazing into the impenetrable curtains that concealed his charge. He swallowed. He had to keep a hold of himself, stay in control.

At least until they got out of the city.

Behind West trailed more of his men and the girl's baggage wagon, which also carried tents and supplies for his men. He glanced over his shoulder, watching the plume of dust rise from their passing, obscuring the city's Georgian walls.

They passed rice paddy fields and small agrarian villages until late in the afternoon, when West declared a halt for the night. "We make camp here."

He dismounted, leading his horse to a nearby stand of drooping trees. He unsaddled his mare, putting all his attention into currying the dust and sweat of the day from its coat.

Not once did he look in the direction of the girl's rising tent. Not once did he look for her.

The plain bleached cotton tent walls concealed Chandari from the rest of the world. She'd eaten alone, in her tent, full of chagrin at being completely ignored by the officer in charge.

She should be used to it now—the blindness of the English toward their half-caste creations—yet still it hurt.

Chandari stood before a tall standing mirror, the mahogany wood dark against the white tent walls. Two lanterns had been lit, casting a golden glow against the canvas and over her light brown skin.

Dropping her sari from her shoulders, Chandari pulled her tight-fitting *choli* over her head. She unpinned her hair, letting it fall in long, loose black curls.

She drew the ends of the sari around her, concealing everything except her bared chest. She studied herself in the mirror. Her light brown skin looked untouched, virginal, the puckering of her dark nipples the only sign of the memories crowding her head.

He had touched her there; her gaze rested on the spot, searching for some mark the man had left. He had tugged at her with his teeth; why was there no sign?

Chandari swallowed, blinking back the rising tears. How foolish to become sentimental about one night. For all she knew, she'd dreamed it—but, no, his scent had been heavy upon her skin when she woke in the morning.

Would he come to her tower room tonight and find her gone? Chandari tilted her head to one side, examining herself. No sign. Nothing.

Someone cleared his throat behind her.

Chandari started, pulling her sheer sari around her. She whirled on him, keeping her breasts covered. "What do you want?"

The red-coated officer swayed. "Thought I'd come and introduce myself." He blinked. "Again."

Chandari drew herself up to her full five feet three inches. "Again? Sir, I believe you are drunk. Leave this tent at once."

He shook his head, weaving with effort. "Won't. And you can't make me." He blinked and squinted to focus on her. "I am drunk, but we have met before."

He pulled something from his coat pocket and tossed it to her. Her eyes widened. A blue lacquered bracelet soared in the air toward her. Instinct kicked in, and she reached out to grab it, her sari falling off her shoulders.

She covered herself, the sari a meager protection against the lieutenant's leering gaze. "That was *you*?"

"Lieutenant Benedict West, at your service, ma'am." He sketched a bow and almost fell over. "It occurred to me that you might be due for a servicing again."

"How dare you!" Chandari retreated a step.

He advanced upon her. "You enjoyed it last night," he cajoled. "My, but you were a beauty in the moonlight."

Meaning, of course, daylight gave the lie to that vision. If he were so disappointed, why did he want to bed her again?

He brushed a lock of her black hair off her trembling cheek. "Pretty," he murmured, distracted by the strands of silken hair lying over his fingers. "So, how about it?"

Tilting her head, she met his gaze. "You expect a woman trained in the ancient erotic arts of my country to be remotely interested in the hog-swiving you call sex?"

He blinked at her, his jaw dropping. The surprise vanished swiftly, and his eyes narrowed. "You enjoyed it last night."

She raised her chin. Admit it to this crude creature? "You, sir, are drunk and in no fit state—"

"Was drunk last night. Did you just fine." He cocked his head to one side. "What say you teach me these erotic arts of yours, if you think I need such improvement?"

"You, sir, are insane. Why on earth should I—"

He grabbed her, and she squeaked. "Because the thought of you burns in my loins."

"Then perhaps you should see a doctor," she replied with some asperity.

West snarled. "I am clean, woman. Very particular, I am. And I want you."

"I'm to join the maharaja's harem. I cannot—"

"You can." He hauled her against him. "You don't belong to him yet."

Her soft curves melted against the hard lines of his body. Her mind whirled. He wanted her, wanted her badly. Nobody paid him for his efforts, and she'd had little chance to bestow her learned skill upon him. Most importantly, he hadn't been paid to want her.

"Your buttons are sticking into me," she whispered, clutching his coat.

"Sorry." His bare hand slid under her chin and tilted it up, his mouth claiming hers in a torrid kiss. She whimpered against his lips, parting her own, allowing him to possess her with that kiss.

In an instant, he made her want him, want him more than even breathing. Her small fingers fisted in his red cloth coat, trying to pull herself up, to reach him. She hooked her leg around his thigh, her anklet jingling. She rubbed her groin against his trapped, hard cock. Forgotten, her sari puddled on the floor.

His teeth caught her lower lip, tugging lightly before releasing her to kiss the fresh hurt. Chandari squeezed her eyes shut. Perhaps he wasn't ignorant of the ancient arts after all.

West broke the kiss and pulled her from him. He stared at her, panting. He wiped his mouth. "Enough," he said, his voice hoarse.

Did he taunt her? Not want her after all? But no, his arousal pressed against her.

"The devil of it is that I don't even know your name."

Was that all? Chandari laughed with relief, the sound tinkling in her own ears, a touch brittle. "I am Chandari Camberton, promised to the Maharaja of Jenalapur."

"Don't remind me," he growled, his blond brows scrunching. He rubbed his head, messing his blond hair. At some point, he'd washed out the white powder that had coated it. His hair brushed his shoulders, a variegated wave of white blond and yellower shades.

He had the lips of a seducer, his lower lip pouty with wanton promise. Freckles spattered over his nose, and a scar made a white trail on his suntanned cheek. His blue eyes, a bit bloodshot, regarded her with some bemusement.

"Do I pass inspection?" he drawled.

"You're not fully in uniform," she observed, giving her heart some time not to pound so hard.

He shrugged. "We're out in the bush. It doesn't matter out here. Don't worry, I'll fully suit up for his highness."

Chandari waved her hand with a dismissive air. She didn't care about the maharaja. Not right at this moment. "Now that you know my name, how do you intend to proceed?"

Again that insolent shrug. "You speak well for a native."

"My mother saw to our education in the English way as well as hers." Chandari gathered the folds of her sari, draping herself. West's gaze lifted from her breasts. "May I make a suggestion?"

West delivered a grandiose wave for her to continue.

Her lips twitched at his mocking gesture. "May I suggest we revisit this question of us . . ." Chandari stumbled over her words, . . . "of us becoming lovers when you are sober?"

He didn't even bat an eye. "Direct little thing, aren't you."

She gave him a beatific smile. "Why, yes, I am. Good night."

West delivered another bow which almost toppled him. "Good night. Sweet dreams." He blew her a kiss and sauntered out of her tent.

Chandari sank onto her sleeping couch. *Heavens.* How had she let her desires get so carried away? Was it her white heritage that attracted her to this . . . this drunken lout?

But she had liked him taking control. . . .

2

Benedict held his swagger until the flap of Chandari's tent fell closed behind him. He slumped into a stumble. How had he ever thought drinking hard his first night on the road was a good idea? The arrack washed away all his good intentions to stay away from the girl.

Awash with drink, he halted in the middle of camp and gazed up at the swollen moon, framed by the dark outlines of leafy branches. The cold light washed over him, purifying him. He shook his head and focused on finding his tent. Drinking led to these ridiculous, fanciful thoughts.

Why shouldn't he turn around and take her? She wanted it—she'd kissed him with such vigor. He pivoted on his heel, staring now at Chandari's tent, light still glowing golden within.

He didn't turn down such opportunities.

He tilted his head to the side, watching one lamp wink out and then another. She wanted to talk of being lovers when he sobered?

He didn't plan on doing the talking part.

With a feral grin that surely would have scared the girl if she'd seen it, he stalked off to his own tent.

In the morning, Benedict decided to lead their little cavalcade. Without waiting for the last tent to strike—Miss Chandari's, naturally—he urged his mount along the narrow trail. A brief gallop cleared his throbbing head of his hangover.

By the time he returned, camp had been struck and the column moving. His gaze landed on the palanquin first, the flutter of the curtains making him wonder about its occupant.

He faced the front again, waving on his men with an abrupt curve of his arm. If the girl insisted on traveling in that dratted palanquin, he'd get no chance for conversation—or other things—until they stopped for the evening.

Benedict's groaning crotch warned him that another unassuaged night without sampling Chandari's delights might be dangerous, maybe even lethal.

Chuckling at his mind's dramatic turn, Benedict heard hoofbeats approach. Reining in, he looked over his shoulder and saw a vision.

She wore a simple gray habit, the long skirt trailing down one side of her chestnut mare's flank. The bodice clung to her bosom, the large masculine buttons doing little to conceal her femininity. A little top hat swathed with gauze concealed her face and streamed behind her. She rode sidesaddle with easy confidence.

Chandari drew her mount alongside his. "You better close your mouth," she observed, "or you will swallow a fly."

Benedict shut his mouth with a snap, nudging his horse into a walk. "You ride."

"How very observant of you." She leaned forward, patting her chestnut's neck, keeping pace with him. "How is your head?"

"I don't get hangovers," he retorted. At least not until after he'd doused his head in ice-cold water and ridden it off.

She sniffed.

"Where did you learn to ride like that?"

"Father gave me lessons when I was a little girl." She gathered the reins firmly in her hand. "I kept them up after he left." She paused, her perfect posture shrinking. Benedict let the silence continue. "I wanted him to be proud of me if he came back."

She'd given him a glimpse of a vulnerability Benedict wasn't sure he wanted to see. He cleared his throat.

Chandari managed a light chuckle. "If you had not asked such a rude question, you would not have received such a personal answer." Her tone grew breezier. "I have no illusions now that my father will ever return. I ride because I enjoy it."

"Why bring the palanquin?"

"I must arrive at the palace in the proper style." Primnness returned to her demeanor.

"Tantalizing and whetting his appetite because you are hidden." His cock gave him a hint of the maharaja's potential eagerness.

"No, because it is improper for an Indian maiden to travel any other way."

"Like riding."

Her smile, visible through the netting shrouding her face, grew. "I am English, too."

Benedict changed the subject, although in his heart he wondered if the maharaja would like a half-English bride. "Indeed. However, as much as I would like to talk about your mixed ancestry, I should remind you that I am sober."

She shot him a puzzled look. "And your point, Lieutenant West?"

"You wished to speak of us being lovers at that time."

"Ah." She sounded amused. "There are ways to speak of such things to a woman. That isn't one of them."

"I've bedded you once. Is there any need to pussyfoot around the issue that I want to again?"

Chandari sighed. "And they say the English are civilized."

"I know. I know." Benedict grinned. "We all swive like pigs."

"That was unkind of me," she admitted.

"You offered to teach me the ancient ways. So, show me."

Her head swiveled to look at him. "Show you now? I will instruct you on the proper way to approach a woman."

"I'm not interested in 'proper.'"

She cocked her head at him. "And that works for you?"

"Most of the time."

Chandari made an odd noise, and Benedict turned in time to see her wrinkled nose. "Englishwomen like their men drunk, rude, and . . . stinky?"

"Stinky?" Benedict lifted his arm and sniffed at his armpit. He didn't smell any worse than usual.

"According to the ancient texts, when a man wants a woman, before he goes to her, he bathes and puts on perfumes, wears his best clothes and attractive jewels. Then he goes to her."

Her lecturing tone irritated him, even though her soft and husky voice aroused him in other ways. He snorted. "And then he rips off her clothes and his clothes, and it's all done. I get it. You want me to take a bath."

"You seem to be efficient in washing your head at least. Why is the rest of your body exempt?"

He placed his hand over his heart. "Milady, I promise to bathe before I come to you tonight."

He wished she'd remove that dratted hat to see her smiling eyes.

"There is a pool just a little way off the road ahead. We should reach the turn off by midafternoon. Do you object to a diversion on our journey?"

"Lady, if it means joining with you, not at all."

She laughed, a free and unfettered sound that resonated deep within him. "Good. Then I will help you bathe properly before the sun goes down. Until then. . . ."

Chandari whirled her horse and trotted back to the palanquin. He watched her go, and, chuckling, gazed at the road ahead. This trip promised to be very special indeed.

None of his men protested at West's order to change direction, and they wound their way through low, green hills festooned with vines and shady trees. Parrots cawed their rude cries, flying in bright flashes of color overhead.

West wiped the sweat from his brow. To reach this damned pool before dark, they'd shortened their midday rest. Everybody drooped, and Chandari had retreated into her palanquin.

The sound of rushing water reached his ears. The trail dwindled away to almost nothing. He looked back over his shoulder. Chandari's palanquin had been lowered to the ground. One of her native bearers ran forward. "Missy Chandari says there is space to camp around the next bend. The pool is farther on. We make camp, yes?"

West peered into the rising foliage. "Yes, we make camp." He ordered four of his men forward to scout ahead to make sure the way was clear.

The area declared safe, tents were erected in quick order. West gathered his few grooming supplies and left his tent, his supplies tucked under his arm.

Chandari waited, with a maidservant three steps behind her, laden with basket and blanket. "That's all you have?" She gestured at his meager leather pouch.

He hooked a thumb in his trouser waistband. "There's more, honey."

She wrinkled her nose and shook her head, almost laughing

at his bravado. "You might as well put that away, I have sufficient soap, shampoo, perfumes . . ."

Without looking, West tossed his razor pouch into the tent behind him. "Lead on. It wasn't my desire to smell like a girl, but if that's what makes you happy."

She turned, glancing over her shoulder. "Oh, you won't smell like a girl, but a man. A clean man."

He followed her and her maidservant along a narrow trail. The sound of falling water grew louder, the sounds of camp faded behind him.

The trees parted to reveal a shaded pool, fed by a six-foot-high waterfall, the white water cascading from some hidden stream. There had been rain recently and the water gushed over the black rock.

Chandari gestured to her maidservant. The girl lowered her basket, overflowing with towels and various glass bottles, onto a flat rock. She shook out the blanket. Bowing to Chandari, the maidservant retreated down the trail.

Benedict approached. "She's leaving us alone?"

"I asked her. What we're about to do . . ." She paused, looking down at her feet, her cheeks rosy. "It isn't seemly."

"Or proper?" Benedict laughed at her glowering blush.

Chandari gestured to the water. "A maiden shouldn't watch a man bathe, let alone help him."

Benedict folded his arms, frowning. "I know how to bathe."

"Really? You do not smell it."

"I bathe when I choose. It's unhealthy—"

"It's unhealthy not to bathe daily. If you have any intent of becoming my lover, lieutenant, you will bathe every day."

Benedict captured her upthrust chin. "Bossy little *bibi*, aren't you?"

Chandari tore herself from his grip, stumbling back. "I am not your wife!"

She ripped a golden ornament from her upswept hair, scattering pins. Storming toward the pool, she ripped off the white silk cravat. Openmouthed, he watched her tear off the gray pelisse of her riding habit, revealing a pale blue translucent *choli* studded with elaborate silver embroidery and showing the smooth lines of her bare back.

At the water's edge, she shucked off the gray skirt, letting it and the petticoats puddle at her feet. She stepped over the material. Benedict stared at her slim legs as they took a running leap into the pond. She dove beneath the dark waters, disappearing from view.

He waited for her to come up spluttering from the cold, but the water didn't even ripple.

"Chandari?" he called out over the water. "Chandari?" A sudden panic seized his limbs. Had she drowned? He stripped off his red coat. Hopping, he pulled off his boots, cursing at his slowness.

He leapt into the pool feet first and waded into the deeper water, his arms sweeping beneath the water in a vain attempt to find her.

"Chandari!" he bellowed. He dove under the water, his hands seeking, seeking. The water tugged at his shirt and his trousers. He surfaced, cursing.

Twisting in the water, he scanned the surface.

And heard laughter echo.

Benedict growled under his breath.

The waterfall parted, and Chandari crawled through, the water thudding on her head and shoulders. She sat on the rock lip, water rising to her waist, her *choli* plastered against her skin.

"How—how did you . . . ?"

"I've visited this place many times," she called to him over the roar of the waterfall. Her smile, sparkling in the filtered sunlight, took his breath away.

"I thought you'd drowned." He waded toward her, the water chest high. He managed an awkward breaststroke. Pulling himself up the rock shelf, he sat beside her, the water pummeling the tension out of his back. "Don't pull a stunt like that again." Relief killed his anger.

She looked at him, pushing glossy, wet black hair out of her eyes. "It got you wet, didn't it?"

"You needn't go to such extremes. The English are not afraid of water."

She merely raised her black eyebrows at him and made a shallow dive into the pool. He watched her swim to the far shore. She rose, water cascading down her golden skin, the ends of her hair plastered against her dimpled buttocks.

She strode without shame, bending to pick up a towel. After she dabbed herself dry, she draped the sari around her. The fine silk clung to her damp form.

She picked up the basket and brought it nearer to the shoreline. Benedict sat mesmerized by her sensual grace, her curves filled with an easy confidence. Her lack of modesty should shock him, but he recalled a shy girl from the previous night covering herself with that diaphanous shawl. Which was the pretense? She covered herself, but the wet silk revealed much.

Chandari slipped back into the pool, her arms outstretched beneath the water, until she seemed to settle on a rock. She beckoned him over.

He made his awkward way across, feeling his clothing drag him down.

She eyed him with warm amusement at his approach. "Do you require help to get out of those wet clothes?"

"You are still in yours."

She shrugged, flicking her black hair over her shoulder. "Your clothes will need to dry. I have plenty of clothing with me. Is it not said the English catch the fever from being wet?"

Benedict didn't want to succumb to a fever, the fear of every

Englishman who came to the subcontinent. Flushing, he shook his head, scattering water drops. "Very well." He pulled himself out of the water. Slipping on a stone, his arms shot out but recovered.

On dry land, he peeled off his shirt and trousers, his back to the pool. He wadded up his clothes, holding them before his crotch.

Chandari's laughter echoed across the pool. "Lieutenant, you will need to lay those out to dry." She pointed behind him. "There's a sunny patch over there."

Benedict turned and walked in a stiff parade march to the indicated spot. He knew Chandari watched him, and it caused a tingle in his loins.

Chandari watched Benedict walk away, his impossibly white butt clenched. He had lovely, muscular legs, lightly dusted with golden hair.

She'd enjoyed teasing and provoking him. Yet it took every bit of her resolve to display her body in the short walk into and out of the pool. The ancient texts said only loose women committed such acts, but she wasn't about to drown in that ridiculous English outfit, not even in revenge for his rude remark.

She watched his return, her frank gaze examining from head to toe but mostly remaining at the groin area. His *lingam* stiffened, rising to a glorious height.

Chandari stifled a gasp. West was uncircumcised! She had heard the English were uncivilized in that respect, but she hadn't realized just how it would look.

It hadn't felt any different.

She ducked her head, busying herself with the contents of the basket.

West crouched in the water beside her, much too close for her peace of mind. His maleness overwhelmed her. No matter how pale his skin, his size and muscles revealed the raw masculine power hidden beneath his stiff uniform.

"Here." She handed him the soap and a natural sponge. "Use this to wash."

He sniffed at the items, crinkling his nose.

"Do I need to show you how?" she taunted in a soft, husky voice.

His bright blue-eyed gaze told her he'd be more than happy to take her up on her offer, but he scowled. "I am not that uncivilized, Miss Chandari."

She watched him scrub himself with the soapy sponge, burnishing his pale skin into a light pink. His hands dipped below the water, between his legs.

Blushing, she ducked her head, retrieving more soap and another sponge with which to clean herself, lifting the folds of her sari to wash beneath.

Beside her, West sank into the water, only his head appearing above the surface, below she saw the white rippling shadow of his arms and legs and . . .

Blinking, she glanced at his face, finding it full of wicked amusement. Her cheeks grew hotter. "Let me wash your hair," she murmured, gesturing he move in front of her.

He tilted his head, dousing his hair before he shifted, sitting with his back to her, and she scooted up behind. His slender hips pressed against the insides of her soft thighs.

She reached for the shampoo, her legs squeezing him. She poured the oil from the bottle into the palm of her hand and transferred it to the top of his head, mashing it into his hair.

Chandari pressed her forefingers against his upper temples, massaging them. She inched along his hairline, her fingers moving in tight circles.

West moaned in pleasure. "Oh, you have the touch."

"Thank you, lieutenant." Chandari's breasts pressed against

his angular back, while she changed her grip on his head. The heel of her palm rubbed his scalp just above his ear, while her fingers worked farther up.

At last she released him, murmuring a suggestion that he slip into the water and rinse his hair. He slid off her lap, floating while he washed his scalp free of the shampoo.

He pushed away from the rocks, still floating, his *lingam* rising above the surface. The gods had gifted him generously. How much larger when fully erect? She remembered him thrusting into her and shivered.

Chandari eyed his bobbing *lingam*, a rising unease making knots in her stomach. Her *yoni* had long turned molten for him. She wanted him with the very core of her being, a fire she hoped would go out with use.

But still . . . "It's getting cold."

West sunk into the water, pivoting to face her. "The water is warmer on the surface."

Chandari headed for the bank, looking over her shoulder at him, aware of her wet, transparent sari. "Dry, and dress. We shall finish in the comfort of my tent."

At that promise, West exited the pool with alacrity, catching a towel she tossed him. He bent and turned and twisted, towel in hand, not shy at showing off his flexing muscles to every advantage.

His broad shoulders tapered to a narrow waist, and when he turned away, she saw an old white scar zigzagging across his hip bone. Fear stabbed her. Her warrior escort might be killed in the next conflict. Not that she might ever see him again.

She picked up the basket. He wrapped the folded blanket around his waist and followed her in bare feet. He caught up with her before they reached the campsite.

Crossing the site, some of the British soldiers jeered at the site of their superior officer's half-naked form. He ignored them, a small smile dancing about his lips. He held the tent flap open for Chandari and followed her inside.

He tied the tent flaps together while she set down the basket. "So, Chandari. I am clean. Now do I grace your bed?"

She blushed. "There are oils and perfumes. . . ."

West stepped back. "Perfume?"

"It heightens the aroused senses." At his frown, she relented. "I will put it on you, if you wish."

He nodded and sat on the couch, letting the blanket fall to the floor.

He really was magnificent when naked.

"Take off your clothes, Chandari."

She frowned at his command. Pity he wasn't so magnificent on the inside.

"Please," he amended, extending a conciliatory hand. "I do not want you to catch a chill."

She unwrapped the sari length from her body, the material only damp now. It left her only in her translucent *choli*, the blouse cropped just under her breasts, leaving the rest of her naked.

She took that off too, trying not to feel self-conscious. She grabbed a bottle of oil and settled behind him. She poured a small amount into her palm and rubbed her hands together, warming the oil before applying it across his shoulders.

She worked to relax his tense muscles. Sitting so close to him, her hands on his bare skin, took her breath away.

She inhaled the scented oil, the sweet jasmine and his muted male odor making a heady mix. She discovered the planes of his back, smooth except for that one scar at his hip.

Such hidden strength, such vitality she never expected to find in an Englishman. Her hands kept moving, while she lost herself in thoughts and dreams.

He twisted on the couch, grabbing her dreaming hands.

"Chandari," he murmured, his voice husky, "you are driving me crazy. See how eager I am for you?"

Chandari glanced down at his *lingam*, straining up from his crotch, semen making a beaded trail from its tip to his thigh. "Oh," she breathed.

He lifted the bottle from her nerveless fingers. "I appreciate you showing me the ancient ways, but if I don't touch you soon, I swear I shall die." He poured oil into his palm, rubbing his hands together. "Lie back, Chandari."

Her gaze fixed on him, she reclined, her head supported by the pillowed arm of the couch.

He leaned over her, his hands brushing her breasts, leaving a sticky trail of oil. She let her breath go in a long sigh. His soft touch was a stark contrast to his barked, clipped commands. He made it easy to succumb to him.

His fingertips brushed her clavicle and slid down, palming her breasts, capturing them entirely in his large hands.

Chandari closed her eyes, abandoning herself to his touch. It hid her from his intense blue-eyed gaze, which ravished her in silent appeal. Everything became the sensation of touch: the oil warming and cooling upon her skin, the rough pads of his hands, feeling her nipples tighten and pucker.

His breath fanned across her skin, hot and cooling. His tongue tip touched her right nipple and withdrew. Touched again and vanished, like some Peri fairy dancing upon a tiny mushroom. She held her breath in anticipation. He skipped to her other nipple with the same tentative, light touch.

His tongue swirled once around her taut nipple, and Chandari expelled a sigh, almost a moan. Oh, so perfect, so good.

West tugged and teased her little nipple until so swollen, its arousal ran in rivulets of need to her belly. He shifted, straddling her, his oil-slicked hands stroking her sides, her breasts, his mouth devouring her.

A shower of rain spattered on the canvas above, and the tent flaps strained against a sudden gust of wind. Chandari shivered, feeling West's thighs tense and tighten about her hips. He leaned even closer, his hands sliding up her goose-pimpling arms.

A small moan escaped her. West cocooned her in warmth. She forgot the rain, the wind, the outside world. Only West existed.

"Tell me," he whispered, "how do your people make love?"

She assumed he meant sex. "I did say I would teach you." Chandari opened her eyes. "It begins, of course, with embraces and then caressing." She gave a small smile. "You are skilled at these already. Then there are scratches, biting, and blows."

West shot upright, staring down at her. "Hit a woman?" He stiffened with outrage. "Are you serious?"

Dare she confess she didn't care for that part of the experience? "You did ask," she reminded him, reaching for his shoulders to draw him back down.

He shook his head, his blond hair shining in the filtered afternoon sunlight. The rain moved on, leaving the air fresh and free of dust.

"Biting, like this?" He bent his head, his teeth tugging on an eager nipple. "Or like this?" He kissed her, drawing out her lower lip, grazing his teeth over her lip.

Chandari curled her arms around his neck, kissing him until her head swam. His embrace tightened, and he deepened the kiss. Chandari writhed beneath him, almost in a frenzy of wanting. His bare chest rubbed against hers, his cock poking her belly, leaving wet smears.

He drew back, gasping. "Witch, you distracted me." He grinned.

She smiled back. "You didn't seem to mind." With one hand, she stroked his cock, her hand soon slicked with his juices.

"As I was saying, light biting and scratching is all very well in the heat of passion, but I would never strike a woman." His brow creased. "Do you mind?"

Her teeth caught at her swelling lower lip for a moment. "Truthfully, no." She tapped him on his bare chest. "It's not that I don't object to a bit of rough play, but I prefer to be aroused, not subjugated."

"Bravo," West whispered, bending to kiss her again.

She dodged his mouth, even though she longed to receive more of his kisses. Emotions she didn't want to feel threatened to endanger her heart. Ridiculous. This was just sex, nothing more. He couldn't help it if he was a natural at it.

3

Chandari closed her eyes and told herself to live in the moment. *Don't think of the future. Don't think that this means something. It is natural attraction that will fade once sated.*

Never mind that Benedict's midnight visit to her room had left her burning for him ever since.

She nipped his shoulder, soothing it with a long kiss, sliding her mouth toward his throat. She tasted the jasmine oil on his warm skin as it filled her nostrils. She wriggled against him. Jasmine always had that effect on her, arousing her when she didn't want to be aroused. Far beyond aroused, wanting fire raced through her.

Benedict placed abstracted kisses on her forehead, thrusting against her, their tangled legs preventing him from gaining entry. He cursed under his breath, using a word Chandari didn't know, and rolled off her. "Chandari, I swear, if I don't bury myself inside you soon . . ."

Chandari gazed on him, caught by the sight of his weeping penis, a long clear trail dangling from its head. The breath left her. She wanted him inside her, too.

He must have read the wanting in her eyes, for he growled. "Turn over. I may last longer."

Her anklets making a musical tinkling, she flipped onto her stomach, drawing her legs underneath her. She didn't expect to take this position, for his *lingam* filled her *yoni* more than sufficiently, but the English did have some odd ideas.

Benedict squeezed between her legs, drawing her hips toward him. His cock slid off the round of her buttock. It bumped against the rear of her smooth *yoni,* sliding beneath her crack and finding her slick and ready.

More than ready. She arched her back, driving her hips against him. The pressure of his *lingam* against her suddenly came from within, and with one sharp thrust, was in her all the way.

She bit back a cry, managing to mute it into a grunt. He filled her, stretched her, and all at a new angle, which alone threatened to give her release. She clenched her *yoni* about him, hearing him groan.

Chandari gasped. He might last longer, but she wouldn't.

He grasped her hips, digging into her soft flesh. He bucked against her, fucking her tight *yoni* with wild energy.

She braced herself, her breasts rubbing against the couch's nubbled surface beneath her. She came with a cry, a wail that told the entire encampment what occurred in her tent. She gave it no thought, soaring on her release, finding bliss again and again with each of Benedict's thrusts. She didn't want it to end: breathing no longer seemed necessary. His *lingam* in her *yoni,* nothing else mattered.

Benedict gave a gut-deep groan, spasming and rigid against her. A fresh wet warmth gushed inside her, and she moaned again with the sweetness of it.

He pulled out of her, slumping beside her, his body sheened with sweat and his bright blue gaze fastened upon her. She sank to the floor, still on her belly, and stared at him over her shoulder.

Brushing back a long lock of her dark hair, he murmured, "Did I pass muster?"

"Yes," she breathed before she thought to deny it, to restore the distance that should be between them. Her skin burned. Who did she fool but herself? She wanted him still. Would she ever not want him?

The thought scared her a little, and she turned her head away, rolling onto her back and staring up at the tent. She wondered if the rain, now stopped, had drowned their love cries.

This Englishman would use her and leave her, just like her father. . . . She sucked in a breath, desperate to restore order. "Tell me," she murmured, "about the maharaja. Do you know anything about him?"

Benedict swung into a sitting position. From the corner of her eye, she saw his body tense. "I've heard reports. Never met the man."

"Nor have I."

He started. "What? Then why—"

"It's an arranged marriage," Chandari told him, calm. "It will bring good fortune and wealth to my family."

She heard the sharp intake of breath, but he said nothing. She rolled onto her side and regarded him. He frowned at his knees, twisting one finger between thumb and forefinger. "Benedict?"

He slanted her a sideways glance. "I never expected us to be alike in that way."

"What way?" She propped up her head with a hand.

"Seeking fortunes for the family. That is why I'm here. To bring back a little fresh gilt for the family coffers."

"Have you been successful? Do you plan to go home soon?" Chandari bit her lip. She didn't expect to ask the last question. What did it matter if he stayed in the country or left? Their worlds would not cross paths again.

"Not really. This trip is a fresh start toward that." He grimaced. "I'm sorry."

She sat up and rested a hand upon his shoulder. "Don't be. It is our destinies that brought us together."

At that, Benedict rose, rummaging through her basket for his wadded-up clothing.

"What are you doing?" Filled with foreboding, Chandari sat up, wrapping her arms about her knees.

"Getting dressed," came his clipped reply. "I've neglected my duties too long." He fastened his breeches and shrugged into his shirt. He delivered a curt bow. "Good day to you, madam."

Madam? Chandari stared after him. What on earth made him bolt? Dazed, she rose and crossed to her small washbasin, crouching to wash.

They set off early the next morning. On horseback, Chandari worked her way up the marching line until she reached Lieutenant West riding out in front.

He cast her a dismissive glance. "You should ride back in the center of the line. It is safer there."

"But you're up here," Chandari pointed out. "I wish to speak with you."

"Is everything not to your satisfaction, madam?" He tried to pin her with an icy look.

Chandari ignored his posturing. "No, it is not. You have avoided me ever since you left my tent yesterday afternoon."

She'd emerged from her tent, dressed in a dry and comfortable sari, and spotted the lieutenant almost at once, only to see him duck into another tent. He'd walked away from the breakfast fires when she arrived to eat.

"Did I say something that made you uncomfortable?" she prodded when he didn't respond.

He urged his mount into an easy canter, and Chandari followed him. He reined in. "Look," he blurted, impatient, "the sex is great, but that it's our destiny? What rubbish."

She took a steadying breath. "You do not believe in destiny?"

"I believe in God." His face filled with surprise. "I also believe in free will."

"Ah yes, the Christian god." Chandari let the topic of religion drop. "You cannot deny the circumstances that brought us together are unusual."

"Unusual, but not fated. You are 'destined' to be with the maharaja, remember?"

"Exactly so, and it seems to me that the reward for my sacrifice is the best sex I've ever had in my life."

He reined in his mount. "Really? The best sex? For all your knowledge about the ancient erotic arts?"

"Passion makes up for knowledge," Chandari acknowledged, aware of the twinkling blue eyes teasing her.

Benedict smiled and urged his mount back into a trot. Chandari followed suit.

Her back straightened, and she strove for a regal pose. "If you don't care to, that suits me."

Benedict reached over the short distance between them and brushed her cheek with the backs of his fingers. "That is the issue. I may care too much."

She flushed, ducking her head. "It cannot be. Know that now."

"I know it."

Chandari wanted to be in his arms to determine the truth of his feelings rather than stuck on horseback. "And will you be able to walk away at the end?"

"I will try." He shot her a glance. "Is that not enough?"

She looked at him then. "It is."

It had to be.

"Please," he said, a conciliatory smile lightening his brood-

ing features, "go back to the middle of the line. It is too dangerous up here. If we happen upon bandits . . ."

"Will you promise to stop avoiding me?"

"I promise." He winked, his scarred cheek twitching. "And
I look forward to more of that great sex."

Laughing, Chandari wheeled her horse and trotted back
down the line. Her heart felt much lighter. She hadn't wanted
to think about being so near to Benedict—Lieutenant West—
and not be able to touch him, not be able to take him inside her.

She didn't have to worry about that now. She slipped into
the convoy behind the empty palanquin, edging out to the side
in order to see her lover up ahead. His broad shoulders encased
in that bright red coat with the broad white straps crisscrossed
over his back, made him seem like a target.

Instead of making her afraid, heat pooled deep in her belly.
She wanted to press her thighs together and increase the pleasure, but then she'd be in danger of toppling off her perch.
Perhaps once they stopped for a rest, she'd switch back to her
palanquin and take her pleasure in private . . . or should she
save it for that evening?

Yes, anticipation heightened the strength of her sexual release. She would wait, but that didn't stop her from fantasizing
about what she would do to him and he would do to her.

They traveled through an overgrown ravine, the narrow dirt
path winding along the bottom.

A shout startled her from her reverie. She looked about to
find the bearers retreating at a run.

Something hot stung her cheek, making a whizzing sound as
it zoomed by. She clapped her hand to her cheek. Had they dis-
rupted a colony of wasps?

Drawing her hand away, she saw blood.

Ahead, West came galloping toward her. "Get down!" he
yelled, his pistol already cocked and firing up at the side of the
ravine.

She slipped off her horse, using the poor chestnut pony as a shield from the oncoming bandits. Peeking over her saddle, she saw them now: turbaned and bearded, running down the ravine's steep sides, rifles at the ready.

Chandari ducked, looking over her shoulder to see if the bandits came down the other side of the ravine.

They did. She plastered herself to her mount, already made nervous by the sporadic gunshots. She grabbed the bridle and patted its neck, murmuring soothing words she did not feel.

Her British escort opened fire, a regular fusillade in opposition to their attackers' more scattered shots. She sought out Benedict and found him yelling orders to his men. He edged closer to her, firing his pistol at the bandits. A halo of smoke and gunpowder residue surrounded him. He bellowed an order to fire.

At his raw look of concern mixed with anger, she sent him back an encouraging smile, letting him know she remained unhurt.

He yelled at her, gesturing with his spent pistol. She shook her head, not understanding. Where did he expect her to go, caught in the middle of this?

A large hand grabbed her throat, pulling her off balance. She let go of the reins, flailing to keep balance. She fell against her attacker. The rank stench of unwashed clothing and old sweat made her gag.

She kicked at him with her booted heels, an irritated grunt her only satisfaction. He hugged her waist, lifting her off her feet and hauling her away.

"Benedict!" she screamed. "Benedict!"

But he had seen. Of course he had seen. He had tried to warn her, unable to reach her because of the milling servants, soldiers, and that wretched palanquin between them.

How stupid . . . oh, how terribly stupid of her. She struggled against her captor, her vision blurring as his burly grip about her neck tightened. Did he intend to strangle her?

She grappled with his thick fingers, trying to pry them off her. Black spots danced before her eyes, and she struggled to gain air. The man kept hauling her away from the convoy, from Benedict.

Her kidnapper jerked, his grip spasming about her throat. Abruptly he released her, toppling back, Chandari falling with him.

At once, she rolled away from him, tumbling down the ravine's side, stung by rocks and bushes. At the bottom, she halted, her head hanging while she inhaled deep, rasping breaths. Her throat hurt.

Glancing back up the ravine, she saw the bulk of the bandit sprawled on the hillside, his body lying at a crooked, wrong angle on the rocks. His head was red with mangled flesh, the blood staining his turban.

Chandari turned away, struggling not to vomit. She didn't look at her attacker again, somehow gaining the strength to stand and stagger back to the line.

Her ears still rang with the sounds of gunfire, but she didn't see any of her military escort shoot, except occasionally. On the hillsides, she saw a few of the bandits return fire, but most had fled or been killed.

Chandari sank to the ground, her legs no longer able to support her. It was over. She was safe. It hurt to breathe, and the gunsmoke hanging in a cloud in the narrow ravine only made it worse.

Benedict galloped up, flinging himself off his horse and onto his knees before her. In almost the same movement, he swept her up in his arms, holding her tight. His mouth found hers, bruising her lips with a fervent, desperate kiss.

She clung to him, returning his kiss with equal ardor, not

caring who saw. Their mouths pulsed together, his tongue re-claiming her mouth.

He drew back. In his eyes she saw the lightness of relief and the darkness of desire. He hugged her to him.

She let him hold her, let his warmth seep into her chilled body. Resting her cheek on his rough wool coat, she closed her eyes, blotting out the terrible sight of the dead and dying.

Pulling away, Benedict looked down at her. "Are you un-hurt?"

"A scratch," Chandari rasped, touching her sore cheek. "Throat hurts."

Benedict nodded. "Let's get you out of here." He hoisted her onto his dark bay, mounting up behind her. With his arm wrapped around her waist, Chandari felt safe.

Benedict yelled orders, trotting past the front of the line. "Round up the servants and let's get moving! Jackson, Pierce, come with me."

The two privates stopped checking the corpses and jogged after him. Benedict urged his horse into a canter. Chandari closed her eyes, the world too unsettling to her eyes.

At last, he slowed to a walk. Chandari opened her eyes, her stomach steadying.

"We'll make camp here. It's far enough from the ravine but not so far that the stragglers can't catch up. Can you get down?"

Chandari answered him by sliding from him and off the horse. She stumbled but quickly regained her balance. She turned to find him down and proffering his canteen.

She took a cautious swallow. Wine, warm from the day's sun, burned her throat. She took another gulp, the wine going down smoother the second time. She handed it back. "Thank you."

He smiled at the improved sound of her voice and plucked

the lacy handkerchief from her riding-habit jacket's pocket. At the center of the lace was a small square of white cotton. Onto this he dabbed the mouth of the canteen.

"This will have to do until camp is set up," he said, brushing her cheek with the doused handkerchief.

Chandari sucked in her breath when he touched the open wound. "Will it leave a scar?"

Benedict shook his head, continuing to dab at her cheek. "It's just a graze. It will disappear in a few days. You were lucky."

Chandari agreed. To have a scarred face meant the end of her career in the maharaja's harem.

"There." He handed her the handkerchief, now red with blood and wine. "That's cleaned up the worst of it." He cast a look around the small clearing. He pointed to a fallen log. "Let's sit over there until the others arrive."

She let him lead her to the fallen tree and sat with relief, smoothing her skirts. Mud splotched it, and bits of brambles clung to the knobby fabric. She picked them off, one by one.

Out of the corner of her eye, she saw Benedict sit beside her, booted legs stretched out. My, she could stare at his legs forever. His breeches clung to him like a second skin, revealing him as all muscle, from powerful thighs to sturdy calves.

She picked out more of the brambles on the side of her skirt. She didn't mind the companionable silence. The forest came to life around them: the call of birds and the breath of wind through the towering trees, the clearing almost glowing green.

Turning to share this peace with Benedict, she stopped short. His eagle-eyed gaze scanned the clearing. He did not relax but remained tensed for action.

He turned toward her and melted a little, a smile rendering his face boyish. Then the mask dropped over his face, turning it into granite. "Miss Chandari Camberton, I must apologize for kissing you."

"What?" One didn't apologize for kissing a lover!

"If I had been less distracted by thoughts of you, we never would have been surprised."

Chandari smiled, unable to help it. "You were thinking of me?"

His abrupt nod and darkened gaze answered her question.

"I was, too." She lowered her voice, soft and husky. "Benedict, this was not your fault. The whole point of an ambush is not to be spotted."

His eyes narrowed. "You could have been killed. It is my duty to escort you safely to your destination. If you—"

Chandari held up a slender hand, astonished it stopped him from talking. "So you wish to put me aside?"

He grimaced. "It is for your own good."

"Is it?" She stood, even though her knees trembled with the effort. Her challenge went unanswered. She stared down at him, his perfect visage blurring with unshed tears. She turned, switching her skirts behind her and stormed away.

The heel of her boot turned under her. Her aloof erect posture fractured, and she flailed to keep balance.

Benedict caught her up about her waist, drawing her against him. "Where else are you hurt?" he demanded, his voice rough.

"Nowhere," Chandari insisted. "Just a little shaky. I will be fine." She attempted to free herself from his grasp.

"Is that all?" He brushed back a dark lock from her forehead, his tenderness a sharp contrast to his clipped words.

"Of course." No point in mentioning the damage to her emotions. She glanced over his shoulder. "The others are arriving." She pulled away.

She kept her back to him, supervising the erection of her tent. Every now and then, the hair on the back of her neck prickled. She knew without turning that he watched her. Probably to make sure she didn't collapse again, and not out of any romantic motive.

Still, Chandari hoped for the latter.

Once her tent was up, she remained inside, rearranging her few belongings unpacked from the cart. She dug out a mirror from a carved chest and stared at the shimmering surface.

She touched her fingertips to her cheek, staring at the red stripe in her reflection. She bit her lower lip. Such an imperfection would not be borne by the maharaja. Her mother had been so pleased with her flawless complexion, and now . . . Chandari hoped Benedict was right and that it disappeared, preferably before they reached the maharaja's palace.

She brought the mirror closer. If it didn't disappear, what would happen to her then? Would Benedict want her after the maharaja dismissed her? She flexed her fingers, her nails grazing her cheek, too light to leave a mark. Dare she take that chance?

Thrusting the mirror away from her, Chandari rose to pace the floor of her small tent. What did it matter? She amused him for the moment, nothing else.

The next day, Chandari rode in the palanquin. In the muted sunlight, she tried to read a small book of poetry, but the jolting ride made it difficult.

She didn't want to see Benedict. She'd half expected to find him in her tent the previous night and reverse his decision, but she waited in vain.

Some hours after they'd started for the day, the procession came to a halt. Chandari waited within the confines of her silken prison. No doubt, the journey would resume in a few minutes.

Someone shoved apart the curtain, bright light blinding her. She blinked to see the dark silhouette of the lieutenant.

"Are you well?" he demanded.

"I am quite well, thank you." Chandari put her book aside and drew the edges of her sari more closely about her.

"You didn't join us in the meal last night, and you do not ride today."

She shrugged. "I ate a little of the fruit I have with me. I do not feel like riding."

He straightened, waving his arm in some sort of signal, and climbed into the palanquin with her. She curled up at one end, leaving him the remainder of the small space. The palanquin lifted and moved forward, rocking from side to side.

"You have avoided me," he said, a cool statement of fact, although he looked half in a rage.

Her chin lifted. "I thought that is what you wanted."

Benedict stared at her, a muscle jumping along his jawline. "Chandari . . ."

"You said it, Lieutenant West, not I." Her head shot up higher. "I will not come running and begging for you to take me back. Did you expect it?" Her lip curled. "Then you are a fool."

His shoulders slumped. "Expect it?" He shook his head and ran a hand through his disordered blond hair. "No, Chandari, not that. I tried to stay away from you as long as I could, and I cannot make it even through one entire day. You have no idea how many times I almost came to you last night." His gaze darkened to an intense blue. "No more games, Chandari; no more denials. I will give you up at the gates of the maharaja's palace but no sooner."

Her breath caught. He meant the words, with no artifice, the agony of his admission writ clear on his face. "And you will leave me then?"

His lips pursed and twisted ruefully. "Possibly not," he admitted. "But we will have to take the chance that I will not make a scene."

Chandari managed a small smile. Nobody had ever made a

scene over her before. Nobody had ever been unable to give her up before either. She swallowed, her throat still aching a little. "Well, then." She kneeled, reaching out and caressing his scarred cheek with her fingertips. "Then we must not waste a moment more of time."

4

He leaned forward, finding her mouth. Her hand slipped to the nape of his neck, curling there. She returned his hungry kiss with eagerness, almost drowning in the taste of him.

The palanquin shuddered. Benedict grabbed her, keeping them both upright and preventing them from toppling out of the conveyance.

"You all right?" he asked, breathless.

Chandari nodded, seeking out his mouth with hers. He drew her onto his lap, loosing her long black hair from its careful pins and letting it escape in waves over his hands and down her back.

Moaning into his mouth, Chandari unbuttoned his jacket, tugging at the knot of his cravat. She bent to taste the bared skin, so pale as compared to his sun-darkened face. She breathed in his scent, an odor she thought not to smell again, and almost cried for the joy of it.

She straddled him, the hard length of his cock pressing against her *yoni* through the strained material of his breeches.

She rubbed herself against him, her arousal growing and dampening his breeches.

He pushed back the sari's edge resting on her head and unwound the long scarf from around her neck, all the while kissing her mouth.

His mouth slipped to her chin and then slid down her neck, pausing to nibble and kiss the flesh. He drew back, taking her face between his two hands.

And paused.

Chandari held her breath.

"Are those bruises?" he asked, his voice choked.

Wordlessly, she nodded. His fingertips brushed the dark purple blooms on her throat, and she closed her eyes, almost swooning at his gentleness.

"Why didn't you tell me?" he rasped.

"I told you my throat was sore." She stopped her swooning and glared at him. "The bruises show why. I am fine, Benedict, honestly."

"You are sure?" His fine features twisted into a tortured expression.

"Yes." She managed a smile. "Now kiss me."

A shadow of a smile crossed his face. "Yes, madam." His mouth swooped down over hers. She kissed him hard, showing him she was able of more than being made love to. She pushed him down, his head bouncing a little from the palanquin's soft mattress.

He unbuttoned his breeches. His hard cock sprung against her dark curls, and she rose up on her knees to sink down upon him.

Benedict filled her, and she let out a soft moan of pleasure. His hands found their way under her *choli*, pushing the silk over her pert breasts. He played with her nipples, tugging and pulling them while she rocked against him, her head thrown back in ecstasy.

His large callused hands covered her breasts, swirling over her soft skin. He moaned at her gentle rocking, bringing her back to herself.

Chandari leaned forward, capturing her mouth with his, teeth colliding as the palanquin bumped forward. They giggled, and Chandari aimed for another kiss.

Benedict held her off. "Chandari, let me see you find release. I want to watch." His hand slid between them, finding her swollen clit.

How could she deny him? She rode his hard cock, pulsing up and down. Swiveling her hips, she ground against him, feeling him thick and hard inside her.

Moaning her pleasure, she let him tease her breasts and clit. Her emotions soared heavenward, receiving a deeper pleasure than she'd ever given. Judging by his soft groans, Benedict's enjoyment matched hers.

The sweet fire rose within her, and she bore down harder on him, driving herself to a release, bracing against his shoulders and riding him hard.

His *lingam* slid in and out of her, going deep each time. She burned from within, a fire that drowned her. The final crest built within her, stealing breath, driving on her perspiring self.

Her back arched, and she cried out, squeezing his cock until he groaned and jerked beneath her.

Falling forward, she kissed him and nestled her head against his shoulder. She wanted to lie like this forever, with him inside her, bathed in this delicious warmth.

A week passed. Benedict and Chandari spent almost every moment together: on horseback, in her tent, or in her palanquin. She rose alongside him this morning. They climbed into the mountains, the palanquin impractical for either travel or sex.

She caught Benedict staring at her, letting his mount pick its own path. In the past week, every time she'd seen him, he'd been smiling. Today, a frown furrowed his brow and the corners of his mouth were drawn down. "What is it?"

"We reach the palace today."

Nausea washed over her. "We cannot delay it another day?"

Benedict nudged his mount closer to hers and reached out to grasp her limp hand resting on her reins. "Chandari, love, I would give anything not to hand you over to him."

"We could simply ride off. My mother has relatives in Agra, on the other side of the country."

"We would not make it nearly that far," Benedict told her, his face serious, although his eyes swam with that wish. "The maharaja will hunt us down. He's a ruthless man, Chandari, not to be taunted. I would not risk you to his wrath, nor to the British settlement's."

Chandari turned away from the drooping green foliage. She thought of her mother and her younger sisters in Calcutta, the wrath of the maharaja falling upon them. Even in the British city they would not be safe.

She turned back to him. "What if he doesn't want me?" Her fingertips traced the faint outline of the scar on her cheek. She examined it every morning, much to Benedict's amusement. The scab had fallen off and a faint red line remained.

"How could he not want you, love? You are beautiful and sensual. Everything that a red-blooded man desires." He shifted in his saddle, and Chandari knew he grew hard for her again.

"Just a day," she begged.

He shook his head. "I wish we could, but we will make camp tonight at the gates of Jenalapur, and then you will be presented to the maharaja in the morning."

"You sound so cold," Chandari remarked with a wistful sense he had already started the process of divorcing his heart from hers.

His fist smacked against his saddle. "Do you think I want this, Chandari?" he snarled. "I have wrestled with this. If there were any other way, I would take it."

Chandari turned away again, wanting to hide her tears. "Very well," she murmured, her head bent away from his.

They rode on in miserable silence, ascending the wide mountain trail to Jenalapur, her new home. Ahead, she caught glimpses of distant rocky outcrops. As they drew closer, the dark gray stone formed the turrets of the maharaja's palace.

On reaching the outskirts of the city, Benedict gave the order to make camp.

Chandari dismounted and saw to the erection of her tent. She heard a commotion, the clatter of rifles coming to attention, and she spun to see the cause of the ruckus.

Indian soldiers, elegantly attired in dark blue uniforms, with matching plumes dancing from their turbans, strode forth from the city gates in perfect double file.

She saw Benedict stride toward them. The lead man saluted. The faint sound of his poor Marathi drifted across the campsite, the words indistinguishable.

Benedict's shoulders and back stiffened. Chandari sensed their time had ended. She turned to her servants. "Cease your unpacking. Get everything loaded onto the cart again."

Glancing aside at the busy servants reversing the process of preparing the camp for the night, Benedict approached Chandari. "You have guessed it," he ground out. Water shimmered in his blue eyes. "Chandari," he gasped, the sound of her name full of agony.

She reached out for him, and he clasped her hands in both his large hands, almost crushing them in a tight squeeze. Chandari welcomed the pain. The maharaja's men would suspect a closer embrace.

"Benedict." His name came out in a sob. "Benedict, don't forget me."

"I don't want to let you go," he said, his voice rough with pain. "I want to hold you, kiss you, make love to you one last time."

Tears fell unhindered down her cheeks, and she pulled a hand free to brush them away. "It cannot be." She must be strong for them both. "My family needs me to do this."

"As does mine." The unspoken reward for his escorting her hung between them, deadening every sense.

She pulled her other hand free of his. The last time they touched and they wore gloves. She wanted his callused hands upon her soft body, wanted all of him. "I need to change."

Her tent still remained upright, and she ducked inside, discarding the English riding habit for more traditional attire. She pulled a flame-orange outfit from her clothing chest, the fabric shining with gold thread. Her marriage gown. She donned each layer, misery settling over her like a funeral shroud.

She swathed a pale lemon scarf about her neck, which still showed the faint green of her fading bruises. Makeup concealed the thin line of her scar on her cheek. She highlighted her dark eyes with kohl and added color to her lips.

The tent flap slapped against the tent wall. Chandari looked up, trying to appear unconcerned when she saw Benedict.

"Don't go," he growled. The tent flap fell shut behind him. He engulfed the space between them in two long strides and took her in his arms. "Don't go."

He saw her painted lips and dove for her neck, pulling away the concealing scarf. He pressed his hot mouth against her skin, and Chandari almost swooned against him.

Almost without thought, she reached for the buttons on his breeches. She undid the first two before she came to her senses. She hugged him close, wrapping her arms around his shoulders.

"You came to tell me they grow impatient, my love," she murmured against his blond hair.

Benedict didn't answer, grinding his hips against hers. A few more buttons and he'd be buried inside her.

"Benedict," she whispered, "Benedict, you have my heart, but you must let me go."

His shoulders convulsed, and he moaned. He pulled away, straightening, a mask of politeness falling over his handsome features, turning them into cold marble. "You are right. The maharaja does not like to be kept waiting, milady."

He bowed, holding back the tent flap so she might make a graceful exit.

It took all her strength to dig down and remember the lessons her mother had taught her about graceful movement. She strode past him, proud and not daring to cast one last glance into his face. That would undo her.

She left behind her escort, her tent, her man, and strode into her future.

Instead of a grand reception, her escort handed her off at the harem's door. An old woman stripped her of all her finery, even her bangles.

A eunuch led her to another room, shoving her to stand before an ornate cedar screen. The eunuch and an old woman prodded at her, making her turn. The woman found the fading bruises on her neck and sent her a sharp, quizzical gaze.

Chandari met them, her heart palpitating. She wanted to run, run back to Benedict, who still camped outside the city, but she had her family's meager honor to preserve.

The old woman gave a sharp nod and continued her survey of Chandari's body. She tugged hard on Chandari's dark nipples, and Chandari gasped, wanting to cry out in pain, but fearing to.

The old woman strode behind her and tapped at her calves and her thighs, wiggling the stick in between until Chandari parted her legs to her satisfaction.

The eunuch knelt at her feet, his thin fingers parting her cunt lips. With a sharp jab, he stuck a manicured finger inside her. Chandari jolted, whimpering.

He withdrew his finger, examined it, and strode to the screen. "She is wet and eager, your majesty," he said in his native tongue.

Chandari gave no sign she understood his words. She'd had a tutor for months to teach her the dialect. Of course she was wet. Wet for her Englishman, not some unseen potentate. Her lip curled before she remembered herself, and she masked her feelings.

Dismissed, Chandari curled up on the couch reserved for her use in the harem. With no way out, it seemed the maharaja didn't want her enough to take her to his bed at once. She didn't know whether to feel relieved or abused.

The chief eunuch stood before her. "You are to come with me," he said in bad English, crooking his finger to make his message clear.

She rose and followed him, her simple white robe masking her lithe form. Had the time come? Would she be pampered, perfumed, and gowned for the maharaja's pleasure?

No matter what he looked like, she decided, she'd think of Benedict, and no other, even if the maharaja was the handsomest creature on Earth.

The chief eunuch led her to a small room, the walls plastered but undecorated except for a small ebony-black grill in the center of one wall at chest height. A high couch stood in the center of the room.

"You are English," he said.

Chandari raised an eyebrow. "Half English," she corrected, her brown skin not even close to the chilled paleness of the colonists.

He acted like he didn't hear her. "The English are a cold

people. The maharaja doubts you have sufficient passion within you to satisfy him."

Rage built up within her. Why had he sent for her, knowing her heritage, if he didn't like English women? "And if he is not satisfied?"

He answered her, giving her a cold look. "He has already paid for you. If you fail, you will become his slave."

She swallowed. "What must I do?"

"Pleasure yourself. If the maharaja is pleased, you will be prepared for his bed."

Chandari thought not of her training, or her erstwhile lover back in Calcutta, but of Benedict, naked and eager before her.

She imagined she performed for him. She moulded her curves with her hands through the concealing folds of her loose gown. The silk material scrunched up between her hands as she cupped her breasts, fingering her nipples.

Benedict loved to make her nipples hard, so hard until they throbbed, swelling under his attentions. She plucked at them, tugging them through the silk.

Desperate for more sensation, she grasped the neck of her gown with both hands and tore it, exposing her breasts and belly. She let the ruined gown puddle at her feet. Chandari no longer cared she'd abandoned the graceful erotic dance of her training.

She grabbed the silken material, pressing it against her breasts, her belly, sliding it down between her legs. She humped the material, her closed eyes filled with Benedict's naked form, his hard cock eager for her.

She moaned, lifting the wadded garment to her nose, inhaling her own scent, wishing for Benedict's instead. She sank onto the couch, legs parted and her fingers busy between. Teasing her already erect clit with her thumb, her fingers delved into her wet cunt.

Chandari imagined Benedict above her, fucking her, but she lacked his weight to anchor her in that fantasy. She flipped onto her belly, rising up on all fours. Rubbing her breasts against the tapestried pillows, she frigged her cunt without mercy, imagining Benedict below her, tasting her tits and plunging inside her.

She wanted more than her fingers. She wanted his *lingam*. She reared back, a desperate moan rising from her throat. Her fingers plucked her nipple, rubbed her clit.

Even without Benedict, the heat rose within. She drowned in hot liquid desire, her cunt making sloppy noises with each haphazard penetration of her fingers. Collapsing onto the couch, Chandari rolled onto her back; her legs bent, she thrust her hips high against her busy hand until her release crested, filling her with a sweet ache. She thrust her fingers up inside her, pressing against the fleshy upper wall of her cunt.

She cried out, her back arching off the couch. She cried out again, the sharp golden release cascading through her body, from her groin still pulsing against her hand, to her head, and back again. Awash in her release, she felt it escape between her fingers, a small gush from her *yoni*.

Falling against the couch, Chandari stilled. Her chest heaved with the effort, her dark hair plastered to her light brown skin.

The chief eunuch stepped into view, reminding her that he hadn't left the room once. Too tired to try to cover herself with the ruined gown, she awaited her verdict.

"You will do," he said.

Behind him, the door opened, and a magnificently jeweled man stepped over the threshold. Despite the gilt, Chandari noticed the sweat on his brow and the spent penis drooping outside his pants. "You will come with me to the festival tomorrow." He looked at the eunuch. "Have her dressed in her finest."

Benedict's first thoughts were to strike camp and march out of sight of Jenalapur, but he stayed his hand. The men under his command needed the rest after a long journey. He needed time to regroup.

Chandari.

He rubbed his hand through his hair and stalked to the edge of camp, gazing up at the palace dominating the skyline. Somewhere in there, Chandari pleasured the maharaja.

It turned his stomach to think of her plying her skills upon someone other than him. She belonged to someone other than him.

Rescue would bring down the wrath of his maharaja and his commander combined. He'd have to abandon his men if he expected to outrun the maharaja's troops.

One of his men approached him, clearing his throat. "Sir? The men want to know if we'll be heading back to Calcutta tomorrow."

Benedict glowered at him. "Of course we are." The private visibly drooped. "Why?"

"One of Miss Camberton's carriers says a big festival starts tomorrow." The private essayed a cautious grin. "Couldn't pronounce the name of it, but it sounds like a great party! Might even get a glimpse of the maharaja himself."

And Chandari? Benedict stared at him, long and hard, his heart pounding, until the man flushed and looked down at his boots. "Very well. You men deserve some reward for your hard work. We'll stay for the festival tomorrow. But be prepared to leave at first light the day after. I want to be away from here, and we should make quick time without Miss Camberton's baggage slowing us down."

The private grinned again and saluted. "Yes, sir!"

Benedict's gaze rose again to the palace. Would he see Chandari one last time? Or would she be unrecognizable in a long veil? She'd know him instantly in his red coat but would she give him a sign?

He rubbed his lips. To be so close to her and yet not have

her? The ache in his heart promised to multiply. But he had to do it.

Benedict let the men go in undress, which, given their meager possessions on this journey, meant going without their heavy red wool jackets. Their light-colored skin and hair alone warranted a concern, let alone the formal military presence.

If Chandari wanted to come, he'd rescue her from this place. He didn't know how to do it, or how he'd even be able to talk with her to discover her needs, but his heart drove him on.

In the last week and a half, he'd fallen for Chandari, heart, body, and soul. He'd never dared to tell her so, choosing to show her with his body. He had little to offer her, nothing when he compared himself to the maharaja's power and riches. And then he had promised to deliver her safely.

Well, he had done that. He'd honored his orders, which said nothing about taking her away again, if Chandari wished. He had a nugget of a plan that might work.

But first he must find her.

He wriggled his way toward the visible maharaja's entourage, pushing through the dense, dancing crowd, the air showering with puffs of colored dust, coating everything in their paths.

Nearest the temple at the peak of the mountain stood magnificent tents of white silk and gold embroidery. Behind the ancient stone temple towered the untamed jungle, its dark emerald green a somber backdrop to the festivities.

The sides of the royal tents were drawn up, rendering the maharaja and his attendants visible to his people. The maharaja, a rotund, imposing figure in silk and jewels, sat upon an ornate gilt throne.

Servants bustled to do his bidding, but Benedict didn't care about them. Where were the women? Where was Chandari?

A second white and gold silk tent stood across from the

first. The translucent sides revealed graceful shadows of moving figures. Was it possible?

Benedict tapped the fellow ahead of him. Ignoring the man's surprised expression, he asked, in a broken version of the local dialect, "Who are they?"

The man's dark, almost black, eyes narrowed in his brown face. "The harem. Even they are permitted to worship on this holy day."

His heart leaping, Benedict thanked the man. He wandered off in the opposite direction, sampling the wares of the various food vendors. Staying away to avoid suspicions, should they rise later.

The open spaces and vegetation reminded him of the overgrown pleasure gardens outside of Delhi. Someone had kept this up, probably the temple's priests.

Spending an hour out of sight of the two royal tents was agony. Again and again, he looked in their direction and forced himself to look away again.

If he rescued Chandari from her fate, it had to be today while she remained free of the restrictions of the harem.

The day wore on. Around him, the denizens grew drunker and drunker, flagons of some local brew waving in their hands. Benedict hoped Chandari remained sober.

Once more, he edged toward the ladies' tent, making slow progress amongst the press of people. The overpowering smells of spices hung heavy in the air, some of which made Benedict sneeze.

At last, he reached the ladies' tent. A loose watch of the maharaja's purpled guard stood between him and the ladies within. He met their gaze with an even, polite smile and continued to look for a way in.

He edged his way toward the back of the tent, still amidst the crowd and thus at a respectful distance.

He stopped short. The tent sides had been raised, giving a perfect view inside.

Except for a serving girl, the tent was empty.

Benedict struggled to find breath. Where was she? Had the harem returned to the palace, and he hadn't noticed? What now?

He backed away from the tent, glancing across at the maharaja's tent to find it still filled with the prince and his attendants. He spotted a girl in a purple sari at his feet, but knew in an instant it was not Chandari.

Benedict lost himself in the crowd. He cursed, kicking a pebble out of the way. He wanted to break something. He had lost his chance.

"Benedict!"

He whirled at the cry, seeing nothing but the milling population of Jenalapur. He turned back toward camp.

"Benedict!"

Why did he have to imagine her calling him now when he had lost her forever? Even so, he looked for her.

He saw her wave from the other side of an old stone fountain, the splashing water partially obscuring her. She wore a nondescript brown shawl over her bright orange sari. The same outfit she had worn on her way to the maharaja.

He grinned and started pushing his way through the crowd toward her. She hovered at the stone rim of the fountain, waiting for him.

His heart caught in his throat. What if she were spotted and taken away before he'd had a chance to hold her?

He reached the fountain and saw the mass of people pressed against the stone sides. It would take him an age to reach her through the crowd.

He swung his leg over the fountain's basin and climbed into the fountain. His feet slipped on the smooth stone, and he struggled to maintain his balance.

Water from the fountain pounded on his head and plastered his ivory shirt to his body. He reached Chandari, extending a hand to her.

She accepted, her face full of wonder, and joined him in the fountain. The plain brown shawl fell off her shoulders, revealing her glorious sari and a length of her raven black hair cascading over her shoulder.

"Chandari," he murmured, knowing the roaring of the water and the crowd silenced his voice. He touched her wet cheek and drew her into him. He didn't care who saw. Chandari had come to him.

She clung to him, her arms slipping higher and higher until they clasped his neck, bringing her mouth up to his. He obliged, kissing her senseless, the heat of his mouth warming the watery chill of her lips.

He never wanted to let her go again. Always, he wanted her body fitted against his, with nothing to come between them. But they had to leave or be caught.

Benedict guided her to the fountain's rim and helped her out. She pressed against him almost at once, every line and curve of her body revealed by her sari, rendered transparent by the water.

Wishing for a coat with which to cover her, he drew her close to him. "I tried to find you," he murmured against her ear.

"The ladies of the harem are free to wander this night." She hugged him tighter. "I wanted to see you again."

Pulling back slightly, he gazed down at her. "Will you come with me?"

Her beautiful face grew pensive, worried. "But the maharaja. . . ."

Benedict gave her an encouraging smile. "I have a plan worth trying. Will you take that risk?"

She nodded, and her smile unfurled like a spring bud. "Yes, yes, of course."

Something red fluttered and landed on her cheek. A rose petal. Chandari looked up in wonder and Benedict followed her gaze. The air filled with tossed flower petals, red and gold.

"This is most auspicious," Chandari breathed.

He hugged her tight. "Let us go before we are found."

It was morning. Benedict delayed in giving the orders to break camp. Chandari crouched in his small one-man tent.

She smiled, tugging straight her borrowed coat. They'd returned to camp and headed straight for his tent, making furtive love, freezing whenever anybody approached. The maharaja hadn't disturbed them yet. Crawling out of his tent, Chandari rose, tugging the too large coat over her crotch. Benedict had insisted she wear a soldier's dress: in her opinion, the tight breeches revealed too much of her to the world, although Benedict seemed to appreciate the view.

Benedict smiled at the sight of her and gestured she sit on a nearby stool. She obeyed, and she saw him nod to someone else.

"C—lose your eyes, milady," said a stuttering private.

Looking up at him, Chandari saw he held a cloth bag. "What are you going to do?"

"Club and powder your hair, my lady. You'll look like one of us, soon enough."

The choking cloud of flour surrounded her, and Chandari closed her eyes, holding her breath. He jammed something onto her head. When it was safe to open her eyes and breathe again, Chandari had become a short version of one of Benedict's men.

Seeing her ready, Benedict handed her a rifle, winking at her, before strolling off to check on his men. She'd heard some of their carousing last night. That had to be the reason for delaying their departure.

He strolled back, his step quickening at the last. "They're all here."

"The maharaja!" the watch cried.

Benedict didn't even start, resting a calming hand on Chandari's shoulder. "Stand with the men. Do what they do. Whatever you do, always look straight ahead, not at me, not at the maharaja, not at any of the men. Understand?"

Biting her lip, Chandari nodded.

Benedict passed the order to fall into line, and his sergeant's bellow made her jump. She scrambled into place with the rest, standing stiffly erect and staring straight ahead.

"Good morning, your majesty!" Benedict flourished a bow.

Chandari strained to see more from the corner of her eye.

"Eyes front," whispered the sergeant, striding past her.

"We seek the maharaja's woman. The one you brought with you," proclaimed a familiar voice. Chandari shivered. The chief eunuch himself had come.

"Saw her briefly last night," Benedict offered. "I was surprised to see her among the crowd. Aren't the ladies of the harem kept in restriction?"

Benedict and the chief eunuch strode into view. Chandari sucked in her breath, wishing herself invisible.

"His majesty always keeps a close watch on his women. Did you speak with her?"

Benedict nodded. "She seemed happy."

The chief eunuch's eyebrow rose. Chandari's gaze shot over the man's head, wanting to avoid eye contact. "Then you have no objection in our searching your camp?"

"Search it!" Benedict bristled. "What is the meaning of this? We have come in good faith and delivered the package. Why would we have her? We wouldn't wish his majesty's anger upon us. Nor my superior officer's."

The chief eunuch said nothing, making a sharp gesture. The

maharaja's guard sprang into life, rummaging through the still-upright tents.

In short order, they returned, reporting their failure to the chief eunuch.

Benedict smirked at him over folded arms. "Satisfied?"

"You will forgive us for our intrusion." The chief eunuch bowed. "We wish you a safe journey."

Benedict returned the bow and watched until the maharaja and his attendants disappeared from sight. He strolled from soldier to soldier, patting them on the shoulder or straightening their gear. He paused before Chandari. "You will be a soldier until we leave the hills," he murmured. "I'll send word ahead to your family to flee to safety. The maharaja will look for you there. We will be watched until then, in case we have you concealed elsewhere." He grinned. "There are no objections to sharing my tent, are there?"

Chandari saluted. "None at all, sir."

His grin grew wider. "Good, lass. This will be an adventure."

A LADY'S PLEASURE

MELISSA MacNEAL

1

Summer of 1899, near the Oregon forests

Ophelia heard the secretive footsteps on the service stairway and smiled. Tonight, as he did several times a week, James Pohl, her husband's personal secretary, was sneaking up to Fanny's room for a quick tumble. They thought they were getting away with it. Thought no one could hear their thrashing and writhing and muted cries.

But here in this mausoleum of a mansion, where it was only the two of them and Ophelia now, every sound was magnified by the silence of the night.

She waited in the darkness, listening. James always paused on the stair opposite her desk, because that one creaked. She imagined him looking through the wall at her right now, as he avoided putting his weight on that step.

Did he know she was naked?

Tonight I tell him, she mused, her pulse quickening. *Tonight he gets a big surprise.*

When she heard his footfalls ascending again, Ophelia lit her lamp and opened the large book on her desk. Its Moroccan leather cover sighed as she opened it. She smiled about the title: *1001 Arabian Knights*.

She hadn't caught the irony of that altered name right away, but the contents of this heavily embellished book had shocked her out of the stupor she'd been in since burying Henry, just last week. James would argue that she shouldn't have been snooping in her husband's study, but this was *her* house now.

It wasn't her fault that she'd discovered Henry's secret life.

And his secret lovers.

And a world of sensual delights these claret leather covers had hidden from her unsuspecting eyes during her entire marriage to Henry Leeds.

As she opened the ponderous volume now, Ophelia was pleased that the pain—the shock—of these discoveries had evolved into curiosity. Fascination. *Longing*.

She wanted what Henry had had. She wanted to romp with those knights—in a slightly different way than her husband had.

Photographs tucked inside the back cover told much of the tale: the *Scheherazade*, a wondrously appointed ship—listed in Henry's ledgers as part of his lumbering fleet—had transported him and his board members and friends to a world of revelry and delight unlike any she had ever known.

But she was about to go there.

She was about to take charge not only of Henry's business, but of his businessmen, as well. She, Ophelia Leeds, now owned the multimillion-dollar Leeds Lumber Company, and *she* would use the *Scheherazade* as transport to her own brave new world of sensuality and bliss.

Lord, when had she ever known *bliss*?!

As Ophelia studied the faces in the photographs, she recognized James and Henry, Erroll Barrymore, the accountant, and a few others. Envy surged through her body.

Here they all were, arm in arm, wearing elaborate Arabian costumes: tasseled fezzes, embroidered vests, and jewel-encrusted caftans that made their harem fantasy *real*. They dressed for the parts they played; they *became* swaggering sheiks and saber-swinging sultans as they sailed the Puget Sound during these forays.

And then there were the ladies. A tinted portrait showed Yen Sin, a Chinese girl with almond eyes and raven hair, and another woman who appeared more demure behind her veils—Lady Jane, she went by. Esmeralda piqued her curiosity, too: the gypsy dancer didn't hail from the original *Arabian Nights*, but with her flowing red hair and bangles and tambourine, she fit right in with the others.

Ophelia had read some very revealing information about these three, and she needed to know *more*.

For Henry, ever the journalist and recorder, had written everything down. He'd listed each man's Arabian name—and, of course, he was Sinbad, the legendary voyager, while James became Aladdin, who made the magic happen. She'd read their accounts of sexual encounters and raucous games, and menus of their sumptuous meals.

Ophelia had also read the ledger, which showed how one-tenth of Leeds Lumber profits had been systematically diverted into this floating pleasure palace, named for the harem wife doomed to die if she didn't entertain her husband. So, clever Scheherazade had told him story after story, night after night.

Just like Henry had told her.

"Tonight's my meeting of the Oregon Lumberman's Association. It'll be long and tedious, so don't wait up."

"I must go to Seattle for new saws and supplies. I'll see you in a few days, my sweet."

"I'll be away for the week, visiting all my mills, Ophelia, dear. I'm taking James along, of course, but you and Fanny will be fine until we return."

And she and Fanny Gault, her maid, were about to become a whole lot finer. A lot more adventurous and outrageous and *alive*!

Because *they* were about to set sail aboard the *Scheherazade* for their own adventures—with those Arabian knights! But *she* would be writing the new script!

Ophelia grinned, shifting in her chair from the excitement of it. Then she paused to listen.

Yes, the lovers were directly above her in Fanny's room. The bed was rocking in that unmistakable rhythm . . . that elemental heartbeat that thrummed through Ophelia's veins as she longed for release.

It was time. She was about to embark upon the most exciting journey of her life—right after she went upstairs to confront those lovers.

And join them.

Ophelia glanced at her nakedness in the mirror, put on a brave smile, and then padded up the stairs with Henry's journal tucked under her arm.

Through the keyhole they looked so beautiful together: James with his long, lean body curled around Fanny's lush backside, fondling her pert breasts while he pumped in and out of her. Her serving girl looked ecstatic, arching her back to complete their lovers' circle.

As Ophelia watched her maid's head fall onto James's shoulder—watched the young couple kiss with a heat she longed to feel—her insides tightened. It was wicked to spy on them this way, but it was her house, wasn't it? They were her employees, were they not?

And if she walked in on them, what could they do?

But she preferred to watch them first, stroking her envy and her hunger the way James was stroking Fanny's passage. In and out, building up for a climax all the more explosive because they had to be quiet. Even so, their moans were growing louder, as was the bumping of the bed against the wall.

James's loose sorrel curls shimmied in the candlelight. The flex of that muscle where his thigh joined his hip teased at Ophelia. By leaning forward to peer though the keyhole, she put herself into the same position Fanny had assumed, with her ass up in the air and her puss gaping open . . . waiting to be filled . . . wet with anticipation. Fanny was gripping the iron bed head, grimacing and grunting until Ophelia could feel the heat and adrenaline and *need* her maid was experiencing.

"Oh, James . . . James, please!" she sighed.

Ophelia moaned, clenching down below.

The couple stopped dead still, listening.

Nipping her lip against even the escape of air, Ophelia prayed they couldn't see her eye through the keyhole.

"What was that?" Fanny gasped.

"Just the house settling. Just the whistle of the wind," James assured her. "Ophelia's asleep. Her light was out when I came up."

"Maybe we should stop, before we wake—"

"And maybe I should just turn you over and throw you down on the bed," the young man teased, doing what he was describing to her. "And maybe I should just kiss you senseless, while I thrust so far into your tight little cunt you can't possibly let me go!"

Fanny giggled, complying by landing flat on her back. Her legs spread wide, welcoming him.

And what a man to welcome! James wasn't hugely endowed, but he was agile. He loved his fun, even if he'd never shown any inclination to marry Fanny after all the years they'd been tiptoeing around, thinking she and Henry were oblivious to their trysts.

Ophelia watched the head of his cock pause at Fanny's opening. Her own insides quivered for that very sort of attention.

James slipped inside, lifting Fanny's hips to his so her knees fell apart and he was fully extended inside her.

Ophelia could stand it no more.

Quietly she twisted the knob. Closed her eyes against the final caution that told her to go back downstairs—to leave all these secrets alone!

But her heart and her hand propelled her into Fanny's room, and into the dare she was about to take.

2

Ophelia swung open the door and stepped in. Held the large leather-bound book across her chest as she looked them both in the eye.

They stopped. Stared at her, in fear of being fired. But then they realized she was naked, too.

That's what made this intrusion a test of her mettle: she was finding out if she had the nerve to carry out a much bolder, more compromising fantasy in the presence of men she'd never met.

"I—I thought I might join you," she began softly, her eyes focused on the place where their two bodies became one.

Even with the softening effect of the candle that flickered beside Fanny's bed, their faces remained wary. Angular.

"J—join us, missus?"

Fanny licked her lips nervously. She was a devout young woman from a poor but respectable family. If it got back to her mama that she was James Pohl's plaything, she might be out of much more than her job.

"I'm sorry if we disturbed your—you must be terribly lonely for Henry, and—"

"No, you didn't. And, no, I'm not."

Ophelia gathered up her courage, amazed she could respond this calmly. "I've known about you two for years—and, as *you* know, my husband and I slept in separate bedrooms. His preference, not mine."

She let out a long sigh, as though her years with this older man were being aired like linens that had collected dust in the closet.

"I'm tired of being lonely," she murmured. "Tired of being portrayed as the poor, sickly wife—or whatever story he must've told his associates."

Pohl's eyebrows flew up. "Oh, no! Henry always spoke of you with the utmost respect and—"

"Respect?" she challenged, stepping toward them. "Is that all I deserved as his wife? Imagine my amazement when I discovered this . . . *interesting* book in Henry's study! A journal of voyages aboard the *Scheherazade*, with men in Arabian costumes and women wearing not much of anything. Women he described in great detail."

Or his personal secretary did, she didn't add. Ophelia would entrust only a few of her secrets to Fanny until James was safely in her pocket.

She paused, trying not to lose her nerve. "He kept these women as his mistresses, while he left me home alone."

James's face confirmed her suspicions: he was aware of all she'd said but was too polite to discuss such things with his boss's wife, even though he'd lived under this roof—had a room next to Henry's—for nearly seven years.

Pohl cleared his throat. "He never let on—I wasn't privy to—"

"Oh, spare me! You know what's written in this book, even though Henry never intended for anyone else—especially *me!*—

to find it!" she spouted. "Don't deny it, Mr. Pohl! You're in these photographs! You signed the minutes of these outrageous meetings! I realized, after I found this book, that my husband truly needed a personal secretary because he had so damn many personal secrets!" She paused to collect herself. To look him in the eye. "And now they are mine."

Silence echoed in the dormer-ceilinged room. Fanny began to quiver and pull away, but James held her fast, his hands still cupping her breasts.

"If you'll excuse us to . . . We'll put on our clothes and—"

"You don't understand," Ophelia whispered. "If you go along with my wishes, you'll see that—"

"Henry requested I remain—"

"Henry's dead."

It didn't hurt much to say that. In many, many ways Henry had never been truly alive for her, the way James and Fanny were alive. So while his passing meant a big adjustment—she now owned a lumbering empire that included seven mills, a fleet of ten ships, and all the employees that kept them running—it wasn't the emotional blow most wives experienced.

She'd been the bird in Henry's proverbial gilded cage. She'd known that from the beginning. But now she was about to fly free!

James slipped a protective arm around Fanny, his expression earnest. "Really, Mrs.—"

"My name's Ophelia," she breathed. "And I want you to be my ticket into this world my husband created aboard the *Scheherazade*."

James gaped. "You don't know what you're asking."

"I'm not *asking*," she said. "If your loyalty to Henry is stronger than your need to remain here, earning your living—or keeping company with my maid—then we have nothing more to say."

Her heart thudded so hard he could probably see her chest

vibrating. Never in her life had Ophelia challenged a man; women weren't allowed, after all. A wise wife knew her place!

But the time had come to get what she wanted—what she *needed*—just as Henry had, when he'd collected his women. He'd considered it his right to be the king of his own business, his own castle, and his empire of secret lives.

"I—I'm sorry you found that book—"

"Before *you* did? So you could protect me from the truth?" Ophelia had expected this ploy, but she wasn't falling for it. "I believe things happen the way they're supposed to in this life," she continued quietly. "Perhaps that loose branch—called a widow-maker for good reason—landed on Henry's head because that was his fate. We can't know such things, can we? But you heard the preacher, same as I did, when he assured us that God is in His heaven and all's right with the world."

Pohl licked his lips. He was still hard, with that *pole* about halfway out now, glistening with Fanny's wetness. He was looking her over very thoroughly. So he was at least interested, which was better than acting disgusted. Or, God forbid, laughing in her face.

Ophelia slowly let the book fall away, to reveal her bare breasts and the curve of her midsection toward hips that swelled slightly . . . over thighs punctuated by a triangle of midnight hair that matched the cascade of curls she'd let fall loose over her shoulders.

James had taken all this in. He remained hard. Listening. Considering his options.

"If you release me from this position, Ophelia, you'll find that Leeds Lumber will—"

"Leeds Lumber?! Is that what you want to discuss right now?"

Maybe she should've stayed downstairs, minding her own business. It was a stupid idea to barge in on these lovers, thinking they'd care what she was feeling or have any inclination to include her.

And now that she'd found Henry's journal of—

"May I see that book?" Fanny asked in a strained voice. "What's in there that dared you to walk in on us?"

Ah, dear Fanny! She appeared the proper, obedient young woman on the outside, but her curiosity had always outshone her halo.

Ophelia grinned. With the two of them determined to know about this secret life—the adventures they'd missed each time the *Scheherazade* sailed—James didn't stand a chance.

Just for effect, she opened the book and removed a small vellum envelope. One Henry had used for an invitation.

Pohl's eyes widened in recognition. "What is it you want, Mrs. . . . Ophelia?"

She looked at him pointedly, right where his pole plugged Fanny.

"Do you like your position with Leeds Lumber, James?"

He blinked. "Yes, of course! I know the business inside and out, and Henry always assured me that after he passed on, I'd be—"

"Do you like what you see, James?"

Somehow she found the nerve to part her legs and cup a breast at him.

His Adam's apple bobbed when he swallowed. Fanny flinched when his grip on her tightened.

"Yes. Yes, ma'am, I do," he said in a voice she could barely hear.

"Good." Ophelia gave him an encouraging smile. "If Henry were alive, when would the *Scheherazade* sail again?"

"In about a week, when the full moon—"

"Excellent!" Her pulse pounded again. This was the tricky part, getting him to cooperate when push came to shove. "I want you to contact all the major players—the mill managers, the crew, the board—and send them invitations to sail, just as you did for my husband." She smiled at him, bubbling with anticipation now. "Henry's about to give them all a big surprise. From the grave, as it were."

"I'm not sure I understand what you're—"

Ophelia reached for the doorknob, looking over her shoulder at him. "Finish your business with Fanny, and bring her downstairs. I can't wait to start our adventure."

3

_____

"Make yourself comfortable on the bed, James," Ophelia said when they entered her room. "I think we'd all enjoy it if Fanny read us a story."

She gestured toward her desk, where the big book of Arabian knights lay open to a page. Fanny looked as puzzled and nervous as Ophelia herself felt, but she leaned over the girl's shoulder to point at the starting place.

"Don't worry, I'm not after your man," she whispered in a voice James couldn't hear. "We simply need to get his attention."

Fanny's face lit up with an impish grin. "Yes, missus. I think we would all enjoy a story!"

As Ophelia straightened, to give James another good look at her bare breasts, she winked at him. Poor fellow looked dazed. Afraid his secrets were about to be as exposed as he was.

But that wasn't Ophelia's intent. She wanted this influential young man on _her_ side through the coming days, and she knew how to keep his allegiance.

"I just thought we could . . . reenact one of the more exhilarating scenes from Henry's book," she said softly. "So feel free to perform as the spirit moves you, Mr. Pohl."

Fanny cleared her throat as though she was enjoying this immensely.

" 'On this particular summer's evening, when the moon shone full, and the Puget Sound reflected the blue of the midnight sky," she began theatrically, "it was my extreme good fortune to come upon a Chinese maiden in dire straits. It seems someone had bound her dainty hands and feet and lashed her to a lamppost on the deck.' " Fanny looked up. "Play along now, James. Use your imagination."

"And the belt of your robe," Ophelia chimed in. Feeling bold and brazen, she whipped it quickly through his belt loops.

James appeared thunderstruck. "How can you let her—?"

"She won't know," Ophelia murmured, assuming the position her maid had described from across the room. "Aladdin signed this account, not you." She put her wrists together and offered them to him. "Make me your slave, kind sir," she intoned. "Allow me to serve you—as happens in the story."

His brown eyes widened. He seemed entranced as he wrapped the flannel band around her wrists and then guided them toward the bedpost.

Fanny cleared her throat and began again. " 'She looked at me with pleading eyes, wet with the tears of her humiliation. "Please, kind sir," she begged me, "my master has left me here as punishment for disobeying him. Can you find it in your heart to set me free? I will remain forever indebted." ' "

James fastened Ophelia's wrists to the brass bedpost with swift, edgy movements, still not convinced this was a good idea.

"Please, kind sir," Ophelia mimicked, widening her eyes. "My master has left me here as punishment for disobeying him. Could you find it in your heart to set me free?"

James swallowed hard, his gaze following the curve of her bare back to the lush cheeks she wiggled in the air.

"You're a naughty puss, indeed, to disobey the master who kept you in his care," he teased.

Fanny's eyes widened. "James! You *know* this story!"

The young man's curls shimmied as he covered for revealing too much. "We—many times aboard the *Scheherazade*—we shared stories with each other, sweetheart. It's a natural thing when men are drinking and sailing on a summer's night."

Satisfied, Fanny continued. " ' "You're a naughty puss, indeed, to disobey the master who kept you in his care!" ' " she read with great feeling. " ' "And what did you do that so provoked him?"

" ' "I stared at his member when he was pissing," she replied remorsefully. "It was not my place to look upon him that way, but—"

" ' "And what did he do then? When he caught you staring?"

" ' "Why," she replied with eyes the size of china plates, "he told me that if I was so enamored of his cock, I should suck it and lick it until it crowed."

" ' "And how did you do that, my tender lotus blossom?" Fanny snickered. She looked up from the book, challenging her lover. "It's your turn, James. But be careful about whacking Ophelia with that pole sticking out of your robe."

Indeed, James was erect and ready for his part in this little passion play. As was Ophelia, who gazed at him longingly.

"You'll have to come closer . . . onto the bed, so I can reach you, kind sir," she whispered. "It's such a large, wondrous cock—bigger than any I've ever seen. I can scarcely believe it's real!"

Boldly—for she'd never done this with Henry—Ophelia opened her lips and leaned down as far as her bindings allowed.

This pushed her backside higher into the air, but she sensed Fanny was enjoying the view, and James certainly didn't seem offended. He stepped forward, pressed one knee to the edge of the bed, and placed his hand on the back of her neck.

Prickles of excitement shot through her. All these years she'd dreamed of doing such things with the handsome young man who slept two doors down the hall, and now her dreams were coming true! As the O of her mouth fit over the deep red tip of him, his sigh encouraged her.

She licked him timidly. Found his little hole with the tip of her tongue.

"More," he breathed. "Don't let it frighten you."

"Oh, James, you're getting ahead of the story!" Fanny exclaimed. But she was laughing, delighted at the little game they played. " 'Indeed, the Chinese maiden pressed her lips tightly around my shaft and began to bob her head up and back, up and back until I nearly lost all rational thought.' Is that how it feels, James? Do you lose your mind when I suck you that way?"

"What? Oh—yes, Fanny, you drive me to—God almighty, woman, I'm going to—"

"Stop! Not yet!" Fanny cried.

Ophelia, sensing she should play along rather than end the story too soon, slid her lips up his shaft and released it with a kiss on its tip.

Fanny was chortling, reading ahead, most likely. " ' "And for *this* your master abandoned you, naked and tied to this post? Why, anyone passing by might take advantage of you, my dear!" '

"Oh, we're going to love this part," she added wryly. "And how do you suppose the lovely Chinese maiden responded, Ophelia? Make it good, now."

Still gazing at the stiff pink erection aimed at her face,

Ophelia heard her pulse roaring in her ears like waves crashing against the shore. She'd told herself she must remain in control of this little drama, but it was damned difficult, now that she was enacting her fantasies with a lover!

"Please, kind sir," she breathed, for she, too, had read this story, squirming in her bed when she pictured the scenes in her mind. "Please, will you look and see what seems to be so wet? Has my master left me in a puddle?"

James was behind her then, his fingers easing cautiously toward her slit. "I—I dare not overstep your master's boundaries, or enter into his private domain—"

"You dare not leave me needy," Ophelia breathed. Her teeth were clenched and so was her puss, anticipating his touch. Feeling ready to explode from the sheer excitement of it.

He chuckled then. Slipped a single finger between her nether lips to spread the pearl of honey that had pooled there.

Ophelia's breath left her in a rush. Her eyes widened, and she pressed back against his hand, begging for more.

" ' "Yes, kind sir, that's where I mean," ' " Fanny continued behind them. " ' "But I now itch where I cannot scratch, for my hands are bound to this pole. Could you find it in your heart to ease my need?" ' "

James was kneeling behind Ophelia now, his breath falling warm on her shoulders as his hand kneaded her swollen, wet flesh.

"Am I at the right spot?" he asked. "Is this where you mean? This warm, open hole I've found?"

"Rub my hair for luck, kind sir," Ophelia breathed, "and then enter my gate. Become my new master, and I will serve you well."

She held her breath. Would he follow the script? Would he play along—for both their sakes?

James cupped her mound in his warm hand, rubbing with

such fervor that hope—along with considerable pleasure—made her sigh softly. While she hadn't imagined she'd enjoy being tied to the bed, where she couldn't reach back and touch her lover, this scenario was apparently a favorite of his!

He spread her wetness again, his soft skin brushing her back now . . . his finger rimming her slit, drawing little circles that made her go dizzy.

"Please," she murmured.

"For God's sake, put it in her!" Fanny said from beside the bed. "Wrap your dog in her blanket before it gets cold!"

With a little gasp, James entered, sheathing himself until Ophelia felt his sac against her damp flesh. From where she knelt, she could see her maid's bare thighs beside her. Damned if those two weren't kissing while James slid himself in and out of her!

This was going so well! Fanny had gotten so caught up in the story she'd joined in rather than sulking in a jealous snit, fearing James no longer wanted her. Never had Ophelia anticipated *this* from her prim and proper maid!

Encouraged—getting even more aroused by the sight of Fanny's gaping legs—Ophelia thrust back in rhythm with James, letting her body take up where the story left off.

She heard their kisses grow more breathless. Fanny kept her balance by placing a hand on Ophelia's back, while James was holding her hips as though he couldn't let go.

And while she'd never in her life imagined having two other people—the maid and her husband's valet—in this solitary bed, Ophelia sensed it was the beginning of an important liaison. A triangle that bound them all together, no matter what transpired in the coming—

And James *was* coming—or close to it, the way he was rutting. He was panting with each thrust, and his balls slapped wetly against her open hole.

She squeezed him. Gripped the bedpost to hang on to her sanity. And then she gaped in amazement when a slender hand slipped down to caress her breast.

While Fanny had helped her dress and scrubbed her back when she was in the tub, *never* had this girl touched her in an intimate way!

Heat surged inside her. Ophelia felt her nerves racing toward a new wave of sensation.

And as James slammed against her, slipping a finger into the top of her keyhole, Fanny's curious fingertips teased her nipple to a sharp peak.

Ophelia's climax made the bed rattle wildly against the wall. Behind her closed eyelids, she saw fireballs. Her puss clenched, and as she felt a warm ooze inside it, she knew they'd cast themselves.

It was the finale of this act, but the beginning of a whole new play.

A short while later, Fanny went to brew some tea, and James was shaking his head at her idea.

"If I send the men these invitations, as though Henry had written them to be sent after his death, no one will come!"

Ophelia smiled. His hair was still tousled, and he looked out of place in her dainty desk chair.

"*You* came," she quipped. "Sheer curiosity will have them boarding the ship—"

"They'll smell a hoax!"

"They'll smell Yen Sin, Lady Jane, and Esmeralda—and be grateful for one last go at them!" she insisted. She wouldn't reveal the other half of her plan—not even to this secretary who would now serve her rather than Henry. "Don't forget to notify the ladies," she added cattily. "I'm sure they're wondering where their next allowances will come from."

James's expression said he was still in doubt, but he picked up his pen.

"And what would you have me say, mistress mine?" he asked in a pointed whisper. "Your wish is my command. Even though I believe you're courting disaster."

4

"There he goes, missus. Off to the office for the day."

"And here we go, as well!" Ophelia smiled at her maid, who remained at the window watching after James's carriage, looking pensive.

"It's the same as the other times Mr. Leeds and James took off—on that fine ship, we now know. But it's different, isn't it?"

Ophelia chuckled. "Well, having you tweak at my nipple last night has changed a few of my previous conceptions, yes!"

Fanny flushed. "I—I never intended to offend, or—or if I overstepped my—"

Ophelia took the fragile hands with which Fanny covered her mouth, smiling at the young woman. She was a pretty thing, in a naive sort of way, with guiless green eyes and brown hair pulled neatly into a twist.

Ophelia had a feeling that, too, was about to change. The naive part, anyway.

"Finding that book about the thousand and one knights

struck me like a bolt out of the blue. But it's given me a marvelous idea!" she said, squeezing Fanny's hands. "We're going to become part of that wild fantasy! If you can play along without breathing a word of this to James, that is."

This suddenly solemn challenge widened the girl's eyes. "Of course, missus! While I've served as your maid—"

"Ever since Henry built me this house. Nearly ten years ago."

"Yes, missus, but... begging your pardon again, if I've overstepped—" Fanny licked her lips timidly. "I always felt I was your friend, as well."

Ophelia's eyes went wet. "And what would I have done without you, Fanny? Marrying a man of means became a lonely undertaking I never anticipated—but he wouldn't want us mourning his death. We have more important things to do."

They went to the carriage house and readied the buckboard, the simplest vehicle for Fanny to drive. The two of them had enjoyed many an hour of happy chatter, while Henry assumed they were at home with their embroidery and cleaning—the very reason Ophelia suspected her husband had never hired a butler or a driver for her. He didn't *want* her out and about seeing how other wealthy wives behaved—and spent their husbands' money.

But that was behind her, wasn't it? She sat taller in the seat beside Fanny, drinking in the sunshine.

"First we'll go to the main offices of Leeds Lumber," she instructed, "and then we'll have ourselves some costumes made. Have you ever fancied yourself a harem girl, Fanny?"

Her green eyes widened. "You've really studied that book, haven't you?"

"I'm only following along with Henry's original idea... the way he entertained his influential friends. Men are so easily confused, you know."

Fanny laughed and clucked at the pair of grays pulling the

wagon. "Why do I think you've got something naughty up your sleeve, Ophelia?"

Ophelia smiled with unexpected pleasure. "I like the way my name sounds when you say it, Fanny. Please, let's drop the 'missus' and be friends in this venture. Confederates and co-conspirators."

"You make it sound so . . . enticing."

"Can't you tell James has been enjoying it?"

Fanny chuckled. "I always wondered why he came home from those 'meetings' so exhilarated. Most men would be falling over from exhaustion."

"Which is why we want him on *our* side. Without divulging our plan for those Arabian knights and their next voyage aboard the *Scheherazade*." Ophelia considered her words carefully as the grays turned down the road to the office where Henry had run his lumbering empire. "Do you recall the purpose of a harem, Fanny?"

The girl smirked. "It seems a convenient way for a man to be married—producing legitimate heirs—while having a lot of women at his beck and call. So he won't tire of the same lover, night after night."

"There's that angle, yes," Ophelia said with a chuckle. "But harems are also fortified households where the outside world never intrudes, and the sultan has absolute power over his wives. Guards at the doors, and male escorts to accompany the women's rare trips into town." She gazed around them, at the vast forested hills and the clear blue sky. "Those wives live in legendary splendor even today, but it would drive me insane, being kept so separated from the world."

Ophelia looked thoughtfully at her maid, who was drinking in this information. "It's to our advantage to keep the *protection* of a harem—and to have James as our keeper of the key. I suspect I'll be receiving several marriage proposals in the coming months."

"They just want your money."

Ophelia smiled ruefully. "Do I look like a fool to you, Fanny?"

The young woman drew the horses to a halt and gazed at her with naked admiration. "I've never known anyone as wise and kind as you, Ophelia. Not to mention quite lovely without your clothes on."

Ophelia's cheeks prickled, but she laughed. "Don't spread that around! It's a secret we're saving for our sail aboard Henry's ship."

She went on with her chat, to ascertain the depth of Fanny's allegiance, as well as to inform the girl of her secret plans.

"Do you recall the character Scheherazade? And why she told those thousand and one tales?"

Fanny grinned with uncertainty. "I confess I'm not a reader like you. Wasn't she married to a man who planned to kill her?"

"Just as he'd beheaded a thousand virgins before she dared to marry him, yes. But Scheherazade was a powerful thinker," Ophelia continued. "Not only a shrewd storyteller, but a woman with strategy!

"So, a thousand nights—and two children—later, she'd reformed her husband from his wife-killing ways. She survived by outsmarting him, Fanny. Winning him with her words."

The maid clucked to the horses as they made the next turn. "That's what you're doing here?"

"Damn right! We're keeping Henry's pleasure palace as a slice of paradise for his friends, but we're covering our backsides, too. Moving into a new future," she declared. "They believe Leeds Lumber won't be the same with a woman at its helm. They'll have all manner of ideas about how to take the reins or circumvent my authority. Or steal me blind."

She looked over at Fanny, satisfied that the young woman was following the sort of talk James, Henry, and other men would never engage them in. "It's in my best interest to play the game they already know, and then change the rules when they *have* to go along."

They turned down a narrow path leading into the massive Oregon forests, toward the camps and office of Leeds Lumber.

"Do you remember the tale about Princess Budur, whose husband disappeared in the desert?"

"Princess Budur . . ."

"It was one of the more obscure tales in Sir Richard Burton's translation of *The Arabian Nights*."

Ophelia smiled at Fanny's flummoxed expression.

"Well, you've had more exciting diversions each evening." Ophelia continued. "And while Henry was in his study or asleep, I've had time to read," she explained. "I admire Princess Budur because when she was left alone in the desert, at the mercy of men who might attack her, she survived by pretending to *be* her husband. She put on his clothes and faked her way into the next city—"

"You're going to dress like Henry?" Fanny gasped. "Begging your pardon, Ophelia, but seven camps full of lumberjacks will be able to tell—"

"No, no! I'm just telling you how Princess Budur survived by her own wits—her clever thinking! Just as Scheherazade did." Ophelia thought for a moment, trying not to lose her maid in this literary discussion. "You probably recall the clever servant girl in the story of Ali Baba, in which those forty thieves stored their loot in that cave?"

"Open, Sesame!" Fanny cried, so dramatically the horses whickered and tossed their heads.

"That's the one."

"It was one of my favorite tales as a child. And didn't the slave girl—"

"Morgiana."

234 / Melissa MacNeal

"—save her master's life by pouring hot oil into those huge vases the robbers were hiding in? So they couldn't attack him in the night?"

Ophelia smiled, patting Fanny's leg. "She was not only clever, she was loyal. Morgiana knew when to keep her own counsel—and her master's secrets."

Fanny's cry of delight told Ophelia her analogy had struck its mark. The young woman halted the horses in front of a modest timber building and then took Ophelia's hands in hers.

"You're inviting me into the game, aren't you? Someone to watch your backside and keep your secrets," Fanny breathed. "And I accept your challenge, Ophelia! You won't be sorry!"

"I knew I could count on you."

5

Ophelia gazed around the clearing they'd come into. When she noticed three other simple log buildings like the one they faced, and caught the aromas of coffee and bacon and roasted meats, she chuckled.

"We were so engrossed in our talk we took a wrong turn," she murmured. "This looks like one of the lumber camps, Fanny."

"I—I'm so sorry! I thought I knew—"

"No, no! This is opportunity knocking! Now that I own such a vast, complicated operation, I should acquaint myself with the camps and—why, I haven't met nearly everyone who works for me!" Ophelia said. "And lumberjacks would be good men to know."

Her maid's expression told her she'd just rambled in a circular sentence, much like the circuitous route they'd taken from the main road. The trilling of birds and the rapid *rat tat tat* of a woodpecker amplified a silence that made the place seem deserted.

"They must be out working," Fanny whispered, even though

no one else could hear them. "Although . . . James mentioned that they eat in silence—by decree of the cook—to keep the men from fighting and carousing during meals. 'Timber beasts,' he called them."

Timber beasts. Ophelia shivered at that phrase, but it wasn't from fear.

"Either way, we've arrived at the perfect time to see what a bunkhouse looks like," she replied quietly. "Pull the wagon over there."

When Fanny halted the grays and set the brake, the two of them clambered down from the buckboard. They were opening the door of the nearest building when a loud, low voice hailed them from behind.

"You, there! You'll get eaten alive if you set one foot inside—"

"He doesn't scare me. It's my camp now," Ophelia muttered.

So Fanny stepped in ahead of her—and let out a disgusted cry. She knocked Ophelia backward in her haste to leave.

"Lord, but it reeks to high heaven! Sorry, missus, I—"

Ophelia teetered, struggling to keep her balance, but she never hit the ground. Two arms like tree branches closed around her midsection, beneath her breasts, which left her feet dangling in the air.

Fanny had doubled over against the side of the building to retch.

It was an awkward start to a conversation with a man she hadn't met.

"As I was saying," he continued sternly, "these bunkhouses are off limits to women. So, who are you? What's your business here? If you've come in from town to sell us some, we're not buying."

Ophelia couldn't speak. She was being held *hard* against a chest that seemed as massive as one of the trees. She looked over her shoulder into a surly, unshaven face. One of the lumberjacks, obviously.

But *smart*: this fellow was waiting her out. Making her answer his question as he penetrated her with eyes as dark as the devil's heart. And he hadn't set her down yet.

"Begging your pardon," she huffed, "but I'm Ophelia Leeds, and this is my maid, Fanny. We were just looking around—"

"And I'm William McKinley, President of the United States," he replied with a smirk. "I'll just be putting you back in your wagon now, because if my men get a whiff of your—"

Ophelia kicked back at his thighs. "Put me down, dammit!"

"Mrs. Leeds? Henry's widow, are you?"

The behemoth let her slide slowly down the length of his hard body until her feet found the ground, which brought his hands over her breasts. He smiled like a tomcat toying with its dinner.

"I'm sorry for your loss, ma'am," he crooned. "But I'm saying you can't go in there because—"

"Because it reeks of sweat and—*piss*!" Fanny added with a grimace.

The Goliath's grin glimmered like a razor. "We timber beasts don't bathe as often as you fine ladies do," he agreed. "But I was warning you about the other beasts. The vermin you don't want jumping into your clothes."

The way I want you to. Ophelia turned a prickly shade of pink at that thought, for this rude, crude man was looking her over closely, even as he was trying to get rid of her.

"V—vermin?" Fanny wheezed.

"Lice, ma'am. A hazard of living amongst men who don't bathe except for the occasional Saturday night in town with women less . . . upstanding than yourselves."

"Women who work on their backs, you mean?" Fanny was all wide green eyes and open mouth. She was dabbing her lips with her handkerchief, trying not to be sick again.

Their escort snickered. "You could say that, yes."

Ophelia blinked. He knew damn well who she was, yet he was playing upon her maid's naive nature . . . playing cat and mouse with *her*. He was obviously a man who wouldn't tolerate being bossed by a woman, let alone become beholden to one.

But that didn't mean she couldn't play puss to his tomcat! Ophelia's insides quivered at such an idea . . . and this lumberjack's brazen gaze told her he was reading her mind.

Then he glanced back to the building behind them, where a stream of large, muscled men in plaid shirts and patched, suspendered pants were coming out. They wiped their mouths on their shirtsleeves, looking her direction with immediate interest.

"Back to work, boys! I'll join you shortly!" her companion called out. "No lollygagging, now! We've got to beat Number Four's challenge by tomorrow."

"Number Four?

The lumberjack grinned at her. "Each camp in this outfit has a quota of trees to fell and send to the river," he said. "As a way to keep up production, we challenge each other, camp to camp. Gets us a bonus to blow on you ladies once in a while."

Ophelia nodded, forcing herself not to watch this man talk. He looked to be seven feet tall, with arms that strained the sleeves of his red flannel shirt. While he wasn't overtly handsome—his lips were fixed in a sneer that matched his attitude—Ophelia had to rein in some rampant thoughts as she stood beside him.

He spoke with the authority of one in charge. A man she should get better acquainted with.

No sacrifice was too large, if it was for the good of her company.

"And your name is?" she queried.

"Judas Rute." He issued it as a challenge, a way to intimidate her. And to mock her further, he bowed.

Ophelia stuck out her hand. It wasn't the socially acceptable thing, for a man of Mr. Rute's position to shake hands with his boss's widow, but she'd overstepped social acceptability long ago, hadn't she?

"Pleased to meet you, Mr. Rute," she said as her hand got swallowed by his large, pleasantly rough one. "You're the boss of this crew, aren't you?"

"The bull of the woods. Yes, I am."

First it was timber beasts and now a bull of the woods. Dear God, just the phrase itself sounded arousingly male and—

Play him for all he's worth.

Ophelia flashed him a coy smile, her gaze lingering along the length of his solid body. "It's been a pleasure to meet you, sir. We've taken up enough of your time, so we'll get back to town. If we drive down that road . . ." She pointed prettily, making sure he saw the rise of her breasts in the gesture.

"Nope. Can't allow that." His large hands landed smack on her shoulders, and he turned her to face the wagon. "You *know*, of course, how a widow-maker put Henry Leeds in his grave. I can't be responsible for another one landing on *your* pretty head, can I?"

Judas made sure Fanny was following. Then he leaned over Ophelia's shoulder so she could watch those bottomless brown eyes as he made his proposition. "But I might drive you a little ways into the forest myself, if you'd like to see my men work their logs."

"Oh, that would be splendid!" Fanny piped up.

So Judas Rute, a man as brusque as his name, boosted Fanny onto the buckboard seat and then assisted Ophelia from the driver's side, so she sat between them.

She had the brief sensation of flying, high and light, when

Rute picked her up. And when he sat down beside her, his broad frame taking up half the seat, she couldn't help noticing how long his thigh was, stretched out alongside hers. And how his pants bulged over legs so muscular and thick from physical labor.

And, yes, they bulged at his buttons, too.

He smelled like fried bacon and like he'd done a day's work, yet Ophelia found Rute's scent invigorating. Very, very male.

"Are you getting along all right without your man?" he asked slyly.

Ophelia heard something sneaking in the back door of that remark, something as scintillating as the way his thigh brushed hers when the buckboard bumped down the hill. His hand slipped around her waist—to keep her from flying over the front of the wagon, of course.

"I manage," she replied with a little wheeze.

As they came to a curve in the road, she saw the vast pine forest stretching for miles around them. Heard the chopping of axes and then a cry of "Tim-berrrrr!"

Men scattered like dwarves in every direction.

A mighty *whump* shook the ground around them.

Fanny let out a little cry of delight, and when Ophelia jumped in surprise, she landed on an upturned hand—a broad, strong hand that squeezed her bottom as though it had no intention of moving!

"That tree'll be cut into sections now." Rute pointed to where they'd heard it fall, which curled his body around hers. "The fallers have done their job, so the buckers will saw the tree into sections the length of boards. Buckers and fallers—they keep this operation going."

"Fuckers and ballers," Fanny echoed in awe. The sight of men cutting branches as they stood on small platforms—which they'd driven into these mammoth trees, several feet off the ground—held her fascinated.

Rute snickered, insinuating his hand deeper beneath Ophelia's backside. "Call them whatever you want, Fanny. Your description fits as well as mine."

Ophelia tried not to giggle at the wide-eyed, oblivious expression on her maid's face—and tried not to squirm on top of this bull's busy fingers. Being squeezed between a behemoth named Judas and the young woman she'd watched in her bed last night was titillating, to say the least!

While James had made her feel quite the woman, she couldn't put Rute's clothes back on him in her mind as she imagined what his *root* must look like. Surely it was proportioned like the rest of him, long and strong and sturdy.

She glanced at his fly buttons. The thought of that thing entering her made the air rush from her lungs.

Or was it the way he'd found that sensitive nub with his fingers? Damned if Rute wasn't rubbing her there, using the friction of her clothes to send her into a frenzy she had no polite way to relieve.

Ophelia's thighs tightened. She thought she might pass out from the spasms shooting through her—and from the effort of keeping Fanny unaware of her agitated state.

Judas cleared his throat, amused by the look on her face, no doubt.

"I'll drive you back to the road now, so I can rejoin my crew."

Somehow he steered the grays into a wide turn with just his free hand. "Promise me you'll not come back into these woods—"

"I'll do no such thing!" Ophelia replied pertly. "We could've driven right down danger's path today, had you not rescued us from our wrong turn. I think I'll stop by the office and recommend a pay raise for you, Mr. Rute!"

Judas looked askance at her as they bumped up the hill. From between the wisps of brown hair hanging in disarray around his rugged face, Ophelia detected suspicion. Perhaps an ulterior motive like her own.

He pulled the horses to a halt. Jumped to the ground— lithely, for a man his size—and placed his hands at her waist to help her down. But then he held her suspended, so her face was mere inches away from his.

Was Rute going to kiss her? Right here in front of Fanny? The idea made her heart pound. Ophelia watched those chiseled lips part with a hunger he could surely read all over her flushed face.

"*Don't . . . come . . . back*," he warned. "And don't raise my pay—unless you raise everyone else's. I already earn more than these other men—"

"Because you're the boss! You take responsibility for their actions—"

"And their lives!" Fanny chirped.

"—and Erroll Barrymore would cause trouble over it. That's what butt-sucking bookkeepers do best."

All the more reason to audit the books, and do as I damn please!

Ophelia smiled up at him, looking directly into those brutally brown eyes. "We'll see about that, Mr. Rute. Thank you again for your . . . *attention*."

6

The road they'd intended to take was about a quarter of a mile from the forest, and it brought them to a modest single-story building with white plank siding. As Fanny pulled up near the door, Ophelia smoothed her dress and mentally prepared what she'd say to Erroll Barrymore.

"I'll just be a moment here, Fanny. I need to—"

"This is where James has his office, isn't it?"

"He's probably out delivering invitations to our party," she replied, to keep a lid on Fanny's romantic notions. "While you're waiting, decide what sort of exotic costume you'd like."

Ophelia gave her a little wave as she paused at the door. Her heart was hammering, for she'd only crossed this threshold into Henry's domain once, when she first became his bride. If she'd gotten the correct impression from that brief meeting with Erroll Barrymore, she was in for some backlash from the errand James was now carrying out.

As she entered the vestibule, a conversation raged in one of the offices.

"What in God's name am I to make of *this*?" a shrill voice demanded. "You can't tell me Henry wrote this note, about one final gift to be delivered after his death! Leeds lived like there was no tomorrow—"

"And he ran out of them, didn't he?"

That was James, defending those notes he'd written last night.

Ophelia remained near the outside door in case one of them came out. Emotions were running high here—just as they would aboard the ship next week.

"As Henry's personal secretary, I wrote these invitations myself, at his request. Now I've dated them and am delivering them as my final tribute to him."

Good answer, she thought with a nod. *Keep it up, James. You're an impressive young man when you're up.*

"And you think the mill managers and bankers will buy this poppycock? *Really*, James?"

The bookkeeper's questions spewed out into the area where she waited, so at least they couldn't accuse her of eavesdropping. The loggers down the road could probably hear him!

"Really, Erroll," came the unruffled reply. "It's in your sister's best interest to show up, as well. One final fling with the knights before—"

"Jane is beside herself with grief! You can't *possibly* believe she'll deck herself out like a harem whore, in the wake of Henry's passing!" Barrymore declared. "She'll smell a trap a mile away! I won't blame her for staying home!"

Ophelia's jaw dropped: the Lady Jane in the photographs— one of Henry's mistresses, who entertained aboard the *Scheherazade*—was Barrymore's sister?

Wasn't *that* interesting?

She stood closer to the door. If James caught her now, he'd never trust her again.

"Seems to me that a man on the Leeds Lumber payroll—

who lives with Henry's mistress in a house Henry built—might want to attend this gala sailing—"

"What are you not telling me, Pohl?" Erroll shot back. "It seems to *me* that the personal secretary who still sleeps in the Leeds mansion—with Henry's widow—might also arouse suspicions from—"

"Leave Ophelia out of this!"

"Oh, it's *Ophelia*, now, is it? My, my, aren't we sounding cozy?"

Ophelia gripped the doorknob to keep herself from strangling Barrymore. She hadn't liked him the first time they met—had never trusted blond men—and his visits to holiday parties at the house hadn't improved her opinion.

Judas Rute might've behaved rudely and crudely, but his description of the company's bookkeeper *fit*, didn't it?

And Erroll lived with his sister, who was one of Henry's mistresses. . . .

"Careful, Barrymore. She's found our book about the Arabian Knights and the *Scheherazade*, so I'd watch my—"

"And why in God's name did she have access to *that*?"

Ophelia held her breath, wide-eyed. Was James revealing this for a reason? If he wasn't careful . . . if he said too much . . .

"It was in her home, Erroll."

"It's still none of her damn business! My God, if . . ."

Barrymore's pause was nearly as dramatic, and damning, as his insinuations.

Ophelia's mind raced with explanations for being there. If either man came out of that office now, she was a caught cat.

"Does she know about these invitations?" Erroll demanded. There was another pause. Shorter, but still damning.

"I don't believe so," James continued smoothly. "I kept those locked in my own desk, awaiting Henry's death, as he instructed. She's been rattling around like a pea in a shoe box, which led her to look for reading material—"

"Well, then you'd by God better marry her! *Soon!* Or *I* will!" Erroll spouted. "If she's got that book, with all its accounts and—and photographs!—well, Leeds Lumber as we know it will cease to be ours!"

Ophelia's eyes widened. Erroll and James knew more about her husband's empire than anyone else, and the immediate way Barrymore had said one of them should marry her smacked of a longtime secret agenda.

And she would be an item on *no one's* agenda. Not anymore.

She opened the front door and then slammed it, walking briskly toward the office. Hoping to appear unaffected by what she'd just heard.

"Anyone here?" she called out cheerfully. "Mr. Barrymore?"

A quick shuffling of feet. The riffling of papers. Urgent whispers.

By the time she stood in the doorway, looking from James to Erroll Barrymore, who held court at the massive desk, the two conspirators had covered their tracks.

Or so they thought.

"And what brings you here, Mrs. Leeds?" Erroll sounded pleasant enough, but his voice cracked.

"It's such a lovely day, Fanny and I decided to get out of that dreary house." Her smile felt pasted on, but they returned it. "And what a nice surprise to see you here, as well, Mr. Pohl."

"The pleasure's mine, Mrs. Leeds," he said gallantly.

"And to what do we owe this rare honor?" The blond bookkeeper sat taller at the carved mahogany desk—which, Ophelia realized, had been Henry's!

Not that it mattered. She concentrated on Erroll's straw-colored hair, so perfectly slicked back from his narrow face; on how neatly pressed his white shirt and frock coat appeared. He seemed elegant and in control here in his little kingdom where the numbers lived and moved at his command. The dark circles under his eyes gave him the poetic eloquence of a tragedian.

"I've come for the company ledger," she announced, her gaze unwavering. "I'll take a day or two to acquaint myself with the Leeds Lumber accounts and then have James return it. If that will be all right with you, Mr. Barrymore."

He stood up, gripping the edge of the desk. "I see no reason for you to fret your pretty head over our accounts—"

Wrong thing to say, butt-sucker!

"—in the wake of your husband's unfortunate passing."

It was the voice of a snake oil salesman. The smile of a cat who'd like to eat the canary—but in a different way than tomcat Judas Rute wanted to devour her.

Oh, Barrymore was smooth. So dapper and courtly. So damned sympathetic.

"Thank you for your concern," Ophelia replied just as politely, "but you see, I kept records for a business when Mr. Leeds first met me, and I've kept our accounts at home. It's my responsibility—my duty to Henry's memory—to educate myself about his lumbering empire. *My* empire now."

That got him! One sandy eyebrow arched like a puma ready to pounce, and as he leaned toward her, he placed both hands on the open ledger.

To cover entries he didn't want her to see?

"I'm afraid that won't be possible, Mrs. Leeds," he insisted in a silky voice. "I'm preparing the monthly payroll for the hundreds of—"

"It's the third of August, Mr. Barrymore. Payday was the first."

Storm clouds roiled in his hazel eyes, and then James stepped toward her. "I'll bring the ledger home with me this evening, Ophelia, if—"

"What are you two trying to hide? What's in these accounts that I don't have every right to know?"

Ophelia crossed her arms, watching them. Noting the rise in their color and agitation as they glanced at each other.

"It's not that—"

"You don't understand—"

"Oh, I understand perfectly, gentlemen!" she said. "I came in the door just as Mr. Barrymore proposed that one of you should marry me immediately! To keep my husband's company under your control! And what would *you* like to confess?"

Barrymore blinked as though he were about to cry!

"Please, Mrs. Leeds," he implored, "you must understand that we who worked with Henry every day—and will remain forever grateful for that privilege!—are still shaken by his untimely—"

"Close the damn ledger and hand it over. Please and thank you!" Ophelia added in a coiled voice. "If you've been hiding nothing from my husband, you have nothing to hide from me."

She, too, placed her hands flat on the desk, which brought her face within inches of Erroll's. It was a smooth, comely face, and yet she found it repugnant. "And I *will* find you blameless, the ideal employee whose integrity shall remain intact. Correct?"

Barrymore slammed the ledger shut, a gesture reminiscent of the illustrious Barrymore family that acted onstage.

But to Ophelia it smacked of guilt. Deceit. *Butt-sucking*, Mr. Rute had called it—but Erroll wouldn't be kissing *hers*!

She held out her hands.

After a moment of strained silence, Erroll thrust the large book at her. "I can assure you, madam," he said in a sibilant whisper, "that you will find every *T* crossed and every *I* dotted—"

"I don't give a whit about your penmanship, Mr. Barrymore. It's your attitude I find so revolting."

Ophelia backed away from those brazen eyes, clutching the

ledger to her chest like a shield. Time this man found out who he was dealing with.

"I have a name, just like you do," she whispered. "What is it? What would you call me if you weren't being such a—a *sycophant*?"

Her *S's* echoed like the *hisssss* of a vicious cat.

"Ophelia," he murmured. "Ophelia Leeds."

"Damn right, I lead!" she replied. "Any questions?"

No response. Just that dramatic stare.

James stood in silence, knowing better than to take sides.

"Let me make this clear before I leave," she said in a low voice, looking from one man to the other. "Your days of keeping secrets for Henry Leeds are over. From here on out, your main concern should be pleasing Ophelia!"

Ophelia left with the ledger then, her footsteps tapping an angry tattoo on the vestibule floor. Her emotions whirled like a hurricane, but she composed her face so Fanny wouldn't suspect what she'd overheard. Things she could entrust to no one until she'd sorted them out.

Luckily her maid was daydreaming in the driver's seat. Fanny jumped, startled, when Ophelia stuck the ledger under the seat and then hoisted herself into the buckboard.

"Finished already?" she asked brightly. "Get what you went in for?"

Ophelia drew a deep breath of the crisp morning air to get herself under control. "More than I expected, yes."

"Are you all right, missus?" Fanny grabbed her hands—with the same fingers that had fondled her breast last night. This recollection helped Ophelia relax, and it relieved some anxiety about what she'd just heard in Henry's office.

Her office now.

"Sometimes we learn more than we want to know, Fanny," she said quietly. "But knowledge is power. Forewarned is forearmed, I say."

"A little learning is a dangerous thing?"

Ophelia smiled to erase the line between Fanny's pretty green eyes.

Dangerous. Yes, Erroll Barrymore, I can be very, very dangerous.

"Let's head into town for those new costumes now!" she said brightly. "Life's a masquerade, Fanny. If we're to be players in the *Scheherazade's* ongoing story, we'd better look the part!"

"Now you're talking!" the maid said, taking up the reins. "But when we get to town—before we make important decisions about costumes—maybe we should enjoy a hot meal and some strong tea. I'll make a more clever Morgiana with my wits sharpened. How about you, Ophelia?"

She heard the girl's hint loud and clear. "You're a good friend and a faithful servant, Fanny. Thanks for watching out for me."

Later that evening Ophelia sat up late, scanning ledger entries.

"Ah, here you are, ladies," she murmured. "What's the going rate for a mistress these days?"

She didn't want to believe the cost for two lodgings: a modest apartment for Yen Sin, and maintenance on a house Henry had built in a highly desirable neighborhood for Jane Barrymore.

Which meant Erroll lived in finer style than the average accountant.

And there were clothing bills for Jane, too. Not so many of those for her husband's ornamental Chinese whore—for Ophelia fully understood the function these ladies served in the life of lumber magnate Henry Leeds.

She left the ledger open and fetched the *Arabian Knights* book from her bedside table. Such reading material she had these days!

Once again she studied the photograph of the three lovelies who entertained aboard the *Scheherazade*: Lady Jane, the dignified blonde; almond-eyed Yen Sin with her midnight braid; and Esmeralda, the red-haired gypsy in her bangles and flowing clothes. The print was tinted with water colors, which told her Henry had prized this memento above the other, more basic photographs. A shot of his favorite tangible assets, as he probably saw it.

In the *Knights* book, her husband had used the ladies' initials to denote special moments he'd spent with them or had watched them perform with his friends. And yet . . . nowhere did she see ledger entries for Esmeralda.

Was the gypsy character a woman of independent means? Seeking adventure and sex with all those men rather than looking for Henry's money?

Ophelia peered more closely at the photograph and then blinked. Esmeralda was wearing so many bracelets and such outrageous dangling earrings, she hadn't noticed it before: a dainty watch pinned to the bodice of the gypsy's embroidered blouse.

Dazed, Ophelia went to the jewelry box atop her vanity and pulled out an identical watch. She sighed sadly. The timepiece had been one of her favorite trinkets, ever since Henry surprised her with it for no apparent reason—which wasn't like him.

So he bought two at the same time. An easy way to delight me while giving his gypsy slave girl a keepsake, too.

Suddenly disgusted—it was her own damn fault, looking for dirt and then finding it—Ophelia rose from her desk. No more gazing at those fake sheiks in their caftans and turbans and jeweled vests! What she needed was sleep.

As Ophelia crept into bed, however, a wisp of diaphanous fabric caught her eye: a remnant left after Mrs. Mulhany had sewn her harem pants and blouse. She stood up and held it in front of her face like a veil, gazing into her mirror. The ensemble would be so revealing she would have *no* secrets from the men on board when she danced—

The door flew open, and James entered. He raked his hair,

warning her of his foul mood, but she was in a fine uproar herself.

"And good evening to you, too," she said, pulling her robe closed. She quickly dropped the fabric, as it was part of the secret she and Fanny were keeping for the party.

"And what was *that* all about?"

"Which 'that' are we talking about? My visit to Mr. Barrymore's—"

"We'll start there, yes!" he fumed. "Why would you need the ledger? To accuse Erroll of hiding accounts or—"

"Oh no, no. The transactions I was looking for were in plain sight," she replied calmly. "They were just coded differently and kept in the back, behind the new blank pages. Not that I call that 'hiding' anything."

James was breathing heavily, as though he'd taken the stairs too fast.

"No, *you*, Ophelia!" he blurted, pointing at her. "What were *you* hiding? It was one thing to take Erroll's ledger and to all but accuse him of crooked bookkeeping! But when you burst in on us—"

"Is there a law against entering my own business?"

"—smelling of sweat and—and *sex*! With your dress rumpled and your hair mussed, as though you'd been—"

"Oooh, we sound jealous, James. Got our feathers ruffled, did we?"

His face reddened. "You'd better watch your reputation, Mrs. Leeds! Riding out among the . . ."

Ophelia scowled, stepping closer to him. "We were on a perfectly proper outing, Fanny and I. And while we were on our way to see Mr. Barrymore, I decided to visit one of my lumbering camps."

She glared, daring him to find fault. No need to admit they'd made a wrong turn that turned out to be so . . . fortuitous.

"You're not saying some lumberjack had the nerve to paw at you and—"

"No, it was a bull. Judas Rute, the bull of the woods."

Even as she said it, Ophelia couldn't help smiling at the way that phrase rolled so boldly off her tongue—and the way it so accurately described the beast himself.

"Rute? He had his filthy hands on you?"

Ophelia shrugged. "He does a dirty job, so his hands—"

"Have no business being on *you*! Why on God's earth . . . When I get hold of Fanny for allowing you—"

"Invite Mr. Rute to the *Scheherazade* party next week, James."

The young man's jaw dropped. "The knights don't share their—that ship wasn't intended for employees who work in—"

"But *you* attend," she pointed out. "And so does Erroll and . . ."

To make her point, she flipped the pages of the leather-bound *Knights* book to where Henry had listed his men. Bankers, lawyers, railroad tycoons—men whose hands were as immaculately manicured as the ones James gestured with.

"What is this party about, Ophelia?"

She smiled with a delight she didn't intend to share. "While you're at it—since we have seven logging camps—it's only fair to invite all seven bulls of the woods—"

"*Ophelia!*"

"Yes, dear?"

His tousled curls shimmied with his attempt to control his temper. "Answer me! If you're going to pull another ridiculous stunt aboard the *Scheherazade* like you did today—"

"I guess you'll just have to come and find out." She let her robe slither down over her shoulders, taunting him with her bare body. "Or perhaps that should be 'find out, and *come*.' And whatever it takes, James—whatever you have to do—Judas Rute will be there."

Ophelia cupped her breasts toward him, smiling. "Good night, dear."

Oh, it had given her a moment's satisfaction, letting James Pohl fill in the blanks about what Judas Rute had done to her. But in the wee hours, when the house lay as still as a tomb, Ophelia rose from her lonely bed. She lit a candle and lifted that remnant of organza, to stand again in front of her mirror.

Ophelia recalled the heat of Rute's hand under her backside, the *need* in his dark eyes . . . although it was a need to dominate her, and she wouldn't allow that. But if Rute played his cards right—if he set aside his aversion to working for a woman—she would make it worth his while.

She swayed before the mirror, watching the fabric shimmer in the candlelight, making her body appear mysterious. Goddess-like. The bob of her breasts fascinated her, as did that black triangle of curls—not something she'd gazed at before.

Yet men couldn't resist that patch of thatch. There always came a point when—even if the woman didn't appeal to him—a man could be reduced to begging for just a whiff of her sex, as long as he believed he'd soon get something more substantial from her.

Ophelia draped the sheer fabric over her head like a bridal veil so both her hands were free . . . hands that went to her breasts and followed the curve beneath them to her belly.

How would Judas Rute touch her here? Would he be all brute force and masculine demand? Or did he have a gentler side he wasn't showing?

She doubted it. Nothing about Rute appeared gentle! And as her mind wandered again to that bulge where his pants buttoned, her fingers wandered into her muff to explore—

"Ophelia! I—I—"

In the glass she saw Fanny standing behind her. The maid's eyes widened.

"I couldn't sleep, either," she confessed. "All I could think of was the way Judas Rute was looking at you—groping at you!—while we rode through the lumber camp." Fanny fanned herself playfully with her hand. "My God, Ophelia, I don't know how you sat through it! Once I realized what he was doing . . ."

Ophelia didn't know whether to cuss or cry! Silly, to think her maid hadn't felt the tremors that had shaken her body like an earthquake.

"Be honest," she said, holding Fanny's gaze in the glass. "When I went into the office today, did I smell of sweat and . . . sex? Was my hair mussed or . . ."

Fanny's brow puckered. "No more mussed than it would've been from a ride without your hat on."

"I don't wear hats. They annoy me."

"I know. But James sees that as a sign of . . . questionable breeding."

"Breeding? That's what he'd *like*! Give a man a sample of your puss, and he thinks he owns it!" She snickered at the expression on Fanny's face. "But I didn't smell of sex or . . ."

Her maid shrugged, approaching in a trancelike manner. "You were ripe and feisty, missus. And no wonder, with Judas Rute fingering your . . . slit."

Her gaze went to that part of Ophelia in the mirror.

"You're going to be so fetching in your harem costume," she whispered. "While Mrs. Mulhany was measuring you, draping you with those gorgeous silks and organzas, I could imagine you dancing! Floating light and free, like a fairy on the deck of the ship, while all the men adored you. Is that what you have in mind, Ophelia?"

Ophelia swallowed hard. Fanny was removing her nightgown as though it were an everyday thing to strip naked and stand so close to another woman who wore no clothes.

"Fanny."

The girl blinked. She came out of her trance but was now kneeling, coaxing Ophelia to face her, so they were both profiled in the mirror.

"Why do you suppose Judas Rute's mother gave him such a vile name?" she asked in a little-girl voice. "Of all the possible names to choose . . ."

"I wondered that myself. But I didn't get a chance to ask him."

Fanny snickered. "What you really wanted to ask was 'Please, Mr. Rute—Mr. *Brute*!—would you stick your finger up my cunt and make me come all over it? Would you throw my dress up over my head—yank down my drawers and *take* me, right here in front of all these men?'"

"Fanny!"

Ophelia's protest wasn't as loud as it had been moments ago. Her maid's voice had softened, too, to insinuate itself into . . . the wet crevice the girl now tested with her fingertip.

And while it fascinated Ophelia to watch that slim finger—now two of them—flicker in and out of her curls, teasing her nether lips, she turned away out of some inner sense of decency—

Only to discover that their reflection in the mirror made a more fetching image—a more heated vision—of this illicit act than watching it straight on.

When Fanny blew her warm breath on Ophelia's thighs, she parted her legs.

And when the maid's hand slipped between her outer lips and began to rub her damp, delicate skin, Ophelia raged with an inner heat she hadn't anticipated.

"Do—do you suppose Judas Rute has a lady friend?" Ophelia mumbled, more for speculation than for an answer. More to focus her randy thoughts elsewhere, so she wouldn't admit how aroused she felt.

"Not that he'd tell you about," Fanny replied in a faraway voice. "Men keep their little secrets. Have you noticed that?"

Oh, the things she could tell this girl! The vows broken, and the social orders upended. Much like she would be, if this maddening massage went on.

"Fanny—"

"Ophelia, may I taste you?" she breathed. "Would you think me indecent if I wanted to watch Judas run his tongue up you? I bet he has an absolutely wicked tongue!"

And I certainly intend to find out, Ophelia mused.

But her thoughts were spinning in loose circles that might make her dizzy, if Fanny kept up her fingering and these improper remarks.

The first spasm took her by surprise. And when the air hissed between her clenched teeth, Fanny moved in, sticking out her pointy tongue and wiggling it.

Ophelia bit her lip, staring at the mirror. Anticipating that moment of hot contact, the sinfully delicious sensation of that warm, hard tongue . . .

"Jesus, Fanny! *Fanny!*" she cried, and then covered her mouth.

The maid flashed her a wet, feline smile. She rose from her knees to coax Ophelia backward, onto the rumpled bed, giggling and squirming—but Ophelia certainly didn't close her legs or swat Fanny's face.

Ah, the throbbing! The searing heat of that tongue on her nub—a tongue that knew what it was doing and then did it some more! Ophelia arched, shamelessly thrusting her hips into the girl's face, invited by Fanny's whimpers of need to serve her this way.

When she gave herself over to it, allowed her body to convulse as she grimaced with the pleasure that gripped her body, it seemed Fanny had become the older and wiser of them. Or at least the more seasoned.

"James says the men don't always hump those three ladies on the *Scheherazade*," she whispered. "He says they go even crazier watching the girls excite each other. Just like we've done here." Fanny paused, her eyes aglow in the candlelight. "If that's what you think we should do to make your point—"

"Oh, plenty of 'points' will be made that night," Ophelia murmured.

"—then I'll be pleased to help in whatever way you need me."

Still groggy, Ophelia raised her head from the mattress. "Fanny, dear, between the two of us, we'll get those men's attention—"

The door opened. James stopped in the doorway, staring at the two of them naked on the bed.

"Fanny, I went—Ophelia, my Lord, I had no idea—"

"Don't stand there stammering, James. It doesn't become you." The maid raised up to look at him, with a hand on her bare hip and her pert breasts protruding proudly. "And hear *this*," Fanny added archly. "If you don't arrange everything exactly the way Ophelia wants it next week, you won't be bedding me for a long, *looooong* time."

James stared as though he might be losing his mind. "I can't believe what I've seen and heard today. First the—"

"Good night, James!" Fanny said with a little wave.

"Good night, James!" Ophelia echoed. "Better luck next time—next week aboard the ship, if you give me what I've asked for!"

8

The *Scheherazade*! She floated high and light, a graceful lady among the ponderous lumbering ships that bobbed in the harbor. Her sails fluttered like mysterious harem veils by the light of the full moon. And, like the legendary storyteller she was named for, this beautiful four-masted schooner could tell a thousand tales.

Ophelia intended to listen carefully, to watch the guests Henry had held in esteem as they cavorted with his three mistresses. Then she would begin her own story, with a different focus—from a new point of view!

"Come along, ladies," James said. He looked around them in the dusk for anyone observing them as they scurried across the pier. "We'll get you on board and into the master cabin before the crew gets nosy. From there, you can watch the festivities and reveal yourselves when you're ready."

Ophelia nodded, wishing they didn't have to hurry past the masts where those tall sails shimmered in the night breeze. Sconces were lit, making the deck nearly as bright as day—except the candle glow lent a more romantic aura to the riggings, ropes, and other equipment arranged neatly around the main deck.

Fanny was behind her, gaping at the wonders they passed. Brass fittings glimmered in the moonlight, accenting panels carved with a crescent moon, stars, and magic lamps—designs echoed in the leaded stained-glass windows. When James ushered them down the polished staircase, the maid sighed.

"Oh, Ophelia! I never dreamed . . . Look at this glorious glossy woodwork!" she whispered. "Not a fingerprint anywhere! Why, it's every bit as beautiful as the staircases and paneling at home!"

"And more costly," Ophelia remarked. "According to the ledger, Henry imported primavera wood from South America, as well as Philippine mahogany and redwood from California. I—I—"

She stopped, gazing around the huge room they'd entered. It was far larger than any in her own home. Because temperatures remained chilly well into the Puget Sound summer, dear, practical Henry had embellished his ship's interior as though he'd be entertaining royalty. And, considering the caliphs, sultans, and sheiks in his photographs, that's exactly who he'd welcomed here. It may have been an elaborate game, but they played it seriously.

And Ophelia intended to get a good look at these men from her hidden vantage point, too—while she polished what she'd say to them. She could get by with a few minor mistakes as Mrs. Leeds, the grieving widow. But if anything utterly stupid came out of her mouth, her lumber company would be affected forever.

Past long tables they strode, hard-pressed to keep up with James, even though he was toting their valises. She and Fanny were swaddled neck-to-foot in Henry's heavy plaid robes, wearing his large hats to cover their hair. Ophelia could take no chance of being spotted before she put on her costume.

Huge gilt-framed mirrors reflected the crystal chandeliers, and the windows were intricate stained-glass tableaux reminiscent of ancient cathedrals. Daylight could come in, but prying eyes wouldn't see much.

After all, this *had* been Henry's sanctuary, hadn't it?

Through a side hallway they went and then up a narrow flight of steps.

"Here we are, ladies. The master cabin," James announced as he unlocked the carved double doors. "Several other guest cabins are arranged below the grand ballroom, but this was Henry's suite. I've been here only once or twice myself."

Ophelia was at a rare loss for words. This master cabin was the hub of Henry's other life . . . a world he'd never invited her to share. Part of her wanted to ignore the sumptuous surroundings: the green velvet comforter on a four-poster of glossy mahogany, a chandelier of alabaster with crystal prisms, a bathroom with a large claw-foot tub and taps for hot and cold running water, and a linen closet that rivaled her own.

But another part of her longed to linger over every luxurious detail—not because she had lacked for any tangible thing during her marriage, but because each choice of color and finish and function would reveal habits of the Henry Leeds she never got to know.

Her husband hadn't lacked for anything while aboard his *Scheherazade*, either. As she gazed around his quarters, Ophelia realized that the accounts he'd written of his days and nights here didn't do his ship justice.

"And here's your view of the rest of our world," James remarked, gesturing at a pair of windows about a yard long and only six inches high. "Lock the door after me. I'll return after I check in with the chef and the orchestra conductor."

Fanny waited for the door to shut. "Chef? Orchestra conductor?" she exclaimed. "My God, Ophelia, it's like living at the opera house!"

They stood at those beveled rectangular windows, peering out over the huge room they'd walked through moments ago.

"I—I'm sorry if my excitement seems misplaced," the girl murmured, running her fingers over the woodwork in awe. "It must be terribly upsetting to learn your husband had three mistresses—and that he entertained them aboard this spectacular ship."

Ophelia smiled sadly. "Yes, I was angry at first. But now that I've reflected upon that *Arabian Knights* book, I understand why Henry built the *Scheherazade*. And why he acquired three other women while he kept me sequestered at home. He'd already done me the greater favor of marrying me, you see. . . . But we've plenty of time to discuss such things, Fanny!" she said with a bright smile. "Off with your clothes! Let's transform ourselves into harem goddesses before James gets back!"

From the valises they pulled yards and yards of folded fabric Mrs. Mulhany had transformed into gossamer veils, airy harem pants, and beaded shirts that tied beneath their breasts.

"I'm nervous," Fanny breathed as she stepped into the wide-legged pants. "Holy mother of God, Ophelia! *Everything* shows through these clothes! I've never—"

"That's the idea," Ophelia teased, but in truth she was just as anxious as her maid. "By displaying ourselves so bawdily—and bodily—we'll distract our guests from who we are and what we're announcing to them. They'll figure it out, but by then we'll be in total control of the situation."

Total control. What a concept *that* was, for two disguised women aboard a ship full of men!

"I like the sound of that," Fanny replied. She smiled as she tied on her veil. "Is this the effect you wanted, Ophelia? Will I pass muster?"

Ophelia turned and let out a low *ohhhhhhh*. Her maid was a comely girl, even in her modest gray uniform. But wearing these shimmering clothes, which flowed with every gesture and draped gracefully over every endowment, Fanny Gault was going to turn heads.

And make points. Lots of points!

"Look in the mirror!" Ophelia said, beckoning with a hand that jangled seductively. Mrs. Mulhany had sewn tiny bells to the edges of their sleeves and pants, so their every move was accompanied by celestial music.

"We're going to tie this tighter." Ophelia tugged the bottom edges of Fanny's shirt taut around her body, so her breasts looked bigger. "And slip this sash lower," she added, baring another couple inches of silky midriff. "And every harem girl needs a ruby in her navel and shiny gold hoops dangling from her ears. And there you are! Mistress Irresistible!"

"Oh, my," the maid murmured. "Mama would faint dead away if—"

"Which is why we didn't invite her!"

Ophelia checked her own clothing, securing the luminous veil just below her eyes. She fastened ribbon roses in her hair and then assessed the results.

"Stuff them in your shirt," Fanny teased. "*That* will make them stare!"

Ophelia laughed. "I'll need more alluring distractions than fake flowers if I trip over my tongue tonight. The invitations James sent have aroused enough doubts about the future of Leeds Lumber, without *me* adding to them."

Fanny stood before her, solemnly adjusting the drape of her veil. Then she stopped. Gazed at Ophelia with a raw hunger that set them both on edge.

"You have the most beautiful blue eyes, Ophelia," the maid breathed. "One look at you and those men won't *care* what you said about the company. If they can even recall the name of it."

Ophelia's mouth fell open. All she could hear was her pounding pulse.

"Thank you," she breathed. "No one has ever—"

There was a rapping at the door. "It's James, ladies. How are we doing?"

They watched the doorknob rotate, holding their breath. While Ophelia knew this was her company at stake tonight—her company, no matter what happened—she also valued James Pohl's opinions. His reaction now could well determine how . . . persuasive she would be.

He stuck his head in. Stared in silence, his eyes widening.

From below they heard the orchestra tuning and the clinking of silver serving dishes being set on buffet tables. And men's voices. *Dozens* of men, by the sound of it.

There was no backing out now.

"While I've never seen a more fetching sight," James breathed, "I must warn you that the men will consider these costumes an invitation to play . . . by their own rules. Perhaps you'd better—"

"By the way," Ophelia piped up; James was *not* going to rain on her games before they even started! "Where's Judas Rute?"

James rolled his eyes, glancing behind him. "Where do you want him? He turned down your invitation, so we had to . . . chemically convince him to come tonight."

From behind him came three burly men—lumberjacks, Ophelia was guessing—who carried a rolled-up carpet between them, followed by three more timber beasts bringing up the other end.

Ophelia saw rumpled brown hair hanging from the front of that roll and boots dangling out the other end. "What on God's earth? What have you . . . I wanted him *alive*!"

"Oh, he'll perk up, ma'am," the closest fellow said. He was tall and stocky, his eyes traveling a wild, weaving circuit from her assets to Fanny's. "We had to shanghai him, is all."

"Shanghai?"

"Yup!" a barrel-chested fellow at the rear chimed in. "Few

dropsa chloral hydrate in his beer, and ole Judas won't be bossin' us for a good long while!"

"Lay him over there on the bed," James instructed. "Put a basin by his head, in case he—"

"I don't believe this," Ophelia breathed. "I make a simple request and—"

"One, two, three, *pull*!" the first lumberjack cried, and the six of them, lined up along one edge of the carpet, yanked mightily.

Out rolled Rute, flopping like a rag doll, to sprawl on Henry's bed.

"Well, now we can say we done pulled the rug out from under ole Jude!" the shortest fellow crowed. "Take 'im a while to live *this* one down!"

"Maybe we'd best not remind him," James suggested from the door. He was pulling a roll of greenbacks from his pocket, gesturing for them to leave. As they rolled up the rug and toted it between them, each man favored Ophelia and Fanny with long, lustful looks.

"Man, oh man, Rute's gonna be real pissed that he missed *this* shindig!"

"We'll have to be sure we eats an' drinks enough for his share, too!"

They filed out then, nodding their thanks as James handed them each some money. Then he turned to give Ophelia one last look.

"Your bulls of the woods, madam," he announced. "Bulls in the china closet, more likely—and they've gotten a snootful of *you* now. Let's hope they behave themselves tonight."

9

"Lord, but he stinks! Those clothes have to go!"

Ophelia peered at the Goliath on Henry's bed, noting the sawdust caked in his hair and in the bristle of his unshaven face. He smelled of liquor and sweat, with a hint of cheap perfume around his collar.

"I'm betting they were in town carousing, and the other bulls—paid well for this little job—took their Saturday baths before they knocked out Judas."

"We've got to get those awful clothes off him! They'll ruin that velvet coverlet," Fanny said.

So, between them, they untied his leaden boots and peeled down socks with dirty holes in their heels.

"Shirt next," Ophelia suggested. So they flopped Judas onto his back to undo the buttons.

"You're just saving the best for last," Fanny teased. She grimaced when they lifted away the grimy, offensive chambray.

"This part's not so bad," Ophelia remarked, ruffling the downy curls that covered his chest. "What a difference it makes to study the beast out of his natural habitat—"

"And out of his head, poor dear."

Fanny ran a finger from his temple along the square line of his jaw and strong chin. "In his way, he resembles a rougher, tougher version of James, wouldn't you say? Clean him up, and cut his hair, put him in a suit and shirt, and you'd have yourself quite a man."

Oh, he's quite a man in his natural state, Ophelia mused, watching the rise and fall of his broad, brawny chest. "Well, onward and downward. Beware of what jumps out when you unfasten his fly, Fanny!"

"Oh, *you* get to do the honors, missus! This was all your idea."

Gingerly, as though something might leap out at her, Ophelia struggled with his buttons and then tugged his encrusted denim pants past his hips . . .

"Mother of God, he's not wearing underwear!" Fanny cried.

"Makes everything a lot simpler." Ophelia chuckled at her maid's modesty. "Frankly, I hadn't noticed the lack of long handles for looking at *that* beast!"

Indeed, Judas Rute had a cock that inspired wicked, wayward fantasies even as it dozed between his muscular legs. His sac looked bigger than her hand could hold, lightly furred with down.

"Well," she breathed, "we'd best get on with it—off with these—or we'll be mooning over him all night."

Fanny laughed nervously. "Might not be a bad idea, Ophelia. It sounds like the orchestra is inspiring quite a stage show, from the way those men are hooting and hollering down there."

Ophelia lifted her head to listen and then went to the rectangular windows, which were opened at the bottom.

"What a sight," she sighed. "And to think Henry always entertained his friends this way, yet behaved like such a recluse at home."

"Resting up for the next voyage, no doubt." Fanny took

Rute's smelly clothes to the bathroom and shut the door on them. Then she stood beside Ophelia, watching the activities with a shine in her eyes. "And it seems our guests are doing his memory proud."

Ophelia nodded, trying hard to take it all in. The buffet tables offered up roasted chicken and chilled shrimp and raw oysters, along with platters of beefsteak and sliced ham and all manner of sauces and side dishes.

And cakes, decorated exquisitely. And puddings and trifles and pies—Lord, the pies! Those sheiks and sultans were piling their plates high, their jewels twinkling like multicolored stars in this universe she'd never before glimpsed.

A bartender and his assistant moved quickly behind the long mahogany bar, which was carved with Moorish arches. Like the rest of the room, it was ornamented with moon and star designs inspired by the Far East.

And, true to their promise, those bulls of the woods were doing Judas proud: all six carried a plate in each hand, exclaiming over the delights to be found on the next tray and bowl they got to.

"Does my heart good to see those fellows indulging themselves," Ophelia remarked quietly. "They work very hard, with their lives on the line every day, making the lumber that makes the money those costumed men only spend and invest."

"They seem reluctant to mingle with our timber beasts," Fanny remarked.

"Yes, well, that might change. A *lot* of things might change before the night's over, and we'd best get to it."

They were turning from the windows when an orchestral fanfare brought them back. A knight in a shimmering caftan of gold and aqua stripes, wearing an elaborate jeweled turban, stepped up on the dais.

"Good evening, Arabian knights!" he cried.

"Good evening to you, Aladdin!" they replied in chorus.

"That's James," Fanny whispered, her fingers fluttering to her veiled face.

"Shhh! We don't want to miss a word of this!"

James, who made a very stunning Aladdin, gazed around the huge room. The crowd of probably fifty men had turned to listen to him.

"It is a sad occasion to meet here without our Henry, and we will *so* miss our Sinbad—"

"Hear! Hear!" several men cried as they raised their glasses.

"—but we celebrate his life and achievements tonight. And he would want us to do that in the fine, high manner to which we've become accustomed!"

Several chuckles and nods brought a tear to Ophelia's eye. Henry *had* treated people well, at least where spending his money was concerned.

"I'm sure you all have questions about those mysterious invitations you received, and they'll be answered in due time!" he continued. "For now, however, I encourage you to enjoy the company of Lady Jane, Yen Sin, and Esmeralda, who will perform a harem dance for your enjoyment!"

Applause filled the room as three scantily clad ladies strutted to the small stage beside the orchestra. The music turned mystical, like reedy snake-charmer songs, accented by the finger cymbals the three lovelies wore.

"Let's see," Fanny mused, focusing on the performance. "The blonde with the jeweled headpiece and veil, wearing the purple tunic, must be—"

"Lady Jane Barrymore. Who just happens to be Erroll's sister."

"*Really*?" her maid replied with a catty lift in her voice. "And the Chinese woman behind her, wearing that gorgeous crimson kimono, must be the Yen Sin who was in that story I read the other night."

"The very one. Far lovelier than her photograph, too."

Indeed, the Celestial's moves flowed with the twists and rhythms of the music, despite the way her kimono was wrapped tightly around her body, until she gave its wide sash a yank. All that gilt-shot silk drifted from her limbs into a puddle on the stage.

The men clapped and called out raucously, obviously enjoying the girl—and their liquor.

Not to be outshone, here came Esmeralda the gypsy dancer, her full skirts and gold necklaces and wavy red hair whirling around her as she twirled on her toes, playing her tambourine in time to the music.

"I bet she colors her hair with henna," Fanny remarked. "You can't tell me that's her natural shade."

"One way to find out," Ophelia teased, ruffling Fanny's muff.

The maid laughed, playfully slapping away her hand. "I don't intend to go looking, do you? Too many fine, fine men in that room to lift a gypsy's skirts."

Nodding, Ophelia watched the three ladies cavort suggestively around each other, a spectacle of grace and motion and color that left her speechless. As the show progressed, Lady Jane's tunic came off, which left her clad in a beaded breast band that matched Yen Sin's; they both wore wide, sheer harem pants that flared away from their legs as they whirled and danced.

As a finale to the song, those two ladies began stripping away Esmeralda's gypsy attire until she, too, wore only the beaded breast band and harem pants.

As they took their bows, the applause vibrated the rectangular windows Ophelia and Fanny were peering through.

"And now our first contest of the evening!" Lady Jane called out in a theatrical voice. "Get cocked, gentlemen, as we're conducting a very special shooting match!"

As she spoke, Esmeralda was tying Yen Sin's wrists with a flourish of leather string. The Celestial let out a mock howl as the gypsy dancer sat her on the edge of the stage and leaned her back. Esmeralda then grabbed the girl's ankles, which opened her pussy wide in front of all those admiring men.

"The object of our game," Lady Jane went on, "is to stand at the line in front of the stage and fire your wads at the target! I'll be the judge of whose cum comes closest to Yen Sin's hole, and we'll declare him the winner. Five at a time, gentlemen! Line 'em up—and of course you must pay to play."

Ophelia glanced at Fanny, whose jaw had dropped nearly to her chest.

"Now we know why we've not been invited to these evenings of fun and frolic," Ophelia murmured. "Boys will be boys. Always flashing themselves to declare the biggest and best. Or, in this case, the most accurate aim for the distance."

"My God, look at the money they're stuffing into that jar."

"And here we go, gentlemen! Round one!" Jane called out. Then she lowered her voice to a more sultry patter for the five men standing at the line, lifting their caftans to stroke themselves.

"Just think about that hot, open hole, waiting for your magnificent cock to fill it . . . wrapping its warm wetness around your girth. Squeezing you . . . *teasing* you, until you just can't hold it . . ."

Meanwhile, Yen Sin was wiggling against her bound wrists and the hold Esmeralda had on her ankles. She whimpered to encourage the contestants.

And they were responding boldly, egged on by the men around them as they worked themselves into full frenzy. Their jewels winked. The tassels on their fezzes swayed crazily as they grunted and stroked, gazing at that pussy edged with enticing black fringe.

"Oh, you're so ready . . . so damn full of hot cum that when you shoot at her cunt, it's going to splatter and coat those pink petals. She's going to moan and writhe with the force of your—"

Yen Sin let out a low wail. She began to rock in rhythm to the suggestive music, which was also setting the pace for the contestants' strokes.

The men began to grimace and shudder, gripping their cocks, now red and straining for release. A wild cry rang out, and a spurt of cream flew toward the stage.

Lady Jane leaned closer to watch.

"Yes, oh, yessss," she taunted them. "Shoot it all over her hole! Fill her with your hot cum and—"

The room rang with a cacophony of cries like wild mating birds or coyotes calling in the night. The contestants spent themselves dramatically, each one watching the stream of his semen as best he could.

Ophelia rolled her eyes. For all their intensity, only two of the five had hit Yen Sin's bare backside.

"Nice show, gentlemen! Doyle, you and Max Madison came the closest," Jane called out. "Replenish yourselves, in case we need a rematch at the end. Next! Five more contestants, please!"

"It seems we have some time," Ophelia murmured. She glanced back to see if Judas had moved. "I'd much rather study Rute—and his root—than watch any more of this contest, so please tell me when they play their final round."

Fanny nodded, giggling. "I'm waiting to see if James competes. He won't want to show them all up with his marksmanship, so he's probably going last."

Already caught up in her study of the behemoth on the bed, Ophelia just nodded. Rute stretched the full length of the mattress. Now that his clothes had been removed from the room, he was much more pleasant to be around.

Carefully she leaned over to stare into his face.

He was out like death itself. Only the steady rise and fall of his chest showed he was alive.

274 / Melissa MacNeal

From this angle, this close, Rute lost the look of the timber beast and resembled . . . perhaps a fallen angel, with that wicked tilt to his lips. It was less of a sneer than she'd seen the other day, and his lashes were longer than she'd expected. Bronzed by the sun and leathered from years in the wind, his face—even with that brown bristle around its edges—was one Ophelia wanted to gaze at endlessly.

Tenderly she brushed the sawdust from his hair, delighting in its surprising softness. She was sorry he'd been drugged and dragged across a barroom floor after refusing her invitation. Ophelia leaned down and kissed him, square on those lips. Might be the only chance she ever got.

"Ophelia! It's the final round and—"

Ophelia went to the slender windows again and gazed toward the stage, where the winners of the previous rounds were priming themselves for a . . . shoot-out. A few of them looked to be in their forties, so a second coming might be a miracle for them!

"Yen Sin's back must be terribly sore by now."

"And look at her . . . well, her *crotch*," Fanny breathed. "I certainly wouldn't want to be lying there, held open, still dripping from the three previous rounds of this asinine game."

Lady Jane was beginning her patter, urging on the finalists to glory.

"You know you want her, big boy," she crooned. "You know how hot and tight and sweet that young cunt would feel wrapped around your cock . . . sucking and milking and squeezing it like she couldn't help herself! Look at her, gentlemen, lush and pink and oh, so lovely. All you have to do is hit the spot. . . . Come on now, boys, pump it up, hard and fast, now. . . ."

"If you were the betting type, who would your money be on, Ophelia?"

An interesting question. Perhaps a worthwhile thing to ponder, as she might be working with those finalists in some capacity.

If she recalled correctly from their holiday parties, Doyle O'Toole was the company's banker, Max Madison was the lawyer, and two of the others captained ships in the fleet. Those six bulls of the woods—easy to spot because they wore denim, rather than Arabian apparel—stood back a ways. As though they considered this contest a crude and tasteless sport.

A point in their favor.

"I'm guessing Madison will make a valiant effort, but—partly because he's right in front of her—I'm thinking Mr. O'Toole has the better chance," Ophelia observed. "Let's go downstairs, Fanny. The crowd's high on the excitement of this contest, so we'd best . . . harness all this energy before it gets washed away at the bar."

They left the windows, glancing at each other apprehensively.

"We'll dance just as we practiced last night, Fanny," Ophelia reassured her. "You saw how exotic we looked in the mirror. Think how amazing we'll be with music!"

Down the narrow stairs they went, while in the main room, the guests chanted their encouragement to the contestants. Ophelia followed the same path they'd come in because it kept them behind the crowd.

She motioned for Fanny to follow her. They walked near the wall, passing a large table loaded with more kinds of pies and cakes and puddings than Ophelia had ever seen. She slipped behind the orchestra.

With her finger on her veiled lips, entreating the musicians not to speak, Ophelia waved at the conductor. His face lit up: he realized they were the surprise for tonight. He kept the orchestra playing a low, seductive beat as he listened to her.

"We'll need some more harem music after James announces us," she whispered.

"Will do," he said—and then a loud roar from the crowd drowned out the rest of his reply.

Ophelia turned in time to see banker Doyle O'Toole declared the winner. His face was flushed. Friends were pressing him with drinks and slapping him on the back.

But it was the action onstage that made Ophelia gape.

Esmeralda had released Yen Sin's ankles. Yet as soon as the poor Celestial laid back on the stage to rest, the gypsy dancer was between her thighs! Damned if Esmeralda wasn't lapping up the spunk those men had shot all over Yen Sin—because she seemed to crave it, rather than to make it the contest's finale.

"Esmeralda certainly has a taste for the—"

But Ophelia lost track of what her maid was saying. From this angle she could see that—like Yen Sin's—the kneeling gypsy's pantaloons were unsewn along the crotch seam, which left her open for . . . whatever business she cared to conduct.

It also revealed that Esmeralda had balls.

Ah, you sly slave girl, she thought. *I know your secret now, you kitty licker!*

10

Ophelia gave James a nod, licking her lips nervously beneath her veil.

He gazed at her and then shooed Esmeralda and Yen Sin from the stage.

"Gentlemen! Good knights, may I have your attention, please!" he cried. "It's time for the revelations we've all been awaiting! The surprise our beloved Sinbad, Henry Leeds, wished to give us!"

At her signal, the orchestra began to play another sinuous, sensuous song reminiscent of the mystical East. Ophelia's heart was pounding so hard she had to squeeze Fanny's hand.

It was the moment she'd been waiting for since Henry's demise.

With her hips swaying brazenly and her hands stretched above her head, Ophelia danced up the stairs and onto the dais. When she reached center stage, she pivoted to face Fanny, who mirrored her actions.

Around they circled, so that the men—now watching in

speculative silence—could see them both from all angles. Could become as enamored of the dance's magic as Ophelia intended.

She canted her hips forward, and Fanny did the same. She raised her arms in a graceful arc above her head, swaying her hips side to side as her arms went the opposite direction.

Then they pivoted, landing back-to-back, so they appeared as one dancer with four arms that now floated up and down in graceful waves.

After a full circle in this position, Ophelia and Fanny turned to face each other, miming the love act as they thrust their faces and hips forward and back, in and out, gazing at each other as though they'd soon be on the floor writhing as one.

The crowd moved closer, absolutely rapt. Ophelia put her hand between their bodies, as did Fanny. They slipped their fingers into the open inseam of each other's pants, still circling, to give the men views from various angles.

Some of the men moaned. Ophelia suspected a few fingers in the audience were dancing the way hers were.

The music grew subtly faster, more intense. As Ophelia followed its lead, she and her maid thrust their hips more provocatively, touching and rubbing each other—until Ophelia gave the signal with her first moan.

Fanny replied, her pitch slightly higher.

Up the scale they went, escalating their cries and the wiggling of their hips until they were at fever pitch.

And their audience was right there with them, breathless for release.

Ophelia grabbed Fanny's hands. Upward and out they extended their arms, arching their backs in apparent climax as their mounds ground against each other. Their heads fell back so their hair swung loose and free, quivering with their final, excited cry.

The music crescendoed to a reedy peak, trembled with them, and then stopped.

The room rang with silence. Then came the low moans and gradual applause—which grew more enthusiastic as their spell subsided.

They righted themselves, smiling in triumph. Fanny released Ophelia's hands to sit cross-legged on the stage in front of her. It was her job to watch the men's expressions and anticipate resistance or trouble, while Ophelia Leeds changed the course of the company before their eyes.

"I bid you a good evening, gentlemen," Ophelia began, her voice rising above their murmurs. "And I'll begin with a moment of remembrance. A toast to my late husband, Henry Leeds, lumber magnate and benefactor of every person in this room."

"Hear! Hear!" a voice called from the sideline.

She blinked her appreciation to James, who raised his glass and led the others in this silent gesture of unanimity. With her own arm upraised in salute, Ophelia let the moment seep into their souls, praying that the respect and camaraderie of this gesture would carry them through. For *her*.

"As of this moment," she went on, "you no longer work for Henry Leeds, or for Leeds Lumber, because the company as you knew it has ceased to exist. I'm sure you understand that no one else could fill Henry's boots."

She gave them a moment to nod and sip.

"If you want a position with this new company—or if you would continue doing business with us—you must interview with me privately. *Now*, while we sail on the *Scheherazade*, into a future as bright as the full moon herself."

The men shifted and whispered. She continued before they could pose any questions.

"My assistant, Fanny, will help you into proper interview attire," Ophelia announced. "You should understand that in my presence, my men wear leather. Or they wear nothing."

She paused to let this sink in. "And please be aware, as you stand there shaking your heads, it isn't *whether* leather, gentlemen. It's leather—or not."

A sea of frowns floated before her. Ophelia didn't dare look at James, nor did she allow her muttering audience to steal her thunder.

It was now or never. They had to understand who would lead and who would follow.

"If you *please* me, I'll assign you a position befitting your abilities. You shall also keep me company whenever—and however—I request it," she added with a sinful grin.

"I've been a lonely woman for too long, gentlemen. I have a large, lovely home—a monument to Henry Leeds and his generosity, just as this wonderful ship is," she continued. "I look forward to sharing my life with you as your new mistress. Just as Henry was, in his way, the master of us all."

The buzzing grew louder, so Ophelia did, too. It was too late to back down. . . .

But then, what could they do? Where could they go? The *Scheherazade* was far from port, in open water. They were her guests—her potential employees and advisers. Her captive audience.

"You came here tonight as Henry's men—some of you as his trusted and *intimate* friends," she said with her arms outstretched. "You may choose to walk away when we dock in a couple of hours. If so, I thank you for the years of service and devotion you've given to Leeds Lumber. We part as friends."

Ophelia watched their faces as these ramifications sank in. Several among the crowd looked ready to leap the deck railing now, rather than wait to go ashore.

But that didn't daunt her. What good was a company—any group of men on her payroll—who didn't serve her with utmost devotion? Ophelia Leeds expected their all, or she wanted nothing.

"I'll await your responses in the master cabin," she went on.

"You have two hours before we dock to interview with me—to state your case and *please* me.

"Meanwhile, enjoy the *Scheherazade* in all her glory, in memory of the man who designed her for your enjoyment! Entertain yourselves as though it's your final night of revelry as Arabian knights aboard this magnificent ship. Because for some of you, it is."

Ophelia paused for a breath, scanning the crowd for Henry's mistresses.

"Lady Jane, Yen Sin, and Esmeralda," she said, extending her arms to them, "when the men have finished interviewing, I want to see you ladies, as well. I'm sure you're wondering about your future, and you need worry no longer.

"Thank you for your attention, and again for your years of devotion to Leeds Lumber," she said with a final flourish. "I am Ophelia Leeds, the company's new owner, as well as its new motto and symbol. Ophelia *leads*, gentlemen. And if you're wise, pleasing me shall become your highest aspiration."

Ophelia exited the stage, her head held high and her gossamer garments fluttering around her body like angels' wings.

11

"You were magnificent! You held them spellbound, Ophelia!"

"We'll see about that when they abandon ship like rats after we dock," Ophelia replied. "There's a chance I just alienated every banker, lawyer, and bull of the woods I need to keep this company running."

The lights were low in the cabin, and Ophelia felt drawn to the figure of Judas Rute, stretched out on the bed. He hadn't stirred. She was beginning to wonder if the chloral hydrate had sent him somewhere from which he'd never return.

"You should go," she murmured to her maid. "Take the valise, and wait for them in the front room. Knock when you have one ready."

With an impish nod, her maid left to do her bidding. Fanny had found Ophelia's plan for harnessing the men's energies and inclinations very clever—but, then, Fanny wasn't fearing for her livelihood.

"And how will *you* react, Mr. Rute?" Ophelia mused out loud. "Will you work for me or be on your way?"

Something prompted her to rearrange him: it seemed disrespectful—downright distracting—to leave him sprawled on the bed in the room where she'd be interviewing.

So Ophelia placed his head on the pillow and his magnificent nude body in a straight line, as if he were laid out for viewing in his casket. Grinning, she pressed his hands together on his chest, in an attitude of prayer and supplication. When would she ever see him this way again, so willing to serve? Such alluring putty in her hands.

Then she pulled one of the upholstered chairs beside the bed, facing the door the applicants would enter. She seated herself, straightening her sheer garments so her assets showed to best advantage.

Then Ophelia folded her hands. And waited.

The minutes ticked by. The clock on Henry's bedside table chimed a quarter past nine . . . nine-thirty . . .

You've done it now! her inner fiend fretted. *You and your big ideas, lording it over those men that they now work for a woman.*

She was about to stand up and stare out those rectangular windows when Fanny rapped at the bedroom door.

Ophelia sat straighter. "Come in!" she called out.

Fanny's giggle—the same sultry sound Ophelia had heard drifting down from her maid's room on many a night—preceded him—but now it was James Pohl entering *her* room—in leather, as she had decreed!

"Mr. Pohl—and Mr. Pole!" she said, gesturing at his erect cock.

It protruded between the harness straps she'd had designed especially for this occasion: leather bands that encircled his waist and thighs, connected to a leather ring through which Fanny had guided his erection.

By the looks of his hard, reddish tip, James had enjoyed his interview preparation—even though his handsome face was flushed with frustration.

"It's fitting that you speak with me first, James," she began, "because—"

"What the hell are you *doing*?" he rasped. "When I saw no one coming up here to . . . The time was flying by! The men are engaged in a feeding frenzy, drinking themselves to—"

"James?"

He blinked.

"Put up, and *get* up. Or shut up."

Although his expression registered displeasure, the tension in his body forced his erection more tightly into its leather collar. This gave Ophelia a full view of his engorged head and shaft—and of his entire fine body, displayed for her gratification.

"How do you propose to please me, dear James?" she purred. "Answer carefully, for the others will follow your lead."

He let out an exasperated breath. "I—what is it you would have me do, Ophelia?"

"Ah, compliance at last. The willingness to ask direction and do my bidding." She motioned for him to come closer, which put his harnessed erection at the same level as her face. "Because I already know you can please me, dear—and because we must use the remaining time to best advantage—I'll excuse you from the favors I expect of the others. For *now*."

Ophelia gazed up into his face, smiling at the tumble of sorrel curls she'd always found so enticing.

"I'm offering you a partnership in this new company, James, because Henry taught you all you know. He was preparing you to carry on when he no longer could," she began. Ophelia watched his expression, the attitude expressed by the body displayed so openly before her. "From here on out, we'll be known as the Leeds–Pohl Lumber Company, and you and I shall be equal partners. As befits this promotion, you should have a home of your own, dear man, and I'm providing you with the house on Henry Avenue. Just in case you take a bride," she added coyly.

James went to his knees, resting his arms on the tops of her thighs. "Are you sure? That's where Barrymore and his sister—"

"Quite sure. We'll negotiate your pay raise later, if you accept," she said with a smile. "So, there you have it. Take it or leave it."

"Leeds–Pohl?" he murmured.

"I thought my name should go first," she replied wryly, "since you men are always leading with your poles. It will remain essentially the same company. Only the perception and loyalties have changed. Can you agree to that—and to what I said on the stage?"

"Of course I can! As you say, Henry was grooming me for—"

"And I believe you will perform well. From every position I ask you to."

Ophelia gave in to the urge: spearing her fingers through his hair, she raised his handsome young face.

"We'll go far, James," she breathed. "But you must go downstairs now and convince our men of that, which you'll often be called upon to do, as this company's co-owner."

He smacked the tops of her thighs, enthusiasm lighting up his face. "Yes, ma'am! It'll be my pleasure to please you, Ophelia. And I thank you for making this dream come true, although in a slightly different way than I'd expected. You won't be sorry."

"Go down and tell *them* that."

He rose and walked quickly to the door and then turned. "I suppose you expect me to remain trussed up like a damn—"

"Leather. Or not," she repeated. "If you can't lead the men wearing the symbol of my new direction, they won't follow you when you need them most. It's no different from the way we women have always endured," she added, arching an eyebrow. "We might wear elegant gowns in the latest styles, but beneath the finery we have *always* been trussed up, James. Seen—and treated—as slaves."

He blinked. Then his glance wandered to Judas Rute on the bed. "He's still not come around? He isn't just pretending to be out?"

Ophelia glanced back at the naked man behind her, so beautiful—and cooperative!—in repose. "He'll serve as a potent warning when the others come in to speak with me. Thank you, James, for your leadership and cooperation. We'll make a fine team!"

Not long after Pohl left, Fanny had another man outside the bedroom door. While Ophelia couldn't make out every word, she heard his resistance loud and clear as her maid showed him his harness.

Then came his low moan as Fanny tucked his cock into that collar. Like a wedding ring, it would remind him he was on call, expected to perform or oblige at all times.

The door opened, and Doyle O'Toole, the company's banker, entered. He was a tall fellow with a complexion like raw beefsteak, suggesting that he and his bottle were close friends. Otherwise, he was a handsome man with some gray stealing into the hair at his temples and shrewd eyes that summed up new acquaintances in a very short time.

She wasn't too bad at that herself.

Ophelia sensed she'd be looking for a different bank soon: Mr. O'Toole, while smiling indulgently at her, was clearly unimpressed.

"Madam, with all due respect for your bereavement, Henry is rolling in his grave at the way you've turned things around! This whole indecent presentation of—"

"You don't look the least bit indecent to me," Ophelia cut in, "but your enthusiasm for squirting all over Yen Sin didn't win you any favors."

His expression went blank. "It was the game of the moment. It was the sort of thing we knights have enjoyed at Henry's encouragement—"

"Well, Henry is no longer in charge," she said evenly. "And if it galls you that *I* am, I'll take the Leeds–Pohl Lumber accounts elsewhere."

"Leeds–Pohl? Since when—"

"Since about ten minutes ago. James and I are partners now."

Ophelia watched his expression as he considered this. Meanwhile she let her gaze wander down his long body, noting the hair on his chest and the way those leather bands directed her gaze to his erection.

Not as enticing as the man behind her but not half bad. If the stories in *The Arabian Knights* were true, he could swill a lot of liquor and still amaze the ladies.

Doyle's eyes widened. "Isn't that Judas Rute, the bull of camp Number One?"

"Yes. Why do you ask?"

"But he looks . . . What the hell—"

"Mr. Rute serves as an example of what happens when men defy—or deny—my requests," she replied, damn glad her veil hid her grin. "I'm not a difficult or complicated woman. I simply ask that my opinions and desires be considered as our company moves into the twentieth century. So how do you propose to please me, Doyle?"

His face grew swarthier. He seemed troubled by the motionless man stretched out on the bed, but he wasn't ready to relinquish his power.

Glancing down at his member, which was sagging a bit, he

replied, "I already spent myself—twice! I won the competition—"

"And in that respect, you gave an impressive performance. Rising to the challenge. Taking true aim."

Ophelia straightened in her chair, cupping her breasts at him. Then she spread her legs so he could see the split seam of her harem pants.

"But now you must consider things from a different perspective, Mr. O'Toole. You must consider how you may best *serve*, as my banker."

To see if he could take direction, she slid her hips forward, opening herself farther . . . watching his eyes and his cock.

"If you and your bank wish to continue your very lucrative association with me, you must consider my *needs*, Doyle. My *desires*. I'll expect you to perform for me even when all your usual ways and means have been exhausted." Ophelia reached between her legs, wiggling her finger. "Remember, dear man, that even if another tree never gets felled, I will live out my days in the luxury Henry has left me. Can *you* say that?"

He blinked, unaccustomed to such words from a woman— or from Henry.

Ophelia sighed. "Must I spell it out, Mr. O'Toole? Must I insist you kneel and please me with your tongue, since your cock isn't responding?"

He fell to his knees, but it was sheer shock that had him staring at her, biting back a frown.

"Come now, Doyle. Surely you don't find me so repugnant you can't kiss my kitty. She's really very tame—and *so* appreciative."

He looked flummoxed but knelt lower. Parted her curls with a finger, as though testing her to see if she was serious.

Ophelia wrapped her legs around his shoulders, opening herself fully.

He closed his eyes, sighing.

At his first touch, she let her head loll back. Focused her thoughts on the tongue that felt tentative on her tender skin. Doyle O'Toole was obviously not accustomed to giving lip service to a woman, but he could probably be trained.

Ophelia parted her nether petals with two fingers, so her nub stuck out in the vee they formed.

"*This*, Mr. O'Toole, is your new target," she whispered. "*This* is the new nerve center of Leeds–Pohl. And if you play the game well—as you did with Henry—we'll have a long and satisfying relationship, dear man."

The sight of her puss, so wide and wet and willing, revived his interest. Doyle applied himself more diligently this time, licking and stroking, following her murmured encouragements until Ophelia convulsed. She shuddered against his shoulders and then fell limp in the chair. It wasn't a stellar climax, but she had other men to interview, after all.

"You'll do," she murmured. "Thank you, Doyle, for learning a new trick to keep yourself in the game."

When she opened her eyes, he was gazing directly at her, wiping her wetness from his face. "But that was just . . . You surely must want me to . . ."

Ophelia smiled. He was like a dog sniffing a bitch in heat now. "That will be all, sir. You've proven you can please me, and there are others awaiting their turns."

He stood, flummoxed—and fully erect. Needy again and not pleased about being denied.

"I had no idea! Henry never let on," he rasped, taking his cock in hand to control it. "He said you were antisocial, tending toward female maladies and—"

"Unfortunately, some men consider 'female' and 'malady' one and the same," she remarked dryly. "So now you know the real Ophelia Leeds. And you know that while Henry had a talent for storytelling, maybe he didn't tell you everything. A lesson we've all learned since his death."

Ophelia gave him a little wave, blowing a kiss at his erection. "Good evening, Doyle. I'll be calling on you soon to review our accounts."

12

As the banker left, Ophelia heard men's voices in the front room. Success! She hadn't scared everyone away with her little speech! To make a prettier presentation for the next applicant, she lifted the velvet comforter on Henry's bed to dry herself with the sheet.

Was it her imagination, or did Rute's eyelids flutter? What a stroke of genius, to leave his body on display! An example to those reluctant to accept the new order of things—to see things her way!

When the door opened she was seated regally in the chair again, facing not one man this time but six of them—all those burly, brawny bulls of the woods she'd met as the *Scheherazade* sailed from the harbor.

"Good evening, gentlemen!" she said brightly. "And may I say I've *never* been in a room with *so* much willing masculinity and strength of character."

"Oh, this one's a character all right," the closest fellow replied with a chuckle. "My name's Burt Hudson, and this here fellow's Burt, Junior." He wagged his leather-ringed erection at her, which prompted the other five to take themselves in hand, as well.

"And I'm Silas Basinger."

"Ted Mahaffey at your service, ma'am."

"Pleased to make your acquaintances," Ophelia replied. And because these men seemed so inclined, she grasped each of them by the shaft they offered instead of shaking hands down the line.

"Peter Short, ma'am," the next fellow said.

Ophelia cast a playful eye at the cock she was holding. "Not so I noticed."

Laughter filled the room, and she realized it had been far too long since she'd heard that. Things were looking up!

"Abner Joseph," the next fellow said, "and I'm a-wonderin' if poor ole Jude is laid out thatta way to meet his maker."

Ophelia glanced back at the naked male on the bed. His color was improving; she suspected Rute was still woozy but aware of what was happening. Smart enough to keep his eyes—and mouth—shut a while longer.

"I appreciate your concern, Abner," she replied, "but I think Mr. Rute will be just fine. He's showing admirable restraint, letting the rest of you timber beasts meet with me before he demands his own interview!"

She paused, sensing an opportunity for information about a man who fascinated her. "I bet Judas is the lone wolf among you, a maverick who leads the pack rather than following."

"Oh, you got that right!" the next man in line piped up. "My name's Earl Washam, by the way, and I gotta say Rute—he's the giant sequoia the rest of us saplins look up to."

When Earl saw the others nodding, he continued. His collared cock bobbed with his enthusiasm. "We lead our own camps, as you know, ma'am, but Jude—he stands head and shoulders above us, far as fellin' the most trees and gettin' the best work outta his crew with the least injuries."

Ophelia caught the merest flicker of Rute's lips and smiled to herself. She turned back to the able-bodied men standing before her.

"I like your honesty and the way you speak so well of your friend, not to mention the hard work you've given to Leeds Lumber," she added. "I also applaud the way you came here tonight and conducted yourselves as gentlemen during that shooting contest."

A snicker rippled down the line.

"Shucks, ma'am, that weren't no sport," Burt spoke up. "If I'm gonna take a lady, I sure don't need nobody to hold her down for me!"

" 'Specially not that Esmeralda, 'cause she's no more a lady than I am!" Silas chimed in.

"No disrespect intended, missus, and we're all real sorry for your loss, when Henry got struck down by that widow-maker," Ted said, "but I'm mighty surprised that Mr. Leeds would have a—a fake lady on his ship as entertainment. If you get my meanin'."

"I do," Ophelia replied.

And despite the muscular bodies that so tempted her—six cocks standing at attention in their harnesses, eager to do her bidding—she restrained herself. Plenty of time to indulge in all these pleasures!

She stood up, smiling at them . . . letting them get a good eyeful. "I hope you men will all remain as my bulls of the woods—"

"Oh, yes, ma'am! We've already talked about that!"

"—and after visiting a bunkhouse the other day, I feel you deserve better working conditions. So I'm offering you quarters in my own home. As long as you keep your crews productive, and as long as you continue to please me," she added, looking at each one of them in turn, "I'll be honored to have you. Does that suit you? Do you have other requests?"

To a man, they looked dumbfounded.

"But, Mrs. Leeds, ma'am, that means you'll have our dirty clothes and meals to see to," Silas said.

"I have a staff to help with that."

"It puts us a distance from our men and from the camp," Mahaffey pointed up. "Travelin' that far every mornin'—"

"I'll see that you're up early—and often," she added with a wink. "I'll provide you a carriage and a team to get you to the woods. "And if you'd still like to join your men in town on Saturday nights, that'll be all right, too," Ophelia added with a sly smile. "While I plan to keep you boys busy—at my beck and call—I can't expect you *all* to please me every night. My bedroom's big, but privacy's a good thing. Don't you agree?"

Grins flickered on their leathered faces. They glanced warily at each other, as though they couldn't believe what they were hearing.

"You're sayin' you want us to work with the men by day and play with you by night?" Abner asked. "Like—like we's in some sorta harem?"

Their expectant silence—their intent expressions—sent a surge of sexual power through her. It was working! By God, these men understood her!

"That's exactly what I'm offering!" Ophelia replied. "High time I had someone to talk to at dinner—men in all the chairs at my long table. Why, Henry will smile down on us because we're putting his mansion to better use than when it was just me rattling around like a bean in a bread box. Do we have an agreement?"

She stuck out her hand.

They grinned like foxes in a henhouse.

"Can—can we touch ya for luck, Miss Ophelia? To sorta seal the deal?"

What woman wouldn't love such an attitude? Such unadulterated loyalty from men who could've crushed her physically—and financially—had they walked away.

"That would be an auspicious beginning to our new arrangement, yes!" Ophelia opened her arms and parted her legs, welcoming them with her smile.

Ted caressed first one breast and then the other, his calloused hand warm yet rasping against her beaded nipple. Confident. Ophelia smiled up into sparkling brown eyes, and, on impulse, she kissed him.

"Don't forget," she said, "that when we dock, you and the others who're staying on may indulge your every appetite. I expect we'll be sailing for the next few days, to get better acquainted."

Silas stepped up then, but he looked doubtful. "What happens when we don't show up for work on Monday? What'll our crews think?"

Ophelia raised a teasing eyebrow. "It'll be the true test of who you can trust to carry on without supervision, won't it? A good time to let the lollygaggers go and hire better men."

Silas's blue eyes twinkled as he slipped an arm around her waist.

She gave in to his kiss. Enjoyed this taste of a playful, passionate man whose finger had found its way between her legs.

"See you later, Miss Ophelia," he said with a wink.

Peter Short kissed her too, grabbing her ass from both sides with an appreciative grunt.

"Oh, feel ya!" he teased. "You and me're gonna get along just fine, darlin'. I like your style!"

Burt and Earl hugged her between them, each man grasping half of her backside and a breast. Abner stepped in then, towering above them, cradling her face in his huge hands for a kiss that tasted ripe with promise.

"Thank you, Miss Ophelia," he said as he trailed the others

out the door. "I was proud to work for Henry Leeds, but for you, ma'am, I'll aim to please!"

"Thank *you*, Abner. It'll be a pleasure having you timber beasts at home."

She smiled at those six bare backsides, so firm and tight as they walked away. Then she turned again to—

Had Rute moved?

If so, he was smart enough not to get caught.

The next rap at her door sent her back into her chair, smoothing the fabric that had crinkled where those lumberjacks had grabbed her. As she sat taller to greet her next applicant, she smiled slyly.

Yen Sin entered first, prodded ahead by Esmeralda, who was followed by Lady Jane. The three mistresses had dressed in full costume again: the crimson kimono and queued black hair; the flowing gypsy garb and loose henna waves; the rich, jeweled tunic and harem veil, so prim and proper like Jane's upswept blond hair.

But Ophelia intended to make them feel far more naked than when they'd cavorted on the stage before that roomful of men.

"Good evening, ladies," she said pleasantly. "I'm sure you're wondering what your future holds, now that Henry's gone. Let's get right down to it, shall we?"

13

The three of them seemed familiar with Henry's finely appointed quarters, but the man on the bed gave them pause. Ophelia let her gaze follow theirs to his deathlike pose.

"This is Judas Rute, the bull of the woods in one of our lumber camps," she remarked. "He lies here as a reminder of what happens when my employees defy me or deny me.

"But then, you ladies are in a different situation, aren't you?" she said in a more sinuous voice. "Paid for the services you perform aboard the *Scheherazade*. Provided with homes and the elevated state of being a rich man's mistresses."

Ophelia studied each of them. She knew what she was going to say, so these moments of silence were a way of asserting her newfound power. For once, *she* sat on the throne, knowing exactly how their precarious position felt.

"You should understand that, until Henry's death, I was unaware he was supporting you," she began quietly. "Yet I wasn't surprised that Henry Leeds had taken you under his wing. That's how *I* met him, after all."

Their eyes shone with hope when they heard this. Not that their vulnerable expressions would change her mind.

"We'll begin with you, Miss Barrymore. I'm sure you'll understand that I have no need of a mistress—"

Jane's eyebrow peaked, as though she were unaccustomed to being challenged. She saw no humor in Ophelia's phrasing.

"—but because this isn't your fault—none of us were expecting Henry to die—I shall allow you to remain in the house on Henry Avenue until the end of the month."

Jane's pale green eyes widened; she glanced at Esmeralda, her cheeks growing pink. "While I understand your severing of our allowances, Mrs. Leeds, I would ask you to reconsider—"

"You're giving us two *weeks*? And then throwing us out into the streets?" Esmeralda demanded. "You *don't* understand, Ophelia! That place has been our—Jane's—home for years, and she couldn't possibly . . ."

Ophelia let the gypsy bluster on, smiling when she saw Fanny in the doorway. Things were about to get interesting, and her maid might as well enjoy these revelations, too.

"While I admire your concern for Miss Barrymore," Ophelia interrupted, "I'm not sure I understand it, Esmeralda. You'll have to excuse my ignorance, for I wasn't privy to Henry's personal secrets until—"

"Ignorance is right!" the henna-haired dancer declared. With an exasperated glance at the blonde beside her, Esmeralda began to yank at her costume. Off came the gold chains, the flowing blouse and skirts—and then, lo and behold, she removed her hair!

And when the wig was dangling in the gypsy's hand, it was Erroll Barrymore standing before her, glaring at her from beneath his artfully applied stage makeup.

"Well, well," Ophelia murmured, "how thoughtful of you to reveal yourself, Mr. Barrymore. I was wondering if you'd come this evening."

It took all her effort not to snicker. With his hair crushed from wearing the wig, and the heavy makeup, and the harem pants and beaded breast band, he'd lost the "presence" he'd exuded as the watchdog of Henry's ledger.

"I had to make my point!" he proclaimed—although, through those gauzy pants, he clearly wasn't on point at all. "You have no right to evict my sister and me from the home we've called ours for nearly—"

"Ah, but calling it yours and paying for it are two different things."

Ophelia waited, watching the anguish color his baby-smooth cheeks. Watching his fake, beaded breasts rise and fall with his rapid breathing.

"I'm sorry if this is an inconvenience, but I have a new tenant for that house, Mr. Barrymore. You and Jane will need to find other lodgings. But with the generous salary and allowance my husband paid you both," Ophelia added, "you surely have the means to rent or purchase—"

"This is *not* what Henry intended!"

"In case you hadn't noticed," she purred, "Henry is no longer in charge. And, just as I told your sister that I have no need of a mistress, I don't need an accountant anymore, either. *I* will keep the books for my new company, Erroll."

Ophelia bit back a grin, continuing in a low voice to further infuriate him.

"I do, however, have permanent guests moving into my home, and I'll be needing an additional maid and a cook," she said sweetly. "Judging from the way you mopped up after those men shot all over Yen Sin, you'll have no trouble at all cleaning for me and my new harem!"

Erroll's eyes nearly popped out of his head. "This is an outrage! You're doing this just to spite Henry's memory! Jane, you tell her how—"

"No, Erroll, let me tell *you* a few things." Ophelia glanced at the Celestial, who stood with her head bowed and her hands folded, and then at Lady Jane, whose face registered her fear and disgrace but whose breeding kept her quiet. "I might not've known about Henry's mistresses until I read his book on the Arabian knights," she went on, "but I know *why* he chose you three . . . *ladies* . . . and why he provided so generously for your upkeep."

Fanny's eyes were bright with curiosity as she stood staring from the doorway. So Ophelia went on.

"I know, you see, that you merely serve as ornaments for a wealthy man's life. You, like I, helped him maintain the appearance of a swaggering ladies' man who couldn't get enough from one woman—God knows, not from his supposedly sickly, reclusive 'wife'—because, in reality, our dear Henry couldn't bed even one of us. Could he?"

All three of them looked at her as though she'd broken some unspoken vow. Had betrayed her husband's trust.

"I found this out when I was keeping the books for a madam in a San Francisco parlor house. The ladies there raised me after my mother died during my birth," Ophelia recounted in a far-away voice. It was a difficult tale to tell, but not to these listeners, who already knew the punch line.

"Henry came in with some friends to have a good time, but he slipped out of sight as they went upstairs with their ladies. Struck up a conversation with me, and was impressed that I had such a head for ciphering." She sighed, wishing that—as the heroine of this story—she'd had a happier part to play. "I was quite a lot younger, so I understood that he married me to protect me from the fate those other ladies lived and died by. I also understood that Henry Leeds had a social life that wouldn't include me and that living in seclusion, in the mansion he built, was my cross to bear."

"Oh, *spare* me!" Erroll jeered. "*You* get to keep your high-

and-mighty home, yet you have no compassion for those of us—"

"Erroll." Lady Jane's voice was low but insistent.

Her brother threw her a wounded look, unwilling to give it up.

"Mrs. Leeds has spoken," Jane muttered. "She's told us where we stand, and while I couldn't expect her to keep paying *my* allowance, you've lost your position because you've never really been the man of this family. You rode in on my coattails when Henry took a fancy to me—"

"He loved me! Loved to watch Esmeralda dance and entertain his friends!"

"But that's behind us now—unless you'd like to clean house for Mrs. Leeds and actually *work* for your living," his sister added.

Jane Barrymore held her head higher, looking at Ophelia with the haughty, regal beauty that would undoubtedly turn another wealthy benefactor's head. "Good evening, Mrs. Leeds. Thank you for your time."

The blonde walked away, and after a moment of indecision, Erroll followed after her, his costume and wig still wadded in one fist.

It was a pathetic sight, yet Ophelia could foresee nothing but trouble if she kept Barrymore on: discrepancies in the ledger had hidden more than the expenses for the *Scheherazade* and Henry's mistresses. Erroll had appropriated several bonuses for himself over the years—and if he'd already squandered that money, that was *his* problem, wasn't it?

"Erroll?" she called after him.

He glanced back at her, his painted face curdling.

Ophelia fingered the timepiece pinned to her harem vest. "At least we have these nice watches to remember Henry by. Perhaps, if you need the cash, the jeweler would take yours back in pawn."

302 / Melissa MacNeal

Erroll stalked out the door in such a huff that Fanny had to jump out of his way. But she was snickering. She'd enjoyed this little drama as much as Ophelia had loved sharing it with her.

She turned then to Yen Sin, her expression softening. The ledger and the book of Arabian knights had pieced together a puzzle that wasn't as pretty as the Barrymores' situation, and Ophelia hoped she did the girl—and Henry's intentions—justice here.

"I'm sorry for the way you were treated on that stage earlier this evening," she began softly, hoping the Celestial understood the nuances of the English language. "From what I've read in Henry's accounts, you're always the one on the bottom of the heap, so to speak."

Yen Sin's eyes, as fathomless and black as her braided hair, widened in surprise. "Is all right, Miss Ophelia. Yen Sin not need . . . I find other work, in laundry maybe, or—"

Ophelia placed her hands on the girl's slender shoulders, guessing her to be no more than eighteen. A pretty piece like this one would get sucked into the whoring life very quickly, even if she had all good intentions of finding honorable work.

"Yen Sin, I'm giving you the *Scheherazade* as your home," she said, "and if you wish to do laundry or conduct other business here, that's up to you. As long as the ship's available when I wish to sail on her—for she's a world unto herself, like no other we've ever seen, isn't she?—you may live on her, with her staff at your disposal. You no longer have to be tied up and taken advantage of—unless you like that sort of thing," Ophelia added with a twisted grin.

A tear slithered down flawless cheeks the color of a golden rose. "I . . . no understand why Missy Leeds . . ."

Ophelia went to the valise and fished out a piece of paper. It made her heart skitter to have this opportunity—her first act of philanthropy, now that the Leeds fortune was at her disposal.

"I found this in Henry's records," she said softly. "It's the bill of sale from when Henry . . . bought you. I read where your family sold you because . . . well, it doesn't matter why!" she exclaimed. "You're a free woman now, Yen Sin! I hope we can become friends, and I'd be proud to hire your sisters, cousins, whoever else needs a chance at a better life."

The Celestial's body vibrated. She gazed at the paper, blinking back tears.

"Thank you, missy! I—I take good care of your ship," she vowed. "Or I work at your home! Whatever you need, Yen Sin want to do."

She gazed up into Ophelia's face, as lovely and fresh as a flower—a miracle, considering the things she'd endured while entertaining Henry's friends.

Ophelia grinned. "Well, for starters, you can bring Judas Rute out of his stupor. I'm concerned about how much chloral hydrate those timber beasts must've given him."

The Celestial went to the bedside to gaze down into Rute's chiseled face. Her lips quirked in a grin.

"He a big man, so they give him big dose. But Yen Sin know just the trick!"

She went into the bathroom and came out with a glass of water. "Yen Sin do this for you, missy, but then she leave! Not want to be here when Goliath raised from the dead!"

With a giggle, the Chinese girl tossed the water in Rute's face. Then she scampered out of the room, taking Fanny with her.

14

Judas Rute came up off the bed cussing and sputtering like a wet cat—a wild lion who might do some damage before he got himself under control.

Ophelia stood out of his sight. It was bad strategy to shrink away from this bull of the woods, so she remained by the bathroom door until he looked around and found her there.

Just for effect, she untied her shirt. It slithered down her arms with the tinkling of those tiny bells, to land in a silken puddle on the floor.

"How nice of you to drop by!" She widened her eyes playfully. "Now that you've gotten an earful of all that's happened here this evening, you can have *your* say."

So long as it doesn't contradict mine, she added silently.

Rute swung his legs over the edge of the bed, glaring at her. As he wiped the water from his face and swept back his hair, Ophelia got a good look at his chest muscles, at the way his entire body moved with an oversize grace and a power she dared not underrate.

"All right, so you *are* Ophelia Leeds. Henry's widow."

"You knew that the other day," she replied coolly, "when you implied I was a whore, peddling my ass in your camp."

He had the sense to wince at that recollection. "You didn't exactly back away, once you sat on my hand."

"You should know, after that meeting and this evening's interviews, that backing away isn't my style, Mr. Rute."

Rute blinked the rest of the water from his eyes, taking in her bared breasts and the triangular patch of black that was visible through her harem pants. "You can't tell me Leeds let his wife wear such a costume—"

"How did he *know* what I wore when he wasn't at home?" she challenged. Then she raised her arms, swaying so the loosened pants rippled down past her hips. "But I like this outfit, don't you? I could wear it—or not—any time I please, now that I'll have a harem of timber beasts living with me." She paused, smiling naughtily. "Your friends made quite a sight, all tricked out in their cock harnesses."

He laughed. Now that his was body fully alert—some parts more than others—Judas Rute was the beast to be reckoned with. And, like a rogue bull, he'd do irreparable damage if she didn't tame him before he got the upper hand.

"So what would you like to say for yourself?" she asked, swaying closer to the bed. "What 'position' do your see yourself in, now that you've heard me interview the others?"

Rute narrowed his eyes. His nostrils flared as he watched her approach.

"The others," he mused aloud, clearly considering himself above their level. "I liked the way you put O'Toole in his place . . . and in yours. Although he didn't do justice to that tongue job, the way I would've."

Ophelia's insides quivered when he licked his lips, looking at her.

"And I damn near got teary eyed, the way you freed that pretty little Celestial. Now *there's* a lady I could get fired up for!"

Ophelia lowered her eyelids. She hadn't missed the way his shaft had caught on fire—for her!

"That's entirely up to Yen Sin," she said.

Not wanting to appear the least bit intimidated, Ophelia stepped close enough that her body brushed his legs. When Rute inhaled, flashing that onyx-eyed gaze at her, she wrapped a hand around his erection. Just to let him know who was conducting this interview.

"And did I treat the Barrymores fairly?" she asked. "Never let it be said that Ophelia Leeds slighted—"

"Ha!" Rute grabbed her shoulders, his face alight with a mirth that softened the edges of his bristled face. Not that she didn't like this man hard in every sense of the word. "I wanted to *applaud* when you sent that pansy ass packing! That pest was going to get himself killed, prancing around in the forest while my men tried to work. Never did trust him," Rute continued, shaking his head. "And he didn't even offer to take care of his sister, now that she's without a man and a place to live! Just confirms what a piss ant he is."

Ophelia looked back into his eyes; she'd watched his lips the whole time he talked. "I like your thinking, Judas, and I'm pleased that we see eye to eye—"

"Not so fast, naked lady."

His hands spanned her waist, and then he wrapped his muscled calves around her legs. "Don't think for a minute you can seduce me into seeing things your way, like you did those other six beasts. I *refuse* to work for a woman. Especially one who knocked me cold to get me onto this ship."

"That was *not* my idea! I just invited you to my party!" Ophelia insisted. "You'll have to take that up with James Pohl, my new partner."

"So I won't be taking orders from *you*?"

Judas ran his hands higher, so they framed her breasts. He watched them bob; grinned when her nipples came out to play. Then he stuck his long tongue out to tease them, one after the other, until they tingled and ached.

Ophelia sucked in her breath. Had to keep her mind on the topic at hand. He was trying to distract her—catch her in a mistake—and he was damn good at it.

"What do I know about . . . fellers and buckers?" she rasped. "I'll just be authorizing the pay for you and your men. *Not* that I think a raise would influence you, but—"

"Already got one of those," he whispered, flexing his hips so his pole rose higher in her hand.

"Yes, sir, I see that. Not that your big, thick cock would influence me, but—"

"What do you plan to do with it, Ophelia?"

His question—the hard, hungry shine in his eyes—told her this was it. This was where she either took control of him and this situation or gave it up forever.

And of all the men she'd met tonight, Judas Rute was the last one she wanted to give up.

"First I'm going to fuck you senseless," she challenged, shoving him backward onto the mattress. "And then, while you're still out of your head, you'll agree to be the Boss Bull— or whatever you wish to be called. The man in charge of all the lumber camps, to whom all the other bulls and timber beasts answer."

"To *whom*?" he mocked her proper talk. Effortlessly, Judas lifted her body above his to hold her at arm's length. "To *whom*?"

Ophelia knew better than to kick and struggle. Her heart raced, and she could barely breathe, balanced two feet in the air above him on the broad hands at her waist. She barely had the presence of mind to gaze from his parted lips down the length of his strong, muscled body . . . halting at that rock-solid erection that grew like a tree between his legs.

"If that nub I showed Mr. O'Toole is the new nerve center of Leeds–Pohl," she reasoned breathlessly, "I can certainly see how that 'pole' of yours should be the foundation we build on for the coming century. The 'root' of our growth."

"Then the name'll have to be Rute–Leeds–Pohl."

"You—you want to be a partner?" Ophelia's thoughts raced again. This was getting *way* out of control! Not going her way at all!

When Judas chuckled, those chiseled lips softened and his face took on that fallen-angel look again, even though he was clearly making fun of her. "If you're going to fuck me senseless, naked lady, that means I'm already your partner."

Why hadn't she thought of that? But it wouldn't do to compliment his powers of logic and observation, would it? She'd never live it down!

Ophelia forced a frown. "So what's the holdup, Judas? You couldn't keep your hands off me the other day when—"

"I've put you on a pedestal," he teased, flexing his arms. "If that's not where you want to be, Queen Ophelia, beg me to put you in your place. Beg me," he whispered, "to make love to you till you can't see straight. Maybe then you'll realize that you can control your company, but you'll never, ever control *me*, little lady."

Those eyes. God, those devil-dark eyes looked right through her and Ophelia *knew* she could never refuse him. All the power and tall talk and pretty ships in the world wouldn't take her where Judas Rute could.

"Please, Judas—"

"Call me, Jude, honey. All my friends do."

Ophelia smiled. If this man wanted her as a friend—and

would still work for her—that meant she really was getting what she wanted. Didn't it?

"Please, Jude," she began again, in her most alluring voice with her prettiest grin. "*Please* make love to me till I can't see straight. That would please me more than you can possibly know."

He lowered her to his chest, devouring her mouth before she even rested along the length of him. Jude kissed her relentlessly, weaving a hand through her hair to hold her head—not that she wanted to get away.

Ophelia grabbed him, accepting the challenge of his tongue in a duel that left her breathless and needy. He still smelled of the cedar sawdust and spilled whiskey he'd been dragged through: bracing, masculine scents that made her breathe deeply and want more.

His hand roamed down to stroke her bare backside. When he arched beneath her, his tip prodded the flesh between her legs.

Ophelia opened to him.

What a joy to have a man—a partner!—who didn't need instructions. Who seemed as eager to fill her as she needed to be filled. It was one thing to have six timber beasts moving in with her at her beck and call. It was another thing altogether to be molded against Jude Rute's hard body, knowing he wouldn't stop thrusting and kissing and grabbing her until he damn well pleased—and until he'd pleased *her*.

"Take me," she whimpered. "Stuff that cock inside me and—"

"Ride it," he growled against her ear. "Only way to tame that beast is to ride it till it stops bucking."

Ophelia sucked air when his cock found her opening. What if he was so big she couldn't . . . What if she retreated in pain when he shoved it up . . .

With a determined moan, she thrust back to take him inside her. Got her knees on either side of his massive body and sat up to challenge him with her gaze.

"You damn well better keep bucking until I fall on my face exhausted," she said, bracing her hands on his shoulders.

He gave her that crooked grin, the one that resembled a sneer. But she saw now that Jude wasn't mocking her. He was taking the game seriously.

"*I* won't be the first one to give up," he replied.

He arched his back, driving himself so deep Ophelia had to gasp for air. She felt stretched to the limit yet ached for more of him. Her need for this was like a rash that, once she scratched it, itched all the more.

When his hands clamped around her hips, she tossed her head back and her body forward, letting him set the pace and the rhythm. Letting Judas Rute put her where he wanted her.

And being *here* sure beat being on his pedestal.

When Ophelia saw his eyes glazing with need, felt him growing harder and thrusting higher, she dismounted.

"Come at me this way, Jude," she commanded, kneeling with her backside pointed at him.

"I might hurt—"

"You gonna make this kitty howl? Or just pet her and tell her she's cute?"

With a low growl, Rute rolled onto his knees and grabbed her hips. He entered Ophelia hard, parting the halves of her ass to open her farther as he thrust into her again and again.

From this angle it felt like a bull truly *had* taken her. He was so big, so powerful—and in this impassioned state, he was damn near out of control.

Then Ophelia felt herself rising from the mattress until Jude rocked back and set her in his lap. Up and down he lifted her, up and down his shaft, until she clenched inside. Her honey smacked wetly between their bodies.

"Want me?" he demanded.

'"Yes—yes, *please*—" She sucked air.

Jude had stopped. He was fully extended inside her, throbbing in the confines of her inner grip. Panting as hard as she was. Yet he held her against his chest, tenderly cupping her breasts. Holding her. Letting his heat seep into her skin as he leaned over her shoulder to kiss her like he'd never let her go.

Never had Ophelia felt so small and vulnerable, yet so protected, with this mammoth of a man wrapped around her. Her lips clung to his bigger ones, opening at their insistence until his tongue had filled her mouth as surely as his cock had claimed her cunt.

He began to rock again. Not letting her go—not letting her come up for air—until she felt she might die first from the need to breath . . . and then pass away from the sheer, extreme pleasure of the climax that quivered from her core outward.

She turned to rubber and went with his rhythm, let Judas Rute have his way with her until he groaned into her open mouth and crushed her against his shuddering body.

When he fell sideways onto the bed, Ophelia went with him.

"Damn, you're good."

Her eyes flew open. She hugged the arms that encircled her, knowing she'd be content if she died like this and never had to get up. Never had to leave this warmth . . . or the heat that would eventually rise between them again.

They made love in the bathtub, while she scrubbed Jude clean.

They were teasing each other into a third time when a knock at the door stopped them.

Fanny poked her head in, grinning.

"James thought you should know we'll be docking in ten minutes," she said in her ever-efficient way. "Which means you have time for another quick one—or another long romp, if you don't care to see people off."

Ophelia blinked. "And just how did you know—"

"Yen Sin showed me a peephole. You and Judas put on a far better show than we saw onstage tonight, missus. And I'm glad!"

"So how many people were watching . . . ?"

Her maid snickered and closed the door.

Jude shook with his laughter. Now that his hair was clean and he'd shaved with one of Henry's razors, the rangy beast had been replaced by an animal Ophelia couldn't stop gawking at. And that beast between his legs seemed to be watching her through that little eye, the way it was pointing at her again.

"Naughty boy," she teased, tweaking the reddish tip of it. "Why don't you get this thing under control, and join me on the deck? While I don't expect those men—or the Barrymores—to say much in the way of good-bye, it would be a solid show of what Rute–Leeds–Pohl stands for."

"Under control?" he quizzed. "You wouldn't like it much if this cock didn't crow when it damn well wanted to. I had you *begging* for it, Ophelia."

"Surprised you, didn't I?" She raised a triumphant eyebrow at him as she slipped into her harem costume again. "Here you thought Ophelia Leeds was some pathetic, sickly little thing—"

"Anyone who walks off this ship doesn't know what he's missing."

Well, *that* was a high compliment, wasn't it?

Ophelia left the master cabin with a confident smile, to venture up to the deck. She watched proudly as her ship eased between the logging vessels that bobbed along the dock. The full moon ruled, directly above them now, and as she leaned against the railing to survey the beauty of the night, Ophelia felt *fine*. Very fine, indeed.

Henry would be pleased, the breeze seemed to whisper. *He wanted you to be happy.*

And, all things considered, this little adventure had turned out for the best, hadn't it? With James and Jude in charge of the areas in which they performed best, Henry's company would continue on firm footing.

And with the money no longer paid to Lady Jane or her crooked brother . . . why, she could entertain in the manner her mansion was built for, couldn't she? She still had a banker. Still had her bulls. So if all the rest of her guests disembarked, Ophelia was still in business.

As crewmen hopped nimbly to the pier to secure the gangplank, James Pohl took his place at the exit.

"He's so proud to be your partner," Fanny whispered from behind her. "And doesn't he look the part? Just as Henry must've imagined."

"You're right, dear. Much better for him than I, to be bidding our naysayers good-bye."

The girl behind her sighed tentatively. "So, what about me, Ophelia? I—I didn't feel quite right putting on one of those harnesses to interview . . ."

Giggling at that image, Ophelia turned to face her maid. Fanny's face glowed in the moonlight, yet there was an edge of apprehension Ophelia had never intended to put there.

"Of *course* I want you to be my personal secretary," she assured her friend, "because with those bulls and beasts moving in—"

"This sounds *so* exciting, missus!"

Ophelia laughed as Fanny grabbed her hands. "But now that

I'm giving James the house on Henry Avenue, you should marry him and live in fine style—if you want to."

The girl's brow crinkled impishly. "I've thought about that these past few days, and I can see an advantage to *not* marrying. You might have the right idea, Ophelia, by not tying yourself to one man again."

Ophelia feigned shock. "Fanny Gault! What would your mama say?"

"That's why we're not telling her, isn't it?" she quipped. "I can still make James wag his tail, of course, but for all Mama knows, I'll be remaining on as your personal servant. Even more devoted, now that Henry has passed on, you know."

"Wicked girl. You couldn't miss a minute of this, could you?"

Ophelia turned when she realized the *Scheherazade* was already gliding slowly out of its slip, turning toward the open waters of Puget Sound again.

The only people standing on the pier were Jane and Erroll Barrymore.

"Shall we go back downstairs, ladies?" James said, offering each of them an arm. "From what I hear, Mrs. Leeds, you conduct quite an interview. And while some of Henry's friends raised their eyebrows at your new . . . living arrangement . . . to a man they applauded your gift to Yen Sin. No one doubts now that Henry's generous spirit is still with us."

Ophelia hadn't anticipated that reaction, just as she hadn't imagined the sea of upturned faces waiting to greet her when they descended into that huge room. In the glimmer of the chandeliers, while the orchestra played a fanfare to welcome her, Ophelia felt happier than she could ever remember. She felt *worthwhile*, like a woman with a purpose and the means to carry it out.

James looked ready to make an announcement, so she pulled him closer.

"What does this mean?" she whispered. "I didn't speak with nearly all these men! I assumed they'd walk away when they learned a woman would be manning the lumber company."

James really was handsome when he smiled, in an endearing, youthful way.

"Most of these men were Henry's associates, not his employees," he reminded her. "Which means you've not only maintained the company rolls, you've kept the respect of some very influential men."

"But mostly, they don't want to miss out on your parties," Fanny murmured. "Where else will they get to pretend they're Arabian knights?"

James flashed her an indulgent smile and then raised his hands for silence. The roomful of bejeweled sultans, sheiks, and caliphs looked at him—and at Ophelia—with expectant expressions.

"Welcome back for our extended sail on the *Scheherazade*, my knights!" his voice rang out. His aqua and gold caftan shimmered as he raised his hands to accept their applause. "You have chosen well, to put your trust in our Lady Ophelia—"

"Hear! Hear!" came a cry from the front. It was Doyle O'Toole, raising his glass high. "A toast to Lady Ophelia!"

Their uplifted drinks and roar of approval gave her such a thrill, she smiled and cried at the same time.

But it was nothing compared to the tremor she felt when Jude Rute stepped onto the other side of the dais. He had brushed the sawdust from his denim pants and chambray shirt. His hair fell in shining layers around his face, and his smile, bracketed by deep dimples, left no doubt that Judas Rute—at least for this moment—ruled the room.

Ophelia couldn't stop staring at him. While not plumed like

the peacocks standing before her, Jude resembled the trees he worked among every day: tall and brawny and damn near invincible.

He gave her a look that melted her harem pants. Or perhaps she was already wet for him again.

"No, gentlemen," he corrected in a sonorous voice, "we shall raise our glasses high and proud to *this lady's pleasure—to Ophelia*, a lady like no other. Let's hope we can rise to that challenge again and again."

Dark, dangerous, and elegantly erotic . . . don't miss
BLOOD RED by Sharon Page,
coming in January 2007 from Aphrodisia.

The earl had spoken in her head. *Tonight, I need you, love. I need to be with you. I need to watch over you.*

And so here she was, gathering the garlic flowers from the side of her bed to toss them away. Images from her dreams raced through her mind as she unclasped the cross from her neck and poured the chain onto her bedside table, beside her glasses. Her hands skimming down his bare back. His mouth on her lips, her throat, her nipples. His erection sliding slowly between her legs.

The images left her trembling, hot, wet.

In three hurried steps, she reached her window and plucked the flowers from there. Althea lifted the sash and dropped the flowers into the dark.

A soft fluttering sound—the beat of wings—told her he had come. She stepped back and he flew out of the dark as a black bat. In a blink, the earl stood in the shadows of her room, and stepped into the pool of moonlight. The silvery light rippled over his broad shoulders, across the planes of his chest, down the lean length of his legs. His erection, long and straight, gleamed like a sword.

"You're nude!"

A surprised, self-effacing smile touched his mouth. "My body can shift shape but my clothes do not." He bowed.

She drank in the flex of his magnificent muscles as the earl bent and straightened. His erection wobbled and she tried to draw her gaze away but couldn't help but stare. Curved like a drawn bow, it bumped his navel. Even to her inexperienced eye, his staff was magnificent. She tightened inside just looking at it.

Her cheeks flamed when she finally met his eyes, glittering in the light.

This was her dream come to life. Did she dare let herself experience it?

The Earl of Brookshire held out his hand. "Come to me, love."

With a soft shy giggle, Althea did, and he cupped her fingers to raise them to his lips, drawing her up against his naked body, against his surprisingly warm flesh. His cock pressed against her belly and she caught her breath.

She would do just a little bit from her dreams. Not everything.

But as the earl's hot mouth stroked over her knuckles, her knees almost buckled. His lips, wet and soft, pressed against her fingers. With a whispered moan, she gazed up into his glowing mirrored eyes.

It was so impossible to guess the earl's thoughts behind his shining, silvery eyes.

At least crinkles at the corners hinted at his delight and Althea smiled in return. A smile that vanished into a startled gasp as he sucked her index finger into his mouth. His tongue twirled around the tip. In her dreams, he lavished such attentions on her nipples. And tonight he would for real.

And heaven help her, she wanted it so desperately she felt she might burst.

Then she flushed, knowing she must do something she hadn't yet done.

"Thank you," she whispered, "For saving my father." Althea had to whisper—their meeting was illicit, forbidden, but also, the moment was magical, and she was afraid to shatter it.

"Anything for you, love." His lordship caressed her cheek and led her hand to his.

She'd never touched a man this way and it was beautiful, strangely sweet, to trace the high ridge of his cheekbone, to slide her fingers into his soft hair. Gathering courage, she laid her hand lightly against his face. Touching him helped her believe he was real. His skin was raw silk and his raspy stubble tickled her palm.

His gaze burned into her. "And you, my beautiful warrior, were magnificent. Courageous."

"How did you send such power out of your—"

"Ssh."

He turned his face in her hand and touched his lips to her palm. Dabbed his tongue in the sensitive center.

"Tonight we are just a man and a woman, love."

Althea's legs weakened again, he caught her by her hips, supporting her. He splayed his hand over her low back. Even through her flannel nightdress, his heat seared her.

But just a woman or not, she needed to know. "What of Crenshaw, the servants, the other guests? How did you—"

"I entered their minds and erased much of what they remembered. They believe your father had a severe stomach upset. Now, sweet, I am beginning to wish I could control your mind with the same ease."

"You can't?"

"If I could, love, we would have been naked, entwined, and screaming in ecstasy long ago."

A jolt of agony shot through Althea's belly at his blunt words. It must have showed plainly on her face because he gave a triumphant grin.

"You have the most tempting mouth, sweet. I imagine that every man you meet hungers to kiss you."

That startled her. She'd never received more than hurried, chaste pecks from men. Nothing that prepared her for his hot mouth on hers.

He lifted her, just enough to allow his lips to slant sensuously over hers. He coaxed her mouth open, the way he did in her dreams. In her dreams, it was so shockingly intimate to kiss with her mouth wide. But the reality was even more scorching and sinful and perfect.

His tongue slid in, filling her mouth with heat and pressure and taste.

She loved it. She pushed forward. Stopped short.

Fangs.

She pulled back.

The hurt in his eyes speared her heart.

Impulsively, Althea arched up and slid her hands around his strong neck. She'd never done this—claimed a kiss, not even in her dreams. He always took her. She was always the one lured and seduced and possessed.

She had no idea how to kiss. Pushing aside fear, she let hunger guide her. She moved her mouth over his, pressing hard, then soft, shifting as he did, savoring his mouth. The earl possessed a heat she'd never known, an intimate taste she couldn't define.

His tongue slid in again and tangled with hers. He kissed her until her wits whirled. Until she understood he would kiss her all night. He kissed her as he tugged the ribbon from her braid and threaded his fingers through her hair. Kissed her as he yanked open the belt of her wrapper and slid it off her shoulders. And kissed her hard as he flicked the first small buttons of her nightdress from their loops, exposing her throat, her chest, the upper curves of her breasts.

She gripped his broad, solid shoulders, her tongue now deep in his hot, delicious mouth. She felt the points of his retracted fangs but forced herself not to retreat.

She wanted to show trust . . . even if she wasn't certain she could trust.

Shadows lengthened, the moonlight disappeared, plunging them into a velvety dark. Althea knew the earl could see her but she was blind and she clung to him tighter. He pulled her closer, until her breasts squashed against his chest and her hard nipples poked bands of solid muscle, beneath hot skin and coarse curls.

His hands slid down to her bottom. Scandalously, he squeezed generous portions of her flesh with both his big hands and chuckled with masculine pleasure into her mouth.

He broke the kiss just long enough to whisper, "What a perfect plump arse you have," before he captured her mouth again.

Gripping her cheeks, his lordship lifted her, slid his leg between hers and lowered her so she straddled him. Oh God, she wore nothing under her nightgown. His naked thigh rubbed her naked nether lips and she blushed as her wetness coated his skin.

He gave another chuckle, this one filled with pride. Just as in her dreams, he was terribly pleased with himself. She was soaking wet, embarrassingly so.

As though he sensed her shyness, Brookshire lavished soft, sweet kisses on her eyebrows and lashes, her nose and cheeks, her forehead, her chin until she giggled helplessly.

He rocked his leg and the pressure felt so good. She let her head loll back as his hot mouth pressed to her throat.

She stiffened and pulled away. "Are you going to bite me?"

Did I ever bite you in a dream?

"No, you didn't but—" Althea broke off, before she said "the other man." She couldn't—absolutely couldn't—say out loud that she had dreamed of another man and him.

"No, angel. I'm not going to bite you. But I do want to taste you. Savor every delectable inch of you." His lips skated down her throat, his tongue licked in the hollow. All the while, his thigh rubbed and rubbed. A wicked hunger blossomed there. He made her throb and she felt as though she floated in air, as though she could fly. Shift shape as he did, spread newfound wings, and soar.

But his hand in her nether curls brought her sharply to earth. He'd slipped his other into the bodice of her nightdress. He cradled her breast, the heel of his hand pressed to her pounding heart. He stroked her curls, dipping his finger lower, into her moisture.

She should stop. Must stop. Or was it far too late? Would he let her stop?

Angel, I will stop when you wish.

"You read my mind!"

Only the signals of your body. Your tension. The startled look in her eyes. I am your servant tonight, love. I do only as you desire.

His finger stayed at the very apex of her sex. Althea fought the desire to tip her hips up, to coax him to slide his finger inside her.

"I don't believe you!" she exclaimed in a whisper, even though she ached more.

And why not, my sweet?

"Because you are a man and every woman knows what a man wants. And because—

What did you enjoy most in our dreams, Althea? What do you want me to do to you?

Yes, she'd done all these things in dreams. But she couldn't tell him. Couldn't say such things.

His tongue dipped into the valley between her breasts. *Did you enjoy my mouth on your nipples?*

"My lord, I—"

"Yannick."

He was speaking, not communicating in her mind, and she felt strangely relieved. She clung to the safer topic of conversation—his Christian name. "It's French, isn't it?"

"You want a French kiss?"

He was teasing, she knew, but she couldn't imagine what a French kiss would be. "Your name is French."

"My mother was French, love, with an English marriage to save her from Madame la Guillotine. And de Wynter goes back to the Conqueror." His lord—Yannick's leg lowered but he scooped her into his arms before her slippers touched the floor. "And I believe you would enjoy a French kiss."

Only when he laid her on her bed, when he slid the long skirt of her nightgown up to the tops of her thighs, when he bent and touched his lips to her nether curls, did Althea realize what a French kiss was.

This they had never done in dreams. He had touched her intimately with his fingers, with his cock, but not with his mouth.

"You can't kiss my . . . there."

"Your sweet cunny. Oh yes, I can. And I will. I never did this for you in your dreams?"

She frowned. "Don't you know? Didn't you have the dreams too?"

"But I don't know if we had the same dreams, sweet angel." To her shock, he breathed deeply. Drank in her scent. Smiled. "I was most remiss if I never kissed your delicious cunny."

"That's what you call it? That crude word?"

Yannick was on his knees on the floor now, gazing up at her from between her thighs. His pale blond hair spilled over his brow, dusted across his darkly lashed eyes. His fingers stroked her inner thighs and Althea could barely think.

His brow quirked. "What would you prefer, then, love? Quim? Pussy? Velvet glove? Pleasure passage? Silken sheath? Grotto of love?"

"Grotto of—?" She stared down at him in disbelief, then dissolved into giggles.

He flashed a playful frown, screened by her auburn curls. She caught her breath at the intimacy of their teasing. How could she be joking with a man—an earl and a vampire!—who had her most private places exposed to him?

He gave an audacious wink. "Women do not generally laugh when I do this."

He traced the tip of his tongue over her curls. Her hands clenched into fists. She almost shot up right off the bed. His hot breath breezed over a terribly sensitive place and she quivered.

Do you wish me to stop?

"Y–yes."

"Are you certain?" He blew across her nether lips and she knew he would *not* stop. In dreams, he knew to make her melt until she could refuse nothing.

And he was a peer after all. Accustomed to having his own way.

Althea tried to say yes once more but her mouth would not cooperate. She truly did not want him to stop. Slowly, she shook her head. Willed the word no at him. Gasped in shock as he pressed his mouth tight to her mound.

Oh yes. Yes. She cried it in her head.

As you command, love. He suckled. She screamed.